The Nabob's Wife

THE NABOB'S WIFE

Phyllida Barstow

CENTURY

LONDON MELBOURNE AUCKLAND JOHANNESBURG

First published in Great Britain in 1988 by
Century Hutchinson Ltd
Brookmount House, 62–65 Chandos Place
London WC2N 4NW

Century Hutchinson South Africa (Pty) Ltd
PO Box 337, Bergvlei, 2012 South Africa

Century Hutchinson Australia Pty Ltd
PO Box 496, 16–22 Church Street, Hawthorn
Victoria 3122, Australia

Century Hutchinson New Zealand Ltd
PO Box 40–086, Glenfield, Auckland 10
New Zealand

ISBN 0 7126 0895 8
Phototypeset by Input Typesetting Ltd

Printed in Great Britain by
Anchor Brendon Ltd, Tiptree, Essex

PART ONE:
THE ENGLISH CAMEL

1

All day the strange sail had lain on the horizon, barely visible to the naked eye yet plain enough through a glass as powerful as the one which young Mr Edward Sweeney, travelling to Bombay to take up his duties as Writer for the Honourable East India Company, chivalrously pressed upon his fellow passenger, Miss Katherine Castlemain, as they stood together at the stern rail, watching the tropical sun set behind that distant menacing triangle.

Kate accepted the heavy brass cylinder, propping her elbows on the rail to steady it, and peered through the eyepiece, but though the sea was glassy calm the image blurred and swam dizzily no matter how hard she tried to focus. After a moment she handed it back, shaking her head.

'It is no use, Ned. I see better with my own eyes. Tell me what you make of her.'

Nothing loath, Ned repossessed himself of his precious telescope and stared earnestly at the horizon.

'French,' he pronounced with great solemnity. Then, shutting the glass with three decisive clicks, he turned shining eyes upon Kate. 'Oh, Miss Castlemain! Do you suppose she will attack us? What capital sport that would be. If only my uncle will not take fright and run away!'

'Captain Foster will find it difficult to run anywhere without a breath of air,' observed Kate. Though she could not share Ned's enthusiasm for the prospect of a fight, she had to admit that any break in the monotony of shipboard life would be welcome. Of all the hazards she had anticipated in this long voyage, boredom was the one to which she had given least thought.

Would time have passed less tediously if her cabin-mate had been more congenial? Kate was fair-minded enough to admit that during seven months of cramped quarters even the liveliest of companions might have developed irritating habits, and Eugenia Hunter had at least the virtue of consistency. At the very outset of the voyage she had constituted herself Kate's moral and spiritual guide, and nothing short of downright rudeness was enough to silence her. She held decided opinions on most subjects and especially on what was and what was not becoming behaviour in single ladies travelling alone.

Kate was tired of hearing that such ladies – even if betrothed – should not converse with, smile at, or even acknowledge the salutations of gentlemen to whom they had not been properly introduced. Not should they proceed at any pace faster than a walk, play cards except with older women, address the sailors, read books other than the Bible or sermons, while as for watching the young men play at leapfrog! That outraged every instinct of propriety.

And she is three years younger than I am! thought Kate with mingled exasperation and amusement. Yet she knew age had little to do with Eugenia's assumption of authority. Daughter of a Dean and betrothed to a missionary whose success in converting the heathen idolaters of Hindustan made him first choice for the Bishopric of Lallakotah, Eugenia's ecclesiastical lineage was impeccable. She had passed her formative years in Calcutta, and considered herself well-qualified to pontificate about India. Besides, even if she had not been so fond of proclaiming it, there could be no doubt that Eugenia was a Superior Female: truly good, effortlessly pious.

If only she would not force her standards upon the rest of us, Kate thought ruefully, as the strains of half-a-dozen voices of varying degrees of tunefulness, led by Eugenia's reedy soprano, floated up to them on the heavy air. Kate straightened reluctantly and turned from the rail.

'I suppose I should go down. Eugenia will be vexed with me for missing her prayer meeting.'

'It beats me how you stand her everlasting jawing,' said Ned with the frankness of a fifteen-year-old.

'Sometimes I am astonished at it myself,' admitted Kate. 'Why do you listen to her?'

7

'Oh, I don't know. For the sake of peace, I suppose. She means well, and one can hardly blame her for wishing to improve the conduct of those around her.'

'I can,' said Ned stoutly. 'When she tells me she is praying for my soul it makes my flesh creep.'

'I know what you mean. Still, you do not have to endure it for many more days. Even the least puff of breeze should take us to Bombay within the week.'

'I would rather have a sea-fight.' Ned's eyes were wistful. Kate guessed he would also have preferred a cornetcy in some dashing cavalry regiment to the prospect of long years of quill-pushing.

She said bracingly, 'You may find yourself in action sooner that you expect! If Colonel Wilson is right, there is likely to be trouble with the Maratha chiefs before long and Bombay will need every man she has to defend her.'

'The Marathas!' He stood straighter, picturing fierce faces under turbans, thundering hoofs, himself at the head of a charge; but a moment later he drooped over the rail once more, saying disconsolately, 'I daresay it is all a hum. The Marathas will not meddle with us after the trouncing we gave Tippoo Sultan. How I wish I could have been there! The fellows who broke open his treasure-house in Seringapatam are all rich as nabobs now.'

'Don't fret.' Kate laid a hand lightly on his arm. 'I warrant you will get your share of adventure.'

'As a beastly writer?'

'Oh, Ned! Have you not read your History? The great Clive began his career as a Writer.'

He grinned at that, but said with becoming modesty, 'I am hardly another Clive.'

'Why not, if you are ready to grasp the opportunity when it offers?' She glanced round to see they were not overheard before saying in a lower tone, 'Consider the case of Major Gisborne, to whom I am betrothed. Two years ago he had hardly a feather to fly with, but he took his chance to transfer to the Civil, and now he is master of a state the size of Wales.'

'A Nabob!'

She laughed at his look of surprise. 'I believe one may call him that. It shows how swiftly a man's fortunes may change in India. I daresay your rise to eminence will be every bit as swift.'

'You really think so?'

'I feel sure of it.'

The subdued murmur of prayers warned her that Eugenia's meeting was about to end.

'I must go,' she said with reluctance. The air was decidedly fresher on deck than it would be in the stifling cabin after half-a-dozen women had prayed there for an hour. 'Eugenia will take her stroll now.'

'Are you frightened of meeting her?'

'For shame!' Her eyes crinkled. 'Do you take me for a coward? I will tell you a secret: this is my one chance to have the cabin to myself! Besides, if she should discover I have been *idling* here with you in preference to attending her meeting, I will never hear the end of it. Good night, Ned. I rely on you to warn me if the Frenchman takes advantage of the dark to creep nearer.'

'I will, never fear. Good night, Miss Castlemain.'

'Oh, pray call me Kate! Miss Castlemain sounds so horridly formal.'

'Thank you.' The colour rose in Ned's thin cheeks. He made her his best leg and watched her disappear down the companionway.

He liked Miss Castlemain – *Kate*. At first he had thought her freakish-looking, even ugly: so tall and thin, with her springy black curls cut short to cluster about her face as they pleased instead of sleeked down and drawn into ear-coils in the accepted fashion. With hair so dark and skin so pale, her blue eyes seemed freakish, too. One would have expected them to be brown. She had a way of screwing them up when she laughed so that her long face assumed quite different planes, and it seemed as if she was laughing at laughter itself. Or was that because her expression was generally somewhat melancholy?

At times he had seen her gazing at the waves with a look so sad and abstracted that it would not have surprised him if she had cast herself overboard. Then someone would speak to her and the lost look would be replaced with a mask of polite attention, the idle hands would take up whatever work was lying in her lap, and whatever dark thoughts had occupied her mind were put aside . . . for the present.

Everything about her struck him as singular. She was a different breed from the other females aboard: a deer among a herd of cows. Then there was the matter of her clothes. Ned would have hesitated to describe himself as an expert on ladies' fashions, but even he could see that Kate's clothes would not have found favour with his mother or sisters. It was not so much that the colours were dull and materials plain, but the garments appeared to have been constructed for a woman of a different shape. On Kate's angular form they hung loose and unflattering, but she seemed to have no interest in making herself appear to better advantage.

Still, if it came to a sea-battle, thought Ned, he would take good care to rescue Kate from the waves and allow Miss Hunter to take her chance with the sharks.

Clamping the telescope to his eye once more, he returned to his contemplation of the distant sail. Hang it, she must be French! Why else would she lurk at a distance without making herself known?

Throughout this wearisome voyage Ned had yearned for an encounter with one of Boney's men-o'-war. Fired by his father's stories of Nelson and the Battle of the Nile (at which the elder Edward Sweeney, now deceased, had used this selfsame telescope to direct *Intrepid*'s guns against Admiral Villeneuve's flagship) Ned had been chagrined to find that his uncle Richard, Master of this wallowing East Indiaman, believed in avoiding trouble and the least glimpse of an unidentified vessel was enough to make him alter course. 'Dodging and ducking like a frightened rabbit!' as Ned put it disgustedly. He thought it all the more strange that Uncle Richard had allowed his precious *Neptune* to stay all day within sight of this particular stranger.

The lack of wind might explain it, of course, but even in a flat calm it should have been possible for *Neptune* to perform her usual vanishing-trick – if her captain so wished.

10

Deuced odd, thought Ned, and fell to dreaming of sea-fights in which he played the most heroic roles. The red ball of the sun slipped into the oily green sea, and all about him the world darkened in the swift tropical dusk.

It was at this point that Ned realized he was no longer staring at one sail, but two. A smaller segment had detached itself from the parent craft and was skimming towards *Neptune* across the darkening water. Puffs of white smoke blossomed against the sides of the distant ship. Ned hung over the rail enthralled, straining his ears to catch the faint thump of explosions.

The small boat skimmed the dark mirror, undamaged. Presently Ned could even make out the figures of two – no, three men aboard. Two strained at long spade-shaped oars while the third lay asleep in the bows. Faintly from the crow's-nest came the lookout's hail; it drew a guttural response in a language that was certainly not French.

As the light high-prowed craft with its sharp bowsprit glided alongside, *Neptune*'s sandy-haired Third Officer hurried to the rail, buttoning his tunic. A prolonged parley began, of which Ned understood not one word, but something in the quick, furtive-sounding exchanges warned him not to advertize his presence. Although the Captain's nephew was accorded a certain degree of leniency by the ship's company, Ned and the Third Officer were not the best of friends.

Presently two seamen were summoned and a hammock lowered. It was drawn up with the weight of the third man slumped in its sagging middle. More parley followed; silver showered down like bright rain, and the native boatmen scrabbled to scoop it from their bilges. They cast off, pulling strongly, and in a moment were swallowed in the dusk.

As the Third Officer and the seamen stood talking in low tones, Ned tiptoed nearer. The rescued man was lying with his eyes closed and one bandaged arm clamped across his chest. He wore a once-splendid tunic of rose-pink silk, badly slashed and stained, girdled with a wide silver cummerbund in which were stuck an assortment of weapons. Round his head was a turban of the same rose

11

silk, threaded with silver and surmounted by a jewel which twinkled enticingly in the rays of the riding-lamp.

But it was his face which held Ned's attention. Pock-marked and dark, with a jutting high-bridged nose and deep eye-sockets, it was bisected by a tremendous scar which ran from below the turban at the left temple right across the face to the right-hand angle of the jaw. It must, thought Ned in fascinated horror, nearly have cut his head in two.

'Is he – is he – dead?' Try as he might, he could not restrain the question.

The Third Officer turned, frowning. 'Oh, it's you, is it, Mr Sweeney? I might have guessed you'd be hanging about where you're not wanted. Cut along now, there's a good lad. This is no affair of yours.'

'But is he – ?'

The older seaman laughed, leaning down to turn back the injured man's eyelid with a calloused thumb and finger.

'Dead? Not likely. Not 'im,' he said hoarsely. 'Got as many lives as a bloomin' cat, 'as Sikander Sahib. Eh, Cuddy? Take more'n a sabre-cut to finish 'im.'

'Then – then you know him?' Ned was as much surprised as relieved.

''Course we knows 'im. Anyone 'oo's ever sailed the Malabar Coast knows Sikander Sahib. Not to say we likes 'im, that ain't. Not to say we wants 'is kind aboard.'

'That will do, Fisher.' The Third Officer rubbed his jaw, staring at the man in the hammock. Abruptly he came to a decision. 'Convey my compliments to Surgeon Matthews,' he said curtly, 'and beg him to attend this man at his earliest convenience. I thought I desired you to cut along, Mr Sweeney,' he added in a threatening tone as Ned hovered.

The boy stood his ground. 'Who is he? Why don't you want him aboard?'

'Why, you young rascal!' The Third Officer clenched his fists, but the cuff was never delivered.

'I can answer the first part of your question, sir, if not the second,' said a voice from the deck. The injured man's eyes were open; even in the gloom Ned thought he detected a glint of amusement. 'Allow me to introduce myself.

Colonel Alexander Quinn of Prince Jaswant Rao Holkar's First Regiment of Horse, very much at your service.'

'We shall ignore him,' said Eugenia in the gentle yet inflexible tone she employed when laying down the law. 'It was very wrong of Captain Foster to take such a scoundrel aboard, but there is little to be gained now by a formal protest. So we shall simply ignore him. That is, provided the wretch has the decency to remain closeted in his quarters. But we should be prepared! Even the most common decency is seldom met with in men of his kind. If Colonel Quinn should have the effrontery to show his face among us, we will have to make our disapproval plain to him *and* Captain Foster.'

There was a murmur of assent from three of the other four ladies gathered in Mrs Bastable's cabin for their daily hour of needlework and gossip. Mrs Bastable herself, voluptuously pale and plump in a loose wrapper of figured muslin, her head enveloped in a mob-cap from which a few blonde curls escaped to cling damply to her temples, nodded and sighed.

'You are quite right, dear Miss Hunter. We will have nothing to do with him.'

'Certainly not. The idea!' agreed sallow, sycophantic Mrs Harcourt, who had not voiced an original idea in all the seven months Kate had known her.

'No, indeed,' echoed mousy little Mabel Davenport, the only other unmarried female on board. She was much in awe of Eugenia.

Kate alone was silent.

Eugenia cast a pleased look round the assembled ladies. 'I must tell you I have already consulted with Colonel Wilson who may, I believe, be presumed to speak for all the gentlemen, and he is in complete agreement.' She snipped her silk with a precise movement. It suggested the wish that Colonel Quinn's neck was between the jaws of her shears. 'Yes, Katherine? You have something to add?'

'Forgive my ignorance, but I cannot see why it should be necessary to treat a fellow passenger as an outcast. Surely

13

such conduct hardly accords with the teaching of Our Saviour?'

So often in the past months Kate herself had been at the receiving end of such reproaches. It gave her a certain satisfaction to catch Eugenia out on so basic a point of theology.

Miss Hunter's pale eyes, the very colour and shape of boiled gooseberries, flashed a warning glance. 'Even Our Saviour does not require His followers to consort with traitors,' she snapped.

'Is Colonel Quinn a traitor?'

'Poor Katherine! How remiss of me to assume that what is plain to the rest of us must be equally plain to you!' Eugenia's smile was gracious. 'Would you not agree that a man who betrays his country is a traitor, unfit for the company of decent men and women?'

Kate frowned. 'How did Colonel Quinn betray his country?'

The paper-fine skin of Eugenia's nostrils fluttered and flared. 'He has taken service with a Maratha chieftain who is our sworn enemy, and with him plunders the lands of those native princes who have committed themselves to British protection. Terrible tales are told of him. I assure you, Katherine, there are plenty of Englishmen, from the Governor-General down, who would be pleased to see Colonel Quinn behind bars. Murder and robbery are the least of his crimes.'

The ladies nodded, eyes bright beneath frivolous lace caps. There was something avid in the glances they darted at her, hens eager to peck until blood spurted.

'If you are right,' she said slowly, 'why has Captain Foster taken him on board? Why does he not clap him in irons and deliver him up to justice?'

'If I am right?' Eugenia shook a pitying head. 'My dear Katherine, you have a great deal to learn about the East. Deliver him up to justice? If only matters were so simple!' She leaned forward, graceful white neck extended, gooseberry eyes fixed earnestly on Kate. 'It is Colonel Wilson's opinion that the wretch has offered Captain Foster an *inducement.*'

Kate digested this. Sea-captains who took bribes were new in her experience.

'May I take it we are all agreed?' said Eugenia into the silence.

Once Kate might have pursued the matter. Jeremy had always encouraged her to argue. Why had God given a woman a brain if He didn't intend her to use it? he would demand. Stand up for your convictions and the world will respect you! But Jeremy was lost to her and the hopes Kate had been foolish enough to build on him had collapsed like a house of cards. For all his liberal notions his own choice of a bride had been conventional enough.

'Well, Katherine?'

The ladies eyed her curiously. Jeremy would have challenged Eugenia's ruling for the sheer love of an argument, but after avoiding conflict with her for seven constricted months, it seemed absurd for Kate to risk one now. What did she care whether anyone spoke to Colonel Quinn?

The heat in the crowded cabin was overpowering. The mingled scents of lavender-water, perspiration and stale breath made the air suffocatingly thick and Kate felt an overpowering longing to be alone, away from beady eyes and gossiping tongues. But where could she run to? On a ship there was no escape from your fellow passengers. Were she to dash out now, Eugenia would certainly follow her; and then she would scold and reason and lecture until Kate agreed with everything she said for the sake of peace, damaging her own self-respect and giving Eugenia still further cause for pitying looks and moral superiority.

'Well?'

'I daresay you are right,' muttered Kate ungraciously; and Eugenia's crumpled brow smoothed into tranquil self-righteousness once more.

'Good,' she said, and laid down her embroidery. 'Now let us continue our study of Bishop Montague's sermons. Mabel, I believe it is your turn to read?'

Self-effacing Mabel, painfully aware of her own tendency

15

to gabble and mispronounce words, shook her head, blushing, and begged dear Miss Hunter to relieve her of the duty.

'Very well, if you prefer,' agreed Eugenia, by no means displeased. She opened the heavy book and bent her sleek head over it, scanning a number of pages before finding what she sought.

'This seems an appropriate occasion to read a passage from the sermon given at the Church of Holy Trinity, Whitstable, on August 19th, 1792, when Bishop Montague took as his text the commandment, "Thou shalt love thy neighbour as thyself".'

As her soft yet penetrating voice filled the cabin, Kate closed her ears. Through the porthole she could see spray flung high as a school of porpoises leaped and frolicked, sleek sides gleaming with iridescence. She caught her breath. How beautiful they were, exulting in their freedom! Watching them entranced, she forgot the sticky itch of her clothes and the headache-inducing airlessness of the cabin. Soon she too would be free, and the sorrows and failures of the past would evaporate like spray in the sun. George would meet her in Bombay. His letter tucked in her bosom promised her new freedom, a new life.

Glancing up from her reading, Eugenia saw her rapt face and nodded complacently. There had been times in the past months when she despaired of bringing poor Katherine to a sense of what was fitting behaviour for a betrothed lady travelling alone. But as always the power of example had triumphed. By the time this voyage was over she felt confident that even this black sheep would be safely within the fold.

Much to Ned's regret, the strange sail had vanished next morning; but he was not one to waste time sighing over what might have been. As the only passenger to have witnessed Colonel Quinn's unorthodox arrival on board, he felt a proprietorial – even protective – interest in him. When two days passed without Quinn's appearance in any of the places one might expect to find a fellow passenger, Ned set out to discover his whereabouts. This was not difficult for one of Ned's particular talents. The seamen were used to his way of hanging about where other passengers seldom ventured, watching the ship's crew about their tasks. With terrier-like persistence he watched and listened until he heard what he wanted: then one afternoon while the rest of the ship's company was partaking of dinner, he made his way down the companionway that linked the passengers' quarters with those of the ship's officers and tapped on a door.

After a moment it was opened by Ali, the Captain's swarthy and taciturn manservant. His face beneath the flattened turban darkened still further on seeing Ned.

'Not coming here, Chota-Sahib,' he said very emphatically, and tried to close the door.

'Oh, I say – ' protested Ned, planting one foot in the rapidly diminishing gap. 'I only wished – '

'Who is it, Ali?'

Over the Mussulman's shoulder Ned could see Colonel Quinn lying at ease on the bunk, his head turned to observe the door. From the clutter of bowls, razors, strops, cloths and the like on the table beside him, Ned deduced that he had been submitting to Ali's ministrations.

'Oh, it's you, my young friend! What can I do for you?' he asked as Ned shoved at Ali's rock-like form. 'All right, Ali, let the gentleman pass. Come in, Mr Sweeney, and bear me company awhile.'

Reassured by the friendly tone, Ned plucked up his courage and entered the cabin. It was, he saw, a part of the Captain's own quarters, partitioned off by a bulkhead, and well appointed with rugs, bookcases, lamps, a small writing-desk and a chair. The bunk was neatly recessed into the ship's ribs. As Ali, his movements stiff with disapproval, began to gather up his paraphernalia, Ned covertly studied his host.

Though in the light of day the livid scar was even more alarming, he was a little disappointed to find that without his turban and gorgeous ruined tunic, Quinn looked less of an Oriental potentate and more like a British officer – ill-

17

favoured, maybe, but nothing out of the common. He wore a plain loose muslin shirt and swamping blue nankeen pantaloons, evidently borrowed from the Captain's wardrobe. His heavy-lidded eyes, unusually large and velvety dark, regarded Ned with equal interest.

Glasses and a decanter stood on the table. 'You'll join me?' he invited.

'I wished only to ask how you did . . . Are you sure I am not disturbing you, sir?'

'By no means! Since Surgeon Matthews has forbidden me to stir from this cabin and Ali enforces my obedience by removing most of my clothes, I am confoundedly tired of my own company,' said Quinn with an unexpectedly charming smile. 'I am glad to see you, Mr Sweeney. Tell me, what news? When shall we make landfall?'

Whatever Ned had expected when curiosity led him to knock at this door, it had not been so friendly a reception. *Neptune*'s male passengers were inclined to treat him in an offhand manner, more as a tiresome schoolboy than one of themselves, and it must be admitted that he had not wholly outgrown the schoolboy fondness for practical jokes which made him less than a favourite with his elders. 'Young varmint' and 'Limb of Satan' were epithets with which Ned was all too familiar. He was more accustomed to being advised to cut along sharpish than have his opinion sought. Sipping his rum in the handsomely furnished cabin, his heart warmed to Colonel Quinn.

'I take it you are a military man yourself?' prompted his host when Ned paused.

The boy flushed. 'Yes. No. That is to say, I only wish I were!' He hesitated, torn between his desire to seek the Colonel's advice and dislike of admitting his own despised profession. 'The truth is, I would like to be a soldier, but I'm nothing but a damned Writer.'

'A perfectly honourable calling, Mr Sweeney.'

'Yes, but – '

'You must be aware that the great Clive himself was once a Writer?'

'That is what Miss Castlemain says,' returned Ned with

undiminished gloom. 'She tells me I needn't be one for ever.'

'Miss Castlemain sounds a woman of sense.'

'But I don't wish to be one at all!' Ned burst out.

'Then why not follow your inclination?'

'Because . . . my mother does not wish it.'

'Ah!'

The Colonel's dark gaze rested thoughtfully upon Ned's eager face and gangling adolescent frame. 'When it comes to choosing a career, Mr Sweeney, I have always believed that the wishes of one's family, however well-intentioned, are less important than one's own. I daresay your mother supposes a Writer's life to be a good deal less dangerous than a career in the Military?'

'That is it, sir. In a nutshell.'

Quinn smiled. 'A common misconception, particularly among mothers. Yet in my experience exactly the reverse is the case. I was born in India, you know, and may claim to speak with some authority when I say that the soldier's life, with all its attendant perils, is a great deal healthier as well as more rewarding than that of any box-wallah.'

Ned's urchin grin flashed, but he shook his head. 'You would not persuade Mamma of that, sir.'

'She is a widow?'

He nodded. 'I have three sisters. I am the only son.'

'All the more reason you should pursue a career suited to your talents,' said Quinn, smiling. Seeing Ned's doubtful look, he added, 'You may take my word for it. I know what it is to have sisters and a widowed mother!'

Lighting a cheroot, he addressed the hovering servant. 'My compliments to your master, Ali. Pray inform him that my wound makes excellent progress.'

'*Ji huzoor, sahib.*'

The man salaamed and left. As the door closed behind him, Ned said diffidently, 'What advice would you give me, sir?'

'I can only cite my own case. My mother wished to make a clerk of me and for two most miserable years to please her I allowed myself to be chained to a desk, writing ledgers. An experience I would not wish on you, Mr Sweeney.'

'How did you escape from it?'

Quinn drew deeply on his cheroot, gazing through the smoke at the small segment of ocean visible through the porthole. 'Since the way to a commission in the East India Company was barred to me, I took service with General de Boigne, of whom you have doubtless heard – '

'A Frenchman!' If he had said a cannibal Ned could not have been more shocked.

'A great gentleman,' corrected Quinn. 'While Benoît de Boigne commanded Scindia's battalions, a finer force could not be found in all Hindustan. I have never known his equal.'

'Why could you not join the Company, sir?'

Quinn stared at him, his expression hardening into suspicion. Seeing nothing but puzzlement on Ned's face, he carefully tapped ash from his cigar and turned so the light from the porthole fell full on his features.

'Why not?' he said softly. 'Look at me, Mr Sweeney. Can you not guess?'

For a moment Ned met that searching dark gaze; then his own eyes dropped and a painful flush crept up his neck. Even before Quinn spoke again he knew the answer. Officers of mixed blood did not hold Company commissions.

'My mother was a Rajput, Mr Sweeney.'

'I – I am sorry.'

'You need not be,' said Quinn icily. 'I am as proud of my mother's blood as my father's. More!'

'I mean, I am sorry if I have been guilty of a want of civility,' muttered Ned, furious in his turn at what seemed wilful misunderstanding of his apology. The pleasure had gone out of his visit. Abruptly he rose to take his leave. But with a sudden change of mood Quinn smiled and laid a hand on his arm.

'Don't take offence, I beg! You must forgive me. My friends tell me I am too quick to imagine a slight where

20

none is intended. Tell me, what decided you to come to India and shake the pagoda tree?'

A little doubtfully, Ned resumed his seat. He liked Quinn, but thought him a bit quick to jump down a fellow's throat. For a moment he was tempted to talk of his own affairs. Though he would not have admitted it, he was homesick, missing his mother's stream of advice and warning and the unflagging curiosity shown by his sisters in their young brother's aspirations. Of all the passengers, only Kate had shown interest in him. He thought shaking the pagoda tree sounded a good deal better than quill-pushing, and the offer of a sympathetic ear was enticing, but he had not come here to talk about himself.

'I would sooner hear of your adventures, sir,' he said politely but firmly. 'How did you come to be wounded?'

'Ah.' Quinn's level brows drew together and Ned wondered uneasily if he had again overstepped the bounds of civility. His mother often scolded him, saying curiosity killed the cat; but unless you asked questions, how could you find out what you wanted to know?

'A tangled tale, Mr Sweeney.'

'I should like to hear it, sir.'

'Alas, without some understanding of the Marathas and their politics, I fear it would make little sense to you.'

'I might understand, sir. That is, if you would be good enough to explain.'

For a moment it seemed as if Quinn contemplated another set-down. Then he smiled and said, 'As you please. I will try to make the matter plain.' He was silent a while, collecting his thoughts. 'Perhaps the first thing you should comprehend is that here in India the highest title seldom carries the greatest power,' he said at last. 'However, those who have the means to exercise power must always do so in the name of its legitimate source. Lip service, if you like. Do I make myself clear?'

Ned was obliged to admit he did not.

Quinn sighed. 'Then let us proceed to particular instances. You have doubtless heard of the Great Mughal? Shah Alam, the present holder of that title is blind, helpless

21

and a prisoner, yet anyone who usurps his power must use it in his name. The Nawabs of Oudh and the Carnatic, and the Nizam of Hyderabad, who were once his officers, have made themselves into hereditary princes, yet they still pay him vassalage. Now that the Tiger of Mysore, Tippoo Sultan, is destroyed, there are only two real powers in India: the Marathas and the British.'

'Who rules the Marathas?' asked Ned, trying to splice this information into what he already knew.

'It is the same situation as with the Great Moghul. The Rajah of Satara, descendant of Sivaji who founded the Maratha nation, is still head of the Maratha confederacy, but his power is in name only. Like the Emperor, he has become a puppet, and his power is transferred to the descendants of Sivaji's five principal officers: the Peshwa of Poona, the Bhonsle of Berar, the Gaekwar of Baroda, Scindia of Gwalior, and Holkar of Indore, whom I serve. Between them, these princes share the territory that stretches from Delhi in the north to the borders of Hyderabad in the south; and from east to west across the breadth of India. Even this great stretch of land is hardly enough to contain them. One day they will clash with the British.'

Ned nodded sagely. 'I daresay they fight among themselves a good deal. I heard Colonel Wilson say that any officer cashiered by the Company could be sure of finding employment with a Maratha prince.'

Quinn grinned. 'True enough. Warfare is the Maratha way of life, and not only among themselves. Of late, they have been wooed by greater powers in the world.'

'You mean England . . . and France?'

Quinn nodded. 'The Maratha chiefs cannot – will not – see it is the path to destruction. Each has his fine new artillery, and his regular battalions trained by European officers, but infantry battles will never be their strength. That will always lie with their cavalry. Until you have seen a charge of Maratha horse you can have no idea of warfare.'

'I should like it above all things,' murmured Ned, eyes glowing.

'The British court the Peshwa, while Scindia intrigues

with Bonaparte's agents. Only my master, Jaswant Rao Holkar, sees that by letting in the French he will lose just as surely as if he signs an agreement with the British.'

'With whom does he side?'

'With no one. He stands alone. But Scindia has the Peshwa's ear, and where the Peshwa leads the Gaekwar and the Bhonsle will follow.' He smiled at Ned's bemused look. 'I warned you it was a tangled tale.'

'I would rather hear how you were wounded,' Ned admitted.

'Ah, that was a brush with Scindia. He blames me because Jaswant Rao will not join his conspiracy with the French. As I rode back from Poona a week since, I fell into Scindia's ambush, and woke to find myself in irons on a French frigate. Had it not been for the courage of Ram Gopal, my bearer, I should now be feeding the sharks.'

Thoughtfully he flexed his injured wrist and Ned gazed at him with envy. This way of life was a world away from his own humdrum prospects.

'What will you do now?'

'To level my score with Scindia? Oh, I assure you I have plans for that gentleman!' Teeth flashed in a grin which made him seem younger and less formidable. 'To tell you the truth I have been thinking of little else since Captain Foster had the kindness to take me up.'

'I wish I could help you.'

'Help me?' Quinn's eyebrows rose. 'Why not?' he said after a moment's consideration. 'I suppose you will not be required to take up your duties the moment you step ashore?'

'N – no. That is,' said Ned uncertainly, 'I am to stay with my father's sister – my aunt Edwin – until the first week in June.'

'You must certainly contrive to see something of the country before burying your nose in your ledgers! Listen: I have a capital notion. I intend to make a hunting trip into the hills above Burhanpur, where there is very pretty shooting to be had at this season. If you care to join me, I should be glad of your company.'

'But what should I tell my aunt?' Ned was torn between delight and bewilderment. Could Quinn really mean it? A man he barely knew? Of course, his mother would be bound to hear of it eventually, but England was a long way away . . .

'Why, tell her the truth,' said Quinn easily. 'Say that a friend has invited you for a few weeks' *shikar*. She will understand. Who knows? We may find bigger game than bison in the Burhanpur range.'

'But – '

'You need not decide at once,' he added as Ned began to stammer incoherent thanks. 'You know where to find me. Think it over for a day or so, then let me have your answer.'

2

I have lost my cavalier, thought Kate wryly when for the third day in succession she took her pre-dinner walk without Ned appearing to offer himself as her escort. It was not surprising, of course, that he should have found a pastime more to his taste than strolling sedately with a woman twelve years his senior. All the same, she missed his cheerful chatter quite as much as the protection his company used to give her from bores and proses such as Colonel Wilson and the Reverend Josiah Evans, mercifully distant today on the afterdeck; or the unwelcome gallantries of Captain Molyneux, an insufferable ginger-crested bantam-cock who fancied himself irresistible though he barely reached her shoulder.

There he was now, smoothing his whiskers and smirking to see her alone. I should have asked Mattie to walk with me, she thought, annoyed at the prospect of being trapped into conversation or forced into incivility; but she knew that any attempt to interrupt the sacred hour of Mattie's dinner would incur her displeasure. Better face it alone, she thought, and quickened her pace.

'A fine day, Miss Castlemain.'

Kate swept on, eyes averted, acknowledging neither his bow nor the ostentatiously raised beaver. This voyage will be the ruin of my manners, she lamented, pinning her gaze on the far horizon though she longed to glance back at Captain Molyneux's outraged face. Unless I change my ways, George will suppose he has offered for a shrew.

The thought of George brought its usual comfort. At least *she* was travelling to India for a definite purpose, with a husband-to-be to meet her when she disembarked; unlike poor Mabel Davenport, whose motive in sailing to India was equally plain but had to be disguised by the pretext of visiting her brother. If only a single lady could be accepted in society without feeling herself rejected and despised! Kate's own experience as a superfluous female in her brother's household was too painfully fresh for her to feel anything but keen sympathy for sad little Mabel.

Kate had lost her mother at an early age, and while her father lived she ruled his estate at Overton, in the steep folded valleys where the Cotswolds swoop down to the Bristol Channel. Neither Sir Gregory Castlemain nor Kate's brother Charles showed the least inclination to hold the reins; indeed they revelled in the freedom Kate's stewardship gave them to hunt and shoot as long as there were horses in the stables and dogs in the kennel.

With Mattie, her mother's housekeeper, to guide her in domestic matters and Jeremy Kingswood with his own farm a mere ten minutes' ride across the fields, Kate had managed pretty well. Hindsight showed her she had leaned too much and too long on Jeremy, taking for granted his readiness to help and encourage. His defection, when it came, was all the more of a shock.

Even now she could hardly bear to think about it. As children they had shared a tutor; after Jeremy's departure for school they spent the holidays playing, dancing, reading and riding together. They shared a private language, laughed at the same jokes, worried over their respective farms separately and together. Kate had always assumed their pleasant companionship would end in marriage. Jeremy, it seemed, had not.

With the destructive force of three swift hammer-blows, her happy world had been shattered. In February of the previous year. Sir Gregory died, flung from an overturned curricle. Two months later Charles married Mrs Laetitia Hallows, a grasping widow with three small sons of her own. In July seventeen-year-old Emily Wetherby came home from her Parisian academy – tiny, delicate, and perfect as a Dresden figurine – and Jeremy fell head over ears in love with her.

Mattie alone understood the depth of Kate's humiliation.

'He's so happy! I can't bear to see him!' Kate had sobbed, returning wet and windblown from riding a week after the

26

betrothal was announced. 'Wherever I go, I see them. I can't bear it.'

Forgetting her dignity and her muddy habit she had buried her face in Mattie's shoulder, seeing no absurdity in the fact that doing so she nearly lifted the little woman off her feet.

'There, hinny. Have a good cry. It'll make you feel better. He's not the only one. There's as good fish in the sea as ever came out of it.'

'There aren't. You know there aren't. Not like – '

It hurt even to pronounce his name and meeting him became a torment. It seemed she could hardly stir from the house without encountering the happy couple, radiant and remote, so wrapped in their love they were hardly aware of those outside it. Kate had been so much in the habit of riding over to Kingswood three and four times a week that her mare baulked if asked to trot past the gates.

Blindly, with the best intentions, Jeremy rubbed salt into her wound. He was in love. He was the luckiest, happiest fellow in the world and wanted his dear Kate to share his happiness. She must love Emmie too. She was young and new to the district. There was so much she could learn from Kate. He would be so pleased, so infinitely obliged if Kate would take his little bride-to-be under her wing. How happy it would make him to see them friends as well as neighbours! Emmie was gentle, obedient, willing to be friends with anyone if it would please her beloved, but –

'I can't do it, Mattie!' cried Kate. 'I can't be her friend, no matter how much he wishes it. I can't bear to see the way he looks at her.'

'There's no such word as can't,' reproved Mattie, but she knew exactly what Kate meant. She too had seen the look and recognized it. Tender, wondering, humble and proud: the look of a man in love.

In the depths of her misery Kate knew that never in their whole long friendship had Jeremy looked at her in that way. They had been friends, nothing less, nothing more. Emmie was a shallow, pretty, frivolous child – but he loved her in a way he would never love Kate.

'I can't stay here, Mattie. Whenever I see him I want to cry.'

'Then we should go away, hinny.'

'We?'

'You don't think I'd stay on here with *that woman* and her spoilt brats?'

'Dear Mattie!' Kate managed a watery smile. The declaration of war between Mattie and the new mistress of Overton had been instantaneous and mutual. Mattie had struggled dourly to keep the upper hand, but Laetitia held all the cards. The importation of a new housekeeper had stripped poor Mattie of her last remnants of authority. If Kate went away there was no doubt that Laetitia would soon find an excuse to dismiss Mattie from the household.

But where could they go?

At first it was easy. The Castlemains had connections. Uncles and aunts, cousins and friends entreated Kate to pay the visits she had never before had time to make. She passed three autumn weeks in Devon, moved to a cousin in Dorset, then took the stage to London where her godmother and her daughter Lucinda gave her a rapturous welcome.

'Dearest Kate! What a pleasure!' Mrs Gisborne enveloped her god-daughter in a cloud of curls, frills and scented warmth. She drew back, holding her at arm's length. 'Dear me, how you have changed, to be sure.'

'For the better, I hope, ma'am.'

'*Certainly* for the better!' What a pity George cannot see her now, thought his fond mamma, assessing her god-daughter shrewdly. I told him she would become a Beauty once she grew into all those arms and legs, but of course he only laughed. Too late, now, of course. I hear she has an understanding with that boy of old Thomas Kingswood's. A pity. She would have done so nicely for George . . .

Following her train of thought, she went on, 'It must be full ten years since you stayed with us. Do you remember? It was when George was to sail for India, and you came with us to see him off.'

'How could I forget? Have you news of him,

28

Godmamma?' Kate felt bound to ask the question, though with a certain diffidence. In the past, news concerning George had not been uniformly good: rather the opposite. Gambling debts; a duel in which his opponent was wounded; the threat of a court martial had dogged George's first years in India. The difficulty of living on his pay had been a recurring theme. But the beaming smile with which Mrs Gisborne had greeted her enquiry banished any fear of a gaffe.

'Wonderful news, my dear! You heard of his transfer to the Civil? He has been appointed Resident in a native state, and advises the Ruler on matters of policy. Such a responsibility! You may imagine how proud we feel of him!'

Kate had murmured congratulations. She was pleased that her godmother need not worry any more about George, the favourite child whose escapades had over the years brought her a good many grey hairs. Kate's own memories of Lucinda's handsome brother were mixed. Gorgeous in the scarlet-and-gold of his new regimentals, George used to take the adoration of his sister and Kate very much for granted. He would tweak their plaits, disrupt their games, and promise extravagant treats which he later forgot.

At the age of fourteen Kate had been a gangling, gawky child, painfully aware of the contrast between her ungainly self and Lucinda's compact grace. George had called her a beanpole, and enquired what the weather was like *up there*; but along with the teasing she could remember acts of unlooked-for kindness: the magnificently dressed doll he brought to replace old wax Nellie after propping her against the nursery fender. The freezing January day he spent patiently teaching her and Lucinda to skate when he might have amused himself with a party of his own friends.

When he boarded the ship he had kissed her, telling her not to cry because he would come back rich as a nabob, with chests full of jewels for them all. She remembered surreptitiously scrubbing her lips behind her handkerchief, for no one had kissed her like that before . . .

Pretty Lucinda was still Kate's bosom friend. It was not long before she extracted every detail of the circumstances

29

that had driven her away from Overton. Either she or her mother must have written to George soon after.

It was nearly two months before Kate left the Gisbornes' cheerful household and travelled to Yorkshire to visit her mother's sister. By now it was high summer and she was becoming restless. These peregrinations were all very well but one could not spend one's life visiting; she was only putting off the moment of facing her bleak and lonely future.

Perhaps, she thought in more optimistic moments, now Laetitia has established herself as mistress of Overton she may resent me less. All I need is a niche where I may live and occupy myself usefully. Perhaps now Jeremy is married and settled I will find it possible to bear the sight of him and Emmie smiling at one another.

But when she eventually returned home on a windy November afternoon she saw at once these hopes were groundless. In the months of her absence, Laetitia had occupied herself in sweeping away all traces of her sister-in-law's stewardship. Her eldest son now occupied Kate's room. Furniture had been moved, trees felled, horses sold. Home no longer felt like home.

Appeals to Charles to stop the rot were met with shrugs and exasperated sighs. 'You can't have things your own way now, Katy,' he snapped, half apologetic, half defiant. 'Letty's mistress here and if you go gallivanting off round the country for months on end you must expect to find changes.'

'So you let her do as she pleases – even to the extent of turning me out of my room?'

Charles' prominent lower lip assumed the petulant droop she remembered from nursery days. 'None of this would matter if you had a home of your own. You had your chances. Why didn't you take them?'

Yes, she had had her chances, and turned them down so she could continue to manage her father's home and relieve both him and her brother of responsibility. A cold fury had possessed Kate. This was the reward she got for her years of hard work.

'Thank you for making the position so clear,' she said in

a shaking voice. 'Since I am no longer welcome in my own home, I will do my best to remove from it without delay.'

'Now, Katy, you know I didn't mean that,' he protested; but she had seen relief flicker in his eyes at the thought of being rid of her. 'I only wondered why you would never look at those fellows who used to offer for you.'

'If you mean Mr Barton and Mr Sievewright, *I* wonder that you would care to be connected with that pair of rogues, even by marriage!'

'Oh, come! Barton was not much of a catch, to be sure, but Sievewright's not a bad fellow.'

'When he is sober.'

'They weren't the only ones, Katy. Be honest. Old Joshua de Havilland was mad to marry you, but you wouldn't have him. Then there was Simon Grant.'

'I did not love him – or any of them.'

'Love!' said her brother disgustedly.

He was right, of course. Secure in the expectation of marrying Jeremy, she had paid little heed to other offers. Now when she cast her mind over the neighbourhood's eligible bachelors, their ranks had thinned almost to vanishing point. Only the brutal hard-riding Alan Barton, whose cruelty, it was whispered, had caused his first wife to take her own life, and poor stammering Septimus Peasbody remained unmarried – the latter was old enough to be her father. Of course she could always set her cap at Parson Stokes, and charge herself with the care of his four ill-favoured daughters . . . She repressed a hysterical laugh.

'Well, I'm glad you find it amusing, for I don't,' said Charles pettishly. 'I can tell you it's no joke to live in a house full of women, each complaining about the others. Between the lot of you I don't get a moment's peace. I've a good mind to cut my losses and sell the whole place. I daresay Kingswood would be glad enough to take it off my hands.'

'No, Charles, you must not think of any such thing,' said Kate hastily, for the Castlemains had lived at Overton since the twelfth century. 'Never fear, I will find myself somewhere to live, and cease to trouble you.'

'Then everyone will accuse me of driving you out.'

'Rubbish!'

But it was one thing to sweep from the room, head high, assuring him she would trouble him no more; a very different matter to fulfil that promise. As the winter tightened its grip on the countryside and they were forced into one another's company, Kate's clashes with her sister-in-law became more frequent, and her brother's temper shorter as he listened to their bickering.

I must go away, thought Kate, but where? What can I do? I can't teach, or sew, or play the piano, or draw. There's nothing in the world I am fit for but ordering servants and overseeing cultivations, and that I'm not allowed to do any more. It was agony for her to watch the flourishing farm and woodlands deteriorate under Charles' slapdash management. Walls crumbled and were not repaired, gates sagged, ditches flooded. Worst of all, the sheep and cattle in which she had taken such pride became lean and scrawny, objects more of pity than envy to their neighbours.

It was in the dark days of January, when the thought of putting an end to her existence had occurred more than once, that she received the letter from India.

She took it to her room and for a while sat staring at it, strangely excited by the thought of the miles of land and ocean it had crossed since leaving the writer's hand. It must be from George. She knew no one else on the Indian subcontinent; but why should George trouble himself to write to her? Of course, she thought, Godmother must have told him of Father's death; this will be the expression of his condolences.

So commonplace an explanation served to dampen her excitement. With no further delay she picked the letter from the table and tore it open . . .

Half-an-hour later when Mattie entered the room to draw the curtains and light the lamp, she found her mistress sitting in the dark by the window which she had not even troubled to close, though wind and rain were blowing in to spatter her dress.

'Why, Miss Kate! Whatever are you thinking of?'

She bustled forward to put matters right then stopped, struck by something unnatural in Kate's seated figure, her pale face and hunched shoulders bent over the sheet of paper in her lap, though it was far too dark to read.

'What ails you, Miss Kate? What's in that letter to upset you?'

'Upset me? No ...' Kate spoke in a dazed voice as if wakening from a deep sleep, and Mattie's thoughts began to run on chest-rubs and possets. Her nurseling's recent pallor and loss of weight had begun to disturb her; but it was easy to see the trouble lay in her mind rather than her body, beyond the reach of such remedies as Mattie's herb-garden could provide.

'Who wrote that letter?' she nagged as Kate relapsed into silence.

'Oh! It is from George – Colonel Gisborne.'

Mattie sniffed. 'What has that young scamp to say for himself?' she asked, and Kate at last raised her eyes from the letter and looked at her directly.

'It's very strange,' she said slowly. 'I don't understand it at all. Oh, Mattie! George has asked me to go to India – and marry him.'

Eugenia believed in punctuality and her appetite was healthy. She had already left the cabin when Kate returned to tidy herself for dinner.

'You're late,' scolded Mattie who was bustling about setting the cabin to rights. 'Where in the world have you been? I've been waiting the best part of an hour. Didn't you hear the gong?'

'Has it gone already? Then I'll go in as I am.'

'With a flounce torn and a great dirty mark on your sleeve? That you will not.' Bristling, Mattie barred her escape. 'Hand me that brush. Whatever will Miss Eugenia say if you go into dinner looking like something the cat brought in?'

Meekly Kate submitted to brush and sponge, and allowed Mattie to hook her into a fresh gown. Laetitia had been unexpectedly generous with cast-offs once Kate's departure

33

from Overton was certain. Though designed for a shorter, stouter woman, this dress of fine green lawn with its simple fichu was a good deal more becoming than the old brown holland Kate wore for walking.

'Now you're worth sixpence more!' Mattie surveyed her with approval, then reached up to pat her cheek before hustling her out of the cabin. 'Hurry now, hinny, or there won't be a bite left for you.'

Kate entered the dining saloon in time to catch the very tail of the Reverend Mr Evans' mumbled grace. With a murmur of apology she slipped into her seat between Colonel Wilson and the parson, and bent her attention on her plate to avoid the inevitable looks of censure from Eugenia and reproach from Captain Molyneux.

Very soon, however, she became aware there was another focus for disapproval in the room, and her own late arrival had gone unnoticed. Beside her Colonel Wilson was puffing and bubbling like a kettle about to boil, while the shrill tones of Mrs Bastable and mincingly refined accents of her friend Mrs Harcourt rose and fell in an outraged counterpoint.

'How dare he come in here?'

'The effrontery! Upon my word, I hardly know what to say!'

'The Captain should be horsewhipped for letting him show his face,' grunted Colonel Wilson.

Kate looked across the room and encountered Ned's agonized gaze. By virtue of his connection with Captain Foster, Ned generally sat near the head of the table where, as his uncle said darkly, he could keep him under his eye. Today, however, he had been shifted from his usual position separating two chubby subalterns, and inserted between Surgeon Matthews and Eugenia Hunter, while his place on the opposite side of the board was occupied by the stranger whose presence was attracting such unfavourable comment.

Kate could see little of him but the back of a dark head bent forward as he leaned across the table to speak to Ned, whose flushed face and crimson-tipped ears expressed social unease, though whether on his own behalf or the

34

stranger's was hard to decide. On either side of Ned his neighbours were turned pointedly away. Eugenia's face was hidden but the rigid set of her shoulders told its own tale, and the surgeon sat with one hand propping his chin and the other twisting the stem of his wine-glass, making no effort to engage the stranger in conversation.

So Colonel Quinn has come out of hiding, thought Kate with a certain admiration, and wished herself better placed to observe the effect of this marauding tiger among the cattle.

'Damned bad form, I call it – begging your pardon, ma'am.' The simmering kettle exploded into steam. 'See that fellow two places away from the Captain? That's your first sight of a Maratha freebooter, ma'am. Name of Quinn. *Colonel* Quinn he calls himself now, though he's nothing to command but a raggle-taggle horde of native troops. Biggest rogue unhung in the Central Highlands. Take a good look at him, ma'am.'

'I am not gifted with second sight. With the best will in the world I cannot learn much from the back of a man's head,' replied Kate rather distantly. It annoyed her that Colonel Wilson should insist on calling her 'ma'am', as if to draw attention to the fact she was no longer in the first blush of youth. Though she knew it was petty, his jocular references to the Fishing Fleet of ladies hoping to catch husbands in India grated on her nerves. What conceited fools men were! As if I had any desire to *catch* a port-nosed old prose like him, she thought angrily. Yet some poor spinster might. To Mabel Davenport, for instance, a proposal from Colonel Wilson would come as manna from heaven, just as George's had to her. The 'Fishing Fleet' was too close to the truth for comfort.

On her other side the parson's unctuous voice chimed in. 'Correct me if I am misinformed, Colonel, but I understand it is Quinn who is responsible for the recent shift of power in the Maratha confederacy? He incited young Jaswant Rao to depose his elder brother, the legitimate heir – '

'Half-brother,' corrected the Colonel. He believed clergymen should stick to religion and leave politics alone. However, he could not resist adding, 'Can't say I blame him. Would have done the same in his place. Kashi Rao is weak in the head and a cruel devil to boot.'

'Yet he was his father's heir. If we British start recognizing usurpers, it will set an unfortunate precedent. For all his faults, Kashi Rao was well-disposed towards us and – ah – amenable.' He smirked. 'It will surprise me if the Governor-General finds Jaswant Rao so ready to oblige him.'

'You're right there!' Colonel Wilson uttered his barking laugh. 'Jaswant Rao Holkar is a stubborn young devil, a chip off the old block, wrong side of the blanket or not. All Marathas are brigands at heart. I saw a lot of him in '94, you know, when we negotiated the boundaries. Used to show me damned fine *shikar*. Never knew a Maratha laugh as he did when poor old Beddington, our Brigadier, was hit on the head by a hailstone in the middle of one of his pijaws. Killed him dead as mutton. No – I can't see this young Holkar taking orders from our Glorious Little Man.'

A sneer twisted his moustache. Like most of his generation, Colonel Wilson thought the new Govenor-General, Lord Mornington, insufferably high-handed, and could hardly stomach his reluctance to accept that anyone might know better than himself how to manage Indian affairs. Decisive Lord Mornington might be: diplomatic he most emphatically was not. In the few months since his appointment he had ruffled a good many feathers, besides laying himself open to charges of nepotism. No one denied that his brother Arthur Wellesley had the makings of a good officer. Nevertheless, it was nothing short of scandalous to set aside his superiors in order to give young Arthur a chance to shine.

As the men embarked on a political discussion in which they made no effort to include her, Kate studied the small social drama unfolding before her at the Captain's end of the table. Despite what she had said, quite a lot could be gleaned from watching the back of the stranger's close-

36

cropped dark head and observing the expression of those seated near him.

Throughout the meal Eugenia maintained the pretence that he did not exist, talking so animatedly to her other neighbour that she allowed Colonel Quinn no conversational opening; but before the cloth was drawn, her position had been seriously undermined by none other than timid Mabel.

Oh, unfair! thought Kate, as she saw the little mouse gently drawn into conversation, but she could not help admiring the Colonel's strategy. So seldom did gentlemen pay the least attention to Mabel that she was quite overwhelmed by finding herself a focus of interest. Hesitantly at first, then with growing loquacity she embarked on the story of her life; oblivious – for the moment at least – of the angry sidelong glances Eugenia directed at her.

Relieved of the duty to keep conversation going, Ned busied himself with clearing his plate in double quick time, while Surgeon Matthews picked his teeth morosely and the Captain, seated between Eugenia and Mrs Bastable, watched from shrewd grey eyes sunk in rolls of fat Quinn's conquest of Mabel Davenport.

At the conclusion of the meal, it was Captain Foster's genial custom to take wine with all his guests, ladies included, before retiring a little topheavily to the study of his charts and log. His departure provided the signal for other gentlemen to propose toasts, and in Eugenia's view it should then have been the duty of Mrs Bastable, senior lady present, to shepherd her little flock out of the dining-room.

But jolly Maria Bastable was too fond both of wine and gentlemen to pay much heed to this convention, and often Eugenia was obliged to recall her to a sense of her duty by rising herself to lead the ladies away before high spirits rendered the gentlemen's conversation unfit for feminine ears.

'Miss Davenport, your very good health! Colonel Quinn! Honoured to have you with us! My compliments, Miss Hunter.'

The Captain was on his feet, drinking to each of his

guests in turn while the stewards hurried round the table filling their glasses. The ladies sipped and bowed thanks; the gentlemen drained their wine in response.

'Now, ladies and gentlemen, I must ask you to excuse me.' With the dexterity of long practice Captain Foster manoeuvred his bulk from behind the table. As the door closed behind him, the other gentlemen resumed their seats and conversation burst out with renewed hilarity, as when children are freed from adult supervision.

'Miss Castlemain. A glass of wine with you?'

A little abstractedly Kate smiled and accepted Colonel Wilson's invitation. Most of her attention was on the other end of the table. Despite the curt refusal he had just received from Eugenia, Colonel Quinn had had the temerity to invite Miss Davenport to drink wine with him, and the little brown mouse's dilemma was painful to behold. It was a standing joke among the male passengers that she would drink with a baboon if it wore Inexpressibles: now her round eyes darted imploring glances between Eugenia and the Colonel, longing to accept yet fearful of dear Miss Hunter's wrath.

'Mabel!'

Softly though the word was uttered, it tipped the balance. Mabel shook her head. 'I must beg you to excuse me, sir,' she said unhappily, flushing crimson.

As the Colonel bowed and turned away, Kate had a fleeting glimpse of him and understood what it must have cost poor Mabel to snub such a man. His mouth was drawn tight, eyes stormy, aware of hostility and its cause. These people hated him, not so much for what he had done as for what he was. Yet he was prepared to risk further humiliation rather than retreat.

Around the table conversation had died. Kate glanced from face to face, noting the expressions of secret glee as the British closed ranks, and suddenly something in her rebelled against their smug self-righteousness, their delight in making others feel inferior.

Raising her head, she looked directly at the Colonel, caught his eye, and smiled an invitation.

'Miss Castlemain!' he said at once, and raised his glass.
'Your health, sir.'

A sigh of mingled outrage and disbelief passed like wind through trees as Kate sipped her wine in response. Ned was grinning broadly, and Eugenia's look of shocked distaste brought laughter bubbling to her lips as it had not for months. Whatever the consequences, she could not regret her small gesture of defiance.

In the hope of evading her cabin-mate's reproaches, Kate lingered in the small saloon after the rest of the ladies retired, but her heart sank as she saw a line of light under the cabin door and knew that Eugenia had waited up for her.

She pushed it open. Though the book of sermons lay open in her lap, Eugenia was not reading. As Kate entered she started up to catch her by the arm, her bony fingers digging in painfully.

'Where have you been? I could not sleep without speaking to you. Oh, Katherine, you have disgraced us all. Why did you not heed my warning?'

In her flowing cotton nightgown, with pale locks cascading down her back, she seemed to fill the cabin. The faintly acrid smell she exuded made Kate's gorge rise. If only she could sleep on deck beneath the stars and escape Eugenia's lectures and her smell! She had hardly expected approval, nevertheless the vehemence of her cabin-mate's reproaches seemed exaggerated.

'You *smiled* at him. How could you do it?'

'I responded to his toast. Surely that is no great matter?'

'No great matter to drink with a *mustee*? When I saw you raise your glass I could have died of mortification.'

'A *mustee*?'

'Oh, do not play the innocent! You put me out of all patience. Anyone with half an eye can see Colonel Quinn has native blood.'

Of course. The dark sombre gaze that was not quite European. The faint lilting intonation. Like a key fitting a lock, small things in Quinn's appearance that had intrigued Kate slipped into place. A streak of obstinacy made her say,

39

'That may be his misfortune but I cannot see it is his fault. Must we shun a man for an accident of birth?'

'You will soon discover the natives are no more liberal than ourselves towards mixed blood,' said Eugenia tartly. She paused, opening her pale eyes so wide that a sliver of white showed above the iris – a gesture that heralded one of her lectures.

'It is a common misapprehension among griffins to suppose that because they are far from home and freed from the stricture of their acquaintance they may conduct themselves as they please in India,' she said in measured tones. 'Nothing could be farther from the truth! So far as females are concerned, any woman who fails to observe the strictest propriety in her relations with the opposite sex will very soon attract invidious comment, besides rendering herself vulnerable to the wiles of natives who are always quick to observe and profit from the least weakness on our part. Should it become known, for example, that you allowed yourself to be inveigled into familiarity with a *mustee*, and should word of this reach the ears of your husband-to-be, it would cause him untold distress.'

'I am sure it would not. George is the most easygoing of mortals.'

'That may have been true when last you saw him, but can you be sure it is now? India has a way of changing the natures even of those we think we know best. Never forget for a moment that everything we have gained we owe not to force of arms but to *moral* superiority. If we allow that ascendancy to be eroded, we put ourselves on a par with the dissolute native rulers and we will forfeit our gains as swiftly as we have won them. Do you understand?'

Anything to bring the lecture to an end! Kate nodded. At once Eugenia smiled and her eyes returned to their normal shape. 'I am so glad. The Devil tempted and you succumbed, so now we will join together in prayer for God's forgiveness.'

Again the bony hand descended on Kate's shoulder. Reluctantly she knelt, trying to ignore the sour smell emanating from beneath the nightgown as Eugenia pressed shoulder and hip against her.

'O Lord God, Who bringeth Light into darkness, we Thine unworthy servants beseech Thee to guide and defend us . . .'

Her face was rapt, her torrent of words filled the small cabin. Very gently Kate eased away until their shoulders no longer touched. Far from going out, the flicker of defiance had grown into a strong flame. For months she had endured Eugenia's bigotry and bullying, listened to her advice, tried to learn from her experience, but all she had been offered was a succession of stifling prohibitions. Eugenia was deaf and blind to anything outside her narrow track of prejudice and propriety. It was time – high time – to strike a blow for freedom.

Quietly she rose and made for the door. Arrested in mid prayer, Eugenia opened her eyes.

'Where are you going? I have not finished.'

'I want to call Mattie.'

'Call Mattie? For shame! She must be asleep. I will help you undress when we have finished our prayers.'

The thought of those bony hands on her skin or hair made Kate shudder. 'It is kind of you, but Mattie will want to take my clothes.'

Eugenia, who was travelling without a maid and often imposed her own little chores on Mattie's good nature, said, 'Really, there is not the least need to wake the poor old woman. I can help you perfectly well.'

The thought of how annoyed Mattie would be to hear herself so described made Kate smile. 'Oh, she does not mind. She likes to know I am safe in bed and will not trouble her again.'

'Wait.' Eugenia laid her hand on Kate's arm and drew her close, staring into her face with an intensity that made her uncomfortable. 'Before you fetch her, give me your promise that you will *never* speak to that man again.'

'Never speak . . . ?'

Kate wondered if she could be serious, but the look on Eugenia's pale face made it clear she was. Surprise gave way to anger. There was no way she could refuse without giving offence, but with a glorious sensation of freedom she realized she no longer cared.

'Promise me! I shall not sleep easy until I have your promise.'

'Then you may expect a disturbed night,' said Kate very clearly.

'But my dear Katherine, I have just explained – '

'I refuse to promise to whom I will or will not speak. You have no right to ask it. I am not answerable to you in any way, Eugenia, and I beg you will allow me to conduct myself as I please. Do I make myself plain?'

Eugenia withdrew her hand as sharply as if she had grasped a nettle. Her face flushed and to Kate's consternation she saw tears glitter in the gooseberry eyes.

'Then all I can do is pray for you,' she said in a wounded voice, and turned with shaking shoulders towards her berth.

3

'You've put the cat among the pigeons and no mistake, my lamb,' said Mattie. She placed the mended brown holland on top of Kate's clean underwear and regarded her mistress with worry in her shrewd brown eyes.

Kate looked very different from the listless creature she had become accustomed to find drooping over a book at this hour. Her cheeks were tinged with colour, eyes bright; even her hair seemed to have acquired an unruly new curl.

'Ah, you may smile, but you'll have to watch your step for all that,' she warned. 'All the ladies and gentlemen are talking about you. I heard Mrs Bastable call you a forward hussy and say the way you carried on last night was a disgrace.'

'Surely you do not believe anything so absurd?'

'What I believe is neither here nor there, Miss Kate, as you well know. There's no saying what some others will credit after living cooped up together for months on end. That Miss Eugenia's out to make trouble for you, mark my words. She and the old Colonel. Once that precious pair gets its knife into you, it'll be no easy matter to pull it out.'

'I don't care for them.'

'Then you should, Miss Kate. Oh, you may toss your head, but I've known ladies like Miss Eugenia before. If you get on the wrong side of her, you'll have no character left when you step ashore. What if Major Gisborne should hear of it?'

'She is making a deal of fuss about nothing,' said Kate scornfully.

'Drinking with a gentleman before you were introduced? For shame, Miss Kate! Your poor mother would turn in her grave.'

Kate put her arms about the little woman, smiling at her worried face. Mattie was never cross for long. She had been

43

guide and mentor to Kate and her brother as long as they could remember. It was only as a last resort that she invoked the spirit of their mother, which showed that however absurd Kate thought this business, Mattie took it seriously.

Mattie was no fool. The youngest of a Derbyshire blacksmith's large brood, she had been reared in dire poverty from which she had escaped at fourteen by going into service at the Big House. There, her willingness and good sense as well as the herbal lore learned from a gipsy grandmother made her a general favourite, and Kate's mother had chosen Mattie to accompany her to her new home upon her marriage to Sir Gregory Castlemain.

At Overton she had risen rapidly through the household. Pretty and spirited, with flashing gipsy eyes and a handspan waist, Mattie did not lack for suitors. None of the Overton lads' blandishments, however, persuaded her to change her privileged status for anything resembling the conditions into which she had been born, and she remained single.

In 1789, the year of France's Revolution, when noble heads had began to tumble across the Channel and French *emigrés* fled to England, Lady Castlemain caught a fever from one of the destitute *aristos* she had taken into her home. The best physician in the district was called to attend her. Waving aside Mattie's remedies he bled his patient repeatedly but despite – or because of – his efforts she died a week later, leaving Mattie to provide her children with all they would ever know of a mother's love and care. The close bonds forged then had survived Kate's rebellious adolescence and the growing difference in their stations after she came of an age to assume domestic responsibility herself.

Though the handspan waist had thickened with the years and the flashing eyes were now meshed in wrinkles, Mattie in her mid-sixties was still as active and nimble as a woman half that age.

'None of your wheedling now, Miss Kate,' she said, but her expression belied the sharp tone. 'I'm not deaf yet nor blind neither.'

'Whatever do you mean? *Oh!*'

'Oh, indeed! I'm not the only one saw you creep out at crack of dawn to walk with a certain gentleman, deny it if you can.'

'I didn't creep.'

'You took good care not to wake Miss Eugenia, all the same.'

'She was snoring,' said Kate defensively. 'The cabin was so hot I thought I would suffocate. Really, it is too bad. Can I not even go on deck for a breath of air without you spying on me and making up nasty tales?'

'Better you hear them from me than from others I could mention.' Mattie's gnarled hands moved deftly, separating Eugenia's creams, lotions, and brushes from Kate's on the tiny dressing-table they shared. 'I declare I don't know why she troubles to plaster these on her face. Won't make a blind bit o'differ to her looks,' she muttered.

Kate gave her a sideways glance. 'I didn't go on deck to meet him, you know. It was quite by chance. Oh, Mattie! He told me such interesting things. I learned more about India in an hour than I would in a hundred years from Eugenia.'

'I daresay,' sniffed Mattie, but Kate could not regret that dawn encounter.

It was in a very different mood that she had woken, with aching head and puffy eyes after a dream-ridden night. Unable to endure the torment of listening to Eugenia's snores a moment longer, she had risen stealthily and slipped out of the cabin. The sky was already paling from grey to primrose, and a turn or two on the foredeck in the delicious pre-dawn freshness relieved her headache. She had determined on a complete circuit of the deck before returning to the cabin when she glimpsed near the aft rail a flaming red head that could only belong to Ned Sweeney. Thinking to chaff him for his recent neglect, she hurried towards him; it was only when she was almost upon him that she saw he was not alone. Seated on a coil of rope, his back against the rail and a cigar between his teeth, very much at his ease, was Colonel Quinn.

To withdraw or pass by was impossible. Both men rose

and bowed; and Ned with an impish grin at once begged leave to present his friend. It was the most natural thing in the world to shake the Colonel's outstretched hand and accept his offer of another coil of rope. Comfortably settled with the breeze cooling her face and raising small silver ripples on the dark sea, she listened to Ned's chatter and covertly studied his companion.

No oil painting: indeed, a face to frighten children, she thought, taking in the full horror of the scar. How could a man survive such a blow? He was an inch or so shorter than herself, muscular and well-made, swarthy but no darker than many Latins. But his eyes were beautiful; large and velvety, they hardly seemed to belong to the scarred and pockmarked face. Seeing her watching him, he smiled with so much frankness and good humour that her spirits lifted.

'I have to thank you for coming to my aid last night, Miss Castlemain.'

'Oh, that was nothing.' It surprised her that he should speak of it.

'On the contrary. I had not realized the depth of feeling against me.'

Embarrassed, she turned to Ned. 'I did not mean to interrupt you.'

Hero-worship shone in his eyes and his manner had a new vivacity. 'Colonel Quinn has been telling me about tiger-hunting. It sounds famous sport! When they are shot the brutes will even jump on the elephant's head to attack the hunter.'

'Hardly astonishing if you have been so uncivil as to shoot them,' Kate observed. The Colonel gave her a measuring look.

'Are you opposed to hunting, Miss Castlemain?'

'I hardly know. Certainly I have no wish to meet a tiger.'

'This was a *man-eater*,' said Ned with a hint of reproach.

Kate smiled. 'In that case I withdraw my objection. Tell me, Colonel Quinn, are you familiar with the Malwa region?'

Interest sparked in his eyes. 'You are going to Malwa?'

'To Attaganj.'

46

'I have a most particular reason to know Attaganj, for I was born there. My father commanded the first of the Raja's regular battalions.'

Kate was puzzled. She had taken the trouble to learn what she could about Attaganj; it was not a great deal, but she knew that the treaty whereby the Raja agreed to accept Company troops for his protection was no more than ten years old. 'But surely, in those days the Company had no troops there?'

'These were not Company troops.' Seeing her mystification he explained, 'My father began his military career in the Company service, but after marrying my mother he was obliged to resign his commission. He took service instead with the Raja of Attaganj. How well I remember the palace! As a child I used to go daily to visit the Raja's collection of wild beasts, and Ibrahim their keeper, who was my special friend, would let me stroke the hunting cheetahs with their golden collars, and sit upon their backs.'

'How long did you live there?'

'Until the Raja's rebellion against his feudal overlord began the troubles that ended by throwing Attaganj into the British lion's mouth. I suppose I was seven or eight when old Madhav Rao, father of the present Raja, tried to break free from the Holkars of Indore. He withheld his yearly tribute, but in the battle that followed his army suffered a defeat and my father was killed. I owe my life to the clemency of Tukoji Holkar, co-regent with the great queen Ahalya Bhai, who found me hiding in the baggage train and carried me to Indore on his saddle-bow.'

'I did not know Marathas were inclined to philanthropy.'

'He was a good man. He brought me up with his own sons, as a huntsman might rear a fox-cub in a litter of hound pups, and with much the same result.'

'What result?'

'Oh, a good deal of snapping and snarling!' he said, laughing. 'Jaswant Rao and I were allies against the rest, even in those days.'

She would have liked to hear more but Ned had begun to fidget. Seeing that Maratha history was of little interest

47

to him, she directed the conversation back to the inexhaustible topic of hunting. She was the intruder in this dawn *tête-à-tête*. It would never do to monopolize the Colonel while Ned sat silent.

When the classic formula 'Pray tell me more of . . .' had worked its unfailing magic, and the two had settled happily to a discussion of guns and elephants, she assumed the listener's role quite contentedly.

Waiting now with more than her usual patience for Mattie to pronounce her fit to be seen, Kate smiled at the recollection.

'Yes, you may look like a cat that's been at the cream, *now*, but you'll laugh the other side of your face when you hear what Miss Eugenia has to say to you,' muttered her maid, dragging the comb through Kate's curls with a brutal disregard for tangles.

'Ow, Mattie! That hurts. There's no need to fuss. Eugenia has better things to think of than my affairs.'

'If you believe that, you're a bigger fool than I supposed,' snapped Mattie with a want of respect Kate could not have tolerated from anyone else. 'There, now. Off you go and don't say I didn't warn you.'

Still smiling, Kate went in search of breakfast. In the dining saloon, white-jacketed stewards went gliding between the small tables dispensing the coffee, toast, devilled kidneys and mutton chops which every English man and woman regarded as an indispensable prelude to a day in the tropics, while in the intervals of munching the passengers indulged in the usual desultory chit-chat of those who, while not actually detesting one another, would not have chosen their present company.

As Kate appeared in the doorway, the rattle of cups and clatter of cutlery ceased. Conversation was suddenly stilled and eleven pairs of censorious eyes watched in silence as she advanced towards her place.

'Good morning, Mrs Bastable. Good morning, Colonel Wilson.'

Her greetings fell into the silence, like pebbles tossed into mud. Good heavens, thought Kate, torn between

48

amusement and disbelief, surely they cannot mean to treat *me* in the way they did Colonel Quinn?

The amusement was shortlived as she realized that was indeed their intention.

'A beautiful day, Mrs Harcourt. Are you going to – ?' Kate stopped in mid sentence. There was nothing to be gained from questioning the back of Mrs Harcourt's head. Ignoring the snub she turned to Captain Molyneux, whose sandy-lashed eyes moved shiftily, avoiding her gaze. Before her civil request for him to pass the marmalade was fairly pronounced, he too had begun an animated debate with his neighbour on the other side.

This is absurd! thought Kate, her temper rising. How dare they refuse to answer me?

'I am obliged to you,' she said loudly to the steward who was silently offering a dish of preserves; and received a startled look from him, since no well-trained servant expects thanks for performing his duty.

'Mr Evans!' Leaning across the table she claimed the parson's attention, sure that he, at least, could not ignore her. 'Can you tell me on which of St Paul's voyages – ?'

'Steward! This chop is cold,' he exclaimed as if she had not spoken. 'It's a disgrace. Fetch me another and look sharp.'

Baffled, Kate relapsed into silence. They were all in it. She would not give them the satisfaction of seeing her lose her temper. On all sides the hum of conversation rose and fell, excluding her. It was as if she had become invisible or – she thought – as if a wall of glass separated her from the other passengers. She felt strongly tempted to rise and sweep from the room, foregoing breakfast, but an inbuilt obstinacy she hardly knew she possessed kept her seated. If this was Eugenia's method of punishing her for extending to Colonel Quinn a perfectly normal civility, she must be shown it was ineffectual. But though she made a brave pretence of eating, Kate's food proved no easier to swallow than sawdust; seldom had she welcomed any sound more than she did the scraping chairlegs that signalled the end of the meal.

Hopes of a return to normality outside the dining-room were soon dashed. This was the hour when the arbiter of morals and keeper of the vessel's conscience habitually withdrew to her cabin to prepare the homily she would deliver at her prayer-meeting later in the day. Jolly Maria Bastable, who never liked to admit her craving for cards in Eugenia's presence, would seize the opportunity to draw the other ladies into a cosy circle to while away the forenoon with a few hands of faro or loo in an atmosphere of feminine merriment, enhanced by the knowledge that Eugenia would not approve such pastimes.

But today there was no lifted eyebrow or nod of covert invitation from Mrs Bastable as Eugenia disappeared towards her cabin. Like a flock of preoccupied hens, the ladies clucked and fluttered away to private nests; the gentlemen shut themselves and their cigars in the round-house; and Kate was left with the choice of sitting alone on deck or braving the cabin and inevitable lecture from Eugenia.

Scolding herself for being a coward, she chose the former, and took a seat beneath the fringed awning on the foredeck which usually provided privacy and shade for Mrs Bastable's card-school. Minutes passed, the sun grew hotter and the horizon dulled to a shimmering haze, but no one came to join her.

She was an outcast. How has this happened, she thought with a kind of despairing wonder. How can so small – so *ludicrously* petty an incident – have grown overnight into a full-blown feud? Am I at fault, or are they?

The oily sea heaved sluggishly; the sails hung in sullen folds as if no breeze would ever fill them again. Kate felt a burning impatience to be done with this interminable voyage and the carping prejudices of those on board. Was this a foretaste of life in India?

She shook her head, trying to clear a creeping fog of despondency. What if George himself had been forced into the Company mould and the laughing devil-may-care officer she remembered had become another Colonel Wilson?

50

'Kate?'

She looked up, blinking against the sun. Ned stood just beyond the awning, regarding her somewhat anxiously.

'Am I disturbing you?'

'Not in the least.'

She patted the seat in invitation and he sat down saying, 'You looked rather grim. I was afraid you wanted to be alone with your thoughts.'

'They were not very pleasant ones.'

'Because no one will speak to you?'

'Who told you?'

'Mr Simkins said it was a disgrace, the way they treated you at breakfast. He heard them planning it before you came in. Miss Hunter and Colonel Wilson decided, and the others copied them. He said it made him boil with rage.'

'Indeed! I am obliged to Mr Simkins,' said Kate, touched to know such tumultuous emotions raged beneath the second steward's sedate exterior.

'I wish I had been there. I would have told them what I thought of them.'

'Oh, no, that would never do,' said Kate hastily. 'It will soon blow over, depend on it. By tomorrow, I daresay we shall all have forgotten the whole silly business. Did you eat in the galley with Mr Simkins?'

'No. Colonel Quinn invited me to share his meal.' Ned glanced at her quickly and then away. From his puckered brow and restless hands she divined that something troubled him.

'Well, out with it, then,' she invited when the silence had stretched a minute or more.

He started. 'Out with what?'

'Whatever is on your mind.'

'Oh!' He fidgeted with a length of twine, twisting it into a tight coil then releasing it. 'There is something you ought to know,' he said at last; and lapsed into silence once more.

'Is it something to do with Colonel Quinn?' She kept her tone carefully neutral.

'Yes. No. Well, yes, in a way. I suppose it is. How did you know?'

51

'Something Colonel Quinn has said to you concerning me?' she hazarded when he showed no inclination to enlighten her further.

Ned's look was anxious, almost hunted. 'Promise you won't be angry if I tell you?'

'Why should I be angry?'

'Well, you know,' said Ned vaguely. 'Gentlemen should never discuss ladies, and all that rot.'

'What did Colonel Quinn tell you about me?'

'Oh, not about you!' said Ned hastily. 'No. It was about – about the gentleman you are going to marry.'

'Indeed?' Her eyebrows rose. 'Is Colonel Quinn acquainted with Major Gisborne?'

'Yes. No . . . I am not sure. That is what I thought you should be told,' said Ned, taking the plunge. 'You see, Colonel Quinn happened to ask me the – the name of the officer you are to marry. I told him it was Major Gisborne . . . and he looked quite angry and said that was impossible.'

'*Impossible?*'

'Yes. He said – ' Ned went on bravely ' – the only Major Gisborne he knew was a double-dealing rogue and deserved to be hanged. I thought . . . I thought you ought to know.'

It was no use venting her anger on Ned. He had only done what he saw as his duty. Kate sat with her hands tight clenched in her lap until a measure of calm returned.

'He must mean another Major Gisborne,' she said at last. 'It is not such an unusual name.'

'Nor a common one.'

'Oh, I don't know. Think of the thousands of Company officers. There may be half-a-dozen Gisbornes, with Majors and Colonels and all the rest of it. Some of them may be related to George, for all I know. The Gisbornes are a large family.'

Ned was silent. Colonel Quinn had enquired if Major Gisborne's name was George, but he had been unable to tell him. Glancing at Kate's set face, he thought it unnecessary to mention this. However plausible she found her own theory about a bevy of Major Gisbornes, the law

52

of probability seemed weighted against more than one of them being called George.

'You see?' she urged. 'A simple case of mistaken identity.'

'I am sorry if I – '

'No, you were right to tell me. But it is very wrong of Colonel Quinn to spread such malicious gossip,' she added fiercely, 'and if I see him I shall not scruple to tell him so. Oh! How glad I shall be when this voyage is over!'

When he left her, she drew from her reticule the sheaf of George's letters that accompanied her everywhere. It was not a very substantial sheaf. George was no great correspondent and in the months since they had become engaged no more than five letters had passed in either direction. So much of George's had been concerned with practical arrangements for her journey that they left little space for introspection or sentiment. Kate told herself she preferred it so. Any declaration of undying love from a man she had not seen for ten years would raise serious doubts of his sincerity. Far better – she argued when her weaker self searched in vain for some hint of romance in George's stiff prose – far better they should be honest with one another than nourish false hopes.

In one passage alone George had addressed himself to self-appraisal, and it was to these lines that she now turned.

You ask what I expect from marriage, and what you may expect in return. We are both mature enough, I hope, to put behind us the extravagant follies of youth and be realistic in our expectations. You have honoured me by your frankness in writing of your disappointed hopes, and I will be equally open in admitting that my life here in India has not been wholly devoid of female companionship, though I need hardly tell you that liaisons of so ephemeral and transitory a nature need cause you no uneasiness.

I suppose I have my share of faults, and to your eyes may seem sufficiently crossgrained for no further explanation of my failure to marry earlier to be necessary; yet in my own defence I must add that never since I set foot in India have I encountered a woman of my own race whose character matched her

53

outward attractions. This is no country for faint hearts, and the exacting nature of my occupation obliges me to seek a helpmeet who will not shrink from living far removed from the society of her own kind. But before I paint too dark a picture let me say that for anyone with the courage and curiosity to seek them, the advantages of this life are manifold and I for one would not willingly return to the constrictions of cantonments.

So to sum up my expectations of you, dear Kate, I look for a wife who will run my household, order my servants, bear my children and share my leisure hours as well as my worldly goods. I hope you will also share the duties and perils as well as the satisfaction of bringing the benefits of our civilization to those whom God has called us to rule. In return, I offer my respect, loyalty and support, and hope you will consider it a fair bargain . . .

No word of love, she thought, putting the much-creased paper carefully away. A fair bargain, George offered her. A business agreement. Was she foolish to wish for just a little more warmth in his declaration? Was it unreasonable to hope that the old fun-loving George she remembered had not been entirely eclipsed by this sober stranger?

Of course, it was difficult to judge people from their letters. If his were the product of as much thought and labour as hers to him had been, it was hardly surprising if they lacked spontaneity. She herself had torn up half-a-dozen sheets of paper, striving to hit on the right note of dignified gratitude with which to accept his proposal. It had been difficult to translate her feelings into words that were neither mawkish nor self-righteous. Certainly George's tone was solemn, but he could hardly treat so serious a subject with flippancy.

A home, a husband, possibly children. A respected place in the world. Any woman who asked more must be decidedly hard to please. It was, as he said, a fair bargain . . .

'Ali tells me it will blow before nightfall,' said Mattie as she dressed Kate's hair before dinner. She had quickly established excellent relations with the other servants aboard, most of whom had found occasion during the voyage to apply to her for panaceas for various ailments, sea-sickness in particular. Through this network she was able to supply her mistress with gossip and information long before they became generally known.

'Wishful thinking,' sighed Kate, thinking of the limp sails; but the Captain's servant was right in his estimate of the weather's mood. After dinner the brassy sky hazed over for the first time in weeks, and before sunset the canvas had begun to flap and strain.

That night and all the next day a wind like an oven blast drove them landward, and so violently did the vessel pitch and roll that Captain Foster forbade any of his passengers to venture on deck until the storm had passed.

Thus the forces of nature succeeded where those of civilization had failed, for Eugenia – a poor sailor – was obliged to solicit Mattie's sovereign remedy for sea-sickness, and this she could hardly do while on unfriendly terms with Mattie's mistress.

An olive branch was offered and accepted. In the cabin an uneasy peace was restored and both ladies studiously avoided further reference to Colonel Quinn.

By dawn on the third day the storm had blown itself out. Kate rose early and hurried on deck, where she found Ned at his usual station by the aft rail, waving his hat to a lone figure seated in the bows of the Captain's launch, which was being vigorously propelled towards the palm-fringed shore by its crew of pig-tailed, nankeen-jacketed oarsmen.

'Has the Captain gone ashore?'

'No, it is Colonel Quinn. My uncle lent him his launch to avoid delay.'

To avoid awkward questions from the Port authorities, more likely, thought Kate, but she said nothing. It was none of her business how Captain Foster and Colonel Quinn conducted their affairs.

'He desired to be remembered to you, and bade me tell you that if there is anything he can do to help you, he will be pleased to be of service.'

'Very civil of Colonel Quinn,' said Kate a little dryly.

'How am I supposed to acquaint him with my need for his help?'

'You can give me the message.'

'Oh, Ned! Once you are at your desk, I fear your employers will not look kindly on your running errands for me.'

His expressive mouth twitched and she studied him more attentively. His eyes were sparkling: half guilty, half triumphant laughter trembled on his lips. Plainly he was bursting to tell her something.

'What's up, Ned? What are you laughing at?'

His bony frame seemed to grow and expand as he straightened his shoulders. 'I don't suppose I shall spend much time at a desk in future,' he said airily. 'I have made up my mind that the life of a Writer would not suit me at all.'

'Why, Ned, whatever do you mean? I thought it was all arranged.'

'So it was. Arranged by my schoolmaster, and my mother, and my aunt's husband. Not by me. I never wished to be a damned *cranny*. I want to be a soldier, and that – ' he took a few prancing steps along the deck ' – that is what I *shall* be.'

She stared at him, astonished. 'But who will buy your commission? I thought you said – ?'

'Not a *Company* soldier.' His eyes shifted a trifle uneasily. 'I mean to make my fortune as a military adventurer.' Even before he added, 'Like Colonel Quinn,' she had realized whose hand lay behind this decision.

'Oh, no! You must not do such a thing. You cannot throw away your whole career on a whim! You know nothing of Colonel Quinn.'

'I know as much as I need to.' Ned's lips set in an obstinate line. 'Holkar is raising new battalions and needs officers. I mean to be a general before I am thirty.'

The unscrupulous devil! thought Kate angrily. How easy a man like Quinn would find it to play on poor Ned's frustrated ambitions.

'Why do you suppose Holkar needs a bigger army?' she

given any thought to how you will feel when you are ordered to fire on your own countrymen?'

'That won't happen,' said Ned confidently. 'Jaswant Rao has too much sense to fight the British. Colonel Quinn says so, and he knows him as well as any man.'

'Since when has a Maratha been known to keep his promises? Everyone agrees they are the biggest liars on earth.'

Ned's face fell. 'Oh, Kate, I thought you would be pleased. I would never have told you my plans if I knew you were going to carp and scold. You remember you told me Major Gisborne had taken his chance? Well, don't you see? This is *my* chance. I won't throw it away.'

'What nonsense! Come, Ned, be a sensible fellow and forget this wild notion. There is no honour or glory in being a mercenary, you know. From what I hear, the Maratha battalions are no better than a rabble of murderers and thieves.'

Ned shook his head. The joyous mischief had drained from his face and his eyes were over-bright. 'I thought you at least would understand,' he said jerkily. 'I see I was wrong. Excuse me, Miss Castlemain.'

Sketching a bow, he walked away, his back stiff with reproach.

'Oh, Ned, come back! I did not mean – '

It was no use. He had gone. Kate sighed and stared at the approaching island, now taking shape in the morning mist.

Shoals of slim, fragile-looking craft loaded high with merchandise were darting out to greet the tall East Indiaman: small predatory fish eager to fasten their teeth in the blubber of a whale. Fruit-vendors held oranges aloft, or dangled great hands of bananas temptingly over the side. Cloth merchants unrolled bales of shimmering silks; shrill cries of, 'Verree beautiful! Verree cheap, memsahib!' floated to her ears.

It would have been amusing, thought Kate, to bargain and haggle a little with the sellers of these exotic wares; to buy a length of silk, a shining brass pot as a keepsake to remind her of this first contact with India. If Ned had been there to laugh and encourage, she would have opened negotiations with one of the smiling half-naked boatmen displaying his wares just under the rail.

'All this stuff is rubbish,' remarked Eugenia's supercilious voice at her elbow. 'If you wish to buy silk, you had better wait until we go ashore. These people will only rob you.'

'I daresay you are right.' Kate closed her reticule and turned away. Cursing Colonel Quinn and all his works, she returned to her cabin.

4

The Island of Bombay and its smaller satellites, which cling to India's western shore like a cluster of teats to the udder of some fabulous animal, were part of the dowry brought by the Portuguese princess, Catherine of Braganza, upon her marriage to Charles II of England.

That merry and impecunious monarch, preferring a bird in the hand to two in the bush, promptly leased them to the East India Company for the far from kingly sum of ten pounds a year. Very turbulent and uncertain the first hundred of those years proved for the infant colony, as successive Mughal Emperors blew hot and cold upon the notion of trade with these thrusting *faranghis* precariously perched on the Western edge of their Empire. From time to time they even made efforts to push them off, but the British clung on as tight as leeches, consolidating their gains as the Mughal power weakened and the great Nawabs who had been the Emperor's officers of State carved themselves kingdoms of their own.

A gadfly may annoy an elephant, but hardly threaten him. In time the descendants of Akbar gave up their attempts to drive the Bombay merchants into the sea. While they dallied by fountains in fretted marble courts, or wrote Persian poems under the red-gold *chenar* trees of Shalimar, the busy bag-wigged, hard-drinking British steadily expanded their influence, building fortifications strong enough to repel Maratha sea-pirates, and airy bungalows to catch the breeze on Malabar Hill.

During the eighteenth century, the predatory power of the Marathas became even more of a threat to Bombay than the Emperor's displeasure had been in the colony's early days. Trained and led by French mercenaries, the armies of the Marathas rapidly learned new techniques in warfare, acquiring steadiness and discipline as well as powerful new artillery. As Napoleon's conquering armies stretched their tentacles eastwards in the last years of the eighteenth century, it took no great leap of imagination on the part of Bombay's Governor to see that a conjunction between the Marathas and the French could prove highly damaging to British interests.

Hot-headed young gentlemen flown with the notorious Bombay Punch might clamour for a confrontation with the Corsican ogre, but Governor Duncan did not share their enthusiasm. Despatches intercepted between the dominant Maratha chief Scindia and Bonaparte's agents left no room for doubt that the French regarded Bombay as the back door to India, which a sufficiently determined push would force open. With most of the Company's strength still occupied in subduing Mysore and propping up the wavering morale of the Nizam of Hyderabad, Bombay could expect no immediate help in the event of an attack.

Despite these worries and rumours, the view of Bombay Island that greeted the sea-weary passengers lining *Neptune*'s rail was a very pretty, tranquil one. As the ship glided past the lighthouse on Old Woman Island and turned her bows towards the harbour, handsome white buildings set off by the dusty green of palm trees fringing the shore brought exclamations of admiration to the lips of those who had not been there before, and murmurs of pleased recognition from returning inhabitants.

To starboard, Cross Island with its beacon marked the harbour's entrance; to port the grave bulk of the castle was surmounted by the cathedral's slender spire. Mirrored in the clear water, the buildings along the Bund seemed to plunge their foundations down to the sea bed, with only the ripple of a passing boat to show where land stopped and water began.

Wait on board until you hear from me, George had written. *I hope to meet the ship myself, but travel in India is an uncertain business. Should I be delayed, my good friends Mr and Mrs Briggs have expressed themselves happy to put you up until such time as I arrive. This will save the expense of a hotel besides making you acquainted with a couple whose friendship I value. Montagu Briggs was the Acting Judge at my first upcountry posting and is a very good fellow. His wife is among the foremost in Bombay society and will, I know, assist you in making any necessary additions to your wardrobe. In Attaganj, goods of European manufacture are largely unknown, and you should provide yourself amply with necessaries before coming here.*

Be assured I will waste no time in joining you . . .

Thus forewarned, Kate was able to wait with a fair degree of composure during the frenzy of disembarkation. Other passengers made their farewells, collected servants and baggage, and stepped ashore. When she and Mattie were the only females remaining on board and there was still no word from George, an absurd new dread took hold of her. Suppose they failed to recognize one another?

He had sent her a locket containing his miniature, but the native artist had given him a decidedly Asiatic appearance. The elongated eyes with downward-drooping lids, arched brows and small pursed mouth framed in a forest of stylized whiskers might just as well have belonged to some Raja as to a British officer.

Nevertheless George had called it 'a fair likeness', and had evidently thought well enough of the portrait to enclose it in a handsome gold locket with their entwined initials set in tiny pearls upon the lid.

'Miss Castlemain?'

A steward approached to hand her a folded chit. With a leap of the heart she glanced at the superscription, but the writing was unfamiliar.

'From Master George – Major Gisborne, I should say?' Mattie craned forward eagerly.

Kate scanned the few lines. In a hand so flowing that it was difficult to discern where one word ended and the next began, Mrs Briggs welcomed her to Bombay, regretted that the doctor had forbidden her to stir from her home until sundown, and begged Miss Castlemain to accompany the messenger to their house.

'Who gave you this?' Kate turned to the steward.

'I'll take you to him, Miss.'

On deck the messenger waited, a gaunt, badger-bearded, barefoot man of middle years and worried demeanour. He wore a plain red turban, neatly folded, wrinkled white trousers and a spotless tunic girdled with the brass-plated belt of a *chaprasi*. Behind him stood half-a-dozen coolies naked but for the cloth about their loins.

'*Salaam, memsahib!*' He bowed with joined palms. 'I am Ram Singh, chaprasi to Briggs Sahib. Please to follow.'

The moment they stepped beyond the shade, Kate felt her head swim. Even in their light slippers her feet seemed swollen to twice their usual size and drawing breath was an effort. Strange smells, most of them unpleasant, assaulted her nostrils as she followed their guide through knots of natives gathered on the quay to where two long box-like conveyances attached to slender poles had been parked in the shadow of a wall. Beside each squatted a team of sinewy natives who rose, salaaming, as the ladies approached.

Ram Singh drew aside the curtain across an opening, and invited Kate to enter.

'Oh, Miss!' breathed Mattie in ecstasy as the glorious realization burst upon her that she was to be carried, too. Through the gauzy curtains of the *palanquin* her bright brown eyes and sharp nose poked out like the snout of an excited hedgehog.

George had advised against bringing an English servant. *In my experience, they become overbearing towards the natives and over-familiar towards their masters,* he had written, but in this matter Kate had ignored his wishes. Mattie was more of a friend than a servant, she argued, and her situation at Overton was too precarious to leave her there.

With a swooping movement she felt herself lifted as the bearers hoisted their poles. They set off at a swinging trot, grunting and chanting as they ran. The motion had a floating, dreamlike quality, decidedly unsettling to one who had barely acquired her land-legs. Thankful to be out of the sun, Kate leaned back against the palanquin's plump cushions, too overcome by heat and dizziness to feel more than a faint curiosity as to where they were taking her and what had become of George.

The reason for the doctor's prohibition against venturing forth in the sun became plain the moment Sarah Briggs rose to greet her guest. Strikingly tall and generously built, she was also in the last month of pregnancy, but she bore her bulk gracefully as she billowed across the dark polished wood floor of the hall to grasp Kate's hands with uncomplicated friendliness.

'Oh, you have come! I am so pleased to meet you, Miss Castlemain – may I call you Kate? My name is Sarah but my friends call me Sal. As soon as we heard George was engaged to be married I made him promise to bring you here. I do wish you happy! George is one of my husband's oldest friends.'

Still talking she drew Kate towards a chaise-longue.

'Come and sit down and tell me all about your voyage. I was so sorry not to meet you, but as you see – ' She glanced at the mound of her stomach. With her fresh, delicate complexion, corngold hair drawn back from her broad low brow and caught in a ribboned knot, and flowing, countrified muslin gown, she might have posed for a portrait of the goddess Ceres.

'It is so long since I talked to anyone from Home. My friends and I are agog to hear of fashions, and plays, and all the things gentlemen take no interest in. But first tell me, when may we expect to see George?'

'Have you not heard from him, either?'

For a moment, Sal looked startled. 'No ... That is to say, he wrote some months ago, asking me to meet your boat. Nothing since then. And you?'

'I last heard from him at Cape Town. He said he hoped to meet me himself, but ...'

Sal said briskly, 'Another letter must have gone astray. It does not signify. All that matters is that you have arrived safely. You may stay here as long as you wish.'

She chattered on, while Kate tried to subdue a sense of foreboding. No doubt it was common enough for letters to

63

go astray. At last, however, she had to say, 'I cannot help feeling anxious about George. Do you suppose he is ill?'

'Oh, there may be a dozen reasons why we have not heard from him. His messenger may have been drowned in the river, or eaten by tigers, or fallen victim to the Pindaris. When you consider the possibilities, it is a wonder messages ever arrive at all.'

Seeing from Kate's expression that such speculations were not reassuring, she added, 'Do not, for heaven's sake, start imagining the worst! We will hear from him soon, and in the meantime we shall enjoy ourselves. It is an age since I talked with anyone from Home. I am become quite a fossil.'

Kate had to smile, for anything less like a fossil than this radiant creature would be hard to imagine. Though worry about George remained, she put it to the back of her mind as she visited the nursery and admired Sal's plump three-year-old son Thomas, strutting about with a wooden sword issuing peremptory orders to his dark smiling attendants.

'We have lost two,' murmured Sal. She called the child to her and hugged him with a kind of yearning.

'Oh, Mamma, let me go! I want to play soldiers.' Thomas struggled pettishly. Kate thought him an unappealing child with his fat cheeks, overlong golden curls and sulky air, but it was plain his mother adored him.

'Off you go, General-Sahib!' She released him and turned to the nurse. '*Ayah*, make sure the baba drinks his milk before he goes to rest.'

'Yes, memsahib.'

'Let me see the milk.'

With the smallest hint of reluctance, the *ayah* produced a muslin-draped jug. Sal lifted the cover and peered closely at the contents, tipping the liquid back and forth.

'Why, *ayah*, whatever are you thinking of?' she exclaimed sharply. 'The baba cannot drink that.'

'It is good milk, memsahib.'

'How can you say such a thing, you wicked woman! It is half water. Throw it away at once. No,' she corrected as the woman prepared to obey, 'give it back to me. I want to

64

show it to the Sahib. Tell me, did you watch the dood-wala milk his buffalo?'

'Yes, memsahib.'

'All the time? You did not turn your back to chatter with the *mali?*'

'No, memsahib.' The dark eyes shifted uneasily, and one thin hand twitched at a fold of her sari.

'Pay attention when I am speaking to you,' said Sal with a snap that surprised Kate. 'Was water in the bucket before he began to milk?'

'No, memsahib. Makee turn upsee-down.'

'Was the milk from the new buffalo?'

'Yes, memsahib.'

For some minutes the catechism continued, but failed to establish how the milk had become adulterated.

'We will have to find a new dood-wala,' said Sal with a sigh as they left the nursery. 'Whatever *Ayah* says, I can see that milk contains water, probably from the nearest ditch. Oh dear, what a worry it is! That is the third dood-wala I have tried in a month, and he seemed such a respectable man. This is a terrible country in which to bring up children. Even with constant vigilance one can never be sure of their safety. Among the servants there is no one – simply no one – upon whom one may rely. My poor Leo! Merry as a grig one morning, and the next . . .'

She left the sentence unfinished and instead asked Kate if she would care to drive out in the evening cool. 'At this time of year, I fear it is the summit of our social lives,' she apologized. 'If one wishes to remain abreast of Bombay gossip, one must not fail to appear on the Esplanade, whatever its olfactory horrors!'

Kate was glad to agree. As if glimpsing a snake-pit prettily covered over with flowers, she saw that behind Sal's tranquil expression lay a multitude of fears and felt thankful – albeit a trifle guiltily – to know that in her own household there would be one servant, at least, on whom she could rely.

The disappointment she had felt on first seeing the Briggs' bungalow (which with its elongated single storey overhung by a thatched verandah resembled nothing so much as a superior cowshed) had soon been superseded by admiration for a building so perfectly adapted to the climate. The site had been cleverly chosen on the slope of Malabar Hill to catch every passing breeze, and with large windows covered by mats of woven grass over which the servants constantly flung water, the air that entered was refreshingly cool, very different from the sultry, dust-laden gusts that tossed the grey-green palm trees.

The front door opened directly into a spacious drawing-room with a floor of polished dark wood. Satin-covered couches and a handsome mahogany bureau with silver appointments consorted happily enough with country-made jackwood tables and stools; there was a work-basket and matching embroidery frame prettily inlaid with ivory, and a folding screen of sea-green silk, measuring fully eight feet long and six high, to separate the drawing-room from the dining area.

On either side of the central apartments stretched wings, the rooms of which gave on to the shady verandah. Here crouched, squatted or lay the *punkahwalas*, whose duty it was to keep in motion the huge fringed frames suspended low over the beds and tables for the purpose of creating a draught. At first Kate found it disconcerting to see so many servants engaged on so trivial and unrewarding a task, but she reminded herself that domestic matters were ordered very differently in India. This had been a central theme of George's letters.

In the three weeks that followed, Kate had ample opportunity to fret over George's continued silence. Day after sultry day went by without a message.

Surely, she thought in her darkest moments, *surely* he would not have brought me all this way if he meant to abandon me?

As the Hot Weather would soon be upon them and Sal's confinement was imminent, the Briggs lived very quietly. The evening airing on the Esplanade formed the pinnacle of the day's entertainment. Comfortably settled in a roomy buggy with a fringed awning, the ladies would drive up and down the dusty track behind a pair of pretty chestnut ponies, with Mr Briggs on a showy hack beside them, exchanging greetings and gossip with other couples. At first Kate enjoyed each new encounter; then as the languid manners and petty tittle-tattle lost their charm, and the faces they met remained relentlessly the same, she began to be glad that in Attaganj, at least, she would not be exposed to so tedious a custom.

'Oh, it will be far worse there,' remarked Sal, laughing, when Kate said something of the sort. 'Just wait until you are obliged to attend a *darbar*, and sit for an hour on the ground without the least notion of where to put your legs! There will not be many Europeans in Attaganj, but you may be sure they will gossip a great deal and probably with less spice than they do here. A year from now, I daresay, you will think Bombay society the most sparkling in the world!'

Kate could not believe her. Anything more stupefying than Bombay gossip was beyond the bounds of imagination.

Though Sal swore she could never outstay her welcome, Kate began to feel she was putting a strain on her hosts' hospitality.

'Oh, George will have his reasons for this silence! A great fellow for reasons, is George,' said Montagu Briggs, as he joined her for breakfast on the verandah one April morning. 'He knows you are safe enough with us.'

Kate could not quite like his tone. Mr Briggs was a strutting self-satisfied little man with prominent chestnut eyes under bushy brows, a dry flaky complexion and an upstanding crest of grey hair. Twenty or more years older than his beautiful wife, he was inclined to treat her like a child. She showed no resentment, but to Kate it was perfectly plain that for all his self-importance, Mr Briggs owed the smooth running of his household entirely to Sal.

'I have no wish to outstay my welcome, sir,' she said unhappily. 'If I had known George would be so long delayed, I would have made other arrangements.'

'Nonsense, Miss Castlemain. We are glad to have you with us.'

His hearty tone grated on her ear. She did not care to

67

be under an obligation to him. Nevertheless, as a member of the Bombay President's Council, Mr Briggs was in a position to know most of what went on, both in the city and the hinterland.

'Have you heard of any disturbances, sir?' she asked tentatively. 'Any account of trouble?'

'No more than usual, m'dear. No uprisings or massacres, if that is what you are afraid of.' He stretched out his legs in their tight breeches and thrusting his hands deep in the pockets of his coat began to jingle coins together. 'Let me see. What can I tell you about the affairs of our turbulent neighbours? Marathas are never so happy as when they are intriguing and fighting, you know. The recent death of old Nana Furnavis, adviser to the Peshwa of Poona, is the most significant event in recent weeks. He was a wise old man and cunning as the deuce. His death leaves his master like a viper without a head.

'What else? The feud between Holkar and Scindia continues unabated. Holkar claims he has the right to levy *chauth* on some of Scindia's villages . . .'

'*Chauth?*'

'The fourth part of the revenue, m'dear. What might more accurately be called protection money. A tribute to be paid for the privilege of not being attacked by anyone else. An iniquitous system, like all Maratha forms of government.'

'It does not sound very different from Company policy,' Kate observed, and had the satisfaction of knowing she had shocked him.

'Not very different! My dear Miss Castlemain! Chalk and cheese are not less like.'

'Does not the Company also extend military protection to native states which are prepared to pay for the privilege?'

Briggs grunted. 'Not the same thing at all. Who gave you that idea? Surely not my wife?'

'Oh, no. I heard it from a – a gentleman I met on the voyage. He was of the opinion that the Maratha chiefs would be ill-advised to sign subsidiary treaties with the Company, for by accepting them they would lose their independence.'

'An Englishman said that? He sounds a thoroughgoing

blackguard!' said Briggs angrily. 'I would strongly advise you not to repeat such opinions. That kind of talk only encourages Boney's agents, who abound in every Maratha court.'

He cleared his throat, eyeing her severely. 'Miss Castlemain, you will forgive my plain speaking, but there is nothing so unbecoming in a female as a habit of trotting out political notions imperfectly understood. When you have been in the country a year it will be time enough to advance opinions.'

'I would rather talk about George,' Kate agreed, restraining the childish instinct to ask Who Began It? 'It is ten years since I saw him. Strange as it seems, you must know him better than I do.'

'Not so strange. After all, we served together for some years.' Briggs' manner unbent a little. He eased himself back in his chair, running a finger inside his neckcloth, and not for the first time she marvelled that Englishmen did not adopt loose clothing in this climate.

'George was nineteen; I was a year or so older, but we hit it off from the start. He was a pretty horseman – of course he rode lighter in those days – and a crack shot. We went hog-hunting together – capital sport for a man with cool nerves and a steady hand. Racing, tiger-shooting – there was hardly a headman between here and Poona who wouldn't call for George when he had a man-eater plaguing his village.

'Then our ways parted. I went up-country. George got into a scrape. You don't want to hear all this?'

'Please tell me. I know so little.'

'It was a duel – some foolish quarrel. I forget the cause. Would have been winked at in the normal way, but instead of winging his man, George damned near killed him and the authorities came down like a ton of bricks. The injured man was Shore's nephew, you see. Governor-General Shore. Bound to be a fuss.'

'But he escaped a court martial?'

Briggs nodded. 'He was well liked, you know. Plenty of witnesses to swear he'd been provoked. All the same, it was a black mark. I was up-country, as I said. Didn't see George

69

for a year or so. Next I'd heard, he'd transferred and was negotiating some treaty with a native state near Delhi. Clever fellow, George. Speaks the language, gets on well with natives, always has – they like him, you know. Laughs at their jokes, respects their customs, always ready to tuck up his legs and enjoy a nautch . . .'

He stopped abruptly.

'Nautch? You mean dancing-girls?'

'Dancing? Caterwauling would be nearer the mark, in my view, but then I'm no connoisseur.' He gave her a sidelong look. 'Don't misunderstand me, m'dear. Custom of the country.'

Was he trying to warn her of something? With a sinking sensation she remembered Ned's unhappy look as he repeated Quinn's verdict.

She said, 'Tell me, Mr Briggs, were you surprised to hear George was to marry?'

He took his time over answering, and the cry of the brainfever bird which formed a background to their talk was suddenly loud.

'Surprised?' he said at last. 'Why, yes. I think I was. When a man reaches forty without tying the knot, one begins to think he don't mean to, you know.'

'There was no other reason?'

'I don't understand you, m'dear.'

'You did not think him unlikely to marry on account of a liaison – a permanent liaison – with another female?'

His eyes became shuttered windows but she read his thoughts. Say nothing. Men must stick together.

'Did you?' she pressed.

'Of course not,' he said irritably. 'That sort of thing – the sort of thing you are suggesting – one doesn't take it seriously. I wonder you are not ashamed to mention such a notion.'

'I am worried, Mr Briggs. Extremely worried.' She pocketed her pride and went on, 'At first I, too, dismissed the notion as absurd. Why should George have asked me to marry him if he had already formed such an attachment?

Now it seems to me the only possible explanation for his behaviour.'

'Good heavens, Miss Castlemain, you have let your imagination run away with you.' The mantle of pomposity fell on him, eclipsing all sympathy. 'Only possible explanation? I never heard such poppycock. You women think the world revolves round you. There may be any one of a dozen reasons why George cannot travel two hundred miles in the Hot Weather. You put me out of all patience.' He rose, tugging his sodden neckcloth. 'With your permission, Miss Castlemain, I, at least, have work to do.'

Her conviction grew that he knew more than he would admit. What can I do? she thought in a kind of panic. I can't stay here. I can't go home and admit George has rejected me. I should have known better than to trust him.

Memories of broken childhood promises rose to taunt her. George had been thoughtless and selfish, even cruel, in those far-off days. Why had she supposed age would reform him?

Apart from the Briggses she knew no one to whom she could turn. The idea of admitting her predicament to Eugenia was utterly detestable. Then a thought struck her and she sat very still, while the questing red ant which had discovered a trace of sugar in her breakfast cup waved his antennae triumphantly before scuttling away to call his companions.

Colonel Quinn had offered his help. He would tell her the truth about George.

How could she send him a message? She watched without seeing as ants swarmed in a thin stream into the cup to devour the sticky treasure. Ned's aunt: Edmunds? Edwards? Edwin . . . that was it. *Edwin*. Kate left the table and hurried to her room to write a letter.

'Certainly I know Mrs Edwin. An excellent woman, something of a gossip, but the very lynch-pin of my Ladies' Committee for the Welfare of the Orphans of Bombay.' Sal pushed damp tendrils of hair from her forehead and smiled wanly. 'This heat! One never quite gets used to it. Do you wish to call on Mrs Edwin? I warn you, it will be very hot. Or will you wait until our evening drive, when we have a fair chance of meeting her?'

Kate agreed an evening drive was preferable to braving the sun, and spent the day in her cool room, thinking how best to frame her request.

She and Sal left the house at sundown unaccompanied by Mr Briggs, and luck was with them for hardly had they completed one circuit of the Esplanade before Sal called to her coachman, who smartly wheeled his ponies under the very shafts of an oncoming vehicle, and whipping them to a spanking trot drew level with an ornate gilded cradle slung between hooped springs and drawn by a beribboned chestnut horse. In it reclined a lady whose ginger curls were crowned with a flamboyant plumed bonnet, and whose long delicate features and translucent complexion proclaimed every bit as clearly as the gap between her two front teeth that this must be Ned Sweeney's aunt.

'My scamp of a nephew?' she exclaimed with great vivacity after exchanging greetings. 'Of course, you were on *Neptune*, Miss Castlemain, were you not? Ned spoke of you most warmly. How sorry he will be to miss you!'

'Has he left Bombay, then?'

Mrs Edwin's plumes dipped like a bird about to fly. 'The naughty boy stayed with us a bare week while his uniform was made before galloping off to Malwa as if the devil was at his heels.'

'To join Colonel Quinn? Oh! I did so hope you would persuade him to give up the idea of becoming a mercenary.'

Mrs Edwin made a *moué* of good-natured resignation. 'Impossible. I tried, of course, but his mind was made up. Mr Edwin is in a rare taking since he promised my sister he would look after the boy, but the moment I set eyes on young Ned, I said, "That's a red Sweeney, Mr Edwin. Mark my words, you'll never make a *cranny* out of him." And I was right. There are red Sweeneys and black ones,' she explained, leaning out of the carriage until her plumes nearly brushed Kate's nose. 'Four of my brothers were red, and they were all fighting men. The others – the black ones –

stayed at home with their noses in their books. I could have saved my poor sister-in-law a deal of heartache if she'd told me the colour of young Ned's hair. What the poor soul will do when she hears he's gone for a soldier, the dear knows. But there it is.' She shrugged prettily and added, 'She'll be pleased enough if he makes his fortune, I daresay, for she's a pack of daughters on her hands and marrying *them* off don't come cheap.'

Her bright gaze travelled over Kate. 'Ned told me you're to wed the Resident in Attaganj. Major Gisborne, isn't it? Well, my dear, I wish you every happiness.'

Kate murmured thanks and was grateful for the deft way in which Sal forestalled further questions about George. For a while she and Mrs Edwin discussed the affairs of the Bombay Orphans as their carriages jogged abreast. Kate admired the gold-laced livery of Mrs Edwin's coachman and the vermilion tip to his horse's tail.

Bowing farewell, the ladies signed to their drivers and the conveyances drew apart.

'What a dark horse you are, to be sure!' said Sal with a mixture of censure and admiration the moment they were out of earshot. 'You never told me you were acquainted with Colonel Quinn.'

'I was afraid you might disapprove,' Kate confessed.

'My husband certainly would.'

'And you?'

Sal said pensively, 'Strange how that man arouses such different passions in the male and female breast! You will find our countrymen breathe fire at the merest mention of Colonel Quinn.'

'And the women?'

'Oh, they incline to the opposite view, and regard his lawless exploits as romantic!'

'Lawless?'

'There can be no doubt of that, I fear. Anyone with the least respect for *meum* and *tuum* must find his activities reprehensible. The Colonel is a brigand, like the robber prince he serves, but – ' Sal's dimples peeped ' – a very dashing one!'

An opinion which would hardly improve Mr Briggs' view, thought Kate. 'Where did you meet him?' she asked.

'Oh, I have only seen him at a distance. We were in Poona, you know, when Holkar and his wild retinue made one of their grand entrances. Such a sight! I shall never forget it. Barbaric, but utterly splendid. It was not long after Colonel Quinn had engineered Holkar's escape from prison, and naturally he wished to impress the Peshwa with his power and glory. The prince's own elephant must have stood eleven feet high and carried himself so magnificently that our poor beasts seemed humble shuffling creatures in comparison. His head and trunk were painted in rich colours and there was hardly an inch of the whole colossal beast that did not sparkle. He wore a frontlet of silver network, silver tassels depended from his ears, and each huge tusk was encased in a solid sheath of silver. Those Maratha elephants! Truly a race apart: as different from our own as thoroughbreds from dray-horses. The horses themselves are just as fine. Colonel Quinn commanded the cavalry which passed right under the balcony where I sat, all plunging and curvetting in no kind of order, with plumes and tassels flying, and every horse carrying a king's ransom of jewels. The men rode them with such an air, proud as Lucifer in their silks and brocades, armed to the teeth.'

She paused, then added thoughtfully, 'It struck me then how irksome and – and *pettyfogging* – such people must find our laws and strictures against their wild way of life. Of course, no Christian can condone the Maratha system of government which is nothing more than outright extortion, but at the same time one can hardly blame Mrs Edwin's nephew for preferring that life to the humdrum existence of a Writer.'

She glanced sideways at Kate, and added, 'I remember Major Gisborne was beside me that day to watch Holkar's entrance, and when I commented on the enthusiasm he laughed and said Indians would forgive their rulers any vice except *dullness*.'

Heads turned for home, the ponies trotted briskly. As

they passed the burning *ghats* by the shore of Back Bay, the ladies were obliged to draw veils across their mouths.

The bungalow was already in sight when Kate said in a low, urgent voice, 'Tell me truly, Sal, do you think George still intends to marry me? Has he changed his mind? I cannot sleep for thinking of it.'

'Oh, my dear!' Sal clasped her hand. 'I hardly know what to say. I am so very much afraid – '

She broke off and pointed towards the bungalow where a crowd of men was gathered about the verandah. A smile lit her face. She said in a very different tone, 'There! I believe you will have your answer directly. Those *palanquins* are George's – I would stake my life on it. He has come to fetch you at last.'

5

Sal was right on one count. The *palanquins* were George's, but he was not with them. He had sent his bearer and a retinue of servants to carry his bride to Attaganj.

Forgive this further delay, he wrote, *but trouble on our frontier obliges me to stay and support the Raja in his struggle against Maratha encroachment. Have no fear. You will be safe in the care of Ram Das and his fellows.*

'It is quite true,' Sal confirmed when Kate voiced doubts about these arrangements. 'I have travelled many hundreds of miles quite alone apart from native servants, and never felt the least anxiety. Indeed I have often been sorry when the journey ended. There is something quite delightful about travel in India, and since George has laid a *dak* for you, there will be no worry about finding bearers. I only wish I could come with you!'

'*How* I wish you could!'

Despite these assurances, Kate was still apprehensive and Mattie could not hide her dismay when she heard how they were to complete their journey.

'Just the two of us with a lot of heathen blacka – natives? Oh, Miss Kate! Suppose they murder us in our beds?'

'Don't be foolish. If Major Gisborne thinks it safe, I am sure it will be all right. Just think what an adventure it will be!'

'I can do without adventure at my age.'

'Would you rather I paid your passage home?'

'I didn't say that.'

Mattie cast a searching glance at Kate's strained face and made no further objection. The uncertainty of the past weeks had told on them both. Mattie had also begun to have serious doubts that the Major intended to come up to scratch, and was well aware of the difficulties they would face if he did not. With only a token show of reluctance she entered her *palanquin* at dusk the following evening.

'Travelling in the dark – whatever next?' she muttered.

'There will be a moon later, and oh, Mattie! Just look at the stars!'

'Goodbye, goodbye!' called Sal, a ghostly figure in white muslin on the verandah steps. 'Write and tell me about your wedding.'

'Write about your baby!'

'Oh, I will, I will! Goodbye!'

At a sign from Ram Das, the bearers swung up their poles. Bare feet rustled on fallen leaves; torches flickered, and the men broke into their low monotonous chant as they jogged steadily downhill towards the ferry.

Kate kept a diary. 'We have sixteen coolies, twelve *palqui hamals*, two armed *chaprasis*, one *ghorawala* to look after the ponies, four *mussauljis* to carry torches, one *shikari*, two *ayahs* – that comes to thirty-seven – now, whom have I forgotten?'

She turned to Mattie, stretched on her own string cot and gazing into the green depths of the mango tope beneath which their tent was pitched. To call it a tent was rather to underestimate the splendour of this canvas edifice some sixteen feet square, with outer and inner walls, fringed awning, lattice-divided bedroom and living-space; but Ram Das referred to it disparagingly as 'littlee tentee', as if he, at least, was used to something more spacious.

Ram Das, Kate had found, linked his own importance directly to that of his master – or, in this case mistress – and refused to allow her to demean him by performing the smallest task for herself.

He would even write my diary for me if he could, she thought with wry amusement. At times she found it irksome to be so waited on that her wants were anticipated almost before they formed in her own mind, but Mattie had adapted to this pampering with great rapidity and was fast learning to communicate her wishes in Hindustani.

'You've left out the cook.'

'Of course! How could I forget Camillo?'

'That dirty Portugee! I caught him using his fingers to beat eggs yesterday and gave him a piece of my mind,' said Mattie darkly. 'One thing you can say for the natives, they are clean, which Camillo isn't – not by a long chalk. Wash his hands? Not him! All he ever does is wipe them on his pantaloons, and they haven't seen soap and water in a month of Sundays.'

'But his food is delicious. Mattie, you shouldn't interfere. I am sure it is perfectly clean really.'

'You wouldn't be so sure if you took the trouble to watch him at work.'

'Which is why I choose not to watch! What the eye doesn't see, you know. Mrs Briggs told me it is ill-regarded for a memsahib to enter the kitchen or cook-tent.'

'Not go in your own kitchen? I never heard such a thing!' But Mattie had to agree that whatever Camillo's shortcomings in matters of hygiene, the food that emerged from his primitive three-stone oven and single blackened pan was always appetizing.

'How he does it, I don't know,' she mused. 'One thing I will say for him, he's got a knack for tasty dishes.'

'It must be the spices,' Kate agreed. 'Oh, Mattie, isn't it glorious to travel like this?'

'Ram Das thinks you should have an elephant.'

Kate laughed. 'Oh, you know what he's like.'

'I think he's right,' said Mattie unexpectedly. 'An elephant would give us a bit of style. Indians respect style.'

'You've been discussing my style – or lack of it – with Ram Das?' Kate was amused.

'I can pick up most of what he says.'

'Then tell me.'

'He's not happy with the servants he's got, that's for sure. Says it's not fitting to your dignity to travel with so few.'

'Few! But, Mattie, we've more than enough to look after us. I wish I could understand them as well as you do,' she added enviously. It was a mystery how Mattie made sense of the guttural blur of sounds.

'Comes easy to me, I don't know why.' Mattie preened

a little. 'My old gran was Romany born, and spoke the old lingo. There's words not so different in this. You don't listen, Miss Kate, that's your trouble. Always did try to run before you could walk.'

'Well, I think this is fine style,' said Kate. 'Who needs an elephant?'

Such moods of euphoria became less frequent as they progressed inland. Dozing in her *palanquin* as the miles dropped behind them, Kate imagined herself in limbo, transported whither she knew not, on a journey that would never end. The heavy heat, the men's low chanting, the rocking, swaying motion broken only when the bearers swung their poles to the other shoulder, all contributed to this illusion. Then she would jerk awake in panic, gripped by the thought that the journey must end, and she would come face to face with George. Everything in her future would depend on George, whose behaviour had begun to seem very far from dependable.

Journeying by night, resting in the day's sultry heat, they followed the flat coastal strip north for ten days before striking inland, engaging fresh teams of bearers at intervals.

After crossing the Tapti ferry, the little procession began the long winding climb from the plain towards the Satpura range of hills which, together with the Mahadeo and Maikala ranges, lie like a coiled snake across the Central Highlands and form the watershed of the great Narbada River.

As the ground rose and vegetation changed from lush green to arid red-brown, the temperature dropped and so did the spirits of their retinue. There was no mistaking the poverty of this wild upland, where the little patches of cultivation ventured no farther than the outskirts of each isolated village. Between these lay deep rocky gorges and forested slopes where the wall of trees pressing close upon the path seemed full of menace. Something more than the region's poverty stilled the coolies' chatter. Passing through the jungle they jostled close to the *chaprasis* with their long matchlocks.

'Here are bad mens and bad beasts,' said Ram Das

79

sombrely. He caused fires to be lit wherever they rested, and when the long quavering howl of a wolf broke the noon silence, Kate was glad of the flames' protection. Glad, too, of Mattie's stout heart. 'Drat the creature! Just when I was dropping off,' she grumbled; but neither she nor Kate felt any further inclination to doze.

There were many tigers in this region, Ram Das announced. In the Hot Weather they spent much of their time near the water. It was too dangerous to march at night any longer. They must move by day and at night seek shelter in a village. Kate watched how carefully he reconnoitred each village before approaching it with his armed guards, and guessed that humans were to be feared here as much as wild beasts.

Despite the increased tension, she found plenty to admire as they climbed deeper into the hills, many of which were flat-topped and crowned with abandoned fortresses. At times the deep belling of a *sambhur* came from the teak forest; a barking-deer would trot, stiff-legged and hump-backed, across their path, and once they rounded a corner to find a she-bear and cubs snuffling and feasting on the fallen blossoms of the *mhowa* tree.

Ram Das checked the procession with a gesture, and all stood in silence while the bear family shambled away.

One evening, the blue haze of woodsmoke overhanging a jungle clearing bore the unmistakable savour of roasting meat. The bearers put down their loads and crowded together, whispering and gesticulating. Kate drew back her curtain and called, 'Ram Das, what is the matter?'

Mattie, listening intently, caught the words, 'Pindari. Fire.'

'They are saying the village has been burned . . .'

'Burned!'

For ten minutes or so they waited then, when nothing moved, went cautiously forward. The ruins glowed red-hot in places. The robbers were not long gone.

Probably only a few inhabitants – those too old or young or infirm to escape into the jungle – had been grilled alive in their huts, but the stench of burned flesh hung heavily.

Charred timbers, broken waterpots, and a few mangy pariah dogs skulking about the ruins were all that remained of the village of Deorigarh, where Ram Das hoped to buy stores and engage fresh bearers.

'Who has done this?' Kate asked him, staring in horror at the smoking desolation.

'Pindaris, tax-collectors . . . who can tell?'

'Why destroy the village?'

He shook his head at so futile a question. 'This is Maratha country, memsahib.'

The words struck a chill. Robbers, Sal had called them. Plundering brigands who lived by despoiling the weak.

'Shall we go on, memsahib?'

Kate exchanged glances with Mattie, then nodded. The bearers were tired but she had no wish to pass the night in this haunted spot.

'Yes. We will go on.'

'*Ji huzoor, memsahib.* Too much danger here.' He looked relieved.

The sight of the burnt village seemed to banish the bearers' fatigue and they set off eagerly enough, but after another two hours Kate called a halt. The moon was in its first quarter and without its light the risk of stumbling or treading on a snake was much increased. Fires were lit and they spent the night huddled round them, listening to the sawing cough of a leopard and wild shrieks from the monkeys he hunted in a nearby ravine.

Soon after dawn they resumed their march, but the ominous blue haze hanging over the little village of Bhorawan warned that fresh disappointment awaited them. Like Deorigarh, every house had been reduced to smoking ash.

'What we do, memsahib?'

Ram Das had lost his air of competence. One glance at his face was enough to confirm that their situation was precarious, yet Kate hardly felt qualified to assume command.

'I suppose we must go on,' she said tentatively. 'Where is the next village?'

'Lacking food, memsahib.'

'Haven't we any left?'

Questioning revealed the existence of a scrawny roast fowl, a loaf, a few dry biscuits. Beyond that their stores were exhausted and the bearers, having marched two days and a night without rest, were on the point of collapse. The nearest place they could hope to obtain supplies was another two days' march distant. Between it and Bhorawan lay unbroken jungle into which it would be folly to venture without food. The alternative of starving amid Bhorawan's smoking ruins was even less enticing.

'Here's a pretty pickle,' said Mattie. 'Why don't you tell that *shikari* to shoot some birds for us to eat? He's carried those guns every step of the way, but I've yet to see him use one.'

Ram Das was doubtful. The *shikari* was old and his eyes troubled him. His duty was to carry the gun for the sahib, and show him where to find game.

'Then *you* shoot something for the pot,' Mattie urged her mistress. 'You and Mr Jeremy were for ever bringing home rabbits and suchlike. He said you were as good a shot as him.'

'That was years ago.'

'Go on with you. You won't have forgotten. It doesn't seem right to go hungry when there's partridges and teal and I don't know what besides.'

'I suppose I could try . . .'

'Of course you could.' Mattie dropped her voice, adding, 'One thing's for sure, those bearers must have a rest. There's three or four of them with shoulders galled like cab-horses.'

'I know.' Kate glanced at the sun and turned to Ram Das. 'We will march for one hour and then camp.'

'*Bahutachha*, memsahib.'

His worried frown smoothed away and even in this situation Kate felt her spirits lift. The self-confidence that had seeped away in the past two years returned in a comforting surge.

'You wait, Mattie! I'll shoot you the best supper you ever

82

ate,' she promised, and took her place in the *palanquin* again.

After consultation with old Jai Singh, the *shikari*, she chose a double-barrelled shotgun from his small armoury. Though heavier than Jeremy's little sporting gun, it balanced easily and the smooth well-cared-for stock felt comfortingly familiar. With this and Jai Singh's small-bored matchlock ready loaded with two solid bullets and six fingers of powder in case of starting larger game, they set out towards the nearest stream just as the light began to fade.

The gaunt old man in his long shirt of ragged jungle green, a dingy turban binding his shaggy locks and wide leather bandolier across his chest, was evidently pleased to be hunting once more. His eyesight might be failing but he had forgotten none of his woodcraft, and led her unerringly to a level grassy strip beside the stream, fringed with bushes and long rushes which gave them cover as they crept towards the birds feeding on the short turf.

Hunger – or the fear of it – provided an effective spur. Two handsome painted partridges dropped dead from the first covey they flushed, and she followed this success with a brace of teal, which Jai Singh plunged into the stream to retrieve.

'*Shabash*, memsahib!' Blackened teeth showed in a grin of approval.

He tucked the birds in his belt and led her along the slope of a ravine, ducking under curtains of creeper while monkeys chattered and scolded overhead. At last he found what he was looking for: a narrow game-trail pocked by the neat slots of deer. From a hide of creeper they watched for twenty minutes until just as the light was fading their patience was rewarded. The striped face of a small buck came bobbing towards them in the gloom.

Too dark, thought Kate. I can't see enough to shoot. Not head on.

Jai Singh uttered a grunting bark. The little buck swung broadside, head raised to locate the challenge.

'Shoot, memsahib,' breathed Jai Singh, and Kate fired.

The buck leaped high, came down stiff-legged, and bounded into the undergrowth.

Missed! thought Kate, lowering the weapon in disappointment. Jai Singh knew better. Crouching low, he vanished after the buck, and in a few moments returned triumphant with it slung about his shoulders.

'I said you could do it,' exclaimed Mattie with as much satisfaction as if she had fired the shot herself. 'Not much a woman can't do if she puts her mind to it, my old gran used to say. While we've got meat, we won't starve.'

Kate nodded and stretched out her feet for the *ayah* to remove her shoes. Tired as she was, it was deeply satisfying to feel useful after being a passenger so long. The sizzling steaks Camillo brought to their table that evening had a special savour.

Though Mattie clicked her tongue over the state of the bearers' shoulders, no one wished to linger in the jungle and soon after dawn they resumed their march. The day was hot and Kate was lying almost asleep in her palanquin when panic-stricken shouts from the coolies at the rear of the procession were followed by a savage jolt as the bearers dropped their burden on the ground.

'*Sher! Sher!* Run!'

Snatching open the curtains, Kate looked out to see the square striped head of a tiger staring down at her from a vantage point on a slab of rock above the path. Time seemed to stand still as she stared back, dry-mouthed, too paralysed by fear even to scream. A deep ruff fringed his neck. The loose glossy hide rippled as he half-crouched, head lowered between his shoulder blades, one huge velvety paw a little advanced beyond the other. His glowing eyes were so intently fixed that she felt drawn towards them, transfixed . . .

'Run, memsahib!'

The spell broke. With a sinuous gliding movement the tiger flowed down from the rock, bounded past the *palanquin*, and struck down one of the fleeing bearers with a single blow of his fore paw. Kate saw the man's limbs flail as the great striped head bent over him. For a second his white-rimmed starting eyes and imploring mouth were visible, then the tiger's jaws crunched. Once – twice – and the victim's backbone snapped.

Growling thunderously, the tiger stood over his kill, pinning the body to the ground with one paw as he stared back at the humans and dared them to interfere with his meal. His muscles tensed as he took the body in his jaws and, arching his neck half-dragged, half-carried it up the other side of the ravine.

As if his departure was a signal, two smaller tigers sprang from the rocks and bounded after the first. With shouts of terror, the remaining coolies dropped their loads and fled.

'The gun. Give me the gun!'

Too late Jai Singh pressed the rifle into Kate's hands. She was shaking too much to hold it and after a moment the old *shikari* took it back. Raising the stock to his own shoulder, he fired it across the ravine where the tigers had vanished.

The empty gesture brought a surprising result. Scarcely had the echoes died away than they heard the crash of another rifle, then another, among the trees on the far side of the ravine. There was a ripping high-pitched squeal, followed by the trumpeting of an angry elephant. The crashing and thrashing of branches at the top of the slope indicated some titanic struggle. Minutes later three elephants emerged on the skyline, and came slipping and scrambling abreast down the side of the ravine, the box-like *howdahs* on their backs swaying dangerously as they forded the stream and started up the near slope.

'Marathas!' quavered Jai Singh. Rifle in hand, he stood his ground bravely beside Kate's *palanquin*, though Ram Das had vanished along with the rest.

'Marathas!' echoed Mattie, her sharp features grey with fear. Her eyes met Kate's and the same thought passed between them: if this was the tax-collecting party their baggage was doomed and they would be lucky to escape with their lives.

Seeing the *palanquins*, the elephants halted then came on at a swinging walk.

85

It was a scene that etched itself for ever on Kate's memory: the first time she had ever been truly afraid. Her childhood had seen moments of danger from the natural world – trees that crashed in storms, horses that bolted, charging bulls and dogs that attacked – but never had she known a sensation of helpless terror such as she felt as the elephants bore down on them. Even if there had been somewhere to run she could not have moved a step.

Despite her terror a part of her mind still marvelled at the sheer physical splendour of the grey monsters. These were not the painted and jewelled animals Sal had described, but working elephants in plain hemp ropes and pads of jungle green, their blunted tusks devoid of decoration, yet their swinging silent stride and majestic carriage proclaimed them lords of the jungle.

Two were huge males standing over ten feet at the shoulder and made taller still by the railed *howdahs* lashed to their backs by means of ropes passed through rings at the four corners and attached to a broad chain girth passing under the belly. Behind each *howdah* stood an attendant holding a parasol to shield his master from the sun, while the *mahout* seated on the great beast's head, bare feet planted behind the ears, guided him by a combination of toe-pressure and the use of a short pointed ankus.

The third elephant was female, lighter in colour, more delicate in appearance and carrying only a plain pad. She held her trunk to one side: as she came closer Kate saw deep claw-marks oozing blood just above her left tusk.

'Hide yourself, memsahib. Be silent.'

The *palanquin* curtains swished shut, cutting off her view. Trembling in the gloom, she heard the elephants' stomachs rumbling as they halted, and the peremptory voice of a man questioning Jai Singh. He answered in a hesitant mumble.

'Ask if the ladies need help, Ghulam Baig. It looks as if their servants have decamped,' said a clear English voice from high above Kate's head, and she nearly fainted with relief.

'Ned!' she exclaimed, pushing back the curtains.

'M – Miss Castlemain! Kate!' He was astounded. 'Wh – what in the world are you doing here?'

'I was going to ask you the same thing,' she said shakily.

Ned's face beneath the rakishly-tied cerise turban looked very young and pleased with life. Several layers of skin were missing from his nose, but his gap-toothed smile had the confidence anyone feels when seated on a ten-foot high throne.

'Oh, Quinn and I are here on business,' he said, recovering his sangfroid, 'and you – of course – must be travelling to Attaganj. But where is your husband?'

'He could not come to Bombay, so he sent servants to carry me to Attaganj,' she explained.

'What, in a couple of miserable *palanquins?* Where are your servants?'

'They – they ran away when the tiger attacked us. He killed one of the bearers.'

'Ran away? The cowardly rascals!'

'One cannot blame them – the tiger attacked so suddenly. Oh, it was horrible, Ned. You cannot imagine how glad I am to see you.'

The occupant of the second *howdah* spoke huskily, and Ned looked abashed. 'Beg pardon, I am forgetting my manners. Allow me to present the Raja of Chhatarpur. His Highness has kindly invited us to shoot in his preserve. An excellent fellow,' he added in an undertone, 'only he don't speak English.'

Kate smiled and bowed in the Raja's direction. He was a short, stout native whose heavy features were redeemed by large eyes of beguiling softness. He smiled back, showing pan-stained teeth, and graciously raised joined palms.

'Where is Colonel Quinn?'

'Over there.' He pointed to the ravine, where two more elephants were just breasting the slope. Beneath the parasol she glimpsed Quinn's scarred face. She thought he looked angry.

'He bagged the big tiger. I never saw a finer shot,' said Ned with enthusiasm. 'The others gave us the slip after wounding poor Moti Mala.' He pointed to the injured

87

elephant. 'We'll go after them again tomorrow, I daresay . . .'

Quinn's elephant halted and stood swaying from foot to foot before the *palanquin*. 'I'll be damned! The Resident's wife!' he exclaimed. 'Is your husband out of his mind, coming here with no warning?'

'Warning? I don't understand you.'

'Where is Major Gisborne?'

'Mattie and I are alone. We are going to meet him in Attaganj.'

'But this is Maratha country!' he broke in. 'Holkar's domain. He knows that well enough. He should have asked for my protection before letting you come here.'

From his seat on the elephant his dark eyes surveyed her with none of his former friendliness. His gaze moved over the stranded *litters* and Jai Singh who stood stiffly, the rifle still in his hands. 'Good God! Don't tell me this is your whole escort? Where are your servants? Your guards?'

'A tiger scared them off,' said Ned quickly. 'That was the shot you heard.'

'I'll be damned!' he said again. 'You mean your husband – '

'Keep a civil tongue in your head, young man!' shrilled Mattie, darting her head through the curtains like an embattled ferret. 'Miss Kate's not married yet, and don't you go blaming her for the pickle we're in. If anyone's at fault, it's Major Gisborne.'

'Be quiet, Mattie.'

'That explains a great deal.' Abruptly Quinn's manner changed. At a word of command his elephant lowered herself to a kneeling position, front legs stretched out, hind legs bent. He opened the door of the *howdah* and stepped out.

'My apologies, Miss Castlemain. If you are alone and have missed your way it is another matter, though it could have had dangerous consequences. You must allow me to offer you an escort for the rest of your journey.'

'Ah, that's talking,' said Mattie with satisfaction.

88

'It is very kind of you,' said Kate doubtfully, 'but I think I must wait for my servants to come back.'

'They will be halfway to Attaganj by now.'

'Oh, poor George! What will he think?'

'What he should have thought in the first place, that it was dangerous folly to allow you to travel through Maratha country unprotected.'

'Didn't I say so all along?' demanded Mattie stridently. 'Didn't I say we should have an elephant and an escort?'

Quinn gave her a curious look. 'You shall have an elephant,' he promised, 'and an escort. I will see you complete your journey in fitting style.'

That evening Kate's ideas of fitting style underwent a great change. Holkar's travelling headquarters was like no camp she had ever seen. It was a canvas town, complete with a main street and countless canvas alleys, a bazaar, military cantonments, horse-lines, camel-lines, and elephant-lines. Each double-poled tent facing the main street was divided into several rooms and surrounded by a complete compound with servants' quarters attached.

The tent into which Quinn conducted her after dismounting from his elephant was furnished with a luxury that astonished her. Handsome tables, chests, carpets, velvet embroidered hangings, screens, porcelain, glass.

'It is a palace,' she said, wonderingly. 'It must take a week to pack the furniture alone.'

'Oh, we can move fast enough when we wish! Jaswant Rao will remain here for a week or so, until he has cleared the country round about of game. Meanwhile, why court hardship?'

His eyes laughed at her, inviting her to share the absurdity of all this luxury among the barren wastes. 'Come and meet Lakshmi, my wife. She will be honoured to receive you. There is so little to amuse her in camp life.'

'I would be delighted.' Kate concealed her surprise at the mention of a wife.

'May I come too?' Ned was close on their heels.

'Certainly not, you insolent puppy!' Quinn aimed a

friendly cuff at his head. 'I've told you before: you must marry into the family before my wife will receive you. I'm sure we can find you a pretty sister or two to choose from.'

'It's not fair. She can see me from behind that damned curtain, but I can't get so much as a peep at her,' complained Ned. 'Confound you, sir, you're a tyrant. An oriental despot, eh, Kate? Keeping his poor wife cooped up without company.'

'But she is about to receive a visit from Miss Castlemain.'

'Without male company.'

'Why should she want male company? She has mine. My wife's notion of freedom is different from yours, my dear Ned,' said Quinn teasingly. 'Come, Miss Castlemain.'

Ned scowled and flung himself down on a couch. Kate followed Quinn through a latticed screen into the scented gloom of an inner chamber. At his shout, a shrivelled old woman appeared and at once a loud argument developed. Though the *ayah* looked frail as a sparrow it was plain that she, not the master of the house, had authority here. Quinn wished to see his wife at once; the *ayah* required him to wait. He hectored. She countered shrilly. All the time scurryings and whispers betrayed intense activity behind the next partition.

Abandoning the argument, Quinn turned to Kate with a wry smile. 'My wife insists on changing her clothes before receiving so distinguished a guest.'

'Please tell her there is no need.' Kate glanced at her own travel-stained attire.

'I *have* said so, but this old bag of bones will not listen.'

'Then I am happy to wait,' Kate assured him.

'But I am not.' He sat moodily switching at his boot until the *ayah* returned and bade them enter.

Several women were grouped in a tableau around a beautiful girl, hardly more than a child, and certainly nearer Ned's age than Quinn's. When she saw them she rose and glided forward, touching her joined palms to her forehead.

She was small and very slender, with delicate features and large dark-lashed eyes in a pale oval face. Wrists and ankles tinkled gaily as she moved. She wore a sari of dark-

90

blue gauze spangled with gold, and the lighter blue shawl gave her the look of an Italian Madonna. On every finger rings sparkled and flashed, joined by tiny strings of seed-pearls to bracelets to form a kind of jewelled glove. Her thumb was adorned with a larger ring set with a looking-glass into which she stole occasional glances to reassure herself that nothing was lacking in her finery. Her black hair was very smooth and sleek, making a rich contrast with the triple row of pearls binding her brow. Kate had seldom felt so shabby or gawky as she did in the presence of this exquisite doll.

She stole shy yet inquisitive glances at her visitor while Quinn presented Kate. The other women rose and grouped themselves at the far end of the room, like a flock of birds settling.

'I am so pleased to meet you,' said Kate, smiling.

Silence. Kate cast an enquiring glance at Quinn.

'I am afraid my wife does not speak English. You will have to address your remarks through me.'

'Please tell your wife I am pleased to meet her,' said Kate, feeling more like a zoological specimen every moment.

Lakshmi indicated a large silken cushion and Kate lowered herself on to it, wondering how to dispose of her legs. With enviable ease Quinn tucked his feet under him and sat as comfortably as his wife. While Kate shifted awkwardly in search of a more tolerable position, Lakshmi leaned forward and whispered to him at some length.

'My wife would like to ask you some questions. I hope you will not find them impertinent.'

'I am sure I shall not! What would she like to know?'

'She asks how old you are, and if English ladies wear gloves all the time?'

More amused than resentful of the girl's naive curiosity, Kate answered a number of questions about her health, family, and lack of adornment as simply and truthfully as she could. It was a slow way to make conversation. Each series of questions was first whispered to Quinn, some

91

evidently rejected on the grounds of incivility, the remainder put to her and her replies translated.

'She asks if you have been married before?'

'No, I have not.'

'She wishes to know if it is customary for English ladies to marry when they are so old?'

Kate bit her lip. Of course, beside this child she must seem old. At twenty-seven an Indian woman might be a grandmother. Would it damage her self-respect less to present herself as an old maid or a rejected spinster?

'Tell her the man I loved when I was young married another woman.'

The answer seemed to strike a chord. Lakshmi sighed sympathetically and observed through Quinn that a rich husband was worth more than a poor lover, no matter how handsome. Again she leaned forward, whispering.

'What else does she wish to know?'

Kate eased her tortured ankles and wondered if she would ever walk again. The strained position had cut off the circulation and both feet were numb.

'She asks if you love the Resident-Sahib?'

That was a poser. Could she claim to love George, whom she had not seen for a decade?

'I hope,' she said after a pause, 'I shall grow to love him.'

'Are you a virgin?'

Why baulk at this when she had answered all the other questions? However irrational, English reticence dies hard. Kate felt the blood rising to her cheeks. As the silence lengthened, Kate looked up to see curiosity in one pair of eyes, amusement in the other.

'Certainly,' she said with dignity.

'The Resident-Sahib is a fortunate man,' said Quinn politely. She could not tell if the comment was Lakshmi's or his own.

Kate threw him a fierce glance. 'Thank you. Now, if you have further questions to ask me, I would be very much obliged if you would find me a chair.'

PART TWO:
THE WITCH OF SARDHANA

6

Not a muscle moved in George Gisborne's florid handsome face as he listened to Ram Das' stumbling account of disaster.

'You have betrayed my trust,' he said sternly as the faltering voice fell silent.

Ram Das bowed his head.

'You saw the memsahib taken captive by Marathas?'

'*Ji hazur*, sahib. By Holkar's men.'

'Go to your quarters. Speak to no one of this.'

Miserably Ram Das withdrew, and George strode to the verandah, shouting for his horse. Within ten minutes he was mounted and clattering out through the gateway of the old fortified city of Attaganj.

Two hours' hard riding brought him to the ferry across the Narbada river that marked the limit of the Raja's territory. Beyond was Maratha country, with strongholds belonging to the Holkar and Scindia families scattered piecemeal between the Narbada and Tapti rivers.

The ferrymen murmured to see the Burra Sahib unattended, but he said nothing to satisfy their curiosity as he ordered them brusquely to untie their flat-bottomed boat from its mooring beside their hut. He stood aloof in the bows, his horse's rein looped over his arm, silent as they poled him across; but he rewarded their efforts with two pieces of silver before remounting to spur on his way.

Another hour through forested hills intersected by rocky ravines brought him within sight of Scindia's fortress of Jumkhola, its immense mud walls frowning down on a sheet of water where ducks and moorhens rose in squawking flocks as he approached.

The gate stood open and no one impeded his entry, though a group of showily-uniformed French officers lounging about the courtyard eyed him warily as he trotted past.

'Here comes the Begum's stallion, damn his eyes,' muttered a tall olive-skinned captain. 'I thought we'd seen the last of him when we crossed the Narbada.'

'With him comes the ruin of poor Baudricourt's hopes,' sneered his companion. 'What would you give me, Étienne, if I put a ball through those golden curls of his?'

'Nothing to what he'd get from the Begum,' grunted a third. 'Patience, *mes enfants*, she'll tire of him in time. Variety is the key to our mistress' heart. We'll all get our turn if we wait long enough. I give the English stallion another month at most.'

George rode past, returning their stares with interest. 'Scurvy frog-eaters,' he muttered just loud enough for them to hear. Without troubling to dismount he urged his lathered horse up the shallow flight of steps leading to the inner courtyard. Two guards in the silver-and-azure uniform of the Begum's household stepped forward to challenge him, but on recognizing him salaamed and let him pass. Only when he reached the inner sanctum of the Dewan-i-Khas did George at last swing down from the saddle. As an attendant led his horse away he strode forward into the latticed coolness, spurs clinking on the marble floor.

Word of her lover's approach had reached the Begum Samru an hour earlier. Reclining on a cushioned divan with her servant squatting behind her, she watched his approach through lazily hooded eyes in an attitude of deliberately sensuous langour. Though the bloom that had captured the heart of the Alsatian mercenary nicknamed 'Sombre' had long faded, the Begum's sexual appetites had in no way diminished since her infamous husband's death. Then she had moved swiftly to seize control of his small army with its nucleus of power-hungry French officers, whom she played off against one another with cynical skill. She kept them in arrears of pay as a huntsman starves his hounds to keep them sharp. Frequent mutinies were the result, and more than once the Begum had suffered the threat of being straddled across a hot gun-barrel to induce her to unlock

95

her coffers. Yet so potent was her allure that she always found a champion to come to her aid.

She made a habit of choosing favourites among her officers, and lavished wealth upon each in turn, fomenting such rivalry that they never combined to overthrow her. These ex-favourites watched her liaison with Major George Gisborne with brooding jealousy. It had lasted too long. Politically it might be advantageous to have the English Resident at the Court of Attaganj in thrall to their mistress; but while she heaped gold and jewels upon him her own officers went unpaid.

The Begum saw their anger and laughed. She had a harlot's knowledge and contempt for men. It amused her to tease and taunt them. She liked to see haughty white men so besotted with lust that they betrayed their wives, their brother officers and their country for the sake of her embraces.

Let them wait, she thought, as Captain Baudricourt sighed and Major de Gonville scowled and the self-styled Chevalier de la Peur vowed to die for love of her. I will change my lover when I please, not when it suits my officers.

She surveyed George coolly, noting how the sweat-soaked curls clung tightly to his skull while his blue eyes blazed with an excitement he could not conceal.

'So, Jowraj Jung, have you tired of your English camel already?' she taunted. 'Why else do you come chasing me in the heat of noon?'

'Send your people away, Heart's Desire. I must speak to you alone.'

She waved to her attendants and they withdrew. George dropped on one knee to seize her hand and press it to his lips. Still with that intense suppressed excitement, he said, 'Queen of my Heart! I had to come at once. My plan has succeeded and Holkar has taken the bait. He holds the English camel captive.'

The Begum's air of studied languor evaporated. 'Who told you?'

'Ram Das returned last night. His party was set on by

Marathas and the coolies ran away. The ladies were taken prisoner – '

'Ladies?'

'Miss Castlemain and her maid. The baggage was looted. Any moment now I may expect the arrival of Holkar's *vakils* demanding ransom. It could not have fallen out better.'

'So you have lost your *bibi* before you could sample her honey!' she mocked.

'What do I care for her? This is the chance we have been waiting for: the chance to clip Jaswant Rao's wings before they are spread. If I handle the business correctly I can bring down the Governor-General's wrath upon that insolent young brigand. Unprovoked aggression. Abduction of an innocent English lady. Miss Castlemain is well-connected, you know. If she should suffer any maltreatment at Holkar's hands the outcry from England will be deafening. The Directors will have to take action against him, like it or not.'

Slowly the Begum's full mouth curved. 'Oh, wilier than the serpent is Jowraj Jung!' Alight with secret laughter, her eyes held his.

George's loins tightened. 'Lovelier than the gazelle is the Begum Samru,' he said thickly. With greedy hands he reached for her. For a moment she lay supine, allowing him to kiss her as he pleased, but as his demands grew more urgent she slipped from his grasp.

'Later, Heart's Desire,' she said, becoming practical. 'My French officers are jealous. If they suspect you of double dealing your plan will miscarry and I shall have no power to silence them. You must return to Attaganj and proclaim your bride's abduction. Until the Lat-Sahib sends his army in pursuit of Holkar, we must not meet. But then – ' She smiled a promise.

'What will you do now?'

'I?' She considered, moving the thumb-ring from side to side to reflect her image. 'I will withdraw to Sardhana, to collect my revenues and make ready for a campaign. I would like to have a part in hunting Holkar down.'

'You should get rid of that fellow Baudricourt,' said

George abruptly. 'He's an insolent devil. I don't care for his looks.'

'Why should I get rid of one of my best officers? Do you fear he will supplant you in my affections? Come, Jowraj Jung, can it be you are jealous?'

'Of course I am, you witch! How can I help it when I see those damned frog-eaters making sheep's eyes at you?'

'You have no need to be. I am the one who has cause to be jealous. How did *I* feel when you told me you would marry this English camel?'

'You knew damn well I was only doing it for the look of the thing.'

'That is as well for you – and for her.' The Begum's eyes glittered. 'Am I to be set aside like a cheap harlot? Did you suppose you could escape me, Jowraj Jung, and let an Englishwoman take my place in your bed?'

'I told you I had to marry to stop the talk,' muttered George.

'Marry!' she said with scorn. 'What do I care for that? Marry her, by all means, but if ever I have cause to think you love her she shall die.' She laughed throatily. 'There are many ways of dying in India, Jowraj Jung. Some are more painful than others.'

Her ferocity frightened and delighted him. Once more he reached for her but she pushed him away. 'Go now, and remember what I have said.'

'Don't send me away, Heart's Delight. I want you. I need you. Let me stay tonight – what difference will one night make?'

'The difference between success and failure, Jowraj Jung,' she laughed, her own desire waking at his touch. She could not wait. She would have him now, whatever the cost. The Frenchmen she took to her bed were mostly striplings young enough to be her sons: slim, pretty boys, eager to please, easy to dominate. Too easy. She found their love-making cloying. This English stallion was a horse of a different colour. Jowraj Jung, she called him: Great George, delighting secretly in his strength and unbridled lust. He was a fierce, even brutal lover, but his wildness matched her own.

'One kiss,' she murmured, drawing him to her while her long sharp nails raked his back through the broadcloth and her breathing quickened. 'One kiss, then you must go.'

Kate was silent as they left the Maratha camp. After several observations had gone unanswered, Mattie gave up trying to engage her in conversation.

Wondering what she'll find at the end of the journey, poor lamb, she diagnosed, and pushed away the unwelcome thought that in entrusting their future to Master George she and her mistress might be jumping from the frying-pan into the fire.

Kate's thoughts were less on her future husband than the man she had just left. Their conversation that morning still worried her.

'Ned and I will ride with you as far as the ferry,' Quinn had said as she prepared to mount the splendidly caparisoned elephant kneeling before her.

'I fear I have put you to a great deal of trouble, Colonel Quinn,' she said, holding out her hand. 'This beautiful elephant! All the men and horses! I only hope one day I may repay your generosity.'

'It is nothing. I am glad to help you.'

'It is very far from nothing! Both Major Gisborne and I must be eternally grateful.'

'I hope you are right.'

Kate gave him a puzzled glance. For an instant it occurred to her to wonder if she was wise to accept favours from a man whose way of life George could hardly approve. Quinn had insisted on making her a present of the tiger-skin, and it seemed churlish to refuse.

On impulse she said, 'Really, there is no need for you to trouble yourself to come with me. I would not like to deprive you of your hunting.'

'I did not mean to hunt today.'

Ned laughed. 'Tax-collecting can always wait.'

'*Tax-collecting?*' The smell of the burned villages was suddenly sharp in Kate's nostrils.

'Why, yes,' Ned went on blithely, ignoring Quinn's frown. 'That is why we are here, you know. We collect *chauth* from all the villages – all the villages that owe tribute to Holkar, that is. Hard work, I can tell you. How they run when they see us coming!'

'Did you collect tax from a village called Deorigarh?' she asked with painful intensity.

'Deorigarh? Where's that?' Ned rubbed his jaw. 'Was that the place where the *patel* swore blind that the Begum Samru's men had been before us? And all the time the money was hidden down the well?' He laughed. 'Rare sport we had with him, I can tell you. Quinn got it out of him in the end – he always does – but we had our fun first.'

Kate's heart pounded. Could this be Ned speaking? Was it possible that he had turned into a monster in five short weeks?

'See to your troop,' said Quinn curtly. 'You talk too much, Ned.'

'Why? What have I said? I only – '

'You call it "rare sport" to plunder helpless villages and steal from poor peasants?' demanded Kate.

'Collecting taxes is not stealing, Miss Castlemain,' said Quinn, and she turned on him in a fury.

'I suppose you would say burning old women in huts is not murder, Colonel Quinn?'

'Burning old women?' Ned looked blank. 'What are you talking about?'

'How can you pretend you don't know after boasting how you amused yourselves?'

'Truly, Kate, I know nothing about any burning. All we did was persuade the *patel* to hand over his hoard.'

'You call it persuasion. Extortion might be more accurate. Can you honestly tell me no force was used?'

Ned was scarlet with indignation, but Quinn's expression showed a gleam of comprehension. He said more to Ned than Kate, 'The Begum's men were not far away, remember? They may have visited Deorigarh in search of plunder.'

'The Begum Samru. Of course!'

Quinn turned to Kate, saying, 'How many villages were burned, Miss Castlemain?'

'We saw two – there may have been more. Do not play the innocent, Colonel Quinn.'

'I assure you I know no more than you do, but you will have to take my word for it. Do you really believe me capable of such infamy?'

'What else can I think?'

'You have been listening to too many stories, Miss Castlemain,' he said with a kind of grim humour. 'I have a fair idea who is to blame for this, but Ned and I must forego the pleasure of escorting you to Attaganj. If we return at once to the burned villages we may pick up a trail before it goes cold. My havildar will see you safely bestowed.'

A tiny flicker of relief tinged Kate's disappointment at being deprived of their company. Instinct warned her a meeting between George and Colonel Quinn was best avoided.

'I hope you catch whoever was responsible,' she said with feeling. 'What will you do with them?'

'Blow them from a gun,' said Quinn and Ned laughed. She could not be sure if they were in earnest.

'Tell me,' she said, 'who is the Begum Samru?'

Quinn answered, with a repressive glance at Ned, 'A most meddlesome and dangerous woman. Vassal to Scindia and mistress of six French-led battalions whose brutality is legendary. She has a *jagir* at Sardhana, near Delhi, from which she derives her revenues, but like the vulture you will find her wherever there is plunder to be had.' He paused, then added, 'For your sake, Miss Castlemain, I hope you never have occasion to meet her.'

It was the Begum's boast that she could exhaust five lovers between *chota hazri* and *tiffin*. A night in her arms combined with long hours in the saddle to take their toll of George as he rode slowly homeward.

101

Jogging towards the Narbada ferry with the westering sun on his face, his mind was busy with a hypothetical chess match in which Holkar sought to exploit the English pawn he had captured. His first move, surely, would be to send envoys to Attaganj to haggle over the price of Kate's freedom. They would try to make conditions. For years the Holkar family had laid claim to *chauth* on a number of villages within the borders of Attaganj, and it had been in order to limit these depredations that the Raja of Attaganj had agreed to receive a British Resident, and support four battalions of Company troops for his own protection.

Doubtless Holkar would see this as a golden opportunity to bargain for a return of the disputed villages – and privily George would encourage this. The more outrageous Holkar's demands, the more heavily the Governor-General's wrath would fall on him when George appealed for military intervention.

If Kate Castlemain was ill-treated or, better still, killed, George's hand would be greatly strengthened.

Nearing the ferry, he saw a dust-cloud ahead and recognized the rakish Maratha turbans with gold scarves securing them under the chin. Holkar's men, by Jove! he thought with a lift of the heart. Events were moving faster than he anticipated. He was glad he had not lingered another day in the Begum's boudoir.

'Ho, havildar sahib!' he called out, drawing level with the leader of the procession. 'Where are you going and what is your business?'

'To Attaganj, sahib. Our business is with the Resident.'

The havildar twirled his splendid moustache and cast a somewhat contemptuous glance at the questioner. George was suddenly aware that he must cut a less than imposing figure in his stained, dusty clothing, mounted on a jaded horse. He had planned to receive Holkar's *vakils* sitting at ease on his verandah, having compelled them to dismount at a respectful distance. If he revealed his identity now, the envoys would look down from the *howdah* to see him tired and servantless, an object of pity rather than admiration.

102

The first move in the all-important chess match would be lost.

Accordingly, he reined back a little to let the elephant pass. He was in the act of drawing a silk handkerchief from his pocket for the double purpose of muffling his face from the dust and their curious eyes, when a woman's voice from within the *howdah* startled him.

'I do declare it's Master George!'

The name stripped away the years and with them his careful dignity. No longer Great George, but reduced once again to Master George, the naughty schoolboy whom that same voice had scolded for tweaking a little girl's pigtails or pushing her doll into the fire.

He groaned. Why in the name of blazes had Kate brought that old tartar with her?

Stifling curses, he looked up at the *howdah*, straight into sapphire eyes he hardly recognized as belonging to his promised bride. Momentarily deprived of speech, he stared at her. Could this be the sallow gawky child he remembered, with her nutcracker jaw and the eyes of a hungry cat? 'Beauty and the Beast' had been his private nickname for his sister and the painfully plain friend to whom she was so much attached. It was the Beast who used to dog his foot-steps in his subaltern days, looking at him during meals with such silent worship that he had begged her – only half joking – to turn her eyes elsewhere.

The change in her was dramatic. The sallow complexion had been transformed to the astonishing rose-gold of an Anglo-Saxon skin newly kissed but not yet cooked by the sun. The strong bones that overwhelmed a child's face now gave her features a distinction to which pretty fluffy Amelia could never aspire. Against all expectation, his bride was beautiful, but the discovery gave him no pleasure. On the contrary his heart quailed at the prospect of the Begum's displeasure. She would think he had deceived her deliberately.

But what could I do? thought George, as every man caught between two women has always thought. With Governor Duncan breathing fire and brimstone against

103

liaisons with native women, and rumours of his attachment to the Begum reaching Poona and Bombay, George had thought that marriage to an unexceptional Englishwoman would quell the tales and resolve his difficulty. Kate Castlemain – plain, awkward, naive Kate – had seemed the perfect choice.

How the devil does she come to be unmarried? he thought. Are my countrymen blind, to leave a beauty on the shelf?

He made an effort to pull himself together. He must say something civil, welcome her to her new home; but first he must get rid of those damned gaping Marathas, watching and listening, ready to report every word and gesture of this meeting to their master. He must recover the initiative and salvage his dignity, but it wasn't easy with her seated like a queen on that damned great Maratha elephant. If this marriage was to go as he intended, he must cut her down to size without delay.

He took off his topi and smiled. 'My dear Kate,' he said expansively. 'How very glad I am to see you safe.'

'George!'

Heavier than she remembered, his square-jawed English good looks no longer clean-cut but blurred by surplus flesh about the jowl and his blue English eyes meshed in lines from constantly looking into the sun, the tight tow-fair curls receding a little, his fresh complexion no longer pink but a uniform brick-red – these changes she noted and instantly dismissed in the overwhelming relief of the thought: I would have known him anywhere!

'Where have you been? What happened?'

'Oh, George, we have had such adventures! A tiger attacked us and your bearers ran away – '

'The cowardly curs! I was shocked to hear of it. Ever since Ram Das told me I have been scouring the countryside for news of you.'

'Poor Ram Das. I am thankful he is safe.'

'A bad penny always turns up. You need not have worried,' muttered Mattie, her sharp eyes noting George's thick body and the bull neck bulging over his collar. He's done himself well these past years, she thought. So long as

104

he treats Miss Kate right, I'm ready to bury past differences. If not, he'll soon find I've not lost the rough edge of my tongue.

'We were rescued by a Maratha hunting-party, just when I thought all was lost – '

Smiling, George held up a hand. 'Later, my dear, later!' He allowed a note of reproach to creep into his voice. 'Little did I think while I was anxiously searching for you that you would arrive in such splendour. To whom do you owe all this pomp?'

Kate smiled. 'To Colonel Quinn! He has been most kind. Did you not receive his message telling you we were safe?'

'What!' exclaimed George angrily. 'You mean to tell me you have been with that rascal Quinn?'

'Why, what is the matter?' Kate was dismayed by his sudden change of tone.

'Matter? I'll tell you what is the matter. My dear Kate, you have put me in a very difficult position. To be frank, I would rather be beholden to any other man on earth. Oh, I don't say you are to blame,' he added as she began to protest. 'He is a plausible devil. No doubt he persuaded you he meant well; but you may be sure his sole purpose in helping you was to put *me* under an obligation I would find difficult to discharge.'

'That's not fair, George. I am sure he intended nothing of the sort!'

'Don't deceive yourself. He must have seen this as a way to bargain with me,' said George curtly. 'Quinn's a slippery customer. If there's one thing less trustworthy than a Maratha it's a half-breed. As for accepting favours from him – *timeo Danaos*, you know.'

Kate stared at him, too angry to trust her voice. In her worst nightmares she had not imagined a dispute with George before she even set foot in his house.

The havildar saw her expression and edged his horse closer. 'Does this man trouble you, memsahib? Shall I send him away?'

'Trouble me?' Kate's laugh held a note of hysteria. 'Oh, no, havildar sahib, don't send him away, I beg! This is the

105

Resident, Major Gisborne, whom I have come all this way to marry!'

The wedding took place two days later in the marble-floored drawing-room of the Residency, its columns decked with marigold and orange-blossom garlands. The Raja was there, with his two sons, and the entire European community of Attaganj, though this amounted to barely fifty souls.

Regimentals splashed scarlet and gold across the rows of country-built chairs; the ladies' plumed and flower-decked hats swayed like a windswept herbaceous border as they tried to catch their first glimpse of the bride's face beneath the veil of Brussels lace which Mattie had cherished ever since it was worn by Kate's mother.

Opinion on the newcomer was divided.

'Odd-looking gal. Freakish,' said Mrs Cornish in the penetrating whisper of the deaf. Her late husband had negotiated the subsidiary treaty for the Company; as doyenne of the British in Attaganj she had appropriated the seat from which the bride could best be seen.

'Certainly very striking,' said Captain Theodore judiciously, though he felt bound to add, 'good thing George is a big fellow or she'd overtop him.'

'Like a lily,' mused Eldred Jones, a superannuated captain who fancied himself a poet.

'More like a beanpole,' snapped Mrs Jones. She had acted as hostess for the Resident on formal occasions and resented her inevitable loss of prestige now that George had acquired a wife of his own.

The service was somewhat erratically conducted by the Reverend James Hopwood, whose barrel-like body filled his vestments to bursting-point. About him clung a strong aroma of arrak punch and this combined with his broad Lowland accent to make even the familiar words of the marriage service barely comprehensible. He looked hot and bothered. Listing the purposes for which marriage was ordained he lost his place, hiccuped gently, and lapsed into silence.

At their backs the congregation tittered. Kate stole a

sideways glance at George, hoping to share a smile, but he faced sternly ahead as if on parade, his expression unreadable. She had learned enough of him since her arrival to know he took his dignity seriously, and quickly mastered her impulse to laugh. Where his scarlet-clad arm touched her shoulder she felt a vibration like a bowstring under strain. For all his apparent composure, George was more nervous than she was. It was strange: despite the solemnity of the occasion she felt light-hearted, even light-headed.

Mattie's cordial! she thought with sudden suspicion. It had tasted of mint, but there had been an underlying bitterness. No doubt some ancient Romany potion to cheer the timid bride. Whatever the cordial's origin, it was certainly emboldening. Mattie should have persuaded George to swallow some too, she thought, and again laughter bubbled up.

' "For the mutual help and comfort of man and woman," ' prompted Surgeon Richardson, acting as Best Man.

'What's that, ye're sayin'? Oh, aye. Thank you, Mr Richardson, the verra words I was seekin' . . .'

The service stumbled on.

When it was over the congregation repaired to the dining-room where refreshments were laid out.

'What a beauty, eh? You have done well for yourself, old fellow!' exclaimed Prince Madhav Rao, a slim fifteen-year-old with a pleasant open face and the assurance of a man twice his age. He stared at Kate with frank admiration, though he had to tilt his head back to meet her eyes.

'Thank you, Your Highness.' George inclined his head and turned to greet the rest of the Royal party.

'George, you lucky dog! Now we see why you have stayed single so long! Welcome to Attaganj, Mrs Gisborne. I hope you will be happy here.'

'Thank you, sir.' Kate curtseyed as Prince Trimbuck, three years older than his brother and already stout, surveyed her with a smile on his heavy features. Both princes were resplendent in long embroidered surcoats over waistcoats of flowered satin and wide trousers of striped silk.

Splendid Cashmere shawls were draped about their shoulders and their turbans were of gold lace twisted with bright colours and strings of pearls.

In contrast the Raja was plainly attired in a tunic and breeches of snowy muslin girdled with a broad jewelled belt. More dignified than his sons, he saluted the bridal pair with joined palms, then stood a little aloof, a fine-looking man of middle years with a grizzled beard and military carriage, amid the shifting kaleidoscope of his retainers.

On the heels of the Royal party came the British, as eager to press the bride's hand and murmur felicitations as they were to sample the champagne and iced claret, ices and syllabubs with which the long tables were loaded. Their duty in the receiving line ended, Kate and George moved among them, bestowing a word here, a smile there, his arm encircling her waist, the picture of married bliss though as yet they had hardly exchanged a sentence.

What do I know of him? she thought; and then, what does anyone know of George? The happy-go-lucky boon companion who would tuck up his feet and enjoy a *nautch* described by Montagu Briggs seemed far removed from this remote authoritarian man.

There had been trouble over the tigerskin. When he heard who had given it, George wanted it returned, but in this matter Kate felt obliged to assert herself.

'It is a wedding-gift. If you send it back I warn you I shall go with it.'

George had given her a measuring look in which she read as clearly as if he had shouted it aloud that once they were married he would brook no opposition. But they were not married yet.

'Very well, my dear. If it matters so much to you, you may keep it,' he conceded.

She accepted the small victory, knowing as well as George did that her threat was an empty one. She could not go back now. Geographically and economically she had cut her links with England. Her future lay in India and she must make the best of it.

'Come, my dear. The Raja is leaving.' George drew her towards the door. She looked at his hand as it grasped her arm – a powerful, well-tended hand, as strong and confident as George himself. Faces might dissemble. Hands were a surer guide to the owner's thought. But what of the other, as yet unknown George? How would that solid powerful body look stripped of its scarlet and gold regimentals? How would her own pale nakedness appear to one used to the sinuous dusky bodies of dancing-girls?

'You look very beautiful, Mrs Gisborne.' George smiled down at her: proud, a little proprietorial, and doubts faded. Suddenly she felt glad to be Mrs Gisborne and belong to him.

'Thank you, kind sir.' She smiled back and his hand tightened on hers.

'*Tonight!*' he said, too low for any ears but hers. She read desire in his eyes and her own heart quickened.

Then a curious thing happened. One instant their hands were locked and his eyes were for her alone. The next he released her as if her touch burned him and his gaze became fixed on a point behind her head.

'Why, George –'

Swiftly she turned; there was nothing behind her but a native bearer in snowy tunic and scarlet cummerbund approaching them with a loaded tray.

'*Simkin*, sahib?'

George took two glasses of champagne from the tray. As he handed one to Kate she saw his hand was shaking though when he spoke his voice was as firm as ever.

'Come, my dear, we must not neglect our guests. Surgeon Richardson is about to propose our health.'

7

'Are you afraid?' whispered George.

He loomed over the bed, enormous in a loose robe, with the mosquito net billowing behind him. As he seated himself the bed dipped heavily and Kate steeled herself not to edge away. The single lamp still burning threw fantastic shadows on the white-washed walls. As he leaned nearer she caught the sharpness of brandy on his breath.

'Why should I be afraid?' His sudden appearance had set her heart pounding. More than once as she lay waiting for him to join her she had imagined she heard movement in the room – soft breathing, the rustle of cloth.

She had called out, '*Koi hai?* Who's there?' but no one answered.

'Easy to see you know nothing of men!' His laugh had a grating edge.

'What should I know?' The strangeness of his manner perturbed her. It was almost as if he wanted her to be afraid. Again she was aware of conflicting forces under that solid exterior.

'Damn it, Kate, has no one told you what to expect tonight?'

'Mattie said – '

'That vinegar-tongued old bitch! Don't take any notice of what *she* says. If I find you tattling to her I swear I'll have her put away.'

'Why shouldn't I talk to her?'

'What goes on behind the bedroom door is our secret – yours and mine. Never forget that.'

Kate yawned. Mattie's cordial had made her sleepy and disinclined for argument. 'Come to bed, George,' she said. 'It's late and you must be tired.'

'Tired? Oh, no.' With a sudden movement he gripped her shoulders, staring into her face with a strange intensity.

'Why didn't they tell me you were beautiful?' he said thickly. 'My mother. Amelia . . . Why did they let me go on thinking – ?'

He left the sentence unfinished. Slowly his hands slid down her arms, dragging the cambric nightgown from her shoulders. As the neckline ripped she gasped and made an involuntary movement to cover herself, but he held her easily.

'Keep still. I want to look at you. Yes . . .'

He bent his head, drawing her towards him, and she felt his lips hot and wet against her breasts, nipping and nuzzling, his bristles scraping her skin until she cried out.

'Stop, George! You're hurting me!'

'God!' he said disgustedly. 'You virgins are all the same. Snivelling and yelping before a man so much as lays a finger on you. Don't you know anything? Can't you see what I want?'

'What do you want?'

'What any man wants. A woman – not a damned ice-maiden.'

Deliberately he removed his robe and she averted her eyes, unwilling to see what the lamplight revealed. He laughed harshly, turning her face towards himself.

'Take a look at your bargain, Kate! Is it what you want? Or have we both got more than we bargained for?'

She couldn't look at him. Without clothes he was more than a stranger, a menacing alien. Holding her wrists pinioned in one hand, with the other he stripped off the remnants of her nightgown, laughing at her frantic attempts to free herself. Greedily he ran his hands over her body, turning her this way and that as she fought him with increasing desperation.

'That's better. That's more the spirit.'

Her struggles were exciting him. Above the harsh rasp of his breathing her ears caught another sound and she looked up past the thick muscles of his shoulder to see another face – narrow, hollow-eyed, turbaned – framed in the mosquito netting. The moment it saw it was observed it vanished, but she screamed with shock.

111

'What's the matter now?' said George roughly.

'Put out the light! There's someone in the room.'

He reared up, listening, then said with menacing softness, 'Don't try that trick with me, my pretty. Do you take me for a tomcat, to make love in the dark?'

'There was! I saw him.'

'Quiet – unless you want the hiding you deserve.'

'*Hiding?*' She could hardly believe this was George speaking to her.

'That's what you'll get, my fine lady, if you don't do what you're told. It's time you learnt who's master here.'

She was scarcely more appalled by the threat than by his calling this crude manhandling *love*. In the glow of the lamp the heavy face bent over her had a terrible absorption; instinctively she knew that nothing she said would divert him now. She was his wife, to do with as he pleased.

'This is part of the bargain, Kate. My part. You can't go back on it now.'

Too late she recognized the trap into which she had been lured – into which every married woman fell. It had been temptingly baited with promises dear to the female heart: a home, children, security. But this was the price she must pay – the surrender of her body – and now it was too late to say it was too high. The truth had been camouflaged under veils of tulle and showers of confetti, but each of those beady-eyed matrons at her wedding today had known what would follow it. They could have warned her: instead they had hugged the secret and encouraged her to step into the trap, as pinioned decoy ducks entice their wild comrades to share their captivity.

Gritting her teeth, she lay passively while with a series of grunting heaves that tore her apart George achieved his climax and collapsed on top of her.

'Good,' he mumbled and, rolling a little on one side, subsided into sleep.

Kate lay motionless, sure that the least movement would split her in two, but finally the numbness of her arm trapped under him made her venture to reclaim it inch by inch. George began to snore. She raised herself on one elbow and looked at him. His passion spent he looked tired, even vulnerable. A moment ago she would gladly have killed him, but now she was conscious of a strange compassion. Sleep smoothed out the crows' feet round his eyes and the deep-cut grooves between mouth and nose. With lips parted and eyes closed, he was recognizable as that younger George she had known.

She did not wish to be reminded of him. With infinite care she eased across to the far edge of the bed and reached out to extinguish the lamp.

When she woke he had gone. In bright morning sunlight, with the song of birds pouring through the shutters and a delicious smell of freshly baked bread stealing into the room, it was hard to believe the night's ordeal had not been a bad dream. She was bruised and stiff and there was blood on the sheet, but her face when she inspected it looked no different from the morning before.

Mattie pursed her mouth when she saw the bruises, but Kate felt disinclined for her sympathy. I have joined the great conspiracy, she thought. I don't want to talk about this with Mattie or anyone else.

When George returned from his morning ride to join her at breakfast it was even harder to believe what he had said and done in the hours of darkness. Freshly shaved and combed, smelling of sandalwood and starch with just a hint of saddle-soap behind it, he bent and kissed her cheek like a dutiful affectionate husband before accepting a cup of coffee and loading his plate with devilled kidneys, eggs and bacon.

'Would you like to ride with me later?' he asked, and she was glad to accept the invitation. For a wedding gift he had given her a spirited Arab pony, formerly the property of the Raja, for which she guessed he had paid a high price.

It will be all right, she reassured herself as they rode knee to knee across the plain. Everything is bound to be strange at first. I must not expect too much.

After their ride, conversation flowed easily at dinner, which they ate alone but for the circle of attentive red-sashed servants hovering in the shadows behind their chairs.

113

She encouraged him to speak of his work: he told her of the Raja's struggle to protect his villagers from the ravages of marauding Pindaris and Marathas, from flood, disease and famine; and his own efforts to promote a fair system of taxation.

'You will find I am away from home a great deal,' he said. 'The only way to discover what needs to be done is to go to the villages and talk with the headmen. They are too much afraid of authority to come to the city, so I go to them.' He gave her a measuring look. 'I hope you will keep yourself busy in my absence. Too many European women sink into idle ways because they have no employment. I am sure you have too much sense for that. My mother was full of praise for the way you ordered your father's estate. She assured me I could rely on you to do the same here.'

Thank you, Godmamma! she thought, though she felt a small pang of disappointment at this confirmation that she had been chosen for her housekeeping skills rather than any romantic attachment. She had guessed it was the case, but it had been pleasant to dream . . .

'Could I not come with you?' she asked wistfully. 'I assure you I have no objection to living rough.'

For a moment he seemed to be giving the request serious consideration; then a shutter dropped behind his eyes.

'I fear not.'

She was disappointed but did not insist, planning to reopen the subject later. After they had finished eating he begged her to excuse him. He must go to his study.

'My work has been sadly neglected since you came. There is a mountain of paper on my desk to be cleared before morning.'

'I wish I could help you.'

'Then try to avoid any further dealings with Colonel Quinn!' he said with wry humour.

'Colonel Quinn? Is it on his account that you have to work late?'

'Principally, yes.'

'Why? What has it to do with me?'

George said with a kind of weary patience, 'Quinn has

114

encouraged Holkar to revive an old claim to five villages between the Narbada and Paungunga rivers, which have been recognized for years as lying within Attaganj territory. Of course, the claim is absurd, but before I make my report to the Governor-General I must delve into the old documents relating to the affair in order to refute it absolutely. Quinn is a cunning devil and if I leave any loophole he will exploit it to his Chief's advantage – just as he seized his chance to put me under an obligation on your account. He hopes, of course, that it may influence my report.'

'I am sorry to be the cause of your difficulty, but I was hardly in a position to refuse his help,' said Kate dryly. 'Would you have preferred me to cast myself into the tiger's jaws?'

George said stiffly, 'If you choose to joke about it that is your affair. I was merely trying to explain to you why I choose not to be beholden to that ruffian. Well, I must work. Don't stay up for me, my dear. I fancy you look a trifle fatigued. An early night will do you good.'

At the time she agreed, but once in bed listening to the regular flap of the *punkah* and croaking of the frogs in the lake, sleep deserted her. Memories of last night which she had succeeded in banishing during the day came rushing back. She lay straining her ears for his step, every nerve strung tight.

Towards midnight she must have dozed, only to wake bathed in sweat for the *punkah* was motionless and the air hot and still as an oven. Brilliant moonlight flooded through the window, laying a path of silver across the floor. Pushing the billows of netting aside, she rose and padded to the lattice that gave on to the verandah, intending to rouse the punkahwala, but on seeing the white heap of cloth snoring gently against the wall, she changed her mind and instead slipped quietly past him into the moonlight.

A gentle breeze dried the sweat on her forehead and moved the tendrils of hair clinging damply to her temples. The tiled floor was smooth and blessedly cool to bare feet as she glided, ghostlike in her pale nightgown, along the

115

latticed length of the verandah that girdled the palace, peering down into the courtyards as she passed.

There were the stables, where Shah Rukh, her new horse, would be picking delicately at the *gram* in his marble manger or dozing hipshot between the pillars of his stall. There was the elephant's stable and long open sheds where camels and buffalo were tethered. That lean cat she could see slinking across the rose garden, neck braced against the weight of the rat in her jaws, must be dam to the litter of kittens under the philadelphus bush. Yes, it was going straight to them. As she watched, the cat cast a furtive glance round, then disappeared beneath the bush; Kate imagined the ecstatic squeaks and purring as the kittens tore at the food.

She moved on. Faintly round the corner of the building came a plangent throbbing music, growing louder as she approached the old *darbar* court. She leaned over the balcony for a better view. Lights flickered under the fringed canopy where once the Raja would sit to hear petitioners. Just outside it she could see a small group of instrumentalists, some sitting, some standing, and in front of them the swaying undulating figure of a girl in a spangled gauzy costume that left her arms and most of her torso bare. Bangles glinted on those sinuously moving arms, bells tinkled about her ankles, and from her mouth issued a strange wailing song. Though the canopy hid her audience from Kate, she could have no doubt of the identity of one of them.

So this was the pressing work that would not wait until morning!

On and on wailed the girl, while the little tomtoms throbbed their insidious message and the viol strayed up and down its eerie scale. Kate stood as though mesmerized, and a voice from the past came back to her as clearly as if it spoke in her ear. The voice of her godmother's butler, half-scandalized, half-admiring.

'A wonderful liar is Master George. I've never known the like. Looks you right in the eye as he does it, too.'

*

'How did your work go last night?' she asked when they met at breakfast.

'All finished! Took me most of the night, but my desk is clear, thank God!' Smiling, guileless, he looked her right in the eyes. 'You look better, my dear, after a good rest. How about another ride this evening?'

*

Chained and blindfold, the cheetah sat on the flat bullock-cart as it creaked along the white dust road. He knew why he had been taken from his cage in the early hours and made to endure this slow rattling progress. His muzzle twitched as the rank warm scent of antelope was borne to his nostrils. Presently, when they were close, the men would take off his blindfold and show him the quarry.

He waited, relaxed yet alert, listening to the guttural murmur of his keeper chatting to the driver, the clopping hoofs of the horses flanking the *ghari*, Prince Trimbuck's shrill giggle and the English sahib's deeper tones.

'Loose him now!' whispered the Prince.

Collar and girth were unclipped, the leather hood swiftly slipped off. For a moment the cheetah's burning gaze surveyed the plain and fixed on the small herd of antelope grazing undisturbed a few hundred yards away. Bullock carts and horses travelled this road every day. They had no cause for alarm; yet a handsome young buck on the edge of the herd raised his head, stamping.

'Go, my lord!'

At his keeper's gentle shove, the cheetah dropped softly off the cart on the opposite side from the deer. Belly to ground, his neat head dropped between his shoulders and topaz eyes intent on his prey, he slunk along beside the shafts, using the movement of the bullocks to conceal his own.

'Ayee! He is clever, that one,' sighed the wizened keeper admiringly. The young buck lowered his head to graze.

Two hundred yards . . . a hundred and fifty . . . still the hunter bided his time with only a spasmodic twitching of his thick long tail to warn that nonchalance was a pose.

Beneath the loose spotted skin every muscle was tensed for action.

Again the young buck stamped. This time his warning was heeded. All the heads swung up, staring fixedly at the approaching cart. A doe uttered a harsh bark of alarm.

As if the sound were a starting-pistol, the cheetah exploded into movement, covering half the distance between cart and deer in long flowing bounds before the startled animals had even wheeled for flight. With stiff-legged leaps they streamed away across the plain, a doe and fawn trailing behind and the cheetah gaining on the stragglers with every undulating spring he made.

'God! Look at that speed!' George marvelled, reining in his horse. Barely a quarter of a mile away, the cheetah seized the straggling doe and brought her crashing down while her fawn, bewildered, circled his stricken dam and then ran bleating after the herd.

'A good *sigharoosh*,' agreed the prince complacently. 'The best I own.'

'Your own breeding?'

'No, he is from Gwalior. One of the royal breed.'

'A gift from Scindia?'

Trimbuck inclined his head, his eyes half-moons of merriment in his heavy face.

'Is that wise?' said George seriously. 'Your father would be angry if he knew.'

'Who would tell him? Not you, I think, my dear George, with your – ah – connections.'

'Damn my connections. I mean it, Your Highness. You are taking a risk. Your brother might find out.'

'Pah! Madhav cares nothing for hunting. All he thinks of is drilling soldiers. *Your* soldiers. He could not tell a *sigharoosh* from a jackal. Look! They have taken the deer from him yet he is gentle as a lamb.'

The cart with the cheetah's attendants had reached the kill. The keeper jumped out and swiftly disembowelled the carcase, throwing a lump of liver to the great cat who seized upon it eagerly. He was sharpset, having had no food for two days, yet he made no objection when the chain was once more fastened to his collar and he was led back to the cart.

'Great work for small reward,' commented George.

'Oh, I assure you he will enjoy a haunch later.' Trimbuck jerked his reins. 'Come, let us see what he has caught.'

Later, as they jogged back towards the city walls, leaving the slow *ghari* to follow, Trimbuck said slyly, 'I am glad the English camel finds favour with you. From the way you spoke I hardly expected you to enjoy your wedding night.'

George stared straight ahead, inwardly seething.

'So her body is as beautiful as her face! You are a lucky fellow, indeed. Marriage is so often a disappointment when one looks behind the veil.'

'Whoever your informant is, he has a strange notion of beauty, Your Highness.' George tried to speak lightly but the blood was pounding at his temples. So there *had* been someone in the room. God! Were there no bounds to Trimbuck's effrontery? It was easy to guess the identity of this particular spy. Amanullah Khan, the prince's boon companion, who had had the gall to dress as a bearer and offer him champagne at his own wedding.

'Amanullah Khan is generally considered a connoisseur,' said Trimbuck, shaking with mirth.

'I would be obliged if Your Highness would refrain from setting your creatures to spy on me,' said George stiffly. 'If my affairs interest you, I am prepared to discuss them but I give you fair warning, I keep a loaded gun by my bed. Nothing would give me greater pleasure than to blow Amanullah Khan's lying head from his shoulders.'

'Bravely spoken!' applauded Trimbuck, unabashed. 'You must understand my curiosity. Tell me, was it English modesty that made you call your bride the ugliest female of your acquaintance? I am a simple black man,' he laughed richly. 'I do not understand English ways. I am very glad, my dear George, to find you have not shackled yourself to a monster. My aunt the Begum Samru has been so anxious. I will send her a message soon.'

'Don't trouble the Begum with your lies,' said George

abruptly. 'I swear I told her the truth. As a girl, Kate Castlemain was the oddest creature you ever saw.'

Trimbuck's eyes brimmed with laughter as he shook a regretful head. 'How I wish I could oblige you! But I must tell her. She demands it.'

'How much do you want?' said George resignedly.

'Pah! Money? What do I care for money?'

'A great deal, I should say.' Since a substantial slice of his salary was already buying Trimbuck's silence, George spoke sourly. His was a handsome salary, but it was not enough. Natural extravagance combined with the habit of living beyond his means to make his present financial situation precarious. Any increased demand would land him in difficulties, as Trimbuck was well aware. Rapacious the prince might be but he was far too skilled a blackmailer to squeeze his victim dry.

It was the Raja's deliberate policy to keep his sons dependent on him for money, hoping thereby to ensure their loyalty. In Trimbuck's case, at least, the plan misfired. Resentful of his penury, the prince was ready to seize any chance of making money and equally ready to espouse any plot that might lead to his father's downfall.

Now he giggled joyously and clapped a pudgy be-ringed hand on George's shoulder as their horses jogged side by side. 'All I ask is an assurance of your friendship, my dear fellow! In writing,' he added after a pause.

'Indeed,' said George coldly. He did not in the least care to be Trimbuck's dear fellow.

'With an undertaking that you will support my claim to the throne should my father die.'

That's more like it, thought George. Now we're getting to the root of the matter. Aloud he said carefully, 'The Raja looks in excellent health, Your Highness.'

'Ah, how deceptive appearances can be!' Trimbuck shook a mournful head. 'You know how dangerous is this wretched climate of ours. Perfect health one day . . . the next, pouf!' He mimed the extinction of life's candle while his fat jowls quivered with mirth.

'Are you telling me the Raja is ill?'

'Accidents happen. Disease strikes at strong and weak alike. Who can say how long he will live?'

'You are the elder son. Why should you need assurances from me?'

'Elder son! Pah! What difference does that make? My father favours Madhav. He has made a will naming him as his heir.'

'Ah.' George blew out his cheeks as he considered this information. If true the consequences to his own plans might be serious. 'Did he tell you this himself?'

'Does my father tell me anything? It is true, all the same. I have it on good authority.'

George nodded thoughtfully. Most of the Palace servants were in Trimbuck's pay. His love of intrigue combined with a talent for amassing information made him both hated and feared.

'If Madhav succeeds the army will follow him – unless you prevent them. Without your support I will be deposed, cast aside ... perhaps even murdered.'

Not before time, thought George, still more sourly. It was true that the Governor-General would probably accept the advice of his Resident regarding any question of succession. Generally the Company upheld the right of primogeniture unless there was a strong reason against it. Only when the eldest claimant had shown himself manifestly unfit to govern was this rule set aside.

Was Trimbuck fit to govern? Wicked, cruel, deceitful, and vindictive as he was, he could not be judged insane. Madhav, on the other hand, was a fine upstanding boy, very popular with the troops, of good character, full of enthusiasm for the British. It was easy to see why old Chimnaji Rao should name his younger son as his successor: less easy to decide his own course with regard to Trimbuck.

What should he do? Offend him, refuse his request, and risk exposure of his own dealings with the Begum? Placate him temporarily with promises? Or do as he asked, with the certain knowledge that once enthroned Trimbuck would break all his treaties with the Company and fling himself into the arms of Scindia's French masters?

Characteristically, George decided to delay. 'I will consider the matter, Your Highness.'

They were at the gates of the Residency. George took his leave.

Trimbuck watched him ride through the paved courtyard, back ramrod-stiff, gaze fixed ahead, the very picture of an officer and gentleman. High-principled, incorruptible, the moral guardian of the people God had called him to govern. The prince's smile faded. A look of malevolence crossed his heavy features; he spat a stream of scarlet *pan* into the dust.

'Think it over, Resident Sahib,' he muttered, 'but if you value your life . . . or your wife . . . do not keep me waiting too long.'

With a growing wonder Kate explored her new surroundings. In the flurry of preparation for the wedding she had seen little of the Residency and certainly nothing in George's letters had prepared her for its size and splendour. Compared to the Briggs' modest bungalow on Malabar Hill it was a palace.

The citadel of Attaganj was planted upon a rocky pedestal which rose abruptly from the surrounding plain. In addition to mud walls twelve-feet thick in which cannonballs buried themselves uselessly (these walls surmounted by numerous towers and cupolas giving an extensive view over the plain), the whole fortified city was surrounded by a sheet of water too wide to be called a moat, since the waterfowl which flighted at dusk on to its islands were out of musket shot either from the walls or the plain itself.

This formidable defence was man-made, controlled by sluice-gates at either end, and in times of siege made available to the defenders a most welcome supply of fish. A banked causeway built across the water provided the only approach to the citadel, and even when that had been traversed, any invader would have to drag his artillery up a mile of steep winding approach under the very walls of the fortress before reaching the main gate.

This was the stronghold from which for two and a half

centuries the Rajput Rajas of Attaganj had successfully defied both Mughals and Marathas. Though it had never been taken by storm, it had twice changed hands through treachery. Bloody feuds between father and son darkened the pages of Attaganj history and Chimnaji Rao had good precedent for regarding his elder son's intrigues with suspicion.

Within these frowning ochre walls which seemed to grow naturally out of the rock on which they were built, the city's grim defensive aspect gave way to narrow bustling streets and a lighter more graceful style of architecture. The royal palace owed its fretted marble screens and airy colonnades as much to Muslim as Hindu tradition, though the writhing gods and demons and lewdly entwined couples in bas-relief against the smoke-filled temple's walls were wholly Hindu.

The Residency itself was a former Royal abode. Of yellow sandstone patchily blackened with age as if by creeping lichen, it stood imposing and four-square on the eastern edge of the city, a bell-shaped cupola at each corner of the roof and in the centre a square tower surmounted by yet another rash of domes. Within, dim cool apartments on the ground floor had intricately vaulted ceilings which made vistas of delicate pointed arches, leading the eye to infinity. Dappled light filtered softly through the richly carved stonework of pillared walkways where every surface was brilliant with inlaid flowers and birds in graceful repetitive designs. There were pavilions and courts to suit every mood, some lush with joyous riots of blossom and greenery; others geometrically formal, their shaven lawns and well-clipped hedges tended by a host of barefoot *malis*.

Through the maze of handsome rooms, white-garbed servants moved with an air of dedication, always busy, though Mattie was quick to note their dedication did not extend to picking up the dust they collected so painstakingly, preferring to whisk it under some convenient piece of furniture; nor could they be relied on to set a table or replace books the right way up.

'How should they know such things?' said Kate in their

defence. 'Since they eat with their fingers and never read a book, our ways must puzzle them sorely.'

'They'll learn,' said Mattie. 'Before I'm much older, they'll learn.'

And learn they did, though the mixture of mime, bullying and cajolery she employed to make her message plain sometimes reduced Kate to helpless mirth.

'You can laugh, but you can't pretend the house isn't a sight cleaner since I took them in hand,' said Mattie with satisfaction.

Kate was happy to give her free rein. Despite George's frequent absences she found plenty to do, and in her heart of hearts admitted a certain relief when she did not have to lie straining her ears for his footsteps approaching the bedroom door. Her marriage had placed her at the head of the female side of the European community; rather to her surprise even such dragons as Mrs Cornish and Mrs Hopwood (whose sharp tongue was popularly supposed to be responsible for the parson's fondness for the bottle) deferred to the Resident's wife, and these two ladies in particular lost no time in acquainting Kate with her responsibilities. It fell to her to provide accommodation and entertainment for visiting dignitaries, or happy-go-lucky young officers of sporting bent, and also to arbitrate in the small disputes and jealousies that sprang up between the ladies of the station.

As George had warned, most of them had too little to occupy them. Their children were cared for, their houses cleaned by willing brown hands. Goods were brought to their door and native tailors sat cross-legged on their verandahs to make and mend clothes. They had unlimited time for the dissemination of gossip and prosecution of feuds. By listening to the former and exercising her diplomatic skills in the latter, Kate learned a great deal in a short time about her fellow countrywomen.

At first she found their passionate interest in one another's affairs disconcerting – even vulgar – particularly when she herself was the focus of their attention.

In the second week of October, the three senior ladies called on her to discuss plans for the Christmas entertain-

124

ment. This was a traditional affair, comprising a nativity play with carols followed by a grand tea-party for the officers' children. Like a file of ducks in their best plumage, the committee members waddled into Kate's drawing-room, quacking among themselves, heads turning from side to side, bright eyes alert for changes wrought by the new mistress of the Residency: Old Mrs Cornish, dignified in dove grey *tussah*, her shady hat trimmed with violets; Mrs Hopwood, neat, prim, and arthritic in maroon; and Mrs Jones, who must have been pretty before she ran to fat, wearing a flounced pink gown and yellow bonnet with the rumpled and slightly raffish air of one who has risen from bed and donned the nearest garments with no thought for whether they were either suitable or becoming.

At first the meeting proceeded smoothly, though Kate was aware of an undercurrent of antagonism between Mrs Jones and Mrs Hopwood which became more obvious when the question of allocating roles in the nativity play was broached.

The obvious candidate for the part of the Virgin Mary was Mrs Jones' daughter Susannah, a raven-haired beauty of nineteen whose charms caused havoc among the station's young and not-so-young officers. However, when Kate proposed her there was an immediate swelling of bosoms and rustling of skirts as Mrs Hopwood prepared for battle.

'I hardly think she would be suitable,' she snapped and closed her mouth in a thin line.

'Why not, pray?' said Susannah's mother, bristling.

'The part demands a certain spirituality and maturity.'

'Nonsense! It is a girl's role. The Virgin was not a middle-aged frump.'

'She should be pure, untouched . . .'

'If you mean to cast aspersions on my daughter's character I would be glad if you would say so plainly,' said Mrs Jones, who believed in calling a spade a spade.

'Aspersions? Whatever can you mean?'

'My Susannah's a good girl,' announced Mrs Jones truculently. 'If you are thinking of putting up that horse-faced niece of yours for the part, I tell you here and now it would make a cat laugh.'

'Mrs Jones!' exclaimed Mrs Hopwood, trembling. 'Withdraw that remark at once, or I leave the room.'

'Ladies, please!' Kate bit her lip. It would never do to laugh, but poor Honoria Macnab's long sad face did look a little like a well-bred horse. Too late she saw the bone of contention: not the part of the Virgin at all, but the handsome person of Captain Lomond Macnab, debt-ridden heir to a Scottish baronetcy, whom Honoria was rumoured to be in danger of losing to Susannah Jones. They had been seen riding together in the early morning while Honoria lay abed, and at the regimental dance he had certainly partnered Susannah more often than his wife.

Kate racked her brain for an alternative candidate agreeable to both parties. The trouble was, apart from Honoria and Susannah, there wasn't a lady under thirty unless one counted twelve-year-old Luisa Gonzalez . . . or herself.

'Why not give the part to Luisa? She is very young, I know, but she's such a pretty child.'

She looked round the table. The faces were uniformly stony.

Mrs Hopwood shook her head. 'A Portuguese? No, Mrs Gisborne. That would not do at all.'

'Or – myself?'

'*You?*' They sounded even more shocked than by the suggestion of Luisa. Even Mrs Jones and Mrs Hopwood were united in opposition.

'Why not? I can sing a little, you know,' Kate felt compelled to add.

'I am sure you can,' said Mrs Jones. 'Please do not think we are questioning your ability, merely your condition.'

'My – my *what?*' Kate looked at them in blank astonishment. As yet she had not mentioned her suspicions even to Mattie.

'Breedin',' said Mrs Cornish plainly. 'Won't do. Can't have a lady in a delicate situation standin' on a stage to be gawped at.'

'How did you know?' asked Kate rather faintly.

'My dear Mrs Gisborne, you will soon discover the impossibility of keeping secrets in a place like this,' said Mrs Jones. 'Why, the news has been all over the station for a fortnight.'

'All over the station?'

Mrs Jones smiled with just a hint of condescension. 'It is nothing to be ashamed of – rather a matter for congratulation. I am surprised no one has mentioned it sooner. Let me see – October, November, December . . . It would certainly be inadvisable for you to take part in the play. Now, if you are agreeable, shall we return to the matter in hand?'

8

My dear Godmamma, wrote Kate on the 2nd February, 1803.

> *By the time you receive this you will be a grandmother. I hope you are not dismayed to hear it! Mattie will scarce allow me to break the news for fear of counting chickens before they hatch, but I am not superstitious and wish you to have our joyful tidings in advance of the Happy Event. I am in good health, though the station surgeon has forbidden me to do more than walk in the garden and drive out in the evening. I find this curtailment of activity excessively tedious.*
>
> *The baby will be born in April, at the start of the Hot Weather. We are fortunate in living high enough for the climate to be perfectly tolerable all year round.*
>
> *George would, I know, send his love if he knew of this letter, but he is away on tour. The threat of marauders keeps him busy on the frontier. Since the Peshwa of Poona was driven from his capital by a rival, the political situation is turbulent. If any of the five warring Maratha chiefs attained supremacy, he would undoubtedly swallow up this little state, and the Company would have to send more troops to support the Raja.*
>
> *As matters now stand, honours are pretty even . . .*

She paused and nibbled her pen, wondering if Mrs Gisborne in faraway London would be interested in the wrangling of Maratha chiefs, or if it would seem as remote to her as the troubles of poor mad King George and his unruly sons did to Kate. It was not only in India that royal fathers and sons clashed. Still, what else could she write about? Since January, when Captain Lomond Macnab and Susannah Jones ran off to Calcutta together, Attaganj had had no gossip worth the telling.

Perhaps she should write more about George. His doting

mother would wish for more than a passing reference. But then again: what was there to say? Dear Godmamma would hardly be pleased to know that as soon as he heard of his wife's pregnancy George had abandoned her bed and she had scarcely been alone with him since.

She could not precisely accuse George of neglecting her. In public he was a model husband. He appeared with her at all social functions. They took their meals together and when she drove out in the carriage he was always ready to escort her. It would sound absurd to say he avoided her when they were so much together, but mentally and spiritually he was as remote now as on the day she arrived.

Any attempt she made to bridge the chasm was politely blocked. You stay on your side and I'll stay on mine, his attitude warned.

'Why can't we talk to one another?' she asked impulsively, after exchanging banalities all through dinner; and he looked up with an air of pained surprise.

'I fail to understand you, my dear. What are we doing now if not talking?'

'Of trivialities. You never discuss anything important with me. I would like to hear about your work, but you never mention it.'

'My work is confidential, as you know,' he said with an air of weary patience. 'I would be failing in my duty if I discussed it.'

'Don't you trust me, George?' She looked at him curiously. 'Do you really think I would shout your secrets from the rooftops?'

'Now you are being absurd.'

'I don't know why you married me,' she said bitterly. 'A housekeeper would serve you every bit as well – and save the trouble of talking at meals.'

He would not be provoked. 'I married you for a number of excellent reasons. If you are disappointed by the arrangement, I am sorry; but you must admit I made the terms of our agreement clear from the start.'

'But we are no longer at the start! We have been married

the best part of a year. I am going to have your child. How long must we continue to treat one another as strangers?'

Her voice had risen; he gave her a look of warning. 'My dear, remember we are not alone.'

'How could I forget?'

The constant surveillance told on her nerves. Wherever she went, eyes watched, ears listened, and no doubt tongues reported what she said and did. Her servants spread the word to those in other households, who in turn reported to their mistresses. As Mrs Jones had said, it was impossible to keep secrets here. Impossible for everyone but George.

A commotion in the courtyard below the boudoir she used as a writing room gave her the excuse to abandon her letter and go to the window. It could not be George – he would be away a week at least – but it might be a message from him.

A posse of gaily dressed native cavalry clattered under the arch. Rose and silver uniforms: not George's bodyguard nor yet Prince Trimbuck's extravagantly dressed escort, yet familiar, nevertheless. When the officers leading the troop swung down from the saddle her spirits leapt.

'Ned! Colonel Quinn!' she called down in a manner that would have scandalized George.

They looked up, grinning. 'Your servant, ma'am.'

'Hulloa, Kate!'

'I am coming down directly.' She dragged a comb through her hair and called for the *ayah* to bring a more becoming shawl. Nothing could improve her swollen figure, but she saw with surprise that her eyes were sparkling and colour tinged her cheeks.

'You're bright and bonny all of a sudden,' commented Mattie as she entered with a pile of linen. 'Who are your visitors?'

'You'll never guess.'

Kate hurried down the wide marble stairs. They were leaning on a latticed balustrade, looking over the garden, Ned's curly ginger head close to Quinn's dark one. At her approach they straightened and bowed.

'Colonel Quinn! Ned!' She took their hands. 'How very

pleased I am to see you,' she said warmly. 'To what do I owe this visit? I hope you have not come in search of my husband, for he is on tour. I do not expect him back for a week.'

They nodded: she had the impression this was not news to them.

'No, we have come to see you, Mrs Gisborne,' said Quinn, and his scarred face softened in a smile. 'Ned would not permit me to ride past without paying our respects.'

Ned opened his mouth, glanced at Quinn, and thought better of the impulse to speak. He bowed silently.

'I am very glad he would not! We have so few visitors. May I offer you refreshment?' She led the way to the little garden pavilion whose low fretted walls overlooked a pool filled with the luminous fleshy cups of lotus blossoms. When they were comfortably settled with tall glasses, she said eagerly, 'Now tell me your news. Where have you been since I saw you last? We hear so many rumours I hardly know what to believe.'

'A tall order!' Quinn lounged in his chair, relaxed as a panther at rest. 'Go on, Ned: here is the chance you have been waiting for. Recount your adventures.'

'About the battle of Poona?' Ned's eyes lit up. 'Do you really want to hear?'

'I should like nothing better – we are all starved for news. Is it true that the Peshwa had Holkar's brother tied to an elephant's foot and trampled to death? Such barbarity! One can hardly believe it.'

Ned needed no further encouragement. He launched into a spirited account of the events leading up to his first military engagement: the Peshwa's treachery; Holkar's thirst for revenge; the stolen march whereby Holkar's army arrived before Poona while the Peshwa and Scindia, misinformed of his movements, waited to oppose him at the Ali Beylah Pass some miles away. Ned had an Irishman's love of words and once started was hard to stop. Allowing no more than half-a-dozen interpolations from Quinn, he described with a wealth of detail the glittering Maratha hosts drawn up on the plain before Poona, and the admirable coolness of

Colonel Close, the British Resident, who refused to leave his post, merely hoisting a Union flag on the Residency roof while he watched the battle. After the first cannonading it had become a question of whose cavalry was superior.

'Twice they broke through us and would have scattered us to the winds if Holkar himself had not rallied our horse,' said Ned with glowing eyes. 'He was wounded, and several times unhorsed, but we kept charging until Scindia's cavalry broke. Long before then, of course, the Peshwa fled from the field, taking his women with him.'

'Ned was wounded too, you know,' said Quinn. He had said little during Ned's recital, listening with an indulgent air, adding a word here and there, encouraging Ned to shine.

'How dreadful! Were you much hurt?'

'A scratch,' replied Ned in the approved tradition of nonchalant manliness. He pushed back his flaming curls to show a long weal below the hairline, barely healed, and Kate exclaimed in horror.

'That looks more than a scratch to me!'

'A sabre-cut,' said Ned with quiet pride. 'I gave the man who did it something to remember.'

Presently, Quinn sent him off to see to the men and horses.

'Well?' he asked Kate, smiling. 'What do you think of your protégé now?'

'More yours than mine, Colonel Quinn.'

'Shall we share the honour? I know you were angry when I persuaded him to join me. I wanted you to see for yourself what a soldier's life has done for him.'

'I am astonished,' Kate admitted. 'He has changed so much. In looks, speech, confidence . . . He has changed from boy to man.'

'An improvement, would you say?'

'Now you are fishing for compliments. Well, yes. Improved out of recognition. But is it not dreadfully dangerous? My blood ran cold to hear of those charges! He is only a boy.'

'Sometimes it is more dangerous to avoid danger than meet it head on.'

'I don't understand you.'

Quinn said quietly, 'When my son Rambir was twelve years old he begged me to take him to war. Begged me with tears, but I would not. I said he was too young. A month later when I came home, he was dead of a fever, and his mother with him.'

'You cannot blame yourself for that,' protested Kate. 'He might also have been killed if you had taken him.'

'Perhaps. But I would not be left with the memory of his tears – he who never cried.'

'I am so sorry,' Kate murmured. 'When did this happen?'

'Five years ago . . . six.'

So the boy would have been about Ned's age. Quinn caught her thought and smiled a little twistedly. 'Oh, I am not making Ned his substitute, never fear. But if he were to be killed tomorrow, at least he would have known happiness. In an office he would have pined like a caged bird.'

'He certainly seems happy,' Kate agreed.

His eyes searched her face with a grave, almost clinical interest. 'And you?'

'Me?'

'Are you happy?'

The question took her by surprise. She hesitated just a fraction too long before saying hurriedly, 'Of course I am.'

'Your husband is kind to you?'

Colour flared in Kate's cheeks. What right had he to ask anything so personal? George's warnings about this man crowded into her mind: devious, treacherous, a turncoat half-caste. Clearly he had chosen a moment when her husband was away to try and worm out his secrets. Anything she said, any breath of criticism, would go straight to his master, George's enemy. Yet how she longed to confide in him her worries about George's long absences and strange secretive behaviour.

'I cannot see that is a matter which concerns you,' she said coolly.

'It interests me, nevertheless.'

'Why should it?'

'Because I like to know my friends are safe ... and happy.'

Kate stared at him, trying to read his meaning. She said slowly, 'You make that sound like a warning – or a threat.'

'A warning, perhaps. In the coming months it will be important to know who your friends are and whom you should not trust.'

'Why, what is going to happen?' All her vague fears suddenly crystallized. 'George never speaks to me of politics,' she said as lightly as she could. 'He – he says he does not wish to worry me.'

'There is going to be fighting,' Quinn said sombrely. 'Did you know the Peshwa has signed an agreement with the British? It is the first crack in the Maratha confederacy. When the Governor-General sends an army to restore the Peshwa to his throne, the other Maratha chiefs will fight.'

Now she understood his worry. 'Will Holkar fight us?' she asked.

'I shall do everything in my power to prevent it. That way lies ruin – for him and the whole confederacy. But Scindia and the Bhonsle will certainly join forces against the British. Their troops are French-trained and commanded: they have everything to gain from a British defeat.'

'Why are you telling me this?'

'I think it is important for you to understand the situation and know where to seek help should the need arise.'

'From you?' She could not help laughing. 'I doubt if George would be pleased to accept *your* help, Colonel Quinn. He still smarts over the loan of your elephant!'

'Was he very angry?' He grinned. 'The opportunity was too much for me to resist.'

'You might have considered *my* feelings! How was I to guess he would dislike being under an obligation to you? From the way he greeted me one might have supposed he would have preferred me eaten by the tiger!'

The moment the words were out, she knew they should not have been spoken. Criticizing George to his enemy? Hardly the behaviour of a loyal wife.

134

'You will please forget I said that,' she said crossly. 'If you are trying to frighten me with your stories of strife, you are wasting your time.'

'I would not dream of insulting your courage,' he assured her. 'All the same, forewarned is forearmed. If it comes to war, the loyalty of Attaganj and the Rajput states to their treaties with the British will be of the first importance. So long as they resist the blandishments of Scindia, the Governor-General need not fear a stab in the back.'

She smiled, thinking of the Raja with his ramrod spine and fierce moustaches. 'Chimnaji Rao is loyal. I would stake my honour on it.'

'What about his sons?'

She hesitated. There was something she did not like about Prince Trimbuck, but it seemed unfair to condemn him for his unattractive looks.

'I am sure they are just as loyal.'

'I am glad to hear it. Well, Ned, what news?' he said, seeing him approach.

'The men are ready to move, sir.' Ned saluted smartly, glancing at Kate out of the corner of his eyes.

'Then we must be on our way. Thank you for your kind hospitality, Mrs Gisborne; I am glad to find you so well,' said Quinn, adding in a lower tone as he bowed over her hand, 'Remember what I have said! If ever you need help, you have only to ask.'

She watched them ride from the courtyard, Ned straight and slim on his chestnut Arab; Quinn short and square, his scarred face unreadable beneath the rakish turban. The clatter of hoofs was suddenly muffled as they met the dust road; faintly she heard a shouted command and the column broke into a canter. Plumes tossing, lances glittering, the cavalcade disappeared in a cloud of dust and she turned back to the garden. How long, she wondered, before George heard of the visit, and what would he say when he did?

Dawn streaked the sky above the placid mirror of lake that surrounded the walled city: brushstrokes of pink and primrose tinged the grey-green horizon where the stars were

135

already fading. Faint and thrilling came the whistle of air through a goose's flight-feathers and George rose swiftly in his hide, bringing the gun to his shoulder in a single smooth movement. The bird landed far out on the water, well out of range, and he lowered the gun again.

'Shoot the one in front of you,' urged Trimbuck in a sibilant whisper from the next hide. 'My God, are you blind? There, on the water.'

When George neither moved nor answered, the Prince exclaimed impatiently and discharged both barrels of his own gun at the black-backed goose floating so temptingly a few yards out on the water. George ducked as the scatter of pellets hissed into the lake too close for comfort, missing the goose which rose and flapped heavily away. As it crossed the mud wall of the jheel, George shot it neatly and the spaniel that had been quivering at his heels bounded out to retrieve the bird.

'Nice shot!' called Trimbuck in fruity patronising tones. He emerged from his hide and waddled across to George. 'Let me try your gun,' he said peevishly. 'Something is wrong with mine. I have shot nothing all morning.'

'Very well, Your Highness.'

They exchanged weapons. George broke open the suspect gun and squinted along the barrel. 'Looks all right to me.'

'It is a rotten little gun. The rascal who sold it to me will have some questions to answer.'

They strolled on to the next tank, where teal and wigeon, pintail, pochard and mallard rose in squawking flocks at their approach. Hardly bothering to aim, Trimbuck raised George's gun to his shoulder and fired into the thick of them. Feathers drifted down and he crowed with triumph.

'It was the fault of the gun. Just as I told you.'

George smiled but said nothing. He looked about for a target. The double report had cleared the tank of waterfowl, but on the close-mown field beyond stood the tall elegant figure of a demoiselle crane, her crooked neck turned inquisitively towards the commotion. It was a long shot, but when George fired a single barrel she dropped without a squawk.

'Nothing much wrong with that,' George remarked, sending the dog forward. Trimbuck gave him a baleful glare.

'A lucky shot, indeed.'

His kohl-rimmed eyes scanned the ground before them. Some sixty yards away a file of women was carrying water from the well, their red and blue saris making a welcome splash of colour in the dull ochre landscape. They swung along with the stately grace of women trained from babyhood to carry burdens on the head, and the sound of their laughter floated across the fields.

Trimbuck caught at George's arm. 'You see those women near the well?'

'Yes.'

'A lakh of mohurs if you can shoot a pot off their heads.'

'Too dangerous. Suppose I shoot her head off?'

Trimbuck shrugged. 'My father does not lack subjects. Are you afraid?'

'Give me my own gun and I'll have a try.'

'No. You must use mine. Two lakhs.'

George hesitated no longer, but swung the gun to his shoulder and squeezed the trigger. The crack of the shattering pot on the nearest girl's head was clearly audible, and for an instant the whole tableau froze: women petrified, shards still upright, only the water moving as it cascaded over the victim's shoulders. Then she clapped her hands to her head and screamed on a high piercing note, on and on, and the other women joined in, dropping their jars and jostling one another as they fled for home, clothes flapping like a flock of screeching parakeets.

Trimbuck laughed until tears rolled down his fat cheeks.

Slightly ashamed of himself, George watched the women out of sight. His hands were shaking. He was reasonably sure he had not hurt the girl but it had been a risky thing to do – not the sort of behaviour expected of the British Resident.

'The gun is yours!' cried Trimbuck extravagantly. 'You have won it in fair fight.'

137

'Thank you, Your Highness, but I prefer my own. Two lakhs of mohurs, you said?'

'I was joking, of course. Surely you knew that? Two lakhs! How could I find such a sum from the miserable pittance my father doles out to me?'

George clenched his teeth to stifle an angry retort. Fool that he was to expect Trimbuck to honour a bet!

'How is the Raja?' he asked in a neutral tone.

'Alas, he is still indisposed.'

'Be very careful, Your Highness. If the Raja dies and there is any suspicion of foul play, I cannot recommend you to succeed him.'

'Foul play? How could there be foul play when I have not seen my father for a week? I send to his apartments for news and get no answer. I even offer the services of my own physician and they are rejected.'

Just as well, George thought. In silence they approached the gate, Trimbuck puffing at the steep ascent.

'Tell me, my dear fellow,' he said putting out a hand to slow George down, 'why would you not shoot the black goose when I called to you?'

'Hardly a sporting shot,' grunted George.

'Not sporting! You mean, too easy? Oh, I will never understand you English!' cried Trimbuck gleefully. 'It is not sporting to shoot when you will certainly kill the goose, but sporting to shoot when it has nearly escaped? Correct?'

'I suppose so. More or less.'

'For the same reason you allow your wife to entertain Colonel Quinn in your home, like a sitting goose, but if she flew away with him you would shoot her?'

'What are you talking about? Do you mean to say that rascal dared show his face in Attaganj?'

'Oh, he did more than show his face,' said Trimbuck happily. 'My word, yes. Private *tête-à-tête* with the Resident's wife while partaking of refreshments, I am told. Laughter, merriment and compliments all round. She told you nothing of this? Dear me, I am astonished. But then, you do not tell her all your secrets, eh, my dear fellow?' He chuckled richly. 'What is sauce for the gander is sauce for the goose.'

'Did *you* invite Quinn here, Your Highness? I would not advise you to make private deals with Holkar behind my back.'

'Nothing could be farther from my thoughts,' declared the Prince with a mischievous look. 'No, no. You need not look at me to find the reason for Colonel Quinn's call. It was made for the purpose of seeing your memsahib. My informer heard it from Quinn's own lips.'

'Did he, now?' George's tone was grim.

Trimbuck smiled. 'It would be as well for you if my aunt Samru did not hear of it.'

'There's no reason she should, unless you tell her.'

'True – very true.' Trimbuck said pensively, 'She has been expressing concern to me that you are forgetting her. She thinks your memsahib has quite bewitched you and you would rather pleasure her than remember your promises to a poor Indian widow-lady.'

'That's rich, coming from her! Damn it, Your Highness, what am I supposed to do? I married to keep my superiors happy. Even the Begum must see I can't neglect my wife completely. It's my duty to provide her with one child, at least.'

'Ah, but when duty becomes pleasure, what then? My dear fellow, don't misunderstand me. I am only wishing to give you friendly warning. Women are strange creatures.'

'Your Highness speaks from experience, of course.'

'No sarcasm, I beg. *Chacun à son goût.*' Trimbuck's soft hand waved in a deprecating gesture. The troupe of supple golden-skinned striplings he kept for his private pleasure was a rich source of scandal at his father's court. He laid an expansive arm across George's shoulders, his smile broadening as he felt their instinctive stiffening. 'You are right, old boy. Why should the Begum hear of your devotion to your wife when a small payment to me will stifle all such ill-founded rumours? Of course, when the child is born you will have to exercise care. Two dependents instead of one! How sad – how tragic it would be if the fury of a Begum scorned were to vent itself on such innocents!'

139

'All right. I'll pay. But I warn you this is the last you'll get. You've bled me white. I can't find any more.'

'Until the triumph of our French allies, eh?' said Trimbuck softly, and laughed at George's uneasy glance round. 'Then we shall both be rich enough to indulge our fancies. I know what mine will be: what about yours? A château on the Loire? A Governorship? Ah, we shall all fulfil our dreams then! Why so gloomy, my dear chap? Don't tell me your wife has caused you to forget your dreams?'

'Of course not.' George threw off the encumbering arm with scant courtesy. First among his dreams was to see Trimbuck's greasy carcase blown from a field gun and it was tempting to tell him so.

'Why didn't you say that blackguard Quinn had been here?' he demanded, striding into the pretty boudoir where Kate sat writing letters. She wore a flowing muslin peignoir with a blue sash and knots of ribbon that matched her eyes. The violence in his tone surprised her even though she had foreseen this question. The striped kitten that had been playing with her pen-wiper jumped off with a startled hiss and hid beneath the desk.

'I tried to tell you about my visitors last night, but you would not listen. If you remember, you were kind enough to say that the way I chose to amuse myself in your absence was my own affair and you did not need an account of all my callers. May I ask why you should be more interested in Colonel Quinn's visit than in Mrs Hopwood's, for instance?'

'Don't play games with me. I want to know why that man came here and why you were ill-advised enough to receive him.'

'Why he came? That is simple enough. Colonel Quinn and my young shipboard friend Ned Sweeney were in the neighbourhood and decided – quite on the spur of the moment – to pay me a civil call. Does that satisfy you?'

'It doesn't explain why you spent an hour hobnobbing alone with a man I regard as an enemy.'

'Be reasonable, George! How could I refuse to receive him? That *would* set tongues wagging: Holkar's comman-

140

der-in-chief turned away from the Residency gates! Why, it might provoke an Incident. I am told the Maratha's pride is delicate and his temper sadly volatile.'

The same might be said for George's, she reflected. His attempts at bullying were so infantile they no longer frightened her.

'As you will discover when you have had time to question the servants, there was nothing in Colonel Quinn's visit to which you could object,' she said firmly. 'If you are considering forbidding me to receive anyone without your approval, I give you fair warning I will make you a laughing-stock.'

'*You* would?'

'Certainly.'

He looked at her with angry dislike. This was not the humble uncritical beast of burden he had wanted for a wife. How had he been tricked into shackling himself to this virago? He would have done better to marry Susannah Jones, mother and all.

His florid face was as easy to read as a sulky child's, and Kate felt an unexpected pang of pity. Poor George! Age and consequence had not really changed him at all. The Indians took him at his own valuation, mistaking bluster for strength. He could not understand why she refused to do the same.

She had to admit the fault was not all on his side. At the age of forty it must be difficult to give up bachelor freedom – just as difficult as it was for her to tolerate his selfish ways. There would soon be a third person to consider: an entirely innocent party whose life must not be blighted by parental strife.

'Forgive me, George,' she said, though it cost her a good deal. 'Perhaps I was wrong to receive Colonel Quinn, but since you were not here to ask, I did as I thought best. I am sorry if you are displeased.'

Since he continued to stare at her and say nothing, she smiled and took his hand, saying coaxingly, 'Can we not forget all about it and make a fresh start? May we not be friends again?'

His hand lay in hers: heavy, smooth, unresponsive. After a moment he pulled it away.

'That will depend entirely on you, my dear.'

Whistling to his dog, he turned away.

9

Drifting towards wakefulness one fine March morning, Kate twisted uneasily on the bed. Her first impulse was to blame the fish. Joaquin had sworn on his mother's soul that it was fresh, but when the thermometer rose towards ninety degrees fish was notoriously risky. Had she been foolish to eat it? She was so tired of stringy mutton and stringier fowl.

She examined her arms in the sunlight slanting through the *khus-khus* matting. No telltale rash to herald food poisoning . . . Perhaps, after all, she had been lucky.

A second twinge brought her fully awake, jerking at the bell to summon the *ayah* and bid her rouse Mattie. By the time she arrived, Kate was groaning.

'Send for the doctor, Mattie,' she gasped. 'Tell him to hurry. I think it is the fish.'

Mattie gave her a curious look. 'You need the doctor right enough, hinny, but it's not the fish troubling you.'

'It can't be the baby yet? Not until April . . .' She drew a sharp breath. 'Call him quickly.'

Surgeon Richardson arrived promptly and confirmed Mattie's diagnosis. 'Bairns pick their own time, generally when it's least convenient,' he said cheerfully. 'Is George away? I thought so. No need to fret. There's as many born airrly as late, and ye're doing fine. Ye're a fortunate young woman, Mrs Gisborne.'

She huddled on her side, unable to find a comfortable position. 'Fortunate?' She had seldom felt more wretched.

'Built for the job. Ye'll have nae trouble, nae trouble at all,' he said breezily, rolling down his sleeves. 'I'll be awa' tae ma breakfast the noo, but I'll mebbe look back later.'

'You're not proposing to leave me . . . like this?'

'Och, it'll be a wee while yet afore ye need me. Ye're not ma only patient, Mrs Gisborne, mair's the pity. Mattie here can do all that's needful, and when the time comes, she knows where to find me. Show a wee bit o' fortitude, noo, lassie. As I said, ye're a lucky young woman.'

His unconcerned footsteps clicked away.

'Unfeeling wretch!' Mattie ruffled up like a defensive bantam. 'If men had the least notion of what they put their wives through, there'd be a sight fewer babies born. Shall you send for the master?'

Kate hesitated. It was the height of the tiger-hunting season and George had impressed on her the importance of this particular shooting party. If she summoned him home it would mean disappointing his guests.

'He ought to know,' urged Mattie.

'Very well, send a message to his camp,' said Kate, and flinched as the next pain gripped her.

Surgeon Richardson was at heart a kindly man and whatever the shortcomings of his bedside manner he knew his job. After tiffin he bustled back, bringing a whiff of curry and tobacco into the bedroom, and expressed himself satisfied with the way things were progressing.

All through that hot afternoon he stayed with her, exhorting and demanding, until Kate put forth her best efforts for the sole purpose of silencing that nagging Scots voice. The baby seemed irrelevant, unreal. All she was aware of through mists of pain was Surgeon Richardson urging her to try harder. Nothing satisfied him.

'Again, lassie. And again. Push harder. Is that the best ye can do? Och, there's no call tae roar at me! Come, try again. Do ye want us here a' nicht?'

Once her labour had begun it did not last very long. As dark fell and the lamps were lit, her son slithered into the world and the sweating torment of the past hours receded like a dream in the ecstasy of holding him.

'He's beautiful,' she whispered hoarsely.

Red, wrinkled, hideous and wailing, but the most perfect baby in all the world.

'Small enough, but aye – he's a bonnie bairn,' agreed the surgeon with his rare smile. He gave her a searching look. 'Ye'll feed him yourself? Good, good. Safest by far. I've known women take a post as wet-nurse when their ain bairns had died o' cholera not twa days syne.'

'Is cholera about?'

'Not yet. Och, we've the odd case, but it's after the Rains that epidemics begin. Feed the bairn yourself and ye'll have nae worries on that score.'

'I will,' she promised.

'I heard a wee while back that George is on his way home. Try to get some sleep afore he comes.'

He bustled away.

George had not wanted to abandon the tiger-hunt that had cost him so much effort. Left to himself, he would have ignored Kate's message, but pressure from his guests forced him home against his will, wasting the weeks of patient tracking which had gone into locating a tigress and her cubs in this maze of broken hills on the Malwa border, and the bribes exacted by the local *thakur* before he would provide beaters to drive the beasts into a suitable ravine.

Today, at last, the complicated operation had been complete. Two pad elephants with experienced native *shikaris* had been sent ahead to block the end of the ravine. Just as George was preparing to see his guests into their *howdahs* and mount his own, the arrival of Kate's messenger spoiled everything. Neither of his guests had any experience with tigers. If he left them the hunt would have to be abandoned and Sir Piers Bolton would go home without his coveted tiger-skin. Sir Piers was a useful ally whose opinion carried weight in the Bombay Council chamber and George would have liked to oblige him with a successful hunt. No one criticized a man who had shown him good sport.

'What's up George, old man?' asked Captain Vincent, strolling up. He was Bolton's aide, a thickset, heavy-browed young officer who was less stupid than he looked. 'Trouble at home?'

'No trouble. Message from my wife, that's all.'

'Expectin' a child, ain't she? Proud papa, and all that? Don't say the little blighter's chosen this moment to arrive?'

Reluctantly George admitted this was the case. 'No

reason it should spoil our hunt, though,' he added, urging them towards the waiting elephants; but Sir Piers looked shocked. He was a gentle, bookish man with a strong sense of family duty.

'Of course you must go home. Never forgive myself if anything went wrong and we were to blame for keeping you here,' he said earnestly. 'Childbirth's a chancy business in this damned climate. George, my boy, your place is with your wife. "Stand not upon the order of your going . . . " Eh? No need to concern yourself about us. Vincent and I will do very well. We'll forget the tigers and see if we can't bag an antelope or two.'

George fumed but had to obey. Sir Piers would have thought worse of him for neglecting his wife than spoiling the hunt. All through the long hot ride he fuelled his anger with thoughts of the opportunity missed, time and money wasted, and arrived home in a black mood.

Kate was dozing with the baby in her arms when he reached her room. Exhaustion had given her beauty a new ethereal quality; blue veins patterned her eyelids and her skin seemed almost transparent.

He paused on the threshold, anger draining away, replaced by a new and quite unfamiliar emotion.

He had never felt any sense of kinship with the dusky infants with which from time to time his mistresses had presented him, nor even convinced he had any part in the making of them. Most *bibis* cheated their protectors with a lover of their own race: it was an accepted hazard. In duty bound he had provided for these children, but with no interest beyond making sure their mothers did not become too grasping. He was quite unprepared for the sudden rush of protective love that swamped him on seeing the small yellow-fuzzed head cradled against Kate's breast.

This was his true-born son, not a shadow of doubt. The wizened face wore a look of profound wisdom; the line of nose and chin uncannily resembled George's father in his last years. Marvelling, he tiptoed closer, and reached out a finger to caress the downy head.

'My son,' he said softly, and Kate opened her eyes.

'George . . .' she whispered.

'I came as soon as I could. Are you all right, my love? Was it very bad?'

Was she dreaming? He had never spoken to her so tenderly. She saw the look of wonder on his face and knew something momentous had happened in his life, just as it had in hers.

'It was . . . bad. But worth it. A thousand times worth it. Is he not beautiful?'

'The most beautiful baby ever born!' he said fervently and she could not doubt that he meant it. 'Thank you, my dear love, and thank God for bringing you both through safely.'

Wordlessly she stretched out her hand. Tears of weakness welled up in her eyes, but they were happy tears. As his hand grasped her strongly he smiled, and she knew it was the promise of a fresh start.

The birth of John George Frederick Gisborne, soon known to one and all as Jacky, marked the beginning of a halcyon period in relations between his parents.

The weather was hot and while Kate slowly recovered her strength she spent the greater part of each day lying on a chaise-longue placed between two windows where it would catch every stray breath of air. George had his own desk brought up in order to be near her and the baby, and they spent many an hour in companionable silence, George working at his papers while Kate read or nursed the baby. His whole manner showed a new gentleness and consideration. Happy at the change and grateful for his company, she tried not to mind that it was Jacky, not herself, who was the focus of his devotion. Sometimes she could not help feeling there was something obsessive about the time he spent gazing into the cradle. For the first month after Jacky's birth he did not leave home, even foregoing the Dewan of Chandarpur's annual tiger shoot, an event for which invitations were eagerly canvassed among the station's officers. Mattie, too, felt he fussed unnecessarily. Jacky must be kept out of the sunlight, bathed only in water that had been boiled, guarded night and day by two *ayahs*, each of whom had been given orders to watch the other.

Kate herself must avoid exertion, spiced food, the heating effect of wine, or anything that might affect her milk and upset Jacky's digestion. But if either of them protested against all these regulations, George's expression hardened and the old dictatorial note entered his voice.

'A child's life here hangs by the most slender thread. I have waited a long time for a son. Now I have him, neither you nor anyone else will be permitted to take risks with his health.'

Soon after this, a letter from Sal Briggs chillingly demonstrated the truth of George's words.

I rejoice at your son's birth, she wrote, *and pray that you, at least, may be spared the heartbreak we have known these last weeks. Ten days ago it pleased God to take our boy from us . . .*

Pale plump peevish Thomas – his mother's idol! With a tightening heart Kate read on:

We were at tea one evening a month ago when we heard a commotion on the verandah. Upon the servant running out to discover the cause, he found the pet spaniel puppy Colonel Lever gave to Tom for his birthday yelping in the jaws of a hyena, which did not seem disposed to quit the premises even when the servants shouted and threw stones. Very reluctantly he dropped the puppy, and my husband coming up with a gun quickly put an end to the intruder.

The puppy was examined. Though smeared with slime he seemed quite uninjured, and for near three weeks continued well and playful as usual. Then one morning the dog-boy reported him dull and disinclined for food, though he drank a great deal.

We had him tied up and watched, but he whined so much that Tom, taking pity on his pet, persuaded the dog-boy to free him. He brought him into the room where I was sitting with some ladies, saying, 'Look, Mamma! Hero is quite well again.'

All listlessness had vanished. On the contrary the puppy was excited, running about the room and constantly leaping up to lick Tom's face. I was occupied in conversation and did not pay heed until I heard Mrs Green say loudly, 'Watch out! That dog is raging mad.'

This gave everyone a scare and chairs and tables were overturned in the rush to get away. I did not at first believe her, but called for the dog-boy, demanding to know why my orders had been disobeyed. He ran in, but had much ado to recapture his charge, being twice bitten before he could leash him. I saw Mrs Green was right and ordered the dog hanged at once.

Alas, too late! That same night poor Tom became fretful and feverish. Doctor Kenny requested permission to impregnate his system with mercury, which relieved him for a time. All night we sat with him, sponging his face to cool the fever, but towards morning the dreadful contractions began and the sight of water seemed to terrify him so much we were obliged to desist. Then, I think, I knew all hope was gone.

Oh, Kate, believe me, there can be no sight more distressing than to watch a beloved child in the grip of such agonizing spasms! As the fits seized him he would throw himself backward upon the bed until his spine threatened to crack, with such violent inspiration and contraction of his chest as to stop his breathing. Then with a stertorous roar like the barking of a hoarse dog, he at last exhaled and lay exhausted until the fit came on him again.

Though mad with thirst he could neither swallow nor drink – indeed, the sight of liquid provoked such terror that it prolonged the fits, and neither morphia, opium or any other panacea could relieve them. Long before the finish I prayed that death might put an end to his pain, but though the doctor begged me to leave I had the strange feeling that to do so would betray him. Some strength I did not know I had forced me to witness his suffering. Through two long dreadful days and nights I did not leave him, though at times he threw himself about so violently we had to restrain him, and he would have bitten my hand could he have reached it.

When at last the end came, it was sudden . . .

149

Kate laid down the letter, her own hand shaking a little. Impulsively she crossed to Jacky's cradle and gazed down at him. He was healthy, bonny and contented, yet what dangers lurked all round?

His eyes were beginning to focus. Wide and blue, absurdly like George's, they gazed back at her and she longed to snatch him up and carry him away from this smiling treacherous land where a child's life hung by a thread. Her heart went out to Sal, who had lost two babies and tried so hard to protect her Baba sahib. All she had left was the baby, Lucilla, a sickly infant by all accounts and unlikely to survive her first monsoon.

George was right. Jacky's life was far too precious to risk. However irksome the precautions, she must suffer them until the first dangerous years were past and he could be sent home to safety in the healthy climate of England.

It was three months before George resumed his visits to her bed. His new forbearance extended to his love-making: indeed, he seemed reluctant to make love at all. Either he was too tired, or he feared she had not recovered from Jacky's birth, or it was too soon to risk another pregnancy. Only when she told him roundly that she was perfectly well did he consent to intercourse, and then in so perfunctory a manner that she was left frustrated.

Had she known this abstinence was the result of Prince Trimbuck's veiled warnings, she would not have thanked him. Her physical awakening had been late and once roused the hungry tiger demanded his due. With secret shame at first and then with growing desperation she tried to convey her needs to George, but he was indifferent.

Mattie, whose sharp eyes had seen veiled forms slip in and out of his study, and whose nose sometimes caught the sickly pungency of opium about his clothes, guessed the reason for this lack of appetite. Why meet trouble halfway, she thought, and kept her suspicions to herself.

One hot night when the moon shed its silver light over the city's domes and towers, and the heavy musk-scented air quickened the pulses with half-conscious yearnings, Kate crouched by the window in her filmy night-gown, looking across the stacked roofs to the wide plain beyond, listening for her husband's footsteps.

Tonight, she thought. I'll try again tonight.

Towards midnight she heard them, heavy and uncertain, approaching along the passage with an occasional soft thud as if he had cannoned into the wall. He fumbled for the door catch, cursing softly.

'Damn thing. Where's it go' to?'

'George?'

'Wha' – wha' you doin' there?' As she materialized from the shadows he blinked in owlish confusion. 'Though' you were 'sleep long 'go,' he said with a hiccuping laugh.

Drunk, she thought resignedly, and took him by the arm. 'Come to bed, George. It's late.'

The sweet pungency hung about him, tantalizingly familiar. Like a docile child he allowed her to divest him of his robe and help him to bed, where he rolled on his back and began at once to snore. She wanted to shake him, force him to recognize her burning need.

Lying close beside him she drew his heavy head against her breast and caressed it. He grunted, whether in protest or appreciation it was hard to say, and emboldened she stroked the tight curls at the nape of his neck; kneading, scratching, hands growing more daring as the vague yearnings crystallized into sexual hunger.

With trembling hands she stripped off her night-gown and pressed against him, skin to skin, kissing and caressing, guiding his unresponsive hands into her most secret places. The mosquito net stirred as if moved by a wind, but she paid no heed. Surrounded by its white mist they were alone, man and woman freed from daytime conventions and taboos.

'George,' she whispered against his lips. 'Love me, George!'

'Wha' – wha' you wan'?'

'I want you,' she said desperately. 'Don't you want me?'

'Harlot!'

Pride forgotten, she writhed against him as desire spread

151

flame through her body, and for a moment felt his loins stir as he tried to respond. But George had serviced four lusty Maratha maidens that evening, singly and in pairs, and now the blandishments of Venus herself could not have roused him.

With a groan he slumped back on the bed. ''Nother time,' he grunted and turned his back.

Burning with shame and humiliation she flung herself across the bed while desire ebbed away. Never again, she vowed. Never again would she beg for love, from George or Jeremy or any man. But how could she quell these urgings of her body that had become a nightly torment? How could she prevent her lust showing when she saw muscular thighs sheathed in buckskin, or bronzed throats rising from flimsy muslin shirts? Society looked with indulgence upon men who lusted after women; it was less forgiving when the roles were reversed. How could she take a lover when servants watched her every move?

That night she dreamed of Jeremy. He was running down a winding road while she pursued him, calling to warn him that a precipice lay ahead. Either he did not hear or pretended not to, and the faster she ran, the faster he fled before her. Just as he reached the abyss he turned and looked back with a mocking smile, and she saw it was not Jeremy at all, but Colonel Quinn.

Two days later George announced his departure on tour. He returned with news that threw Attaganj into a ferment. Poona had been recaptured from the Marathas. Despite the protests of senior officers, the Governor-General's brother, Colonel Arthur Wellesley, had been given command of an army which had marched with unbelievable speed from Mysore and stormed into Poona just in time to prevent Amrit Rao, the puppet-regent placed there by Holkar, from setting the city on fire.

Amrit Rao had fled. As soon as the Peshwa could be persuaded it was safe to return, he had resumed his seat on the *gaddi*, though it had taken a good deal of tact on the part of Colonel Close, the British Resident, to restrain him from punishing his disloyal subjects with all the barbarous mutilations and other atrocities which his fertile brain had devised during his months of exile.

Poona was now protected by the British, and the Peshwa, head of the Maratha confederacy, firmly under British domination. Enraged by this betrayal, Scindia and the Bhonsle of Berar had withdrawn their armies to the frontier and were prowling there like savage dogs, raiding the Peshwa's villages, destroying crops and terrorizing peasants while awaiting their chance to attack the isolated British force. The opposing armies were about evenly matched, and the Marathas had the advantage of the country.

'What of Holkar?' asked Kate with some anxiety.

George smiled contemptuously. 'Holkar? Why, at the first sign of trouble he bolted for home like the cur he is. Worried about your friend the Colonel, eh? I don't advise you to lose any sleep over him, my dear. He's a mercenary through and through. He won't risk his precious neck until he sees which way the dice are likely to fall. The first thing any adventurer learns is how to stay on the winning side.'

She was relieved to hear there was no immediate prospect of Ned being called upon to fight his countrymen. George was probably right about Quinn: his loyalty would be to his pocket. Even so, she had a strange sense of *déjà-vu* as George outlined the situation. It was so precisely what Quinn had predicted four months earlier.

'Will the Attaganj battalions be called out?'

'Possibly. It is what we have trained them for.'

'Can you be sure of their loyalty? There are so many Marathas among the sepoys.'

'Why, what a worrier you are, to be sure!' he said in a patronizing tone that suggested such matters were none of her business. 'Don't you think the people here are contented with our rule? They know very well they are better off than they would be under Maratha domination.'

'Yet it is only a few years since Holkar laid claim to the state.'

'I see you have been listening to Colonel Quinn! Not the most reliable source of information, my dear. In fact, if you will accept a word of advice, don't believe a word he says.

153

There! That is quite enough discussion of politics. Let us talk of more interesting matters. How is Jacky? Has he acquired any new teeth?'

His moods puzzled her: she never knew what to expect. As the Hot Weather dragged on he was alternately elated and irritable, like a man waiting for some great event but frustrated by minor obstacles. Two months of inconclusive negotiations between the British Resident in Poona and the Maratha chiefs on his frontiers ended in early August, when the newly-promoted General Wellesley lost patience and formally declared war on Scindia and the Bhonsle. As his army supported by that of Colonel Stevenson advanced into the broken hills and ravines of the Deccan, the Marathas kept just out of reach, sometimes enticing him on, sometimes circling behind him. In a sinuous course of loops and zigzags, the opposing forces played cat-and-mouse; the British pursuing doggedly, intent on a general engagement, while the Maratha cavalry made lightning raids on baggage trains and supplies, melting away before anything more than a skirmish developed.

Messengers came and went in a constant stream from the Attaganj Residency, charting the campaign's progress in the Deccan, and bringing news of General Lake's attacks on Maratha strongholds in Hindustan. It was difficult to predict which snippets of news would please George and which plunge him into depression; Kate soon learned that it was not advisable to comment on his moods.

'One would almost think you favoured the Marathas!' she remarked, half joking, when news of a British reverse not thirty miles from Attaganj was received by George with smiling equanimity.

The smile vanished. He turned on her with an anger quite disproportionate to the remark. 'That's a damned silly thing to say.'

'Then why are you pleased to hear of poor General Wellesley's troubles?'

'Because he's a cocksure young ass who should never have been given this command,' said George cuttingly. 'Never would have been, either, if he wasn't the *Lat Sahib's* brother. Damned Irish: cling together like burrs. There's half-a-dozen officers who outrank Wellesley, but were any of them offered the command? Oh, no. Our Glorious Little Man gives it to his own brother even though he's still wet behind the ears. Of course I can't help laughing when he makes a fool of himself.' He gave her a lowering look. 'But I'll thank you not to spread any rumours about favouring the Marathas. If that kind of talk gets about I *will* have something to worry me.'

Privately Kate thought that considering the difficulties of heat, hostile and ill-mapped terrain and the near-impossibility of obtaining food supplies, General Wellesley's conduct of the campaign was remarkable for its success; but clearly professional jealousy clouded George's view and it was a subject on which they would not agree.

His reluctance to discuss outside affairs with her soon led her to establish other avenues of information. Mattie's nose for gossip was invaluable; from her and snippets gathered by other officers' wives, Kate was able to piece together a fair picture of what was happening. Despite the numerical superiority of Scindia's French-led forces, the disciplined Company troops were gradually gaining the upper hand.

Two days after the declaration of war, General Wellesley had captured the important fort of Ahmednagar, belonging to Scindia, while farther north General Lake invested and successfully stormed the supposedly impregnable stronghold of Aligarh.

Meanwhile, where was Holkar? Rumour declared him to be flitting from one unprotected city to another, taking advantage of his rival chiefs' preoccupation with fighting the British to raid both Scindia and the Bhonsle's territory, and extort huge sums in ransom. The city of Mandesar alone had paid him a *crore* of rupees to take his plundering troops away. Tales of atrocity abounded. Had Quinn ordered the torture of rich banyas to make them reveal their treasure-hoards, thought Kate, shuddering. Had Ned torn the rings from their wives' ears and noses?

With fighting so close, George had forbidden her to go beyond the city walls. There were times when she thought she would give her eye-teeth for accurate information and when in mid August the rivers spilled over their banks and became impossible to cross, her sense of claustrophobia made her pace the long walkways of the Residency like a caged she-wolf.

As General Wellesley's successes mounted, George's temper became so uncertain that the only thoroughly safe subject of conversation was Baby Jack.

Six months old now, and the possessor of four fine teeth, he was his father's delight. Even Mattie, who had reared enough children to know they all caught up with the early achievers in the end, had to admit he was an exceptionally strong and forward baby as well as a bonny one. His wide eyes were the very colour and shape of George's, cornflower blue against the rosy peach of his skin. Lint-fair curls clustered on his neat skull and his fat arms were creased into appealing bracelets about the wrist.

Lately he had learned to roll over, arriving with an expression of surprise on his stomach after being placed on his back, and now he endeavoured manfully to raise himself on hands and knees.

On the second day of September, Mattie brought him bathed and fresh in a pin-tucked gown of white lawn to join his parents for the sacred hour of play after tea. However busy he was, George would not miss this evening ritual, but today Mattie found Kate alone among the tea-time paraphernalia.

'Where's the master, then?' Mattie took the baby from his *ayah* and handed him to Kate.

'In his study.' Absently Kate began undoing all the tiny buttons the *ayah* had just been at pains to do up. 'A messenger arrived just as he sat down to tea. He won't be long . . . There, my precious! Doesn't that feel more comfortable? Lie there and have a nice kick while I finish my tea.'

She laid Jacky on a folded quilt of peacock-blue silk. Mattie clicked a disapproving tongue. 'He'll ruin it,' she warned. 'You shouldn't take off his napkin. There! What did I say? Some folk haven't the sense they were born with.'

156

'It doesn't matter. He looks so sweet on the blue. Oh, all right.' She picked up the gurgling baby and hugged him close. 'Come here, precious, and let Mamma clean you up. Your Papa will be here soon, and we want you fit to be seen.'

'As he was until you took off his pretty clothes. Here's the master now. I'll be back in an hour to put Jacky to bed, so don't you go getting him all worked up, or he'll never drop off.'

'Really, Mattie, how you do fuss! Sometimes I wonder if he's your baby or mine.'

'Why, mine, of course! I thought you knew that by now.'

They were both laughing as George entered, but a glance at his face was enough to banish their smiles.

'Is it bad news?' asked Kate as Mattie quietly left the room.

'Bad enough! That damned impetuous fool Wellesley!'

'Why, what has happened?'

For once he took no notice of the baby, but said in a tight-clipped voice, 'There has been a major engagement at Assaye, with heavy losses on both sides. Wellesley found the Marathas encamped on a tongue of land where the Juah joins the Kailna river – an impossible place to manoeuvre – and attacked without waiting for Colonel Stevenson to come up. It was nearly a disaster. They say the seventy-fourth suffered terribly – cut almost to pieces.'

The Seventy-Fourth was his own regiment. He was torn between pride and anguish.

'Did we win?'

'If you can call such slaughter victory. At all events, Scindia is in retreat. Some of his troops, from the Begum Samru's battalions, are making for the Kahira ferry, to join their comrades in Hindustan.'

'Then they must pass through Attaganj!'

George nodded. 'I am ordered to take three battalions to guard the frontier. The second battalion will remain in cantonments in case of trouble. We march tonight.'

'So soon!' Kate turned very pale.

Seeing her alarm he said more temperately, 'Now, my

157

dear, there is no need to worry. You will be safe enough here.'

'I am more worried about you.'

He smiled. 'Never fear, I can look after myself. But listen, Kate. Should anything happen to me, you must leave here and go at once to Bombay to seek out my man of affairs, Mr Bapuji – I will give you his direction. He will advance you money, and the valuables I have deposited with him over the years. You will find it enough to keep you in comfort when you return to England. No – let me finish. I want no scrimping, mind. Jacky must have the best education money can buy. Ponies, guns . . . Give me your word on it.'

'Most gladly, though I hope I shall not have to honour it, ' she said, forcing a smile. 'Don't worry, George, Everything shall be as you wish. I daresay in a few days when this scare is over, we shall wonder what the fuss was about.'

'I pray you are right. It is all a confounded tangle. I wish – ' He stared at her and she thought him about to say something revealing, but the long habit of secrecy prevailed, and he changed the subject abruptly. 'You must excuse me. I have much to do.'

'Kiss Jacky, at least, before you go.'

She held the baby up to him and for a moment the two fair heads merged as he embraced his son with more emotion than she had ever seen him show. When he handed him back she thought there were tears in his eyes, but quickly dismissed the notion when he said in his usual curt way, 'I hope you will be sensible and conduct yourself with dignity while I am away. I do not wish to find you have been entertaining Colonel Quinn in my absence.'

She bit back an angry retort, saying instead, 'And I hope you will keep me informed of your doings. You cannot imagine how agitating it is not to know what is happening.'

'I will write when I can.' He stooped to give Jacky a last caress as he lay kicking on the quilt, then bowed formally and left her.

Fife and drum and clattering hoofs roused her from sleep

before dawn. George was booted and spurred, his charger held at the steps as he bade her a hasty farewell, pressing into her hand his letter of instruction to Mr Bapuji of Bombay.

With Jacky asleep in her arms, she stood on the mist-wrapped verandah to watch him ride away to join the troops who had already begun to stream past the Residency, dark faces proud and excited beneath turbans and tall shakos, pipe-clayed crossbelts gleaming white against scarlet tunics.

The earth trembled to the steady beat of their feet. This was the first time the native troops of Attaganj had been called on to show their mettle. Officers and men were united in determination to give a good account of themselves.

She wondered which of the various ferries and river crossings George would choose to guard, or whether he meant to string men all along the frontier. If he did, the line would be a thin one. The Begum Samru's men might slip past. What kind of woman was this mistress of mercenaries? A vulture, Quinn had called her, to be found wherever there might be plunder. Kate thought if she were in George's shoes, she would concentrate her infantry in two or three places, and rely on native cavalry to patrol the rest . . .

Were she in George's shoes! The thought made her smile. Not a word of his intentions had passed his lips, and after eighteen months of marriage she had known better than to ask questions. How much I should enjoy discussing such matters, she thought, instead of being labelled Female, and unfit to voice an opinion on anything beyond the domestic sphere.

Yet the Maratha queen Ahalya Bhai had reigned here for thirty years of peace and prosperity; and Good Queen Bess for forty-five of England's most glorious years, and no one pretended *they* had no political understanding.

Why was George afraid to let her into his secrets? She had supposed from his constant urgings or economy and complaints of lack of funds that he spent his pay faster than he earned it. Now she learned of valuables salted away with a Parsi whose address in the city's seediest quarter made it unlikely that he was the kind of man of affairs of whom George's superiors would approve. Curiosity burned in her to know more of George's dealings with Mr Bapuji. If only she could discuss the matter with Sal, or even Colonel Quinn!

With nothing but the 2nd Battalion – and that under strength since several officers were sick – left to defend Attaganj, the city was edgily nervous. Mattie reported that rumours were rife in the bazaar. Holkar had raided neighbouring villages. He had joined forces with Scindia. There had been a great massacre. Holkar was marching on Attaganj . . .

Kate tried to stay calm. True to his promise, George sent her scribbled notes at intervals, but the news in them was not reassuring.

Scindia has given us the slip, he wrote. *He avoided the Kahira ferry and crossed the Narbada on a bridge of boats. We are going in pursuit. I may not be able to write for some days . . .*

What might happen in those days? Panic threatened but she forced it down. George would not have left her and the baby if there was real danger. Colonel Quinn had promised his help if she needed it, but how could she contact him?

As if summoned by her wish, he came.

She was sitting at her desk one morning, writing letters, when Ahmed entered with his soft tread to announce in a tone of deep disapproval that Colonel Quinn was below. 'I tell memsahib Not At Home?'

'Certainly not,' she said composedly. 'Show Colonel Quinn into the Long Room and bring *Lal sherâb*. I will join him there directly.'

10

He was pacing the floor of the long light room when she entered. 'Forgive this intrusion, Mrs Gisborne,' he said, bowing over her hand. 'It is kind of you to see me.'

'I am always glad to see a friend. Is Ned not with you?'

'We are marching for Indore. He is with the men.'

Then why had he called? He saw the question in her eyes and said with a kind of suppressed irritation, 'The truth is, I have a favour to ask. Frankly, I am in the devil of a hole.'

'Then let us see if I can pull you out,' she said, smiling. 'It is not so long since you pulled *me* from the devil of a hole.'

This brought a reluctant grin. 'I did not intend to ask *quid pro quo!*'

'Nevertheless, tell me what is the matter.'

'Very well. As I said, we are marching to Indore with all speed. This morning as we waited at Kahira for a crossing, Ned rode a little upstream where he chanced to notice a crowd gathered on the river bank. You know what a jackdaw he is, always curious.'

'I know.'

'He rode up to see what they were about. He saw a corpse on a funeral pyre, and as he watched the mourners helped the two widows mount up beside their husband. By Ned's account one was a grey-haired crone who climbed the ladder unassisted, but the other widow – a young girl – had to be carried by men of the family, and he noticed her hands were bound. He went nearer, not liking what he saw, and as soon as the flames sprang up he heard her scream, and saw her try to struggle free.'

'Oh, horrible!' Kate pressed her hand to her mouth. The practice of widow-burning known as *sati*, though deeply repugnant to the British, was too deep-rooted a custom to be suppressed entirely.

'Ned lost sight of her as the smoke billowed up and supposed she had perished; but a moment later he was amazed to see the poor creature spring from the pyre with her hair and clothing ablaze, and fling herself into the river where the current at once carried her away. The mourners rushed to untie a boat, meaning to drag her back, whereupon Ned – without the least thought of the consequences – spurred his horse into the river. He reached the girl first and pulled her across his saddle. Then with difficulty, for the water was deep and swift, he brought the charger back to the bank, pursued by stones and curses. Though much frightened and scorched, the girl was alive and most piteously begged him not to return her to her family.'

'I should think not!' Kate considered. 'So now you are encumbered with a camp follower you do not want, but duty requires that you look after her?'

'*Ned* requires it,' he corrected with a ghost of a laugh. 'I fear knight-errantry has gone to his head.'

'So you have brought her to me. Of course I will look after her. I am astonished you should have any doubts on the score.'

'You mean it?' He threw her a look of pure gratitude. 'I shall be for ever in your debt. May I bring her in? I warn you, she is in a woebegone condition.'

'Small wonder after such an ordeal!'

He went out and in a few minutes returned with a slender and very bedraggled girl in her early teens, wrapped in a sari still daubed with ash and dried river-mud, the material so badly scorched in places that it was only rendered decent by the addition of an officer's cape, probably Ned's. Most of her hair had been lost to the flames, and the remainder grotesquely frizzed so it stuck out in a kind of halo, but under the burns and dirt brilliant dark eyes glowed in a face of such astonishing loveliness that Kate could hardly believe Quinn was unaware of it.

Though her hands and throat bore angry red weals where

the burning timbers had pressed, her swift immersion in the river had saved her from serious injury.

'Her name is Serinda,' said Quinn, leading her forward.

'Come here, my poor child. You are safe with me,' said Kate in her careful Hindustani, but the girl cringed as if fearing a blow, and would have fled if Quinn had not held her.

'She is quite unused to *faringhis*,' he said apologetically. 'I am afraid she may cause trouble among your servants. Though she was born a Brahmin, what she has done will render her casteless, lower even than the sweepers.'

'She is very pretty,' said Kate, foreseeing trouble of quite a different kind. 'Have you no eyes, Colonel Quinn?' She laughed at his look of surprise. 'Never fear, she will soon become used to me and if the servants here dare to abuse her in any way they will have to answer to me. I will put her in Mattie's charge and she can work in the nursery where we can keep her under supervision.'

She summoned Mattie and instructed her to see to Serinda's burns and find her some fresh clothing. The girl went with her willingly enough, and Quinn turned to Kate with an expression of profound relief.

'Mrs Gisborne, you are an angel. I cannot thank you enough.'

'I assure you there is no need for thanks. One good turn deserves another, and for my part I feel quite proud to be associated with Ned's chivalrous deed!'

'I will be sure to tell him so,' said Quinn, rising.

She saw he was anxious to rejoin his men, but could not resist detaining him a moment to ask if the Attaganj battalions had yet succeeded in catching the Begum Samru's troops.

'Oh, no. There was never any chance of that!' said Quinn rather dryly.

Kate frowned. 'Why not?'

'Because in my opinion they had not the smallest intention of doing so.'

'But George –' Her eyes narrowed. She said

163

suspiciously, 'Are you accusing my husband of – of *cowardice*, Colonel Quinn?'

He smiled and shook his head. 'Even his worst enemy would not call Major Gisborne a coward.'

'Then why – ?'

'Pray forgive my haste, Mrs Gisborne, but I must leave you. As it is I shall be lucky if I catch up with Ned before nightfall. Thank you again for pulling me out of the hole!'

She watched him ride away, still puzzled by the dismissive, almost contemptuous tone in which he had spoken of George. Could it be that Quinn resented being under an obligation as much as her husband did? Well, the tables were turned now, she thought, and the debt of gratitude paid. George must be pleased by that, at least.

Smiling at the strange ways of fate, she made her way to the nursery.

Serinda quickly recovered from her ordeal and showed herself such a bright willing worker that she won golden opinions from Mattie.

'Nice little thing – does twice the work of that Nasi Bhai and in half the time. Clever, too. She's picked up some words of English already, and she's that good with the baby. She'd play with him all day if I let her.'

From Mattie, too, came further details of Serinda's earlier life. Far from regretting her change of circumstances the girl seemed delighted by her new environment, which was not surprising since her marriage had been an unhappy one.

'Forced to wed a man old enough to be her grandfather, and she not fourteen years of age – the things they do to these girls! She says the other wife was jealous; never stopped scolding and made her do all the work; and then the old man would take his stick to her. *I* don't know! Can't hardly wonder she didn't care to be burned alive for his sake.'

'How did they persuade her to it? Was she drugged?'

'That she was. Told me all about it – all she remembers, that is.'

'Do tell me.'

164

Mattie settled herself in her chair with the pleased expression of one with horrors to recount.

'Seems that when a man dies his widows are supposed to tear their clothes and break all their pretty trinkets as a sign of mourning. Well, Miss S didn't want to do that, and who can blame her? She'd been given some nice bits of jewellery, bracelets and such, when she married, and didn't see why she should spoil them on account of a man for whom she cared not a brass farthing. So as soon as she heard the old man was dead, she dug up a corner of the woodshed when no one was looking, and buried her jewels, thinking they'd make a nice little nest-egg when she married again; but the other wife must have suspected something and told her brothers-in-law, for the very next day they came shouting and nagging at poor little Serinda, saying a woman who stripped off her ornaments meant to become *sati*, as they call it, and how the family would be shamed if she refused.

'On and on they went till she was fair mazed with their shouting. When one stopped, the next would start; but she stuck it out for two days and nights. Say what they liked, she wasn't going to burn herself, not for anyone.

'When they saw she wouldn't give in, they changed their tune. Said it didn't matter; they'd only been thinking of her. All my eye! The old woman offered her a cup of warm milk as a peace-offering and she drank it because she didn't want to offend her. Next thing the poor girl remembers is waking up with a pain in her head and the smoke choking her. Well! I've heard some strange goings-on since we came here but that beats all!'

Kate found it a mystery how Mattie understood so much of the girl's soft rapid speech, but she was thankful the two had become allies and willingly agreed to Mattie's proposal that Serinda should be promoted to nursery-maid in place of the amiable sluggard Nasi Bhai.

The Hot Weather was over and the rains were petering out. At six months, Jacky had been introduced to solid food and since he no longer supplied his early meal, Kate made the most of this freedom by rising daily at dawn and riding

165

for an hour or so in the delicious morning freshness. The exercise improved her spirits. Though messages from George were scrappy and infrequent, she found it easier to dismiss worries after a good gallop. It was easier too, since Colonel Quinn's visit, to ignore bazaar-gossip regarding Holkar's intentions. *He would not allow them to harm us,* she thought. It was comforting to know her family was under his protection, whatever George might say.

Returning to breakfast one morning with a good appetite, Kate was met by Mattie with disturbing news. Jacky was unwell. He had vomited in the night and again this morning. His bowels were loose and he was feverish.

All desire for breakfast fled; a cold finger seemed to touch Kate's heart. 'Send for the doctor at once,' she said and hurried to the nursery.

The baby tossed and turned in his frilled muslin cradle, drawing his knees to his chest and straining with a look of painful concentration before relaxing again with a moan. His fluffy hair was darkened and clung damply to his skull and the lovely rose-gold skin looked angrily flushed. From the cradle rose a foetid pervasive smell.

'His bowels are that loose we can't keep him clean, not two minutes together,' said Mattie defensively as Kate's nose wrinkled.

She picked the baby up, cuddling him against her shoulder, but he wailed and struggled fretfully and she felt heat radiating from his skin.

She was thankful for the prompt arrival of Dr Simon Grant, the civilian doctor who had taken charge of the station's health since Surgeon Richardson had been recalled to Bombay. Grant was a thin, beaky-nosed young man with dark deep-socketed eyes and stooping shoulders, and his experience of human frailty both physical and mental had given him a somewhat acid tongue; but his patience with children was inexhaustible and he had lived long enough on the subcontinent to become a competent amateur illusionist, much in demand at social evenings. What child would refuse to say 'Aaah!' for a doctor who produced silver rupees from his ears, or resent being bled after seeing a real live dove hop out of Mamma's reticule?

Jacky was too young to appreciate such tricks, but he was a favourite with Dr Grant, who turned to Kate with a grave face after concluding his examination.

'Tell me, Mrs Gisborne, when did this vomiting begin?'

'Tell the doctor, Mattie.'

'It must have been one in the morning, sir,' said Mattie, her own face pinched with worry. 'The *ayah* woke me because he was crying and would not settle. I thought at first he was teething ... Then he brought up a little. It wasn't much, not at first.'

'You should have called me,' said Kate.

'I didn't think there was cause to. You know he's sometimes fretful when he's teething. The moment I saw him this morning I could tell it was more than his teeth and I would have called you to him then, only you'd gone gallivanting off on your horse.'

Anxiety made Mattie aggressive; Kate knew there was little use in recrimination and turned again to Grant.

'Is it serious?'

He shook his head. 'I am afraid so. I can't be sure but it looks very much like cholera.'

'*Cholera!*' she exclaimed, dismayed. 'But – but how could he catch cholera here in his own nursery?'

'I know. It is strange – and worrying. There are no cases in the city just now that I know of.' He tapped his teeth with a pencil, his gaze roving round the room. 'Tell me, have you made any changes in Jacky's diet lately?'

'None.' Kate glanced at Mattie who nodded confirmation.

'Or his daily routine? Have any strangers been admitted to the nursery – your friends, for instance, Mrs Gisborne?'

'No.'

Again his eyes moved over the large airy room, noting the well-polished floor, the covered jugs and utensils, the shining metal bucket from which soiled napkins were immediately removed for washing. Nothing here to harbour germs, and yet ...

He said in a lower tone, 'I do not recall seeing that young

ayah on my previous visits. Where is Nasi Bhai whom I recommended to you?'

'Her work was unsatisfactory. I was obliged to dismiss her.'

'Ah. And the young *ayah?*'

Briefly Kate explained the circumstances of Serinda's rescue. The doctor listened with a look of angry surprise.

'You mean you allowed this girl to look after your baby without taking the most elementary precautions to assure yourself she was healthy?' he said incredulously. 'Upon my word, ma'am, you have only yourself to blame for this.'

Kate stared at him, stunned by the accusation. 'But there is nothing wrong with Serinda! She is perfectly healthy – you can see for yourself.'

'Yet she may carry the disease,' he answered grimly. 'It is not uncommon for carriers of cholera to exhibit no symptoms themselves – indeed, to appear in perfect health. Come here, girl.'

Serinda gave him a frightened glance, but obediently left her place in the corner and came to stand before him. Good food and pleasant work had made a dramatic change in the appearance of the woebegone waif Ned had plucked from the river. Her burns had healed well and were now no more than faint pink patches on her glowing olive skin, while the mutilated hair which Mattie had trimmed into shape had a raven's wing sheen. Kate thought she had never looked lovelier, but the stern gaze bent on her by Dr Grant took no account of her beauty.

'I am told you lost your husband recently?' he said in slow Hindustani.

Wide-eyed, she assented.

'Tell me, what was the cause of his death?'

Serinda bowed her head so that the soft rapid answer was unintelligible to Kate, but Mattie drew her breath in sharply.

'Cholera,' said Grant heavily. 'Just as I thought. Mrs Gisborne, I shall do everything in my power to save your baby, but I fear you should prepare for the worst.'

*

That day and the next Kate dared to hope. Jacky was a strong child and when Dr Grant had bled him and lanced his gums to reduce the fever, and applied leeches, he seemed to rally. For two days and nights she never left him, giving him barley water and kaolin when he would take it; but he vomited more than he drank and by evening on the second day he was noticeably weaker, his skin waxen where it had been red, and his eyes disproportionately large in his pinched face.

'You must rest, Mrs Gisborne, or you will make yourself ill too,' said Grant with brusque kindness, but Kate refused to leave the baby. Now she understood what Sal had meant when nursing her own child. If she turned her back a moment she had a superstitious fear that his spirit would slip away.

Jacky was not going to die. Somehow they would pull him through. She clung to that thought though the baby was changing before her eyes. So swift and inexorable was the decline that she could not tell exactly when the truth came to her; but as dawn broke on the third morning she knew there was no more hope. A fire that burns low can be rekindled only while it retains a certain heat: beyond that point it must go out. Jacky's vitality had passed that crucial point, and yet –

'What can we do?' she said desperately to Mattie. 'There must be some way to save him. What else can we do?'

As their eyes met across the cradle it struck her that Mattie had become an old woman overnight. Her skin stretched tight over her sharp features and the snapping black eyes had an inward look. She held herself a little bent, as if scared of sudden movement, though her voice was as brisk as ever.

'One thing you're not doing, my lamb, and that's sitting there a moment longer. Off to your bed, and don't let me see you again until you've bathed and rested. It's not a bit of good wearing yourself out worrying, and it won't help the poor mite either.'

It was the tone Kate had obeyed since she was a child. She knew Mattie was right, yet she lingered.

169

'I don't want to leave him. The doctor – '

'Don't want to leave him with me? What nonsense! Look at him, bless him! Sleeping like a little angel and the doctor won't be here for an hour or more. I'll wake you when he comes, never fear.'

'If there's any change? If Jacky should wake, you'll call me? You promise?'

Mattie bent over the cradle. Her face was hidden as she said in a muffled tone, 'I promise. If he wakes I'll call you. Be off with you now. You're asleep on your feet as it is.'

When Kate rose she found this was true. The long vigil had made her lightheaded so that the walls seemed to approach and recede and she had difficulty walking even the short distance to her bedroom. Once there, it seemed too much effort to undress, so she lay down on the bed fully clothed until a violent internal commotion forced her to rise and stagger to the closet.

Returning, she looked in vain for a servant to help her. Bedroom and verandah were deserted, which was strange because there were always white-robed figures squatting there until they were needed. She had become so used to their silent presence that she took it for granted: without them the long corridors had a curiously naked look.

'*Koi hai?*' she called, clapping her hands, but no one answered.

Her muzzy brain struggled to find a reason for this unusual state of affairs but before she reached any conclusion another spasm gripped her. The closet seemed a mile away; after she reached it she had hardly the strength to drag herself back to bed.

Mattie was right, she thought. I have made myself ill. I must rest until she calls me.

A jug of lemonade stood beside the bed. Her tongue was parched, her throat moving spasmodically as she reached for it, but she spilt more than she conveyed to her mouth and, having drunk, dropped the glass with an exhausted sigh. Soon the spasms came on her again but this time she could no longer rise.

Time passed; the room darkened about her. The *mussaul*

170

should come to light the lamps, the *ayah* to dress her hair and help with her bath – where were they? Where was the *punkahwala?* The air hung heavy and still as a damp blanket as she lay there in the gloom, too weak to go to her baby, too weak even to escape from the soiled sodden clothes from which emanated that same foul miasma she had smelt on Jacky. She could not tell how many hours had passed before she became aware of the doctor's face looming over her – now huge, now impossibly small – and heard his angry voice:

'Run off, the lot of them! It's a damned disgrace, but you can't blame the poor devils. Why should they stay and die with their masters?'

She felt herself lifted and laid back on something cool and dry, and a moment later the blessed relief of water on her cracked lips.

'Trust George to be away when he's needed,' said Grant dourly, and a voice behind rumbled agreement.

She wanted to tell him she must go to Jacky. She had been asleep. She should not have left him so long, but Mattie had promised to wake her. As she tried to speak, the water she had drunk rose burning in her throat and choked her. Strong hands held her head as she vomited helplessly. Grant's voice said, 'Don't try to talk, Mrs Gisborne. You are all right now. We will look after you.'

171

11

'Urgent message for Gisborne Sahib,' said the *hircarrah* on the rope-galled camel at the gates of Gwalior fortress.

'Give it to me, brother. I will deliver it,' said the guard.

Though the words were civil enough, the glance that accompanied them was not friendly. The *hircarrah* hesitated. Already he had done more than duty demanded, and done it willingly for the sake of the doctor sahib who had saved his small son from smallpox. When he failed to find Major Gisborne with the Attaganj army encamped on the state's northern frontier, he had persevered in his search, following him north into the heart of Maratha territory in order to deliver his message. Now he could follow no farther. What Gisborne sahib did in the enemy camp was his own affair. Neither gratitude nor duty required a humble messenger to put his head into the lion's den. These Marathas were a treacherous thieving lot, all too likely to beat him and steal his camel if once he let those massive gates clang shut behind him. Besides, they had a harsh way with the bearers of bad tidings, and judging by the expression on the doctor sahib's face when he gave him the letter, the news it contained was very bad.

The guard said impatiently, 'Where is this message? Give it to me.'

With some reluctance the *hircarrah* drew the letter from his pouch. It was stained and crumpled after seven days' travel on a camel's hump, but the seal was intact.

'Be sure Gisborne sahib gets it without delay,' he said peremptorily as he handed it over.

The tone was a mistake. The guard frowned and lifted his muzzle-loader. 'Begone, Mother-Defiler, unless thou hast a wish to dance on an elephant's foot!'

With more haste than dignity, the *hircarrah* wheeled his tired camel and started to retrace his footsteps. He had done the best he could. If Gisborne Sahib chose to consort with Maratha scum he could not expect others to share his company.

The Begum was smoking her hookah when the message was brought to her. The pungent smoke wreathed her shawled head, mingling with the scents of musk and sandalwood to lull her limbs into langour while her mind ranged, cool and alert, over past and present preoccupations. Jowraj Jung had made love to her before mounting his horse for the day's hunting, but she thought his ecstasy had seemed a trifle forced. Could it be that she was losing her power over him?

Like any woman entering her fifth decade, the Begum constantly sought reassurance from her mirror. No matter that her breasts were still firm and her dancer's body as flexible – if not as slim – as when she had captivated Sombre. Her face gave the game away. The smooth ivory skin had begun to crumple a little. Fine lines flanked her glistening voluptuous mouth, and the shadowed hollows behind her large eyes had a bruised purplish tinge no cosmetics could wholly conceal.

Strive as she might to mend the ravages of Time, they were apparent to her, and George's wife – over twenty years her junior – had begun to seem less an object of contempt than a rival and a threat. Little as she trusted her nephew Trimbuck, she could not altogether ignore the testimony of the spies he had placed in the British Residency in Attaganj. This painted an unpleasing portrait of a domesticated Jowraj Jung, devoted to his wife, besotted with his son. No man can serve two mistresses. It was time, thought the Begum, drawing on her hookah, that one of those lamentably common accidents – bamboo in the curry or a scorpion lurking in a slipper – put an end to the life of young Mrs Gisborne.

Then I will marry Jowraj Jung myself, whatever my French officers' objections, she thought. They hate to see anyone set above them, but I am their mistress: I shall do as I please. Lafayette will make trouble, of course. He will threaten to leave my service and sell my secrets to the British. Well, I can deal with Lafayette.

Conveniently she allowed memory to blot out the disaster of her second marriage. She had allowed her heart to rule her head when she tied herself to the handsome, weak-willed Le Vassoult. Her angry officers had mutinied, forcing the Begum and her husband to flee. They had made a suicide pact, vowing never to be captured alive, but when the mutineers caught up with them, Le Vassoult had honoured the pact and she had not. Even so, after his death she was chained to a gun for seven days by the mutineers, dependent on her maids for scraps of food, and rescued from this ignominious position by the impetuous daredevil Irishman, George Thomas, the self-styled King of Hansi.

He had been a man! she thought, smiling at the memory. But Thomas was dead, victim to his one fatal weakness. He had died of drink before his forty-seventh birthday. His wife and numerous progeny had found refuge with the Begum, and his eldest son held a commission in her army.

George Gisborne was big and blond and lusty as George Thomas had been, but his fatal weakness was for gold, not drink. How delicately she had bribed him at first, with gifts of jewels hidden in baskets of fruit; and he had grasped the bribes like a greedy child who never dreams he may one day have to redress the balance of payment.

Now the Raja of Attaganj was sick and the Resident's help was required to set her own wicked nephew on the *masnad*. It was time to call in the account.

Fortune had not favoured the Begum of late. She needed a triumph to take away the bitter taste of her submission to General Lake after Aligarh was stormed and taken. Fearful of losing the rich *jagir* at Sardhana from which she drew her revenues, the Begum had offered submission. Her lip curled in contempt as she recalled how eager the jolly red-faced general had been to receive it. He had even forgotten the decorum due to her sex and embraced her heartily on both cheeks as if she had been some bearded chief.

Her escort had been shocked and there might have been trouble, but with great presence of mind she had accepted the salute gracefully, remarking that it was the kiss of a father to a daughter, and implied no disrespect.

She had charmed General Lake, as she charmed all susceptible Englishmen who saw in her diminutive person a fitting object for chivalry. Lake had confirmed her in possession of her *jagir*, though it irked her to know she held it through his indulgence.

In defiance of this token submission, she had sent five of her six battalions secretly to join Scindia's host in the hope of halting General Wellesley's advance into Malwa, though as usual she had prudently warned her commanders that in the event of a battle they must keep their men in camp on the pretext of guarding it until they could be certain which side would win.

She had had cause to bless this prudence when Wellesley's swift attack took the Maratha army by surprise at Assaye: all but one of her officers followed her orders and saved their battalions. Only the swaggering Gascon Armand Petitpierre was unable to resist the chance of glory and disobeyed. In consequence his battalion was cut to pieces while the others escaped to tell the tale. The Begum's battalions were her jewels – the source of her pride. She had transformed Sombre's rabble into a disciplined and formidable army, the loss of any part of which caused her far keener regret than the loss of a husband or child. She cursed Petitpierre's folly, and thought that if a British sword had not conveniently ended his career in her service, she would have terminated it herself.

With an almost sexual craving she looked forward to the day when she could add the fine Attaganj battalions to her own. Trimbuck was no soldier. George Gisborne would make her as good a commander-in-chief as he would husband, when once she had disposed of his wife . . . That wife! The Begum frowned, her musings suddenly soured.

'Approach,' she said to the hovering servant, and took the envelope he offered, turning it delicately between finger and thumb before breaking the seal with a sharp movement. She could understand more English than she pretended, and the message was short.

175

My dear Gisborne,

    I am sorry to have to tell you your wife and child are gravely ill with the cholera. I must advise you to return without delay if you wish to see them alive.

                                Yours etc,
                                Simon Grant

That wife! The Begum sat very still, considering how best this news might serve her purposes.

'Has Gisborne sahib returned yet from the hunt?' she asked.

'No, Highness.'

'Tell him I wish to see him as soon as he returns.'

'Yes, Highness.'

She gave orders that the letter should be resealed and delivered to Gisborne sahib in her presence. Then with an uplifting feeling that events were moving in her favour, she told the maidservants to prepare her bath.

Oiled and scented, her gleaming black hair dressed with flowers and her face so subtly painted it could have passed for twenty years old in the warm flattery of lamplight, she waited for George in the musky shadowy room, reclining on a bank of silken cushions while behind a screen zither and finger-drum throbbed like a quickening heartbeat. On a low table stood wine-jug and goblets. Rustlings in the shadows told where the nautch-girls awaited her summons.

'You are weary, my lord,' she said, gliding up as he entered, a little stiff-legged after long hours in the saddle. 'How was the hunt?'

George's eyebrows showed pale against his sun-flushed face. 'Very successful, thank you. Antelope, bison, gaur . . . A rare day's sport . . . and a rare turn of foot that horse you gave me can boast.'

'You like him? He is yours.' She smiled. 'Major Lafayette wagered me a hundred *mohurs* that he would throw you.'

'Not for want of trying,' said George, dryly. No doubt Lafayette had tried to secure his wager by putting thorns under the poor beast's saddle or powdered ginger up his rectum. George made a mental note to serve the Major as well some day.

'Sit and eat and tell me all that befell.' The Begum drew him to the cushions. With her own hands she eased the tight cutaway from his shoulders and herself knelt to serve him wine. He accepted these attentions without comment, knowing what they portended, wondering for the first time if he would be capable of playing his part. A nagging doubt plagued him: could he satisfy her again tonight? Her appetite seemed to grow as his diminished. It was a ravening beast that would devour him; a consuming flame that would leave him a charred husk. And why not, since it was the only exercise she indulged in? While he sweated and sweltered in the saddle, she had been lolling on these cushions, weaving sexual fantasies.

Clear in his mind he saw the sequence the evening would follow. First she would serve him food spiced with every aphrodisiac known to her cook's inventive brain. Then she would ply him with wine which he would drink for no better purpose than deadening his senses and suppressing that frisson of disgust that threatened to impair his performance when he touched the crêpey skin beneath her arms or saw the diamond-meshed wrinkles on her neck, and smelled beneath the perfumes and unguents the clinging musty odour of an ageing body.

Even the scented oils with which her skin was anointed now repelled where they used to attract him. She must not suspect. He was too deep now in her debt to risk incurring her enmity. Treachery, stupidity, incompetence, dis-obedience – all these she expected in the men with whom she had to deal, but instinct told him none of them would rouse her to such wrath as an affront to her sexual vanity. Hell hath no fury . . .

Besides, those French cut-throats who surrounded her would be quick to profit from his fall from grace. Somehow he must play out the charade to the end.

Once Attaganj was in the Begum's hands and the prom-ised *crore* of mohurs in his, he would quit India. He had been luckier than most, but after twelve years in this infernal

177

climate an Englishman lived on borrowed time. He had no more wish to lay his bones in the European cemetery at Attaganj than he had to see his son turn into a pale, peevish, over-indulged *baba sahib*, pampered rotten by the servants, his character ruined even before it was formed.

No, he resolved, Jacky should grow straight and strong in the bracing air of England, and have the best education money could buy. There would be plenty of money. Enough to buy him a seat in Parliament, a country estate, respectability. No one cared to enquire too closely how a returned nabob's wealth had been amassed – not unless you were Clive, or Hastings . . .

And Kate: would she ask questions? Would she wonder at his sudden affluence?

'Share your dreams with me, Jowraj Jung!'

George returned to the present with a start. Share his dreams? He'd be hanged first, he thought.

'I wish I could,' he said, nevertheless, stifling a yawn. In truth he wished more than anything in the world for clean sheets and solitude.

'Because you are dreaming of your English camel?' The provocative pout that accompanied the words would have been charming on a girl's fresh face; on the Begum's it was grotesque, but not for the first time her power to read his thoughts disconcerted him.

'Why should I dream of her when I have you?' he countered, drawing her down beside him, and she curled against him like a cat that wanted to be stroked. Absently he caressed her hair, his blood stirring to the half-heard throb of the drum. Perhaps it would be all right after all. No one knew better than she how to pleasure a man into arousal. So long as he did not look her in the face he could imagine her young and desirable, and serve her as she wished . . . if he did not fall asleep first.

Wine and exercise were taking their toll. That damned horse and thrice-damned Lafayette! There was still the *nautch* to come and the Begum would be offended if he snored all through it.

His head nodded forward . . .

A man may sleep in the saddle or on the march, but it is a rare individual who can slumber peacefully through the piercing shrieks and wails of a sextet of brassy-voiced Kashmiri nautch girls, from whose beautiful throats issued sounds more appropriate to asses or peacocks. Professional pride and fear of their august patroness – as well as hope of a handsome present if they pleased her – stimulated the girls to give of their best, but in vain. Their harshest and most discordant clamours acted on George like a lullaby, and the louder they wailed the sounder he slumbered.

An hour later he woke refreshed, to find the room all in darkness but for a single lamp set some four feet in front of him, illuminating from below the face of the woman who sat crosslegged above it in the classic pose of harlots offering their charms for sale in the House on the Wall.

The filmy gauze of her bodice softened without concealing the lines of her arms and torso, drawing the gaze to the deep mounds of her breasts with dark nipples standing erect, while the mysterious dark pools of her eyes reflected twin stars of lamplight.

When she saw he was awake she began to move her arms, slow and sinuous at first, then with a growing passion that brought her to her knees and then to her feet, swaying and beckoning in an ecstasy of invitation. With an inward groan he recognized the dance performed by temple prostitutes when they offer their bodies as vessels to be filled with the god's life-giving force. She, the Begum, was offering herself to him in the manner of the lowest temple whore while he lay there paralysed, unable to respond.

Nearer she came and nearer. He was seized with a kind of panic. The moment was coming when he must seize her and tear off her clothes, splaying her legs apart on the cushions. Already his nostrils were full of her scent; her arms entwined his neck, but all he felt was a sick revulsion. He must do something quickly, feign illness . . .

Tearing himself free from those clinging arms, he staggered upright, clutching his throat.

'The wine!' he croaked. 'Poisoned!'

It was enough. She stood stock still, breasts heaving, her

179

eyes no longer lustful but narrow and bright with suspicion. With a swift movement she picked up the goblet that had fallen as he rose, sniffed the dregs, and inspected the contents of the half-full wine-jug. Then she clapped her hands.

'Attend my lord,' she ordered as servants came running, and herself held his head as George pretended to retch into a basin. He wondered if she would see through the sham, observing her beneath half-shut lids as he lay on the cushions she had prepared for a very different climax to the evening. It would be imprudent to stage too swift a recovery. She had picked up the goblet again and stood with shoulders a little hunched and head bent looking, he thought, like a small but dangerous raptor.

After a few minutes he ventured to open his eyes and smile suitably wanly.

'Forgive me, Highness. It – it came on me so suddenly.'

At once she was at his side, bending to stroke his brow. Her hands were like talons; he repressed a shudder. 'I rejoice to see you recovered,' she said huskily. 'Was it the wine?'

'I should not have drunk so deep . . .'

Turning to her cupbearer who had watched the exchange with a frightened expression, she demanded: 'Whence came this wine?'

'It is good *lal sherâb*, Highness.'

She stamped her foot. 'Whence came it? From my own cellar? Speak, fool!'

'From the cellar of Lafayette sahib, Highness.'

'Ah.' For a moment she reflected, then said sharply, 'Summon Major Lafayette to attend me.'

'Highness, it is late. The Major sahib sleeps.'

'What do I care for that? Bring him at once, awake or asleep.'

Bull's-eye! thought George gleefully, on hearing Lafayette named. His accusation had not been wholly at random. The Begum never touched alcohol and was shamefully swindled by her purveyors who filled her cellars with wine which was at best distasteful and at worst downright

180

dangerous. Her servants were in the habit of purloining bottles from her officers' private stores to offer her more important guests. As soon as he tasted tonight's claret he knew it could not have come from any cellar of the Begum's. It looked as if Lafayette would be repaid for his trick with the horse sooner than expected.

When the Frenchman appeared between two armed bodyguards it was apparent he was furious at being thus rudely snatched from the arms of the pretty Maratha maiden with whom he was attempting to console himself. He was a thickset, muscular fellow whose aggressive stance with head lowered and thrust forward, legs braced, gave him the look of a bull of dubious temper.

'*Ma foi*, but you choose strange hours to summon your officers from their rest, Madame!' he said in a tone of loud complaint.

'Rest, Major?' Her ironic gaze took in his rolled sleeves and half-buttoned breeches.

'In what can I serve you, Madame?' There was a faint emphasis on the word 'serve' and a disdainful glance at George, still reclining on his cushions.

'Major Gisborne and I have been debating the quality of a certain wine. Knowing you are a connoisseur, I would like to know your opinion.'

'What wine, Madame?' Lafayette's expression became guarded and George was hard pressed not to laugh aloud. The Frog was no fool! Already he guessed what was in the wind.

With considerable reluctance Lafayette accepted the goblet offered by the Begum. 'Drink, Major!'

He bowed. 'Your health, Madame. And yours, *mon brave*.' Warily he sipped while the Begum watched with bright assessing eyes.

'Drink it all,' she commanded.

'As Your Highness pleases.' Lafayette drained the goblet and set it down with a flourish.

'Well?' she asked, disappointed.

'A respectable claret, Madame. A little young, perhaps. If I may hazard a guess, it has come from my own cellar.'

181

'You do not deny it?'

'Why should I?'

'Do you also admit you gave that wine to my *khansamah* for the purpose of making Major Gisborne ill?'

'Is that what the rascal says? I deny it absolutely,' said Lafayette vigorously. 'If your thieving rabble of slaves persist in stealing from my cellar I am powerless to prevent it. I cannot stop them any more than I can teach your English stallion how a gentleman holds his wine.'

A bright spot of colour flamed in each of the Begum's cheeks. 'How dare you speak to me like that!'

'It is time someone had the courage to tell you the truth, Madame. You are making a fool of yourself over a man who will betray you without a second thought,' said Lafayette, stepping close to speak urgently in her ear. Furious, she waved him back. Her hold on power was far too precarious for her to allow any public familiarity from those who served her. With the memory of tender moments still fresh, Lafayette had made the mistake of confusing her private image with her public one, and this she could not forgive.

At a signal, the Frenchman's arms were seized by burly armed guards before his hand reached his sword. Suddenly aware of his danger, he fought furiously, but was overborne by sheer numbers while the Begum watched with a cold impassive face that showed not the smallest pity for this man whose embraces she had enjoyed. An embittered lover, liable to foment disaffection among the rest of her officers, was a danger she could not tolerate. Any man who allowed jealousy to override respect was better out of her service.

'Madame – I beg you – !'

'Take him away.'

Her hand moved in a gesture Lafayette understood quite as well as the guards. His ruddy face blanched and he dropped on his knees.

'No, Madame. Not that. Anything but that.'

'Take him away.'

In desperation he appealed to George. 'Tell her, Englishman! It is a lie. There is nothing wrong with the wine. It is a lie. Tell her!'

'I cannot help you, Major,' said George with genuine pity and Lafayette's shoulders drooped.

'You are making a mistake! A terrible mistake!' he yelled as he was dragged from her presence, but the Begum disdained to answer.

She glided to where George lay and took his hand. 'Come to the window, my lord. Together we shall watch him die.'

Sickened, he turned his face away. The last thing he wanted was to see the bewildered elephant hopping about the torchlit courtyard, trying to avoid stepping on the struggling man strapped to its forefoot, while the crowd yelled and drove it hither and thither.

'It was true,' he said dully. 'Lafayette is innocent. There was nothing amiss with the wine.'

The Begum regarded him with the indulgent smile one might bestow on a beloved but foolish child. How charmingly naive were these Englishmen! Lafayette might be innocent of this particular crime, but in his heart at least he was guilty of sedition and for that he must die. Gently she stroked George's brow, smoothing the disordered curls with a loving, almost maternal hand.

'My lord, you are not yourself. Rest now until your strength returns. I will watch the execution alone.'

Grateful to be rid of her, however briefly, George closed his eyes. When he opened them again a servant was standing before him, a letter in his hand.

'For you, Major-sahib,' he said and bowed.

George turned it over, staring at the unbroken seal, while his heart began to pound heavily. He had covered his tracks so carefully. Who had known where to find him? With a presentiment of doom he ripped it open. A moment later he was on his feet, shouting for his horse.

The Begum hurried in, followed by a posse of servants, and he had no doubt she had been watching the delivery of the message.

'What is it, my lord? Where are you going at this hour?'

'My wife!' he cried distractedly, snatching up the coat he had discarded and brushing off the hands that sought to detain him. 'My son! I must go to them at once.'

Her face hardened. 'What are they to you? Did you not swear to me a short while since how much you wished to be free? Well, you have got your wish.'

Her knowledge of the note's contents hardly surprised him. Realizing he had betrayed too much of his true feelings, he said with all the firmness he could muster, 'Nevertheless I must go at once. My absence will look suspicious. Once it becomes known that I am here . . .'

She smiled reassurance. 'You have nothing to fear. My guards killed the messenger before he had gone two miles. You are safe here as long as you care to stay.'

But George's anxiety was too acute for him to delay his departure even as long as dawn. An hour later he left Gwalior in brilliant starlight, accompanied by two *sowars* of the Begum's second battalion, and before noon the following day had crossed the river on his way back to Attaganj.

'We buried him here in the children's corner, alongside the Cattistock twins and little Milly Dale,' said Dr Grant gruffly. 'My wife thought you would prefer him to have young company.'

Kate's vision blurred as she gazed at the row of small graves with their neat borders of white marble and the headstones recording pitifully brief lives.

Sacred to the Memory of
EMILY FELICIA DALE
Beloved Daughter of Capt. HGW Dale, BNI
Died August 10, 1800, aged 2 years and 7 months
'The lovely Babe within this Tomb was cut off in the Bud
But she in Paradise will bloom and ever live with God'

was engraved on the nearest.

Sacred to the Memory of James and David Cattistock
Beloved Twin Sons of Mr and Mrs H C Cattistock
Who died April 7, 1798, in their Seventh Year

> 'Lovely and pleasant in their lives,
> In Death they were not divided'

Between them lay an even smaller grave with fresh flowers on the newly-turned earth and no headstone. She could not look at it.

'Where is Mattie?' she said in a choking voice.

'Not far away. Over here.'

He led her to another fresh mound just beyond the children's corner. 'Call if you want me. I shall not be far,' he said gently, and left her to mourn alone.

Tears would not come. She sat on a stone bench in the quiet cemetery, with a light wind stirring her veil and the guttural murmurs of the *malis* grubbing weeds from nearby graves the only sounds to break the silence, and felt numb, stunned, curiously detached, as if in a dream she watched a black-clad woman sitting by Mattie's grave, but knew in her heart it was all a dream. Mattie the dauntless. Mattie the indestructible. She could not be dead. She would not have left without a word of farewell. Did that mourning woman really believe Mattie was dead, and Jacky, her beautiful baby, lay cold and still in that small mound? It was only a dream . . . a bad dream . . .

Presently she would wake and go to the nursery, and find the big room full of sunlight and laughter, with Mattie scolding the *ayah* while Jacky lay kicking on a mat, crowing and gurgling with delight as Serinda stooped to tickle him.

No, that was wrong. Kate frowned a little. Serinda could not be playing with the baby. She had vanished, no one knew where. The doctor had frightened her and she had run away.

Why had she been frightened? Because she had brought cholera into the Residency, and Kate herself had nearly died, while Mattie and Baby Jack . . .

Reality crept closer. Hard as Kate clung to her dream, a fog of misery rolled in to engulf her. Now watcher merged with mourner, and she knew she could not pretend. It was all true, horribly true. Her child was dead and poor loyal Mattie, who should have laid her bones in some green

English churchyard, was buried in the dust of a strange land.

They were dead, and she had killed them. As the burden of grief and guilt settled on her shoulders she bowed her head and tears came at last.

Where, oh where was George? Why didn't he come to share this grief and comfort her?

'Murderess!' said a voice behind her and she turned with a gasp. George stood there, bare-headed, wild-eyed, his face streaked with dust and sweat and his fists clenched.

'You killed my son,' he said in a hard flat voice that carried more menace than a shout. His big hands opened and closed convulsively on her shoulders. He began to rock her back and forth, slowly at first, then with increasing violence. Her hat fell off, and her teeth clamped on her tongue.

'No, George! Listen, please listen . . .'

He was beyond hearing. Foam flecked his mouth as the bitter words spewed forth. 'You killed him, you dirty whore. You and that blackguard half-breed. Now I'm going to kill you. I've nothing left to live for.'

Dear God, he has gone mad, she thought in terror. He worshipped Jacky. Hearing of his death has turned his brain. Her head snapped back and forth – he was going to break her neck.

Through mists of pain she heard the *mali's* shout: 'Sahib, sahib! Come quicklee!'

Then the scrunch of running feet on gravel and Grant's shocked voice. 'Stop it at once! George, old fellow, let your wife go. You are not yourself.'

Grant was a wiry young man and he had boxed at school. When his appeal evoked no response, he very coolly threw off his coat and jabbed a flurry of stiff uppercuts to the Resident's jaw. George reeled back and sprawled senseless on the gravel. Kate sank down on the bench, moaning and clutching her head.

Grant bent over her. 'Has he hurt you, Mrs Gisborne?' He examined her quickly, then turned to kneel beside George, who was breathing stertorously through his mouth.

186

Grant rolled back his eyelid, nodded briefly, and stood up dusting his hands.

'Poor fellow! The shock was too much. When he wakes he will regret this. I will give him a sedative to calm him. Come, Mrs Gisborne, let me take you home.'

12

News of the struggle in the cemetery spread like wildfire through the station, and most of the sympathy was for George. Kate's dangerous folly in exposing the little community to the risk of cholera was widely condemned, particularly by the women. Mothers who lived in daily fear of India's deadly diseases could not forgive anyone who put their children's health in peril. The buried resentment that had smouldered in them ever since this outsider arrived to marry the Resident surfaced in barely veiled hostility.

Her relationship with the notorious Colonel Quinn was not allowed to pass unnoticed.

'No smoke without fire,' said Mrs Bateson darkly to her friend Mrs Clark. 'If you ask me, it would have served her right if he had throttled her, the baggage.'

For several days, Dr Grant kept George in his infirmary under sedation, explaining that he was suffering from heat-stroke. It was true that the shock of Jacky's death combined with an eighteen-hour ride had taken its toll of George, and when the doctor allowed him home he was strangely subdued.

Kate had dreaded the meeting, but seeing him so changed – his features blurred with laudanum and his eyes mere slits of blue between puffy lids – her fear was replaced by pity. She accepted his stumbling apology without reproaches.

'I must have been mad. I don't know what came over me. Can you forgive me?'

'There is nothing to forgive,' she told him.

He grasped her hand and she felt tremors run through it. 'It was when I saw his grave. So small a grave . . .'

'Don't speak of it now,' she said, feeling tears choke her throat. 'Our darling boy is safe with God, where nothing can harm him.'

His head came up. For an instant she thought she saw a flash of anger in those blue slits of eye, but it was gone in a trice.

'That is what we must try to believe,' he said heavily.

During the next weeks he was busy dealing with the pile of papers that had accumulated during his absence. Every night his study lamp burned late. It crossed her mind that by burying himself in his work he hoped to alleviate his grief, and she did not complain of neglect even though at times she felt she was living with a stranger. Jacky had been their one shared interest. Now he was gone their lives moved on parallel lines that never touched, and without Mattie's companionship Kate felt lonelier than ever.

When George left once more to inspect the army, now permanently deployed on the state's northern frontier, the whispering campaign against her grew until she could no longer ignore it.

Alone in the front pew of the Mission church, she listened to low voices behind her, spreading poison.

'Look at her. Butter wouldn't melt in her mouth. It would be a different story if Colonel Quinn happened to pass by. The things I've heard, you wouldn't believe!'

'Poor Major Gisborne is the one I feel sorry for. If he knew the way she carries on the moment his back is turned, he'd go white overnight.'

'Should never have married her. Told him so, but he wouldn't listen. Never does to bring outsiders into a tight community. Well, he's paying for it now, poor chap. To see that bloody half-breed sniffing round like a dog after a bitch makes my blood boil. But what can one do? Made his bed: now he must lie on it.'

Major Vance, she thought bitterly, identifying the last speaker. She had not bothered to disguise her contempt of his drunken bullying ways, and this was his revenge. She half turned her head to see who the other whisperers were. Mrs Bateson and Mrs Clark leaned close together, the flowers on their hats mingling.

'Poor Major Gisborne! He worshipped that child.'

'The way *she* behaves, you'd think none of us knew what

189

it was to lose a baby,' hissed Mrs Clark, who had buried four of her own.

'Shhh!'

Seeing Kate's eye on them, the ladies drew a little apart and folded their hands in prayer.

Sick with anger and disgust, Kate sat through the rambling sermon without taking in a word. Did those poisonous tongues believe what they said? How could they accuse her of adultery without the least shred of evidence? A dark abyss seemed to open under her feet as she recognized the depths to which envious women would sink in their desire to topple an interloper from her perch. 'Sling enough mud and some of it's bound to stick,' Mattie used to say. How she longed now for Mattie's support. Without George's protection or Mattie's unswerving loyalty there was no one to give the lie to such slanders.

Once her ears were tuned to listen for them, she heard whispers wherever she went. Riding, walking, sitting in the garden or her own bedroom – there was no escape. Her servants watched every minute of her day – and sold their tales to other memsahibs who embroidered them to their own fancy before passing them on. Colonel Quinn figured large in these fables.

When Kate heard the clatter of hoofs in the courtyard one sunny November morning and saw a troop of horsemen clad in rose-pink tunics trot smartly under the gate-arch, she knew a moment of utter despair. He had come again. If she received him, her reputation would be gone for good. Yet how could she turn him away?

'Gentleman to see you, memsahib,' announced Ghulam Singh, his upswept grey mustachios bristling with disapproval.

'Tell him I am not at home.'

'Very good, memsahib.'

He went away. Soon after she heard a loud commotion on the stairs and a bellow of pain from Ghulam Singh.

'Not at home?' exclaimed a well-known voice. 'I'll see about that.'

Tall and debonair in a rose silk tunic with a pale green

190

turban perched rakishly aslant his carrot curls, Ned Sweeney swung jauntily through the door and paused on the threshold. 'Servant, Kate!'

He sketched a bow, then strode over to clasp her hand warmly. There was a new confidence about him and his freckled skin glowed. She thought he had grown an inch and put on a stone.

'By George, but it's good to see you. How are you, and how's the son and heir? Flourishing, I trust?'

Her mouth opened but no words came. Ned rattled on: 'Great news! I'm a captain now. Didn't I say I'd be a general before I'm thirty? The best of it is that we'll be in cantonments for a while, so I can take Serinda off your hands. I hope Baby Jack won't mind losing his *ayah*? Tell him my need is greater than his!'

He paused, struck by something strange in her silence. 'What's up, Kate? You look deuced queer all of a sudden? Ain't you pleased to see me? Have I said something wrong?'

Brooding discontent clouded Prince Trimbuck's heavy features as he sprawled on a heap of cushions with one plump courtesan, naked to the waist, kneeling before him. Her scarlet mouth like sea-anemone, sucked at his private parts. With one hand he caressed her hair, while the other fondled the full round breasts of a second flimsily clad damsel whose supple body arched backward across his knees. He flipped the nipples back and forth, teasing them to stand upright against his fingers, and their owner moaned in simulated ecstasy.

Behind the lattice Hamesha Begum, mistress of this House on the Wall, signalled to the musicians to quicken the beat, and filled a goblet with her best French wine to refresh the prince after his exertions. She was an astute businesswoman who trained her girls well, and was justly proud of her reputation for running the best brothel between Bhopal and Burhanpore. But her practised eye could see all was not well tonight. Despite the courtesans' efforts Trimbuck's penis remained limp and his mouth drooped petulantly. He had invited the Resident to share the fleshly delights of this house, and Gisborne Sahib had refused him.

That much Hamesha Begum knew. Where Gisborne Sahib was now could only be guessed; she thought it most likely he was entwined in the arms of the Witch of Sardhana.

Trimbuck thought so too, and it troubled him. He had few illusions regarding George, who would, he knew, doublecross him as readily as he would doublecross George. The thought of him hatching plots with the Begum Samru was not a pleasant one, and it effectively stifled any desire for these greasy, heavy-breathing harlots.

He gave the girl's nipple a painful tweak and rose, kicking both would-be seducers aside.

'These ugly hags are no use. Get them out of my sight!' he shouted as Hamesha Begum hurried to attend him. Hastily she shooed the girls away.

'Would my lord prefer a young boy, quite unspoiled? The dealer from Kabul spoke highly of his charms.'

Trimbuck's eyes bulged dangerously. 'Don't try to foist your dirty Afghan whelps on me! The last one you found me stole a valuable jewel while I slept.'

Hamesha Begum searched her brain. She had an entertainment planned for such an emergency, but would have preferred longer to rehearse it before putting it on view. However, this was a moment of crisis and she had no wish to lose so valuable a client.

'If Your Highness pleases, I have a new dance I believe will amuse you.'

'Dance? What's new about a dance? I am tired of your girls and their dancing,' said Trimbuck ungraciously, but he sank back on the cushions and Hamesha Begum smiled.

'This, my lord, is different.'

She slipped away. Presently, a very curious cacophony struck up behind the screen. Harsh and discordant though it was, a discerning ear might have detected a mangled rendering of *The British Grenadiers* played on Indian instruments.

Into the circle of lamplight skipped a slender female figure wearing a flowing wig of flaxen tow and a low-cut, tight-waisted ball gown in the European style. Her face was whitened with flour and she strutted with out-turned toes holding her skirt clear of the floor to display her high-heeled slippers.

Behind her swaggered a slim boy, equally bepowdered and bewigged, with an absurdly large yellow moustache stuck to his upper lip. He wore a scarlet uniform jacket that had undoubtedly been purloined from some quartermaster's stores and thigh-length boots from the same source.

The couple faced one another to bow and curtsey; when the boy bent over it became apparent he wore nothing between tunic and boots, while the petal-shaped panels of his fair companion's gown opened like a flower to reveal that she, too, was entirely naked underneath.

Clasping one another about the waist, the pair began to hop and cavort to the music in a dance that grew increasingly wild, at least below the waist. For while their faces remained studiously devoid of expression and the clothed upper parts of their bodies moved with apparent decorum, their naked lower limbs performed lewdly suggestive gyrations, now welded together, now coyly apart, the male's thrusting advances being alternately accepted and rejected by the female until at last in a frenzy he bore her to the floor.

Crude though the display was, it tickled Trimbuck's fancy – as did anything that ridiculed British habits or punctured the bubble of British superiority.

'Wah! Wah!' he applauded, grinning. His loins tightened at last. Stumbling to his feet he kicked aside the periwigged youth and knelt to straddle the girl himself, while behind her screen Hamesha Begum nodded with satisfaction and signalled to the musicians to play soft languorous strains.

Trimbuck would want the girl now, no doubt of that, and her own investment would be handsomely repaid. It had been a gamble to take an untrained girl fresh from European employment, but Hamesha Begum's instinct was seldom wrong when it came to knowing what would please men, and in Serinda she had recognized a very special kind of allure.

She would be sorry to lose her so soon, but in this

business there was no room for sentiment, and providing she continued to please the wayward prince, Serinda's future was assured. The only problem was how much to ask for her.

Hemesha Begum smiled into her thumb-mirror and twitched her spangled scarf to fall more becomingly across her plump shoulder. She thought with pleasure of the bargaining to come.

*

After a week of fruitless searching, Ned had to admit defeat. Serinda had vanished. Neither bribes, threats, nor painstaking questioning could elicit any hint of her whereabouts.

'I can't stay and look for her any longer,' he said gloomily, as he joined Kate on the verandah. 'A messenger rode in this morning. Look. I'm ordered back.'

He handed her the despatch. *Colonel Quinn presents his compliments to Captain Sweeney and requests his immediate return.*

Below the *munshi's* careful copperplate was scrawled in spiky black penstrokes which she guessed were Quinn's own: *Come at once. Cyclops is feeling his oats.*

'Cyclops? Oats?' She handed it back.

Ned grinned. 'A private joke. Holkar lost an eye when his musket blew up in his face, though he sees as much with one as most men do with two. If he's feeling his oats, it must mean we're off campaigning. No rest for the wicked.'

She thought he looked pleased.

'Tell me about Holkar,' she said curiously. 'One hears strange stories. Is his temper as violent as they say?'

A shadow crossed Ned's ingenuous face. 'To be honest, Kate, he scares me. You never know what to expect. One day he's full of good fellowship; the next some demon gets into him. He'll fly into a rage and order awful punishments. Quinn's the only person who can handle him . . . they were brought up together, you know.'

He saw her frown and said, 'Quinn's had some narrow escapes. Holkar's a devil at times. Once he tried to have Quinn blown from a gun for some trifle – I forget what.

194

Luckily he changed his mind before the order was carried out. When four of his officers deserted him for Scindia, Jeswant Rao tore the carpet with his teeth!' He laughed rather mirthlessly. 'I don't mind admitting I steer out of his way when I see the storm-cones hoisted.'

'Oh, Ned, do be careful! He sounds a perfect monster. I don't like to think of you near such a man.'

'You sound just like Mamma,' he told her, grinning. 'I can take care of myself, never fear, so long as Quinn keeps the right side of our lord and master. And remember, his star is rising. Since General Wellesley got Scindia and the Bhonsle fairly on the run, their troops have been flocking in droves to join Holkar. That's the reason Cyclops is feeling his oats! He's top dog, now. The only undefeated Maratha chief – and wouldn't he just like to take a crack at the British himself!'

'I hope he'll do nothing of the kind!' she exclaimed.

'Quinn won't let him,' said Ned cheerfully. 'Don't worry. I expect he means to spend the Cold Weather harrying the Rajput princes. That always puts him in a good mood.' He added with a concern that touched her, 'It's *you* I worry about, Kate. Stuck here in the middle of nowhere with a lot of cackling old hens for company, and the country in turmoil all about. I hoped I'd meet your husband. Is he often away?'

'Oh, he comes and goes. I never know quite when to expect him,' said Kate as lightly as she could 'He's very busy, you know. I'm all right, Ned, really I am. You must not worry about me.'

Ned wondered if he should mention the rumour he had heard linking George and the Begum Samru, but after a moment's reflection decided that the least said was soonest mended. Quinn was always urging him to keep his mouth buttoned.

'I suppose I should go.' He hovered uncertainly. 'You will send for me if you hear anything . . . about Serinda?'

'Of course.'

'And if ever you need my help – or Quinn's –'

'I would not ask Colonel Quinn's help if he was the last man on earth,' she said with sudden passion.

After a moment's silence Ned said quietly, 'Don't forget it was I who persuaded Quinn to bring Serinda here. I am as much – nay, more – to blame for your son's death.'

'How can you say so? You knew no more than I did of the risks involved. Colonel Quinn is country born. He knew – and I find his silence hard to forgive.'

He realized the subject was too painful for further discussion and took his leave, promising to visit her again very soon. From the balcony she watched him ride away and wondered what scandal the gossips' busy tongues would invent concerning him. Would they accuse her of adultery with a boy of seventeen?

The following night was heavy and still as she wandered restlessly from room to room, unable to contemplate long solitary hours in the great muslin-canopied bed. At ten she settled to write letters in the little study whose French windows gave on to the balcony, where during Jacky's brief life George had often brought his own work, devouring accumulated heaps of documents while the baby rolled and gurgled on a quilt at his feet.

Outside in the street a dog howled on a wavering ascending scale that echoed her aching loneliness. Since Jacky's death she had often woken from uneasy dreams and thought she heard breathing close at hand, though when she reached across the bed was empty. Then she would watch the moon trace its silver path across the tiles, unable to sleep, until the crows outside her window began to salute the dawn with a croaking cacophony.

George slept in the dressing-room, pretending it was out of consideration for her health.

'Dawn parade, my dear, and I don't wish to disturb you. You look a trifle peaked.'

'I don't mind waking early. It is the best time of day.'

'Even so, you need your sleep. Allow me to know what is best for you – after all, I have lived here a good deal longer! This climate plays the deuce with an English constitution.'

'I am perfectly well, George.'

'Good. I am glad to hear it. All the same, I shall sleep in the dressing-room.'

The howling dog moved away. Kate finished a letter to her brother and pulled another sheet of paper towards her, determined to keep writing until sleep overtook her. Beyond the golden circle of lamplight the curtains across the French window stirred and she glanced up uneasily, sensing an unseen presence.

'*Koi hai!* Is anyone there!'

Again the draperies rustled. A fold seemed to detach itself and glided swiftly towards her as she froze in sudden fear, unable even to scream. Then she saw who it was, and expelled her pent-up breath in a sigh.

'Serinda!'

'Where is the Major Sahib? He must call out the troops! There is treason afoot in the city.'

Even in the first shock of recognition, Kate noted the richness of the girl's gold-bordered *sari* and the many jewels winking on hands and wrists. With glittering eyes ringed in kohl and mouth painted a dark luscious red, she looked sensual and exotic, very different from the self-effacing young *ayah* who had tended Baby Jack, and the sight of her obvious prosperity fanned Kate's anger.

'What are you doing here? Where have you been? How dare you burst in like this!'

'Tell me where he is,' repeated Serinda with an impatient stamp that set her anklets jingling. 'He must call out the troops at once.'

'Are you mad, girl? Have you been smoking *bhang* to give you bad dreams? What do you know of troops or treason?'

Serinda said with a quiet intensity that dispelled any notion that she might be drunk or drugged, 'Listen, memsahib. I have come here at great risk to warn you of danger. The Begum Samru's army is marching on Attaganj. Unless the Major Sahib calls out his troops at once, you and every *Angrez* in the city will die before morning. It is

197

true, I swear it! I heard the orders from Prince Trimbuck's own lips.'

'Trimbuck?' Kate frowned. Little as she liked the Raja's fat son, she could not suppose so ineffectual a figure posed any threat to the state.

'Oh, do not ask questions, memsahib! There is no time to lose. At midnight the Begum will meet the Prince in the ruined temple outside the Kashmir Gate. If the *Lat Sahib* calls out his men he can capture them both.'

'The *Lat Sahib* is not here.'

'He must be here!' Serinda's frightened eyes searched the room as if she expected George to step out from the shadows. 'The Prince said he had returned.'

'He was wrong. There is only Major Vance. The Second Battalion is still in cantonments, but – '

She hesitated. Major Vance was no friend of hers. Besides, he was certainly asleep at this hour, carried to bed by his servants after draining his second bottle of brandy, and would not rouse until the native barber finished shaving him tomorrow morning. No doubt the conspirators were aware of Major Vance's weakness and planned accordingly.

Who else was here?

Rapidly she reviewed the remaining officers but found little comfort. Darcy Knowles, the Adjutant, skeletal and lugubrious, a superannuated captain who was popularly supposed to need orders in triplicate before he dared to blow his nose; Joss Fetherstonhaugh, sixty if he was a day, and blind as a bat; fresh-faced Humphrey de Salis, still shaky after his first bout of malaria . . . The young, the old, the maimed, halt and blind. The officers George had left because he thought them unfit for active service. Would any of them risk Major Vance's wrath and act on his own initiative? In her heart she knew they would not.

'Memsahib, I must go,' said Serinda hurriedly. 'If I am missed – '

'Wait!' Kate put out a hand to detain her. 'Tell me more. Tell me everything you know. Where did you hear this rumour?'

'In the house of Hamesha Begum.'

'Ah!' Now Kate understood why Ned's search had been fruitless. The activities of Hamesha Begum were a subject of scandalized interest to the British community, particularly the ladies, who were always urging George to clamp down on her trade in smooth-skinned Afghan boys and dusky beauties from Rajputana.

'It is a disgrace! Such things should not be permitted in a state under our protection,' Kate had heard Mrs Dewhurst exclaim; and George had replied stiffly: 'I am entirely of your opinion, ma'am, but my hands are tied. I have no power to enforce our laws here, more's the pity.'

'Surely you could persuade the Raja to bring pressure to bear?' persisted Mrs Dewhurst, whose own husband's sexual proclivities gave her good reason to wish for the closure of such premises as Hamesha Begum's.

'Ah, that is another matter. Believe me, ma'am, I am doing what I can.'

But whatever George's measures against her, Hamesha Begum's house continued to flourish; though she operated on the very fringes of legality, she had powerful friends to ensure her survival, by no means all of whom were Indians. If Serinda had got wind of this plot in Hamesha Begum's establishment, there was likely to be at least enough truth to warrant it being taken seriously. Still, Kate was puzzled.

'Why have you told me this? Why risk your life to come here?'

Serinda gave her a curious look, half pleading, half defiant. 'I have no reason to love the French, memsahib,' she said softly. 'You were good to me and took me in when my family would have killed me, and I – I repaid good with evil. Tonight I saw my chance to level the score.' She paused, then as Kate stood silent and irresolute, added urgently, 'Hurry, memsahib. There is still time to saddle a horse and escape. My friend will open the gate for you.'

'No.' Kate came to an abrupt decision. Better risk appearing an hysterical fool than perish through apathy. She knew the ruined Jain temple outside the Kashmir Gate where the conspirators planned to meet. It was a lonely place, high on a rock above the lake: ideal for a secret rendezvous ... or an ambush. If she could verify and confirm Serinda's story, she could force Major Vance to act.

When dealing with snakes or Marathas you must strike at the head, Quinn had told her. Do this, and you need never fear the tail.

'How many battalions has the Begum brought here?' she asked, hardly expecting Serinda to know, but the answer came immediately.

'Three, memsahib.'

'So many!' Kate's heart quailed. Even if Major Vance called out his men at once they would be outnumbered.

'She has promised to set Prince Trimbuck on the throne if he delivers the city to Scindia ... to the French. Memsahib, Colonel Quinn is at Amarpur, no more than three hours' ride. He will come to your aid.'

Unthinkable. George would have good reason to complain if she summoned his avowed enemy to settle trouble in Attaganj. She could see only one solution, and that was to send for George himself. He might accuse her of crying Wolf but even that was better than doing nothing.

Abruptly she came to a decision.

'You must return to Hamesha Begum's house before you are missed,' she said, 'but first go to the stables and wake Hussain. Tell him to saddle Sultan and meet me at the Kashmir Gate.'

'Will you ride to Amarpur?'

'No. Hussain shall ride to warn my husband. I shall go to the temple secretly and watch for the Begum Samru.'

'I will come with you, memsahib.'

'No.'

'Yes.'

Brown eyes met blue in a brief tussle of wills, then Kate nodded. 'Very well, but we must hurry. Go now and wake Hussain.'

Soon after eleven two shrouded female figures slipped out of the Residency's side gate and mingled with the flow of pedestrians and shoppers in the network of narrow alleys

200

attention: for the first time since coming to India, Kate knew the delight of anonymity. Though tall by native standards, her slender build and olive skin favoured the disguise. With eyes demurely lowered, she attracted no curious glances as she followed Serinda past the rows of tiny cluttered booths where silversmiths and leather workers, vendors of sweetmeats, pots and cloth, grain-merchants and makers of reed baskets sat cross-legged in the midst of their wares, silhouetted against the golden glow of lamps which lent the scene a strange enchantment. Hot spicy smells filled the air: there was a mood of anticipation and gaiety which affected her own spirits. Never before had she walked these streets by night, or been able to pause before a stall without at once being importuned by beggars and over-eager salesmen; never before had she felt the pulse of an Indian city after dark.

So much life was here. So much vitality in the raucously chattering housewives and traders going about their nightly business after lying comatose throughout the day's heat. This was the real India – a country the British conquerors never saw or wished to see. George should walk the streets like this, she thought, instead of galloping past these stalls sending traders and pariah dogs scattering before his horse's hoofs. If he had troubled to listen to the people instead of poring over papers in the gloomy splendour of the Residency, he might have got wind of this conspiracy himself and left more than a token force to protect Attaganj. She felt a spurt of anger against George – against all officers who galloped gaily off to war leaving their women to fend for themselves.

'Come!' Serinda's thin fingers plucked her sleeve, drawing her ever deeper into the labyrinthine alleys. She, at least, had not forgotten the urgency of their errand. Kate followed where she led, regaining her bearings only when the stark outline of the Kashmir Gate loomed black against the star-bright sky. It was open. Silently they passed through.

By the shadow of the outer wall, Hussain stood holding the big bay charger, Sultan, whose bit chinked softly as he snatched mouthfuls of grass from the roadside. She went towards him.

'Is all well, Hussain? No one hindered you?'

His anxious bearded face stared at her; he gave a muffled exclamation. 'By the Prophet, you startled me, memsahib. For a moment I thought – Yes, all is well. None sought to stop me, but there is mischief afoot. See! The guards have left the gate, on whose orders none can say. The bazaar hums with rumour. They say the Raja is dying and the British have suffered a great defeat.'

He was her favourite among the grooms: a lean, grizzled man in his fifties, fiercely loyal to George. Despite his years he had the bearing of a much younger man, and could lope all day at her stirrup without tiring.

'Mount, memsahib, and let us go at once.' There was barely suppressed agitation in his voice. 'Truly, there is great danger here.'

For an instant she was tempted. He was offering a way of escape. What did she care for the bickering women of Attaganj who had made their dislike of her so plain? Let them fend for themselves! Should she not search for George herself rather than leave the task to Hussain?

He pulled off the flysheet and folded it, and she saw he had put her sidesaddle on Sultan, the very one she had brought out from England.

'Mount!' he urged, and cupped his hands, ready to throw her up.

Kate stepped back, shaking her head. 'My place is here, Hussain. You must fetch the Sahib. Do not argue!' she said fiercely as he began to protest. 'Take off the saddle and go.'

'But, memsahib – '

'Do as I say.'

Reluctantly, he unbuckled the girth and lifted off the heavy sidesaddle. Sultan snorted and stamped, impatient to be off.

'Here is the letter. Remember, our safety is in your hands.'

He salaamed and tucked the paper in the breast of his

202

robe, then vaulted easily upon the horse, clamping his bare legs about the shining flanks. Sultan wheeled and with a clatter of hoofs they were gone, slipping and sliding down the steep path to the causeway, then out across the plain.

For a moment after they vanished the two women stood in silence, half expecting shots and angry voices, but no one else had seen Hussain's departure and Kate sighed with relief.

'Come,' whispered Serinda.

Treading with care over jumbled rocks, she led the way uphill towards the old Hindu temple. Creepers brushed their faces and plucked at their clothes as they pushed along the overgrown path which opened out on a bare rocky outcrop high above the city, where buildings, once extensive, were crumbling slowly into decay. Only a single domed roof was still supported on vaulted arches, while around it a complex of broken walls and marble floors had been forced apart by tree-roots to make a refuge for pariah dogs and jackals.

In daylight Kate had seen peacocks perform their stately pavanes in the dappled sunlight cast by lattice-work of pierced marble. Now she shut her mind to the probable presence of snakes as she followed Serinda into the shadow of the dome.

At the foot of a flight of steps leading to an upper gallery, the girl touched Kate's arm and pointed.

Kate nodded and tiptoed after her. Sinking down on a stone bench, they let the thick warm silence settle round them. Nothing moved as their pulses slowed to normal. The deep watchful stillness even seemed exaggerated, as if the temple was holding its breath, waiting to see what the intruders meant to do. Then by degrees the small night-time sounds which their coming had interrupted began once more. Frogs croaked in the tank, cicadas strummed and a dry rustle over leaves told Kate her fear of snakes had not been fanciful. The moon was past its height. It must be nearly midnight. Any moment now the Prince and the Begum should arrive.

Ten minutes crept by, and another ten; nothing moved

and nagging doubts crept into Kate's mind. Could Serinda be mistaken? Had she lied to her? Had she been lured to this spot for some quite different reason – to get her out of the way while Serinda's accomplices ransacked the Residency? What a fool she would look if the story got out. What a gullible hysterical coward and fool!

She imagined the sniffs of Mrs Bateson and the delighted titters of Mrs Clark. Their mockery would be bad enough; ten times worse would be George's anger at being recalled on a false alarm.

She shifted uneasily on the stone bench. Serinda sat so still she hardly seemed to breathe, but in Kate fear and tension had begun to produce that bane of childhood games of hide-and-seek, the urgent and entirely inconvenient need to relieve herself. As the minutes crawled by she tried to ignore it, concentrating her attention on every tiny sound about her, but it was no use. The longer she waited, the worse it became.

It was difficult to judge how long they had sat in silence, but from the angle of the moon Kate guessed an hour had passed when she decided enough was enough. Serinda must have lied – what a fool she had been to trust the girl!

'Why did you bring me here?' she whispered. 'Who bribed you to tell me that story?'

'Patience, memsahib. They will come. Listen!'

Kate strained her ears but heard nothing. Abruptly she rose.

'Memsahib, wait!'

Ignoring the agonized whisper, she hastened down the steps, too desperate for a moment of privacy to look about her and see the bulky shadow of a man by the temple wall. He froze into utter stillness as she passed. After a hasty glance round to be sure she was alone, the watcher left his post and crept after her, noting where she vanished into a small gully overhung with creeper.

Squatting by the path, he settled to wait.

Soon his patience was rewarded. The tall shawled figure emerged cautiously into the moonlight and began to walk down the path towards the city. Something about the gait puzzled him – something alien in the carriage of head and swinging arms – and he hesitated briefly, but his orders were clear. Anyone discovered in the temple must be brought to his master.

Running forward on bare silent feet, he made a sudden pounce, clapping one hand over Kate's mouth to stifle her scream, and pulling her tight against his chest with the other. The attack took her completely by surprise.

For a moment she struggled, driving sharp elbows into a midriff as unyielding as seasoned oak, and kicking at his shins, but Trimbuck's bodyguards were chosen for their brawn and she realized very soon that she was hurting herself more then her assailant. With the smell of garlic and rancid grease in her nostrils, and lips crushed against her teeth by the pressure of his hand, she felt herself half dragged, half carried back up the path to the temple.

From her perch in the gallery, a terrified Serinda watched as her mistress was manhandled up to the feet of the great statue of Vishnu, where a dark oblong marked the entrance to the subterranean quarters of the temple priests. As the entwined figures passed through it, Serinda moaned softly and fled.

13

Flickering shadows cast by a single oil-lamp bestowed an illusion of movement on the writhing limbs and contorted faces of a hundred deities carved into the walls of the chamber below the temple, but the two living figures seated facing the wide window which commanded an extensive view of the plain stiffened as if turned to stone as the guard dragged in his prisoner.

Kate clutched her shawl about her face in a desperate attempt to escape recognition as she stole fearful glances at the conspirators.

Prince Trimbuck, resplendent in sky-blue pantaloons and a crimson silk tunic sashed with cloth-of-gold, his thick neck encircled by a dozen strings of pearls and a sapphire the size of a small bird's egg in his elaborately swathed, gold-threaded turban made a startling contrast to the tiny sombrely clad woman perched on a cushion beside him; but despite the gorgeous clothes the Prince had an anxious – almost hangdog – air. It was plain he was greatly in awe of his redoubtable aunt, the Begum Samru.

The most dangerous woman in Hindustan, Quinn had called her. It was not difficult to believe. There was a malign power in that diminutive imperious figure with its beaky profile, hooded deepset eyes and tight contemptuous mouth.

'Highness! I caught this woman in the temple!'

Trimbuck's heavy-lidded eyes swivelled languidly to focus on the shawled bundle at his feet.

'Why was she there?'

'Why, Highness?' The guard looked perplexed.

'Answer me, fool! What was she doing?'

'Why, nothing. Walking.'

'Was anyone with her?'

'She was alone, Highness.'

'Then why have you troubled us, imbecile? A woman

206

walking alone – where is the harm in that? Beat her and let her go.'

'Pull back the veil. Let me see her face.'

The Begum's incisive voice pierced Trimbuck's soft rumble. Without glancing at his master for confirmation of the order, the guard stooped and pulled off Kate's shawl. She put up her hands to cover her face, but the damage was done.

'So the memsahib comes to spy on us!' said the Begum and laughed softly. 'Do you know her, nephew?'

'It is the Resident's wife.'

'Ah, I said there would be trouble from that quarter. First the groom, now the mistress. Truly, there have been strange doings in the Residency tonight.'

'Great is the Mother of Wisdom,' Trimbuck purred. 'Shall we kill her as we killed the other?'

'Discover first what brought her here and if our plans are betrayed.' The Begum darted a bright malicious glance at her nephew. 'Perhaps I should withdraw my troops. I have no wish to risk them needlessly.'

'We will never have a better chance than this! If you desert me now and my brother mounts the throne, all I have schemed for, all I have risked, will be lost.'

'Question her, then,' snapped the Begum. 'Find out what she knows. Guard! Bring her here to me.'

Kate had only half understood the soft rapid exchanges, but the word 'Kill' grated unpleasantly on her ear. The guard dragged her up and across the floor until she stood before the small dais on which the Begum was seated. At this range their eyes were level: the bright dark gaze examined her with more than passing curiosity and Kate felt instinctively that this woman had none of Trimbuck's softness. She was cool, clear-headed, merciless: the only hope was to bluff her into believing she knew nothing at all.

She turned to Trimbuck, saying in as ordinary a tone as possible, 'Good evening, Your Highness. I did not expect to find *you* admiring the ruins by moonlight. Magnificent, are they not? If this man is your servant, I would be glad if you would tell him to take his hands off me. No doubt he means no harm, but I find his attentions excessive.'

She had succeeded in disconcerting him. He frowned petulantly and snapped an order. The guard released Kate, who rubbed her wrists and turned a bright social smile on the Prince.

'I am obliged, Your Highness.'

The Begum spoke in careful but adequate English. 'Tell me, memsahib, do you often walk alone at night?'

Kate's heart beat painfully fast. Trimbuck she could deal with, but this tiny predatory woman was a tougher proposition. 'Oh, I come here when I can! I prefer to walk at night. You know how we British love exercise! Moonlight gives ruins such *particular* enchantment.'

'You do not think it dangerous?'

'*Dangerous?*' She gave the word all the incredulity she could muster. Though the Begum's face gave little away, Kate thought the bluff was working. If she could establish the character of a harmless eccentric, she might be allowed to depart unharmed ...

'I have always felt quite safe in my nocturnal wanderings,' she said with a laugh that barely carried conviction. 'I was startled just now when your servant took hold of me, but I see he was only trying to guard your privacy.'

'Do you often assume native dress?'

'I – I find it convenient. It attracts less notice.'

'I understand.'

Kate had an uncomfortable feeling that the Begum understood rather too well. She said, 'I must return home now, before I am missed.'

'One moment.' The forward movement of the Begum's head was horribly reminiscent of a snake about to strike. 'I think you should stay here a while.'

'Stay? For what reason?'

'You will soon know.'

'This is outrageous!' said Kate, trembling. She turned to appeal to Trimbuck. 'Your Highness, you have no right to keep me here. My husband will take a serious view of any attempt to detain me against my will.'

As they exchanged glances she realized that indignation was the wrong tactic. Fawning though Trimbuck appeared, she guessed that his dislike of British rule ran deep. He would enjoy seeing one of the hated race discomfited. If she was to regain her slender advantage, she must appear to accept the detention with good grace, and hope for a chance to escape and warn Major Vance.

She said with forced brightness, 'Do you really wish me to stay? Nothing would please me more. May I have a seat?'

Trimbuck grunted an order, and the guard left his post behind Kate and disappeared into an inner chamber to fetch a cushion. As soon as he was out of sight, Kate stepped forward and, before either of them guessed her intention, dashed the single oil-lamp to the floor, plunging the room into darkness.

With the sound of the crash and Trimbuck's startled cry echoing in her ears, she darted through the door and slammed it shut, shooting home the long wooden bar that acted as a bolt, then fled up the sloping passage that led to the temple.

Behind her she heard confused cries and orders. The acrid fumes of oil-smoke crept up the passage after her, but no one came in pursuit. She reached the top of the passage with a heart pounding fit to burst, and stopped to recover her breath, hardly daring to believe she had escaped so easily. The cries had given way to pounding thumps against the door, but it was solid and should give her time to get clear away.

After the gloom below ground, the starlight seemed unnaturally bright. She slipped cautiously through the priests' entrance and stood once more among the jumbled ruins, debating whether to return by the main path or make a detour round the side of the hill. Speed was essential . . .

As she stood undecided, straining her ears for movement on the path, she felt rather than heard the thump of hoofs approaching at a steady trot. On a bend in the path they came into view, a dozen troopers riding single file up the hillside. She stepped behind a rock, crouching low, to wait while they passed.

Metal jingled and leather creaked as they approached. The leading horseman was singing under his breath. With an incredulous jolt of relief Kate recognized the tune.

'*Drink to me only with thine eyes,*

And I will pledge with mine . . .' he sang softly, keeping time with taps of his whip against the saddle-flap. His charger's white blaze shone clear in the starlight. As Kate stepped from her hiding-place and laid a hand on his bridle, Sultan shied violently, nearly unseating his rider. Behind him, the *sowars* jingled to a halt.

'Hell's teeth!' George Gisborne raised his whip.

'George!' she said faintly, 'thank God you have come in time!'

He drew in his breath with a hiss, and leaned forward to peer at her. Then he swung down from the saddle.

'Kate! You fool – you damned interfering fool! What the *blazes* are you doing here?'

His anger could not spoil her overwhelming sense of relief at his opportune arrival. She began to stammer out her story, words tumbling over one another in her eagerness. He listened while the troopers murmured among themselves and their horses blew and stamped.

'Alone?' he said incredulously when she paused for breath. 'You expect me to believe you came here alone at dead of night to trap these dangerous conspirators? My dear, you never cease to astonish me! May I ask why you did not communicate this dastardly plot to Major Vance, whom I left in command of the garrison precisely in order to prevent such wild happenings?'

His sarcasm stung. 'It is true!'

'Why didn't you tell Major Vance?'

'You know he is never sober after eight o'clock. Even if I had told him he would not have believed me.'

'Did you even try? Ah, I thought not. You preferred to indulge your dramatic fantasies and send messengers flying the length and breadth of the land.'

'I sent Hussain to warn you. What else could I do?'

'I might suggest a number of alternatives,' he said dryly. 'Well, my dear, I congratulate you. Single-handed you have destroyed a promising operation against Scindia, not to mention depriving me of a night's sleep. I hope you are proud of yourself.'

'George, you must believe me.' Weariness and frustration brought her close to tears. 'Unless you act now, Trimbuck and the Begum will seize Attaganj as soon as the old Raja's death is announced. She has three battalions encamped a few miles away.'

'As you say, but I take leave to doubt.'

Kate stamped her foot. 'They are there, in the temple. All you need do is take them for questioning. Ask the Begum why she is here.' She added without thinking, 'Strike at the head and you need never fear the tail.'

'I can guess where you got *that* advice.' George handed his reins to his *daffadar*. 'Very well, my dear. Let us descend to the lions' den and see what you have caught. It is a little late for me to remind you that this is hardly the approved manner of treating our native allies – the Begum *is* now an ally – locking them up in temples without so much as a by-your-leave. Prnce Trimbuck will have every right to be angry . . . but why should that cause *you* any concern?'

Chastened and furious, she allowed him to lead her back to the temple; she was mildly surprised to find he needed no guidance to the door of the underground chamber, but of course he had lived in Attaganj long enough to be familiar with all its archaeological remains. There might well have been moonlit nights when he, too, climbed up from the city to enjoy the night breeze on Temple Hill . . .

'In here,' she said, as he paused before the door with its wooden bar still solidly in position. No sound came from within, but she had the impression of a listening silence.

'Careful!' she warned. 'Shouldn't you wait until your men – ?'

He gave her a strange look. 'I know what I am doing,' he said, and jerked the bar loose. The door swung inward. 'After you, my dear.'

The invitation was almost a challenge.

'Very well,' she said, and stepped across the threshold.

The lamp had been relit yet Trimbuck and the Begum

seemed hardly to have stirred from the positions in which she had first seen them. Only the faintest tensing of muscles betrayed surprise at her reappearance: after a single glance at her all their attention focused upon George, magnificent in scarlet and gold, broad shoulders straining at his faultlessly cut tunic, boots gleaming, spurs twinkling, the very personification of British power and glory.

'So you have come, Jowraj Jung,' said the Begum, and laughed.

'I have come.'

George stepped forward until he stood at the foot of the dais where Trimbuck sat with his fat thighs spread and feet tucked under him.

'Maharaj!' he said, and bowed low.

Trimbuck's sleepy eyes regarded him for a moment before he spoke.

'It is over, then?'

'An hour ago your father breathed his last. I have come to proclaim your accession and escort you to your palace, Highness.'

Proclaim your accession? Dumbfounded, Kate stared from one to the other. This must be a dream. George had come to arrest Trimbuck, not proclaim his accession. With a dizzying sense of unreality she saw why George had left the city undefended, and why he had returned so opportunely.

'What of the Second Battalion? Will they fight?'

George smiled. 'Maharaj, you have nothing to fear. The barrack gates are shut and the officers under arrest. I made sure of that before I came here.'

'*Traitor!*'

Trimbuck's lazy gaze swivelled to rest on Kate. 'Your memsahib is a troublemaker. Be sure to keep her under your eye. She has caused me much annoyance by her meddling.'

'Meddling?' George's light eyes examined his wife as if seeing her for the first time. The cold speculative assessment struck fear into her heart. Her husband was a stranger to her. She had married him, lived with him, made love to him and borne his son yet she had never known him – never guessed his ambition or where it would lead.

Almost to himself he murmured, 'She will not meddle again, that I can guarantee.'

'George, *please* – ' She stopped. He was not listening. He had closed his heart and mind against her. She was nothing but a minor inconvenience to be dealt with as expediently as possible.

It is no use, she thought. Nothing I say will move him. All the same, she had to try. Tentatively she laid a hand on his arm. It felt rigid and unresponsive under the scarlet cloth.

'George, you must listen to me,' she said in a low hurried tone, very conscious of the Begum's contemptuous smile and Trimbuck's unconcealed enjoyment of her humiliation. 'I am your *wife*. I have your interests – your true interests – at heart. Don't do this thing. Change your mind, I beg of you! It is not too late. For my sake – for the sake of Jacky's dear memory – '

'Don't speak of him!' he said with sudden passion. For a moment she thought he would strike her, then he mastered his anger and said in a lower voice, 'When Jacky died you forfeited any claim you ever had to my protection. You brought this trouble upon yourself by your infernal meddling. Why couldn't you stay out of politics, like other women?'

'So we could all be butchered together?' she flashed.

'Butchered?' He frowned.

'My dear fellow, pay no attention to her,' said Trimbuck smoothly. George gave him a suspicious look.

'You promised safe-conduct to Burhanpore for all the women, Your Highness.'

'Of course, of course.' Trimbuck's tone was testy. 'They shall have an escort as far as Company territory and any British officers who care to accompany them are free to do so. My word upon it. Send your wife with them by all means, old man, but a word of warning: do not permit her to spread tales of alarm among your compatriots. If they do not depart quietly I cannot answer for the conduct of my men.'

213

George hesitated. He knew the fat prince well enough to place little reliance in his promises.

'Send her to Sardhana,' said the Begum, seeing him irresolute. 'Among my people she will have no chance to make mischief.'

George's face cleared magically and Kate realized with a sinking heart that he would do anything this woman asked of him, even to the extent of betraying his country and sending his wife to an unknown fate. Trimbuck he could resist, but the Witch of Sardhana had him in thrall.

'Don't send me away! Let me stay with you,' she pleaded, catching at his sleeve again, but this time he shook her off impatiently. His mind was made up. The minor inconvenience was settled to his satisfaction. It was time to turn to more important affairs.

'Come, Your Highness,' he said curtly. 'My men are waiting.'

'By all means, let us go.'

'Don't leave me, George! Don't let them take me away!'

The look he turned on her was regretful, almost pitying. 'I never thought you would have changed so much,' he said, and the words sounded to her like an epitaph.

'George, *please!*'

He turned his back on her and bowed, first to the Prince and then the Begum; then turned and left the chamber, shoulders stiff, spurs jingling. She realized with a feeling of utter despair that he did not even wish to know what became of her.

The Begum clapped her hands and gave shrill orders. Kate made no resistance as her wrists were bound with a length of cloth and a bandage tied over her eyes. She was hustled outside and bundled into a *palanquin* which set off downhill at a smart jog. Sinking back into the musk-smelling gloom, Kate abandoned all hope of rescue.

PART THREE:
THE MAD DOG

14

Holkar's single eye gleamed bloodshot beneath his slanted turban as he set down the cherry brandy with a crash and roared for music. He was a short, dark, active, strongly built young man, an excellent shot and fine horseman, not unhandsome in feature apart from a certain wildness of expression which, together with the nervous tic working spasmodically below the blind eye, hinted at a mind precariously balanced on the edge of sanity.

Tonight he was in tearing spirits. The Rajput prince of Naipur had resisted a demand for *chauth*, depriving Holkar's emissary of his sight and his manhood before sending him staggering back to the Maratha camp with his testicles crammed in his mouth. Trusting in his treaty with the British, Naipur had then sent urgent messages for Company support, but these had gone unanswered.

For ten days Naipur held out against Holkar's onslaughts, the cannon mounted on his battlements inflicting considerable damage on the attackers; but when a raiding party led by Colonel Quinn – acting on information from a disaffected cousin of Naipur's – crept up a hidden pathway in the cliff behind the fortress and scaled the walls from the rear, the Raja had been forced to surrender.

It had been an expensive act of defiance. Ten waggon loads of gold and jewels from his treasure-house, along with the pick of his horses and six elephants with ceremonial trappings of scarlet and silver had been removed to the Maratha camp. Now the Raja sat glumly, a spectre at the feast, waiting to learn his own fate.

The mutilated envoy had been a nephew of Holkar's. The more he drank the more certain it became that the Raja's demise would be a painful one.

From beneath his sandy lashes, Ned Sweeney stole occasional glances at the dejected figure in his gorgeous tunic of peacock blue and gold, but was careful not to catch his eye. He hated these victory feasts. He felt sick to know that the Raja of Naipur would soon be a screaming bloody lump of flesh, unrecognizable as a man. Moodily, Ned pushed morsels of spiced lamb about his plate. The head wound he had sustained during the assault ached fiercely; he longed to throw himself down on his *charpai* away from the heat and noise and light, and let sleep blot out the memory of the post-battle butchery. Fighting he loved, but the cold-blooded settling of scores made his gorge rise. Only the knowledge that any movement away from the feast would bring that single malevolent eye to rest on him kept Ned in his seat. He prayed most fervently that Holkar would not single him out for attention tonight.

The prayer went unheard.

'You are eating nothing, Captain Sweeney,' said Jaswant Rao with wicked amusement.

'I am not hungry, Your Highness.'

'The food is not to your taste?'

'No, no. I have had all I want.'

'I am told you conducted yourself with great gallantry today, Captain Sweeney. Without your courage the assault would have failed.'

'Thank you,' muttered Ned, thoroughly uncomfortable to be the focus of attention. From the corner of his eye he saw Colonel Quinn's grin and knew to whom he owed Holkar's compliments.

'In recognition of your services, you shall have the honour of devising how this traitor shall die.'

'I'd rather not, if you don't mind,' Ned mumbled, his face as red as his tunic.

'Come, Captain Sweeney, you disappoint me. Can you think of no novel means of execution? Would you prefer him to die as Sambhur Khan did?' Sambhur Khan had been dangled over a precipice and his fingers cut away one by one until he fell.

'No.'

'Then what can you suggest?' Holkar's tone was silky. 'Am I to understand that my officers are weaklings, afraid of blood? Ho, guards!' he roared suddenly. 'Tie the Raja to a stake and we will have some sword practice.'

Ned shot a pleading glance at Colonel Quinn, who had sipped his wine with an air of detachment during this exchange, comfortably cross-legged in the posture Ned still found unbearable for more than ten minutes at a time. Now he responded promptly.

'Why kill the goose that lays golden eggs? The Raja of Naipur is rich. Spare his life now and you can milk his treasury for years to come. Kill him, and you will bring the British buzzing like hornets about your ears.'

'What do I care for the British? You have the soul of a banya, Sikander Bahadur, thinking always of money.'

'Money pays troops and troops win battles,' said Quinn imperturbably. Holkar fidgeted with his pearl necklace and his cheek twitched convulsively. Ned watched with deep apprehension: plainly the prince was working himself into a rage.

'Spare the life of the wretch who maimed my nephew?' he demanded. 'Blood cries out for blood. Heat the irons. I will put out his eyes myself if you jackals are afraid to, and any man who dares object will get the same treatment.'

'Hardly your favourite nephew, Jaswant Rao?' said Quinn gently.

The bloodshot eye swivelled to give him a long stare. 'Explain yourself,' said Holkar with menacing softness.

'Oh, I merely observe that it is strange that a youth who caused you so much disquiet when he was whole should excite your sympathy now he has received his just deserts,' said Quinn carelessly.

'Just deserts? Are you implying my nephew was a traitor?'

'Why else should you make him your messenger?'

Don't do it, pleaded Ned silently. Don't twist the tiger's tail. What does it matter what happens to the bally fellow? Let Holkar chop him in little pieces if it keeps him sweet.

But Quinn seemed determined to provoke. He continued with maddening deliberation, 'In my view, it would be more appropriate to thank the Raja of Naipur for ridding you of a dangerous troublemaker.'

He had gone too far. Holkar's face became congested; he signalled to armed guards who stepped smartly forward and seized Colonel Quinn by the elbows, dragging him to stand face to face with the angry Maratha.

'I demand an apology.'

Quinn smiled. 'I never apologize for speaking my mind. You know me well enough for that.'

What would have happened next was uncertain, but Holkar's restless eye, roving about the crowded pavilion, was attracted by a commotion in the farthest corner near the entrance, where a number of his followers were closely packed, as much to see and hear their betters as to await their own turn at the left-overs. Through this throng a woman was trying to force a passage, scolding at those who blocked her way.

'Let me through, blockheads! Let me through. I must speak to Sikander Bahadur. Out of my way.'

Wild-eyed and dust-stained, her hair in disarray and her feet bleeding from rough roads, her appearance would have scandalized Hamesha Begum, but Ned knew her at once.

'Serinda!' he cried, starting up and pushing away the hands that clutched at her. 'What has happened? Where have you been?'

Sobbing with relief, she collapsed at his feet. Gently he raised her, pushing back the disordered hair and gazing into her face.

'Who is this madwoman? What does she want?' Holkar's shout cut through the hubbub. His anger had vanished as quickly as it erupted; he seized on the chance of a distraction.

The crowd parted to let Serinda approach the dais. 'I come from Attaganj, Your Highness,' she said loudly. 'The city is betrayed to the French. Prince Trimbuck has ordered the slaughter of all the *Angrezi*. The Begum Samru – '

'Slaughtered! The French!'

Serinda's voice was lost in the commotion. The pavilion buzzed like an overturned hive.

'To horse!' shouted Holkar, leaping up, his single eye ablaze with excitement. The fate of the Raja of Naipur was forgotten as quickly as his quarrel with Quinn. Amid the shrilling of bugles and neighing of horses disturbed from their rest, the Maratha camp mobilized with a speed that paid tribute to the efficiency of Holkar's mercenary officers.

'You damned young fool – where do you think you're going?' Quinn strode up to Ned who sat swaying in the saddle, his face deathly white beneath his turban. 'Get off that horse at once, and away to your tent.'

'But I'll miss all the fun.'

'Fun? I can tell you you'll miss more than fun if you ride all night with a hole in your head.'

Ned clenched his teeth. 'It's – it's Kate,' he said indistinctly. 'I can't stay here while she – while all those poor defenceless creatures . . . If that blackguard Trimbuck has hurt them I'll – I'll never rest till I've hunted him down.'

'I know,' said Quinn more kindly. 'But you won't help her by killing yourself, you know. We'll save them if we can, you have my word on it, but I won't take you with me. I've better things to do than act as your nursemaid. The state you're in, you're no use to me. If you don't get that cut seen to, you won't be much use to her, either.'

He nodded at Serinda, who smiled boldly back at him.

'I will take care of my lord, Colonel Sahib.'

'Minx!' he said, laughing, 'I don't doubt you will.' He hurried away.

Soon after, Ned heard them gallop out of camp. He raised his head, but could not altogether regret his exclusion from their ranks while Serinda's smooth hands were on his brow, and his bearer was scurrying to and fro with dressings at her orders. She gave him a draught of warm wine spiked with opium and watched, smiling, while he drank.

Quinn was right, he thought drowsily. There were times when heroics would not answer. If anyone could save Kate, he would . . .

Before Serinda finished winding the bandage about his head, Ned was fast asleep.

At the junction where the Nanpani river flows into the more turbulent waters of the Ivory Gorge, Holkar and Quinn went their separate ways. The former led his column directly towards Attaganj, while the latter struck north in a flanking movement designed to prevent the Begum Samru bringing in reinforcements from Hindustan.

As Quinn had been quick to point out, this was the best chance Holkar would ever get to establish his own claim to Attaganj. If he could overthrow the rebels and restore order, there was little doubt that Lord Wellesley – furious at Trimbuck's treachery and the mistreatment of his allies – would accept the *status quo*, for the time being at least. With two armies in the field against the insurgent princes and the Company Directors pressing for a reduction in expenses, the Governor-General would be grateful to any Maratha prince who showed himself well-disposed towards British interests. In time, of course, the question of subsidiary treaties was bound to be raised again, but by then Wellesley might have been recalled to England, and his successor could well pursue a less expansionist policy towards the Marathas.

In the meantime, the rescue of the British women in Attaganj was all-important, and it was vital that Holkar himself should be seen as their saviour. Rather reluctantly, Quinn agreed to play a minor role in the rescue, and led his men at the best pace he could towards the Attaganj frontier.

An hour after dawn he called a halt in a grove of trees half a mile from the main crossroads on the way to Kerouli, along which he expected the Begum's reinforcements to pass. They had made good time, covering nearly thirty miles in seven hours over difficult country. Both men and horses deserved a rest.

As cooking fires were lit and the low buzz of voices drifted across the grove, Quinn smoked and fretted, unable to rid his mind of the images which had haunted him throughout the night ride. Women's faces, pale and sleep-blurred, mouths open in terror as they woke to find their beds surrounded by armed men. Screams as dazed, uncomprehending children were torn from their mothers' arms. Brains splattered on white walls, the flash of steel . . .

One face dominated the rest: a pale oval face with wide eyes and cloudy dark hair that made him think of a big dusky moth, beating her wings against a window as she tried to reach the sunlight. A headstrong, reckless, heedless moth. The kind which would flutter at the pane even when the window was open.

I tried to warn her, he thought. I showed her the window was open, but she would not listen.

It was no good telling himself that Trimbuck would not maltreat so valuable a hostage. The prince's capricious cruelty was well-known. He might prefer the amusement of torturing his prisoners to any advantage gained by keeping them alive.

The hours crawled past as he fretted for action, but the messages that arrived from Holkar at intervals ordered him to stay where he was. Reinforcements from Sardhana were on their way and he must be ready to intercept them. Shadows lengthened. His patrols returned reporting that all was quiet. It seemed as if the whole landscape had fallen asleep.

By evening when not so much as a bullock-cart had passed the crossroads, Quinn's restlessness became intolerable. He decided to try for a brace of jungle-fowl. Throwing away the stub of his cigar, he called for his gun and accompanied only by Daoud Mohammed, his grey-bearded bearer, strolled into the dark jungle.

The small sounds of the camp faded as the tangled gloom engulfed them. He loved the jungle at this hour, when hunters and hunted alike were preparing for the business of the night. Birds chose their roosts and deer their grazing-grounds. Predators yawned and stretched and flexed their claws. Green parrots flashed squawking across his path as he moved deeper into the shadowy undergrowth, stooping low beneath festoons of wild vine. In a small glade a troop of monkeys leapt and played on the crumbling ruins of a shrine. They pelted him with debris, chattering disapproval.

Grinning at their noisy demonstrations, he crossed the glade and plunged into thicker cover, following a narrow game-trail for a mile or more until it intersected a track

222

that was plainly used by humans. It ran almost parallel to the road he had left, and it struck him at once that he should post a patrol here. He would look foolish if the Begum's reinforcements slipped past on this trail while he waited at the crossroads. Perhaps they had done so already? It might account for the absence of game in the vicinity.

Kneeling, he examined the tracks, but none were recent enough to mark an army's passing. Abandoning the notion of shooting, he turned and was about to go back the way he had come when, in the distance, he heard the faint chant of approaching runners. They came from the direction of Attaganj.

Quinn stepped into shadow, curious to know who preferred this obscure jungle path to the open road.

Soon six bearers came into view trotting steadily and keeping up their rhythmic 'Ho-hum-*ha!*' that was half a grunt and half a song. The litter they carried had gilded poles and silk curtains, drawn close. A female, then, travelling at night, without escort? Quinn's interest quickened. Decidedly, this required investigation.

As the litter drew near his hiding-place he stepped out to block their path. The bearers halted.

'Greetings, brothers,' said Quinn pleasantly.

They glowered and said nothing, though their leader, a burly fellow with a deep chest and leg muscles like twisted ropes, growled and spat and tightened his grip on his cudgel.

'Whither bound, brothers? The road is lonely and night coming on. Are you not afraid of wild beasts, that you travel so late?'

'Our mistress is sick. We must carry her to Chatagarh before morning,' grunted the leader.

'Who is your mistress?'

'That is none of your business, sahib. Step aside and let us pass.'

Quinn saw this was no cringing peasant to be easily intimidated. The team, responsive to their leader's mood, growled in their throats and moved a pace forward. They were six to two and in any fight would have the advantage.

223

They knew as well as he did that he had no authority to delay them.

The curtains of the palanquin shook and bulged. Quinn looked at them more closely, seeing that the curtain edges were tightly laced together, the ends knotted. Now his curiosity was thoroughly aroused. This was carrying modesty altogether too far. Even a bride was permitted to peep through the curtains on her way to her husband's house.

'What ails your mistress?'

'Huzoor, it is the smallpox,' quavered an older bearer who shouldered the rear of the left pole. 'Do not approach too closely lest the infection should spread to Your Honour. Truly she is very sick and has not stirred these past hours.'

'Out of our way!' demanded the leader.

The team advanced purposefully. Quinn came to a decision. At whatever cost he must see inside the litter. It could be the Begum herself, travelling north in secrecy. How she would mock if she succeeded in slipping through Holkar's close-drawn net!

Stepping back, he raised his shotgun, holding steady aim on the burly leader's chest.

'Put down the litter.'

Indignation showed plain on every face – indignation and a glimmer of fear. For a moment Quinn thought they meant to refuse, and his finger tightened on the trigger; then slowly they lowered their poles to the ground and stood waiting, eyes fixed on him balefully.

'Give me your knife,' said Quinn in an undertone to Daoud Mohammed. 'Take the gun. If anyone moves, shoot him.'

Without taking his gaze off the leader, Quinn handed over the gun and grasped the slim-bladed skinning knife the *shikari* wore at his belt.

'Move away from the litter,' he ordered the sullen team. 'Further. That's right. Sit down. If any man moves, he will wake in *Jehannum*.'

They squatted on their haunches, angry and watchful.

Quinn went up to the litter and slashed the laces on the curtain, ignoring their growl of outrage. Pulling the silk

224

hangings aside, he bent and peered into the darkness within, holding his breath against the foetid stench.

The woman lay comatose, just as the bearers had said. He was conscious of a sharp pang of disappointment. Not the Witch of Sardhana: just a dying woman swathed in many shawls, her face muffled so all he could see were two desperate eyes gazing up at this violator of privacy.

Ashamed, he drew back, and was about to close the curtains once again when the sick woman made a violent thrashing movement, raising both feet beneath the covers and kicking so strongly that the litter rocked. She emitted a strange strangled moan.

He looked at her with renewed attention. Her movement had disturbed the covers; now he saw cords tied across the litter from side to side. She lay prone not through infirmity, but because she was lashed to her couch, and the reason she did not speak lay in the twist of cloth tied over her mouth.

With a surge of excitement, he sawed at her bonds. As they fell apart she struggled to raise herself.

'Tiger! Behind you! Watch out!'

The shouts took Quinn by surprise. Worse, it distracted Daoud Mohammed, who spun round to stare into the undergrowth. Before he realized the deception, the leader of the bearers sprang on his back with a yell and bore him to the ground. Daoud Mohammed struggled fiercely: both barrels went off with a crash that sent birds screeching from their roosts.

'Run! Hide!'

Severing the last cord, Quinn ran to his servant's assistance.

He might as well have told her to fly. Blood had long ceased to circulate in Kate's numb hands and feet. Painfully, she rolled off the litter, away from the heaving, cursing knot of struggling bodies, and dragged herself on hands and knees across the track towards the dark wall of jungle. Into its sheltering gloom she forced her way with frantic haste, heedless of thorns and clutching vines, and collapsed in the nearest small hollow, knowing she had not gone far enough for safety, but quite unable to stir her limbs any further.

For what seemed an age she listened to the thuds, grunts and groans, unable to tell who had the best of the fight, though with odds of six to two it was easy to guess. At last came a scurry of fleeing feet and silence, broken only by heavy breathing. She cowered in her inadequate hiding place, waiting for discovery.

'Mrs Gisborne! Where are you? They have gone.'

How could she ever have thought his face would frighten children? Nothing could have been more beautiful to her at that moment than the hideous scarred features of Colonel Quinn, filthy with blood and dust, his hair full of twigs, shirt ripped half off, stooping to examine the prostrate body of his *shikari;* nothing more melodious than his curt instruction to raise the old man's head while he forced the neck of his flask between his teeth.

'Can you walk?' He gave her a brief worried glance. 'I fear Daoud Mohammed is badly hurt.'

It was no time to complain of her own aches. She said, 'Of course, but first let me look at that wound. I have done some nursing, you know.'

Blood oozed in a dark sluggish stream from the contusion on the back of the old man's head. A cudgel-blow had split his scalp with such force that white skull gleamed through the matted hair.

'Can you find me some water?'

She washed the wound as best she could and bound it with strips of silk torn from the litter's hangings. Daoud Mohammed breathed stertorously, muttering curses.

'How shall we carry him?' she asked, straightening from her task.

'He is no great weight, poor old fellow!' Quinn stooped and hoisted the limp body across his shoulder. In silence broken only by groans and muffled curses, they set off along the jungle path.

It was slow, difficult going and when at length they reached the abandoned shrine they were glad enough to rest. The moon had risen, and shed a clear silver light across the glade. Above the little temple's tumbledown cupola, the monkeys huddled and chittered. Kate listened in silence to the story of Serinda's dramatic arrival in Holkar's camp and the Maratha's march upon Attaganj.

'I should have come to you myself,' she said. 'If I had known – if I had had the least notion where George's sympathies lay . . .' She broke off and he waited for the inevitable question.

'Tell me, Colonel Quinn,' she said with painful directness, 'how long have you known that my husband is a traitor?'

'I suspected it but had no proof. He was always careful to cover his tracks, you know. Yet there were straws in the wind. Two years ago, when he was in Delhi, his association with the Begum Samru gave rise to a good deal of comment. Then he was appointed Resident in Attaganj and I heard no more of it.'

'Yet you suspected it continued?'

'My dear Mrs Gisborne, a leopard does not change his spots because he is wearing a golden collar! Yes, I suspected his marriage to you might be no more than a blind, to conceal the true state of affairs from his superiors.'

'So you tried to warn me.'

'To warn you?'

'Do not be disingenuous, Colonel Quinn,' said Kate sharply. 'You must have known Ned would repeat your judgement to me.'

In the darkness she guessed he was smiling. 'Possibly, though for all the notice you took, I might have saved myself the trouble. The question is, what will you do now?'

What, indeed? In the past twenty-four hours shocks had come on her so thick and fast she had hardly given the question a thought.

'I – I hardly know. Return to England, I suppose.'

'Forfeiting all your property? All your rights? For shame, Mrs Gisborne! I did not think you so poor-spirited.'

She looked at him with dislike. 'What rights? What property?'

227

'Even abandoned wives have a claim on their husband's estate. Major Gisborne is no pauper!'

'He is always complaining that he has no money.'

'His man of business in Bombay could tell a different tale!' said Quinn with a soft laugh. 'Why he has been taking bribes for years! You must not return to England penniless, Mrs Gisborne. I advise you to make careful enquiries of Mr Bapuji before you leave the Begum mistress of the field.' He paused, glad to see he had given her something to think about. 'In any case, there can be no question of travel until the countryside is settled.'

'How long will this dreadful fighting last?'

'Not long, by my reckoning,' said Quinn promptly. 'General Wellesley has the rebel princes fairly on the run. I prophesy that Scindia will sue for peace within the month, and when he does the Bhonsle will soon follow suit. By the New Year all will be quiet – as quiet as it ever is.' He laughed softly.

'It sounds as if you enjoy fighting,' she said disapprovingly.

'Do not forget I have lived most of my life among these turbulent gentlemen! Fighting is meat and drink to Marathas, and my livelihood depends on it. Their quarrels flare up like fireworks, and are as quickly extinguished.'

There was a moment's silence, then he went on, 'Let me make you a proposition, Mrs Gisborne. Until it is safe to travel, be my wife's guest. No, hear me out! Lakshmi is lonely and will be glad of your company. Besides, the Begum Samru is not noted for constancy. You may find your husband returns sooner than you expect. What do you say?'

Night had fallen, but the wide arch of stars spanning the glade provided light enough for him to make out the line of her bent head. She was silent so long he thought she had drifted into a trance.

'Well?' he prompted, touching her shoulder.

'It seems I have little choice,' she said flatly. 'Thank you, Colonel Quinn, I shall be glad to accept your hospitality. I only hope one day I may be in a position to repay such kindness.'

15

Any reservations Kate had about committing herself to a stay of indefinite length in a strange household quickly evaporated in the warmth of her reception, though she found Lakshmi sadly changed. Still childless after four years of marriage, her beautiful black eyes seemed haunted by the spectre of infertility, and her lack of fulfilment was evident in her nervously plucking hands and brittle chatter. The fear that her husband might put her aside in favour of a better breeder was ever in her mind. Though at first she regarded her English visitor as a welcome distraction, it was not long before Kate became aware of dark undercurrents below the household's surface serenity.

Even while Lakshmi and her wizened, *pan*-chewing mother, aunts, and other female dependents were over-whelming Kate with kindness, she felt that beneath their outward courtesy there lurked an unspoken fear of Quinn's motive in thrusting this stranger into their midst. Despite her apparent friendliness, Lakshmi was jealous, anxious lest her husband's glance should stray too often or linger too long on the interloper, and this jealousy betrayed itself in small ways however hard she tried to hide it.

Not that Quinn provided any substance for her anxiety. On the contrary he treated Kate with perfect indifference and showed her no more attention than he did his wife's ugliest aunt. Devoted as he seemed, and tolerant of Lakshmi's whims, there were moments when his face was sombre as he watched her chattering and posturing. Kate wondered what thoughts, what regrets were passing through the brain behind that twisted mask: then he would smile and answer her inconsequential questions, and so great was the change of expression that Kate would scold herself for imagining the sombre mood.

Questions were something Kate found difficult to escape.

She was astonished by her hostess' interest in the most trivial details of the lives of white women. Her curiosity, particularly in biological matters, was so frank and childishly inquisitive that Kate often blushed but could not be offended.

They had some strange misconceptions.

'Tell us, tell us! Is it true that white women have tails under their skirts?'

'And *faranghis* have hair all over their bodies? Do they make love ten times a night?'

'We have heard it said that French women swallow live fish so they may bear sons, and hide them from their menfolk who feast on newborn infants.'

Naive though they were in some respects, these Maratha women had a freedom and force of character that impressed her greatly. At times when their men were absent, the women took up the reins of government and few of their decisions were subsequently reversed. Their model and inspiration was Ahalya Bhai, the great Maratha queen whose thirty-year reign had given her people peace and prosperity such as they had never known before or since. The spirit of democracy that pervaded Maratha justice was never more evident than in *darbar*, when the chief admitted even his humblest followers to approach with petitions. Arbitrary as these judgements sometimes seemed, they were accepted without complaint.

Before she had been with them a fortnight, the siege of Attaganj was suddenly lifted as Holkar turned his mercurial attention to an easier target. A neighbouring *thakur* had gone hunting, leaving his home unguarded. Away galloped Jaswant Rao to take advantage of this unlooked-for prize, leaving the punishment of Prince Trimbuck to the British army which was advancing swiftly from the south-west.

Kate fretted, thinking of the imprisoned British women. Would Trimbuck honour his pledge to send them to Burhanpore? Did he understand the very notion of honour?

Two days later, Holkar and his men rode into camp laughing, their saddles loaded with booty. Gifts for their women, elephants, goats, cattle, and cheetahs from the *thakur*'s menagerie. To Kate's surprise and pleasure, Quinn presented her with a fine Deccani mare, dun with black points.

'For me?'

'Try her,' he said, laughing at her astonishment. 'If you like her, she is yours.'

'She is beautiful.' Kate laid a hand on the mare's silky neck and she blew gently through her nostrils.

With her came two attendants, an old man to cut her feed, and a lean young *syce* who rarely smiled but ran tirelessly beside the horse and knew instinctively where game was to be found. Together they ranged the wide grasslands teeming with game around the Maratha camp, and sometimes ventured into the dark teak forest, where they might catch a tantalizing glimpse of noble heads with long-tined antlers before the shy *sambhur* melted into dappled shadows.

Such rides were an antidote to the claustrophobia engendered by the constant proximity of other women. She felt ashamed of her craving to be alone, but could not help being glad that Lakshmi never wished to ride with her.

Only on the days when Holkar replenished his larder was Kate careful to stay in camp. Ned warned that she would surely be sickened by the sight of frantic beasts struggling in the hunters' nets. Every visitor of note was entertained with a hunt whose degree of ceremonial was a barometer to the regard in which Holkar held him.

One crisp December morning when the mist still lay in hollows and cobwebs sparkled on every branch, Kate watched the hunting procession stream out of camp. She wondered that all this dazzling, glinting, trumpeting splendour should be deemed appropriate for the sallow, undersized native with the face of a dissatisfied rodent who hunched close against Holkar's shoulder in the swaying *howdah*, muttering earnestly in his ear.

Proud as Lucifer on his long-striding elephant, Holkar stared straight ahead. Around him horses pranced and curvetted as their riders engaged in mock skirmishing; elephants raised their trunks in clarion challenges, and one great beast advanced upon his knees to demonstrate his

231

rider's skill. All was dust and glitter and turmoil; but the centre of the line where Holkar rode had the ominous stillness of the eye of a storm. Though he glanced neither to left nor right, she felt he was aware of every movement – almost every thought – of the men around him. His menacing presence cast a shadow as he passed. She well understood Ned's anxiety to avoid the attention of that single smouldering eye.

When they reached the hunting-ground, she knew, he would exchange his great ceremonial elephant for one plainly harnessed for the chase. The hunters would fan out in a half moon several miles wide and advance in line abreast, crashing through low scrub to drive every creature sheltering there towards the long nets.

'Who is with Holkar?' she whispered to the woman at her elbow, and the answer came back with a mixture of revulsion and dread.

'Sirji Rao is beside him. Sirji Rao Ghatke.'

The name meant nothing to her. She watched the procession until the rolling dustcloud swallowed it up, then went to join Lakshmi and her ladies. There would be no ride today.

In the evening disquieting rumours flew round the camp. The hunt had not been a success and Holkar was angry. The guest of honour had shot nothing and heads – the chief *shikari*'s among them – were likely to roll.

'Quinn will go too far one day,' said Ned on his regular evening visit. He paced up and down, unable to relax. 'I'm not sure he hasn't done so already. Talk about twisting the tiger's tail! He scares me: I'm not ashamed to admit it. Can't he see the man's insane?'

'Jaswant Rao? Insane?'

Ned nodded, his face uncharacteristically solemn. She thought how suddenly he had grown up and felt a pang of regret for the carefree boy aboard *Neptune*.

'Tell me what happened today.'

'Oh, the usual thing, only worse,' Ned said fretfully, 'It's courting trouble to provoke him, especially when that vile reptile Sirji Rao Ghatke is here, whispering poison in

Holkar's ear. Did you notice him today? There's nothing he'd like more than to see Quinn's head on a plate.'

A chill ran through Kate. 'You mean that rat-faced man in the green surcoat? Who is he?'

Ned said with suppressed fury, 'The last man in the world Holkar should listen to. Scindia's father-in-law, one of the greatest villains who ever lived, whom he uses to do his dirtiest work.'

'Why does Holkar receive Scindia's emissary? I thought they were at daggers drawn.'

'So they were,' said Ned gloomily, 'at least, until General Wellesley licked Scindia and the Bhonsle. Now it has all changed. Holkar is the only undefeated Maratha chief, and the others are cringing round like beaten hounds, wooing him with promises.'

'Promises? For what?'

'They want him to lead a new uprising against the Company, and chase the British out of Maratha territory for good.'

'Chase out the British? Surely Holkar won't agree? Can't he see he would be defeated too?'

'When he's sober he knows that well enough, but how often is he sober nowadays? When the brandy gets to him he's ready for any mischief. I tell you, Kate, I don't like the look of things. For two pins I'd resign my commission and take service elsewhere.'

'You wouldn't leave Colonel Quinn?'

'No – o . . .' Ned looked undecided. 'He still thinks he can twist Holkar round his little finger, and so he can nine times out of ten. It's the tenth time that worries me. Sometimes I see him look at Quinn as if he hated him.'

Kate had seen that look, like a bull planning a charge.

'It's plain as a pikestaff to everyone but Quinn,' Ned went on. 'I tell him he'll play with fire once too often, but he only laughs.'

'What put Holkar in a black mood today?'

Ned sighed, as if it was too much trouble to explain, then unexpectedly launched into the story. 'We were driving deer in the grasslands, with most of them going towards the nets.

I didn't see what happened – I was out on the wing – but I heard a lot of shouting, and then a bunch of antelope, a dozen at least, broke back through the line and headed straight for Holkar's elephant. Everyone waited for him to take the shot, but he was slow in getting up the gun and before he could fire, Quinn dropped the biggest buck right under the trunk of Holkar's elephant. You may imagine now pleased he was.'

'Oh *dear!*'

'That wasn't the worst of it. Later we hunted a tigress in the long grass. We had her surrounded, and she was just going nicely towards Sirji Rao, who was waving his gun about to everyone's peril, when she sprang on a bearer and began to maul him; whereupon Quinn cantered up on his horse and speared her clean through the heart without giving Sirji Rao a chance to discharge his weapon.' He shook his head. 'There'll be trouble at tonight's feast, mark my words. Jaswant Rao has been made to look a fool, and he won't take that kindly.'

She remembered his gloomy prophecy that night as she tossed and turned on her string cot, listening to the squalling of nautch girls and roars from the revellers. Quinn could look after himself, she thought. It was no use fretting over him. He had lived with Marathas so long that he must be allowed to know his own business best.

But whenever she heard a shout her heart leapt in dread lest it heralded Quinn's execution, and when she rose next morning, dull and listless, she was so convinced that some misfortune had overtaken him that it came as a shock of relief to see him standing in the doorway, waiting to intercept her on her way to Lakshmi's quarters.

His face was pale, unshaven, the eyes dark-shadowed.

'A word with you, Mrs Gisborne,' he said, and beckoned her outside. His manner scared her. As she followed him into the shade of the spreading peepul tree that overhung the tent, she felt a sense of impending doom.

'Sit down,' he said as if he hated the task ahead of him. 'We had news last night from Attaganj. Soon it will be all over the camp. I wanted to warn you first.'

234

'Warn me?' Her heart bumped uneasily. 'What has happened?'

'I am afraid what I have to say will distress you.'

White-faced, she stared at him. 'Please do not keep me in suspense.'

'The British have captured the city – at a cost. General Wellesley sent a force under Colonel William Hackett. They broke down the gate and took the place by storm. They found Trimbuck inside the palace. He had died by his own hand.'

Wellesley, Hackett, Trimbuck ... the names meant nothing to her. There was only one name she wanted to hear. Controlling her voice with difficulty, she said, 'Was George captured?'

'As far as I can ascertain, your husband and the Begum made their escape before the city was surrounded. Where they are now, no one knows.'

Kate drew a deep breath. After all, what had she expected? While the Begum wanted him, George would not come back to her. She saw from Quinn's face that there was more to come.

'Tell me the rest.'

'I fear it will shock you.'

'Tell me, nevertheless.'

He said in a clipped unemotional tone that told her more clearly than words how deeply he himself was shocked, 'Major Vance and the officers of the second battalion had been butchered by their own men. The British women and children were taken prisoner on Trimbuck's orders and confined in a Bibighar near the Palace. At first they were treated well enough. But when Trimbuck saw the British meant to storm the city, he sent an envoy to Colonel Hackett, threatening to kill his hostages unless they withdrew.'

He paused. Kate bit her knuckles. 'What was Colonel Hackett's answer?'

'He refused to negotiate unless the women were freed. When Trimbuck heard this, he ordered the guards to tie

235

the women in pairs, back to back, and fling them from the walls.'

Kate's head swam dizzily; she whispered, 'The children? Surely they would not – ?'

'The same.'

Sickened, she bowed her head. Mrs Bateson and Mrs Clark, their chattering forever silenced. Fat Ma Walpole and little Tommy. Luisa Gonzalez. The frail, pale Judson twins. All dead because she had not warned them of their danger.

'My fault.' She was hardly aware of speaking aloud. 'I killed them.'

'You must not think that.'

'It is true.' She sat very still, imagining their screams as they were hurled off the battlements, fighting down the hard dry sobs that threatened to stifle her. She must not cry in front of him.

'Mrs Gisborne, are you all right?'

Though his voice seemed to come from far away, she was conscious that he had moved close to her. Too close. His hand clasped her shoulder, and she struggled against the mad impulse to cling to him, sob out her guilt upon his shoulder. Blindly she stumbled to her feet.

'Where are you going?'

'I – I want to be alone.'

'Wait, Mrs Gisborne. I have something more to say.'

He saw her surprise and went on quickly, 'I am concerned for your safety.'

'Mine?'

'Let me explain. Last night the *vakil* sent by my master to Colonel Hackett brought back his answer. He dismisses Holkar's claim to Attaganj, out of hand. If we had been there at the storming – But no, it is too late to conjecture about that. My advice was not heeded. Hackett's decision has inflamed Jaswant Rao. Until the storm blows over, I cannot guarantee your safety here.'

'Because I am British?'

He nodded. 'Colonel Hackett's refusal comes at a bad time. For months Scindia has been inciting my master to

236

lead a new Maratha rising. This latest affront may tip the balance.'

'Cannot you prevent it?'

'I?' His laugh had a bitter edge. 'You over-estimate my powers of persuasion! I am beginning to believe I have lost any influence I ever had with him. While Sirji Rao is here to flatter and insinuate I can do nothing. Yet there was a time – not so long ago – when Jaswant Rao was as deaf to flattery as he is to my counsel now.'

'Ned thinks he is insane.'

'Insanity is the curse of the great Maratha families.'

'What will you do?'

He did not pretend to misunderstand her. 'If he declares war on the British? I will face that trouble when it comes . . . if it comes.'

'That is no answer, Colonel Quinn.'

'It is all you will get, Mrs Gisborne.'

'Why do you stay with him?'

A pause, and she feared she had overstepped the line between interest and impertinence. Then he said coolly, 'Because I serve him. And because of a promise I made to Ahalya Bhai.'

Their eyes met. After a moment's silence, he said, 'In the meantime, we must find somewhere safe for you. I suppose you have no wish to return to Attaganj?'

'No. A thousand times no.'

'In that case, I suggest the best place is the mission hospital at Chandargarh. Samuel Barnes is a good man. He has lately suffered the loss of his wife and will be glad of any help you can give with his patients. Will you go there?'

'Yes.' After a moment's consideration, she added, 'You are very kind.'

'Few of your compatriots would endorse that judgement.'

'Then they are worse than fools,' she said warmly.

'Believe me, Mrs Gisborne, my concern for your well-being is purely practical. I would not like Jaswant Rao blamed for any harm that befell you, but it is impossible to tell what follies he may commit in his present mood.'

She felt rebuffed, and said, 'I am capable of forming my own judgement without anyone's endorsement. When do you wish me to leave?'

He glanced round, lowering his voice. 'As soon as possible.'

'Today?'

'As soon as you can make ready.' He added with evident constraint, 'I must warn you to say nothing of your departure or destination to anyone, not even my wife. It is best she should be ignorant of your whereabouts. Make no mention of leaving. Simply ride out as usual with your *syce*, and I will meet you by the river.'

There was an urgency in his manner she had never seen before. Ned was right, she thought with a sinking heart. Colonel Quinn has lost his influence with the Maratha. I have become an embarrassment because he can no longer protect me.

'You are very pale, Mrs Gisborne. Are you fit to ride? The distance is no more than twenty miles.'

'I am perfectly well.'

'Good. Then I will tell Tuka Ram to saddle your mare.'

'If you do, word of my departure will be all over camp within an hour,' she said dryly. 'Why should you concern yourself with such a matter? Let me give the order myself.'

They had been speaking in low voices, standing so close that they almost touched. Now, as she moved past him to duck beneath the tent's low entrance, her eye caught a flicker of movement in the shadows, the faint glint of gold thread as a *sari* whisked away behind a screen. There were few secrets in a Maratha camp. She wondered which of Lakshmi's confidantes had been sent to spy on them, and how much of their conversation she had understood.

At the edge of the *sal* forest where the river disappeared into a foaming gorge between black sheer cliffs a hundred feet high, Quinn dismounted and signalled Kate to do the same.

'From here you must go alone.'

238

'Alone?' She could not believe he would abandon her in this dark sinister place.

'First I will show you the way to the mission. Give your mare to Tuka Ram. Come!'

Stumbling a little from stiffness, she followed him up rock-hewn steps to a promontory overlooking the thundering gorge.

'There.'

He pointed across the river to a group of white-washed buildings half-a-mile away, gleaming in the evening sun. A low central block stretched welcoming wings towards the river and round about were clumps of trees, cool green against the burnt earth.

'You see the path? The bridge?'

Kate nodded.

'Can you walk that far?'

'Walk? But my mare – '

'She must go with me. I need her to lay a false trail.'

He saw her astonished look and went on, 'Tonight your mare and Tuka Ram will return to camp with a sad tale. An accident in the forest. A springing tiger, a fall . . . His story will be believed, never fear.'

The long hot ride had dulled her wits. She said, 'How do you know?' and Quinn laughed.

'Because it is the story Holkar has bribed Tuka Ram to tell me! Fortunately, your *syce* had the good sense to inform me of it, and together we contrived this way to frustrate Holkar's plot.'

Hence the hurried departure, the secrecy. Kate bit her lip. 'Then I am more than ever in your debt – and Tuka Ram's.'

He brushed aside her thanks, saying, 'Samuel Barnes is a good man. He will look after you – if you will let him. I must return to camp before my absence is remarked. Can you go on alone?'

Never had she felt less inclined to go anywhere. She heard her voice say, 'When will I see you again?' and marvelled at its composure since all her instincts were crying out, begging him not to leave her.

239

'As to that, I cannot say, but I will send news whenever it is safe to do so.'

'Will you tell Ned where I am?'

He shook his head. 'It is best no one knows. Goodbye – Kate.' He took her hands, holding them in a warm firm grip. 'Do not be afraid. You are safe here. And before I go – '

Instinctively, she yielded as his lips came down on hers with a hard demanding sweetness. For a long moment her body pressed tight against his, aware of the pounding of his heart, hard muscle beneath the sliding softness of silk, the faint sharp tang of cardamom mingled with leather.

He released her and stepped back with his twisted smile. 'Are you angry? I should not have done that, but I have wanted to for so long.'

She analysed her feelings. 'Not angry. Surprised.'

'That I should dare to kiss you?'

'That I should like it.'

His grunt of amusement sounded spontaneous. 'Oh, Kate!' He held her hands tightly, and said, 'Now I must go. Tell Samuel Barnes I sent you, and I will call when I can . . .'

She watched the dark head and rose silk tunic take the steps in a few quick bounds. A moment later the clink of metal and soft thudding of hoofs on the forest path told her they had gone, and his kiss melted into the misty unreality of a dream.

Picking up the skirt of her habit and straightening her shoulders, she began to walk down the path towards the bridge.

16

'We make a good team, you and I,' said the Reverend Samuel Barnes with a sidelong look at Kate as she sat sewing, her dark head bent under a lamp, one steamy July evening. He appealed to his mother: 'Wouldn't you say so, Ma?'

'What's that, Curly? What's that you say?'

Samuel's grin broadened. Fifty years old, weathered and gnarled as an oak, he looked more like a village blacksmith than a priest. Only a narrow half-moon of pale fluff was left of the golden curls of his boyhood, yet Curly he remained to his mother and it had not been long before Kate, too, adopted the nickname.

A year had passed since she had stumbled exhausted into his garden; looking back she thought it had been the happiest year of her life. Working beside him in the hospital, sharing his simple home, she had found a purpose and contentment she had never known before. Even in the midst of poverty and famine, the strength of Curly's faith provided an inspiration to the destitute peasants who dragged themselves to the bank of the Chambal river, trying to escape the drought in the Deccan. Though the rains had come at last, it was too late for many of the starving peasants, who had eaten their buffaloes and seed corn – sometimes even their own children – in their desperate struggle to survive, but whatever their condition Curly took them in and fed them before sending them on their way to Gujerat. Sometimes, his mother scolded him for giving away too much of their own slender food-stocks, but he only smiled and said, 'God will provide for us as He did for Elijah in the wilderness,' and against all the odds he was right.

Now he raised his voice to answer his mother. 'I said Kate and I make a good team. I don't know what I'd have done without her, this Hot Weather.'

'Oh, very true, dear; very true. No need to bawl at me, Curly. I'm not deaf yet.'

Mrs Barnes raised her faded blue eyes from the sock she was darning and smiled at Kate. Though she was seventy and bent with arthritis, there were still moments when Kate glimpsed the gallant high-spirited girl who had followed her missionary husband to this wild place and helped him found his hospital. Of the five sons born to her, only Samuel had grown to manhood; and proof that he, too, had known tragedy lay in the row of small graves to which had recently been added the larger one of his wife, Annie.

He grieved for Annie openly, as he did everything, but had no hesitation in admitting that the pretty wife whose portrait smiled down from the sitting-room wall had been of little help in his work.

'She wasn't brought up to hardship,' he said, excusing her. 'She used to say the smell of sickness made her ill; and ill she was, poor love, most of the years she lived here. Her mother brought her up to be a proper lady. To hear her play the piano fair went to your heart. She never complained, but it's my belief she pined away, without all her pretty things. But there! What was I to do? I couldn't leave Ma here on her own after Father died.'

'Of course not. Still, you made her the garden.'

He smiled. 'Aye. She loved the garden. You like it too, don't you, Kate?'

She did more than like it. To her the garden with its rosebeds and carefully trimmed lawn, its little paths bordered with lavender and marigolds brought back the scents of home. It was a healing haven to which she repaired whenever the tide of human misery washing against the mission walls became too much to bear.

The Hot Weather had taken its usual toll, and the monsoon which followed filled the wards to overflowing. After the first week, new patients' cots had to be placed on the verandah, a prey to insects and the miasma of decay rising from the flooded river. But though the rains brought disease, they also gave hope. It had been the failure of the

242

previous year's rains that had caused the terrible famine now stalking the Deccan.

Stick-thin children with swollen bellies and huge resigned eyes came daily to the mission, and were given whatever nourishment Samuel could spare to help them on their way, but Kate knew that most of these unfortunates would never reach Gujerat. Yet how could they stay, when the constant passage of marauding armies over the devastated land had deprived them of seed-corn and buffaloes to rebuild their future?

Peace: the land cried out for peace.

Looking at Samuel, Kate thought he had lost two stone in weight since April had sent the thermometer soaring and brought refugees flooding in. His cassock hung loose on his big frame, and there were fresh grooves round his mouth and eyes. But now they hoped the worst was over. This year's rains had been abundant. There had been no fresh cases of typhoid fever for a whole week. Though smoke still drifted from the burning *ghats* across the river, blades of tender green had begun to spring from the mud as the water receded. If only the land could be granted six months' peace and the harvest safely gathered, it might sustain its inhabitants once more.

Six months' peace; it seemed little to ask. But always the threat of armed men descending like locusts to strip the countryside brought Kate's heart to her mouth whenever she heard hoof beats.

Situated as it was at a river crossing, the mission attracted snippets of information from the outside world. These were frequently contradictory and confusing, but one thing was all too plain. Undeterred by the defeat of his fellow chiefs, Holkar was out to make trouble and the patience of the Governor-General was wearing thin. It could only be a matter of time before Lord Wellesley decided to teach the Marathas another lesson.

Where, thought Kate, would Colonel Quinn's loyalty lie then? In all her months at Chandargarh she had heard no word of him, though only this morning an Afghan horse-dealer, bringing his son to the mission for treatment to

243

an infected camel-bite, had given her unwelcome news of George. By his account Jowraj Jung was still high in favour with the Begum.

'Aiee! He drives a hard bargain, does Jowraj Jung!' said the dealer admiringly. 'Fifty of my best horses, he bought, and the Kabuli stallion, for only a quarter of their true worth. It is said the Begum will marry him and give him command of all her troops.'

Fool that she was to imagine he might have begun to regret his defection! Kate kept her face expressionless and busied herself dressing the boy's leg.

The dealer was still bursting with news.

'Have you heard how the Sircar's cavalry was defeated at the Mokundara Pass? They say five hundred *sowars* died and Lookhan Sahib – he who betrayed Scindia at Aligarh – was taken captive and cut in fifty pieces.'

She disliked the man's tone, half-awed, half-gloating. He was trying to frighten her. Any show of interest or alarm would encourage him to further flights of fancy.

'I have heard nothing', she said shortly.

'What does he say about the Mokundara Pass?'

She had not realized Samuel was at her elbow. 'Something about a massacre. I expect he's making it up.'

'Tell what thou hast heard, brother,' said Samuel quietly.

Under his patient questioning the tale emerged: even allowing for exaggeration it was a disturbing one. The uneasy peace was over, and the British now openly at war with Holkar.

At the start of the rainy season, General Lake had despatched a strong force consisting of five battalions of infantry and three thousand Irregular Horse under the command of Colonel Monson, with orders to act vigorously against Holkar, confiscating his possessions and driving him back to his capital at Indore. At the same time, a second force under Colonel Murray marched from Gujerat, with the intention of forming a junction with Monson and catching Holkar between the pincer's jaws.

Monson had advanced and Holkar – in classic Maratha fashion – retired before him until he judged the British force sufficiently isolated, whereupon he had doubled back on his tracks and confronted Monson, who in his turn retreated to the Mokundara Pass.

'The fool! The shatterbrained addlepate!' groaned Curly, but he spoke in English for Kate's ears alone. 'Did no one tell him you must never, *never* retreat before a Maratha?'

It seemed no one had. Dismayed, they listened to the rest of the story: the British force split up, their rearguard routed, the capture and death of Lieutenant Lucan.

'Aye, they would have singled him out for revenge,' said Curly, nodding. 'He was in service with Scindia once, you know, and repaid him with treachery by admitting the British into Scindia's fortress at Aligarh. Well, he is hoist with his own petard and I cannot be sorry for it. If there is no trust between our races, how can there be peace? But Monson, now – that is a bad business. This will undo all Wellesley's work.'

The Afghan could add little more. He thought the British were retreating north in disarray with Holkar hot on their heels, and every Bhil, Pindari, and dispossessed Maratha who still owned a horse was flocking to be in at the kill.

'All last year's work undone. When will it ever end?' said Curly that evening. She had never seen him so depressed. 'That blockhead Monson! Brave as a lion and about as much sense. Heaven help this poor country while dolts like him are put in authority.'

'You know him?'

'Aye. I have the honour of the Colonel's acquaintance,' he said dryly. 'I was not always such a stay-at-home, you know. When I was chaplain in His Majesty's service I saw enough of fighting men to last me a lifetime, and Monson had no more sense then than he has now.'

While his mother sat with them after supper they talked of other matters, but when the old lady had retired to bed, Curly returned to the subject of the Afghan's news.

'Forgive me, but I could not help hearing him speak of your husband,' he said with his usual directness. 'Did he give you hope of seeing him again?'

'Hope that he would return to me?' She found it restful

245

to talk to a man with whom there was no need to tailor her answers. 'On the contrary! George must have played his cards well. It is said the Begum intends to marry him.'

'She can hardly do that while he is married to you! She professes the Catholic faith, you know. I daresay she finds an assumption of piety useful in fending off unwanted admirers, though in this case she must find herself in something of a cleft stick.'

He paused, then added with a hesitancy that was rare with him, 'Do you still care for him, Kate?'

Had she ever cared for him? It seemed doubtful now if he had ever cared for her. Perhaps for the few brief months of Jacky's life . . .

'What difference does it make? I am married to him.'

'There is such a thing as divorce.'

Divorce. The word lay between them like a double-edged sword which neither cared to grasp. Divorced women were a breed apart, objects of lewd speculation, pity, or shame.

'He has given you ample grounds to seek a divorce.'

Kate said edgily, 'How can I divorce him when I do not even know where to find him? The courts would laugh at me. Besides, I cannot see I would be better off than I am now, even if the action was successful.'

'Can you not?'

There was no mistaking his meaning. Kate looked up, seeing his face flushed with hope, his shining eyes more like a boy's than a man of fifty.

He rose and crossed the room. Standing behind her chair he placed his hands firmly on her shoulders as he said with almost painful intensity, 'I want you, Kate! I want to marry you. I've kept silent as long as I could, but today when I heard there's trouble on its way, I made up my mind to speak out.'

'Is trouble on its way?'

He raised his hands a little and let them fall again. 'Bound to be. That's why I want to get matters straight between us. I want you to know that whatever happens you're not alone any more. What do you say, Kate? Will you divorce Gisborne and marry me?'

With a strangely constricted throat she tried to give the answer he wanted but the words would not come. He was good, kind, strong, patient – and he loved her. He was everything George had never been. She had only to say yes and her problems would be solved, her future assured. Curly would take charge of everything. He would know how the divorce should be managed and how to bring George to a sense of his obligations. He would extract a fitting settlement so she did not come to him penniless – and even if she did, he would not care. He had taken her in before when she was destitute.

She made herself think what marriage to Curly would be like. She would be safe with him, happy and fulfilled as she had never been with George. Perhaps they would have children – strong healthy children able to withstand the Indian climate. She pictured a row of curly golden heads, rosy-cheeked faces with their father's open smile.

'Would you marry a divorced woman? What would your mother say?'

He laughed, she thought with relief. 'Ma? You don't have to worry what *she'd* think! Why, she's been nagging me for months, telling me I'd miss the boat. She wants to see her grandchildren before she's too old.'

'And you?'

'How can you ask? Divorced, widowed, single – it makes no odds. I've loved you ever since I saw you hobbling across that bridge, almost too tired to walk. I looked at you then, and I looked again, and I thought, that's the woman for me. I'll wait for her if it takes a lifetime.'

The simple declaration went to her heart. Why, then should the hideously pocked and scarred face of Colonel Quinn take shape in her mind's eye, so plain she could see the particular twist of his mouth as he had said, 'Samuel Barnes will look after you – if only you'll let him.'

She closed her eyes but the image lingered and she knew why she could not accept Curly's proposal. Damn Colonel Quinn, she thought. Damn myself for a treacherous, double-dealing, deceitful coward.

Curly misinterpreted the spasm of self-disgust that crossed her face. 'Forgive me, I have spoken too suddenly.'

'No . . .'

'You need time to reflect.'

She sensed his disappointment and cursed her own inability to respond with the warmth he expected – and deserved. It was the best offer she was ever likely to have. Why couldn't she accept as simply as he proposed?

'I am sorry – ' she began, and he cut her short as if to stifle the refusal he dreaded.

'That you cannot answer me at once? No, no. It is I who should ask your forgiveness. I did not mean to force a decision upon you – heaven forbid! So long as you allow me to hope I am content to wait for your answer.'

If I was not such a miserable coward I would answer him at once, she thought with bitter self-disgust. Waiting will only make it worse. But she could not bring herself to blight his hopes with a flat rejection, and instead turned to lay her hand over his as it lay on her shoulder.

'I am honoured, dear Curly – more honoured than I can say. If you will give me a little time . . .'

'All the time you wish,' he said stoutly.

She was relieved to see his usual expression of resolute optimism replace the anxious supplicating look. He gave her shoulder a final pat and, murmuring something about checking the wards, went towards the door.

'Shall I come with you?'

Usually he was glad of her company on his late rounds, but tonight he shook his head. 'I'll go alone.'

Standing by the window, she watched his lantern bob across the patch of glistening mud that had once been lawn. The patients were housed in the long wings running at right-angles to the central block of bungalows. Somewhat to Kate's surprise the bobbing lantern carried on past the wards, past the small wooden chapel, and turned sharp left in the direction of the stables.

Rain drummed on the tin roof of her bedroom, and the dank humid air trapped inside had saturated clothes and furnishings so the mouldy smell of decay pervaded the room. White ants swarmed round the legs of her string cot, which were set in bowls of water to prevent the ants gnawing the wood, and weird creatures blundered about the lamp, singeing wings and legs in reckless self-immolation. As she began to undress she noticed with a shiver of disgust that one of the soft leather slippers Curly had given her at Christmas was host to a thriving colony of maggots; however, she was glad to see that the family of musk-rats she had reluctantly ejected from her only sun-bonnet that morning had not deserted her but had set up house again behind the tin trunk in which her few possessions were stored. She was fond of these gentle rodents – not rats at all but *sorex coerulescens*, the heavenly shrew – whose warbling and chittering accompanied her preparations for bed. Their quiet domesticity was as appealing as their determination to rid her bedroom of cockroaches and beetles. Blowing out the lamp, she watched until their small shadowy forms emerged for the night's hunting: mother first, followed by her four babies, each grasping the tail before it between its teeth, so the whole procession wriggled across the floor like a many-legged hairy dragon.

Her heavenly shrews would spend the dark hours teaching their children how to find and hunt their prey, so that in the morning she could step with confidence across a floor scoured clean of grubs and bugs. Less welcome tenants of her room were the mosquitoes whose high-pitched warning sounded intermittently round the net shrouding her bed, while the steady rasp of teeth against the bathroom door told her it was some rat's ambition to escape the relentless downpour. Twice she sat up and clapped her hands, and once threw a hairbrush at the source of the noise. Each time it stopped, waited a while, and then began as steadily as before.

After four years in India such noises had ceased to bother her. Throwing back the damp sheet she spread herself face down on the bed, limbs outstretched for maximum coolness, and fell into an uneasy sleep.

When she woke at dawn the rain had stopped, leaving a

warm unrefreshing fog wrapped about the buildings. She rose and walked down to the river for her usual morning stroll, glancing in the stable as she passed. Only one stall was occupied, not by Curly's heavy-boned countrybred but a horse of very different calibre: a fine-skinned, long-tailed bay Arab, racked up to the manger, picking at cut grass.

A traveller's horse, she thought. It was not unusual for people to stable their horses at the mission when the river was too high to ford. They would then cross the footbridge to transact their business at the village on the opposite bank. It was strange that Curly had not mentioned this visitor. So fine a beast must belong to a man of consequence. Wondering a little at his silence, she walked on.

This was the best – indeed, the only – time for exercise. Before she reached the bank she glanced round and saw her shadow was with her: ten-year-old Amos, the orphan who tended the mission garden, tousle-haired and bandy-legged, his bandolier across his chest and the long-barrelled matchlock slung on his shoulder. He placed his palms together in silent greeting and slipped past to walk in front of her, eyes alert for snakes or the blunt-nosed muggers who hauled themselves out of the water at night to lie like logs across the warm sand. At this time of day they were sluggish, needing the sun's warmth to quicken their reflexes. Birds hopped impudently within range of their terrible jaws at dawn, but were careful to give them a wide berth at noon.

Wild life teemed on the banks. Once she had come upon a cloudy-grey and black-striped fishing-cat in the very act of scooping a fish from a pool; and often a stealthy approach to a favoured drinking-hole was rewarded by the sight of a dozen deer gathered by the water, their reflections meeting their bodies to form strange heraldic images in the limpid mirror.

Today she walked quickly, head bent, busy with her thoughts. Curly's precipitate proposal had pushed worry about the rumoured massacre at Mokundara to the back of her mind, yet this morning she realized that the one had provoked the other.

Trouble was coming, he said, and no one was better able

to recognize the signs. If Holkar had declared war on the British, neither persons nor property would be safe. Quinn had lost his long struggle: would he break the promise he had made to Ahalya Bhai and quit Holkar's service? Would he be allowed to? And what of Ned, Lieutenant Vickers, Captain Dodd – all the riff-raff of cashiered Company officers who had attached themselves so profitably to Jaswant Rao's service? Would he let them go – as Scindia had allowed Lieutenant Lucan to go – and place their knowledge at the enemy's disposal? Holkar had seen how such generosity was repaid: he would not make the same mistake.

Trouble was coming. Last night she could not see why Holkar should bother to molest the mission hospital, but this morning her brain was functioning again. The Mokundara Pass lay no more than fifteen miles distant. It was all too likely that survivors and stragglers from Colonel Monson's army would be brought to them for treatment. What if Holkar descended upon them then?

Unconsciously she quickened her pace, almost treading on Amos' heels. She should not have gone out without telling Curly. Perhaps he would want to move his patients to a safer place and needed her help. She must find him quickly, discover if he shared her anxiety. Perhaps he had learned something from last night's traveller. It was curiously out of character for him to say nothing about the horseman's arrival . . . curious and sinister.

'Stop, Amos. We will turn back.'

He looked round in surprise. Her usual walk was twice as long as this, a five-mile circuit that brought them back to the mission from the other direction.

'Back longee same, memsahib?'

'It is going to rain.'

She turned and began to walk fast the way they had come. Mist swirled about her, warm and heavy as a Turkish bath. Through it she heard the confused rumble of thunder and the sky darkened from lead to gun-metal bronze, warning of a fresh torrent about to break.

'Run, Amos!'

As she broke into a trot lightning split the sky and the rain came sluicing down, soaking her in a instant. With hair plastered to her skull and the wet folds of her cotton dress hampering every stride, she floundered through the puddles, oblivious to the branches whipping across her face and Amos' cries receding behind her. The path had become a stream along which she slipped and splashed with a single thought in mind: to get into shelter as soon as she could. Though these storms seldom lasted long, their violence was dangerous. River banks caved in and trees were uprooted to sail downstream like wrecked galleons, destroying all in their way.

She had outrun Amos. With bursting lungs she dropped to a walk, seeing with relief the blurred outline of the mission buildings through the veil of rain. The stable was nearest. She ducked under the low doorway and stood shivering and dripping on the mud floor.

The bay horse jerked nervously at his rope, rolling his eyes. Frowning, she stared at him, her memory teased by that white-rimmed eye. He stamped impatiently and she moved out of range of his heels.

Standing in the entrance, she surveyed the back of the hospital wing where the female patients were housed. Abruptly as it had begun, the rain slackened: the storm was over. In a few minutes the ground would steam like a pan of drained cabbage, giving off much the same gaseous vapour. As she gathered breath for a last dash across to the bungalow, she heard a shout, and simultaneously a tongue of flame rose above the roof of the women's wing.

Her first thought was that lightning had struck the thatch and set it ablaze. Then she saw the horsemen gathered by a corner of the building, and knew that trouble had come sooner than expected.

Head and shoulders taller than his guards, Curly stood watching his life's work burn. She saw the rat-face of Sirji Rao Ghatke bending to question him, and whatever answer he got was not to his taste, for he raised his whip and struck the missionary full across the mouth.

What happened next was difficult to make out. There

252

was a sudden flurry of movement and Sirji Rao's gold turban vanished abruptly into the crowd. Like swarming bees, the tightly packed bodies swayed to and fro, scattering and rushing together. Then through a gap she glimpsed Curly. With a sword in one hand and a lance in the other, he was laying about him more like a berserk Viking than a man of God, towering above his foes as he cut swathes in the ranks of those nearest to him.

'Come, dogs! Come and get me!' she heard his exultant shout; but the dogs were reluctant to accept the invitation. With one last sweep of his sword, Curly cleared the way to the nearest horse and showing an agility astonishing in so big a man, sprang on to its back. The horse squealed and plunged, trampling the men who clutched at Curly's clothing, trying to pull him down. He burst through the crowd and was away at a gallop, heading for the river, while a dozen horsemen streamed behind him in pursuit.

The water's too high. He can't cross the river, thought Kate, watching in horrified fascination.

But Curly had no intention of swimming the raging brown flood. Instead, he turned towards the narrow footbridge made of cantilevered tree-trunks that spanned the gorge above the waterfall.

He could hardly have staged a more theatrical exit. The lowering pewter sky which heralded the next cloudburst was undershot with streaks of lurid orange light, in which the wall of jungle beyond the river assumed a deeper, more virulent green. As always before rain, the air had a peculiar clarity. Against the black cliffs the bridge looked a mere fragile thread, a strand of gossamer casually spun from bank to bank across the foaming torrent.

Yet for all its apparent fragility, the bridge was solidly constructed, strong enough to bear a horse's weight if the animal could be persuaded to step on to it. And now Kate and the watching Marathas saw a feat of horsemanship that held them silently spellbound, united in hope that daring would be rewarded with success.

The white stallion was Holkar's favourite mount, famed for speed as much as his courage and beauty, and he easily

253

outpaced his pursuers. Arriving at the bridge two hundred yards in front of the foremost, Curly drew rein and without apparent haste allowed the stallion to lower his head and sniff the planks before urging him forward. Gingerly yet boldly, placing his hoofs with deer-like delicacy, the horse stepped on to the narrow bridge and began to cross.

Silhouetted against the black cliffs, like an insect crawling along a cobweb, he went steadily forward until he reached the dangerously sagging middle, where the planks were slippery with rain and imperfectly joined. Only then did his courage fail. He baulked, turning his head back to where the other horses now milled about on the bank he had left, and neighed shrilly.

On his back Curly sat motionless, his long legs hanging below the horse's belly, unable to risk a clash of wills on such treacherous footing. For a long moment the tableau held.

Kate found she was holding her breath. Whenever in the future she had cause to think harshly of Marathas, she would remember this moment and qualify her opinion in its light. It would have been easy – so easy – for one of Curly's pursuers to dismount and run up behind the stallion on foot, frightening him into plunging forward into the abyss, but whether from chivalry or mere curiosity, the horsemen made no attempt to follow. Instead, they withdrew a little from the brink of the gorge, and silently watched the bulky figure on the small horse precariously balanced above the water.

'Go on!' Kate breathed, digging her nails into her palms. The horse half-reared, trying to turn and rejoin his companions. Curly left the reins loose, sitting apparently unconcerned as the animal danced uneasily on the slippery footing. Then his quarters bunched and he jumped lightly over the gap, landing as neatly as a cat on a wall. With no further hesitation he picked his way up the slope until he stood safe on the farther bank.

'*Shabash!*

The spontaneous shout of applause could not have carried above the noise of the water; nevertheless, Curly turned to look back. He raised his fist in a gesture half of defiance, half farewell. Then he patted the little horse's neck and trotted away to vanish in the trees.

Kate leaned on the stable door, heart thumping, legs weak with reaction. When she looked up, the mad dog himself stood before her.

'A brave man.'

He was sober, the twitching muscle temporarily still.

'Where is Sikander Sahib?' he demanded. 'Tell me where to find him and we will not harm you.'

She stared at him: so that was why the bay horse seemed familiar. As the reason for this callous wanton destruction sank in, anger overcame her fear.

'Is that why you came here? To find Colonel Quinn? Is that why you have destroyed these poor people's only refuge and driven away the only man who cares for them? Well, you have wasted your journey. Colonel Quinn is not here. Your spies should have told you that.'

The single smouldering eye held her transfixed, a rabbit before a stoat. 'Then we will take you instead,' said Holkar, and signed to his guards.

'When the milk-white doe bleats, the tiger leaves his lair,' leered Sirji Rao Ghatke and Kate's heart sank. Quinn had escaped but only temporarily. They planned to use her as a bait to lure him back.

George Gisborne's lips curved in a beatific smile. His eyelashes were pale half-moons against the brick-red skin of his cheeks as he lay, dead to the world, on the Begum's couch, his curly yellow head pillowed on the bosom of her prettiest serving-maid.

The Begum sighed, suspicion confirmed beyond doubt. What fools men were! She could have made him a king, yet he threw away the chance of power and glory for the sake of a pretty slut. Silently, she let the curtain fall into place.

Gliding back to her boudoir, she called to the servants to take up the rug in the centre of the floor and bring spades.

'Dig deep,' she ordered, watching them labour.

When all was prepared to her satisfaction, she called for her officers to attend her.

'You sent for me, Highness?' George stood before her, freshly bathed and shaved, still glowing with the special radiance of sexual satisfaction, but there was a question in his eyes. She had told him her journey would take a month. Ranged behind him stood her French officers, tense and expectant. Word of the digging had flown round the camp, though no one had spoken of it to George.

'It seems, Colonel Gisborne, I am back sooner than expected,' she said coldly.

'Your return can never be too soon, Highness,' he said, smiling into her eyes.

'Liar!' She spat in his face.

George stepped back, rubbing at his cheek, alarmed and confused. He glanced round. The French officers were not troubling to hide their grins; behind them the dark Maratha faces were closed and hostile.

'Arrest him!'

George struggled unavailingly as his arms were gripped from behind. 'What are you doing? What have I done? Your Highness, there is some mistake. Tell these men to release me.'

'Bring in Bhagirthi.'

As the girl was led in, unveiled and dishevelled, her pretty face blotched with tears, George realized the nature of his peril and turned deadly pale. He began to bluster.

'Let me go! I can explain! You are making a terrible mistake.'

'Do you deny lying with this girl?' demanded the Begum. More than ever she resembled a fierce small hawk, hooded eyes glaring, nose and chin implacably curved.

'Yes. No. Never seen her in my life. Don't pay any attention to those Frog-Eaters, Highness! They'd tell any lie to get me put away. Madam, on my honour, it was nothing. A passing fancy – '

'Which you may indulge as long as you have breath,' said

256

the Begum very sweetly, and turned her face from him. 'Bind them,' she snapped. 'Throw them in the pit.'

Two of her guards bent swiftly and drew aside the rug before her dais. Under it the black hole yawned emptily. As the soldiers dragged him towards it, George struggled frenziedly, roaring like a wounded bull.

'Highness, you can't do this! Black bitch! Murdering whore! Let me go! You'll pay for this! Save me, save me!' he appealed to the French officers in an extremity of terror; but they shrugged and would not meet his eyes. They would not risk the Begum's displeasure, and George had never been popular.

It took a dozen guards to bind him to the sobbing girl and carry them bodily to the pit. Even when his head was below the level of the earthen floor George continued to curse and blaspheme, calling the Begum every foul name he knew, while she listened with her face set as hard as that of a temple goddess.

'Fill in the pit,' she ordered.

The guards seized spades and worked with a will, flinging spoil over the pair in the pit, while they ducked and dodged and tried to keep the suffocating earth from filling their eyes and noses. Hardened though they were to atrocities, the French officers murmured among themselves, but a single fierce glance from their mistress was enough to quell any move to George's aid. As his shouting empurpled face vanished under the soil, two of the younger mercenaries fainted and most of the others turned pale.

When the hole was filled and the earth stamped down, it still trembled, like a molehill about to erupt. With a contemptuous glance at her green-faced officers, the Begum ordered the rug to be spread over it, and called for her hookah.

Seating herself upon the rug, she dismissed the stunned Frenchmen, telling them she would appoint a new Commander-in-Chief the next morning. Silently they filed out, leaving her alone to smoke and brood, seated upon loosened earth that gradually ceased to tremble.

17

General Lake's jolly red face creased into a smile of welcome as Colonel Quinn, tight-lipped and travel-stained, wearing a borrowed tunic and plain white pantaloons above his dusty boots, came into the tent and saluted.

'Come in, Colonel, come in!' he said genially. 'I am glad to make your acquaintance at last. I knew your father – a gallant officer.'

'Thank you, sir.' Quinn saluted.

They measured glances. Lake said bluffly, 'No use pretending we've not had our differences in the past, eh, Colonel? I've cursed you often enough, but that's all water under the bridge. Now we must put those differences behind us.' He gave Quinn a straight look. 'One thing I must make plain. His Excellency has offered an amnesty to British officers who've served native princes, whatever the circumstances. All right and good. Glad to have you join us. But I warn you I will not tolerate divided loyalty – is that understood?'

'Yes, sir.'

'Excellent.'

Lake was not a man to harbour grudges nor, at this low point in British military fortunes, was he inclined to look a gift horse in the mouth. Colonel Quinn's escape from the massacre of Holkar's officers was a piece of luck, in his view, and the offer of his services more than welcome. In his kindly way he set about putting the newcomer at ease.

'I won't disguise from you, Colonel, that we're in the devil of a mess,' he said frankly. 'This unlucky retreat of Monson's has cost us dear. Bad business, bad business! Nothing succeeds like success in a Maratha's eyes. Until we inflict a damaging blow, Holkar's prestige will increase. His cavalry runs rings around us. I must force a general action, but how to pin him down?'

When Quinn was silent, he went on, 'Half our native allies have reneged on their promises already. Unless we bring Holkar to heel the rest will follow. You have heard the Begum Samru tore up her treaty?' His smile was indulgent. 'Of course, the lady is a law to herself. I should never have trusted her. Still, it's an ill wind blows nobody good. The latest despatch from Sardhana informs me that rogue George Gisborne has got his just deserts at last. Seems the Begum caught him *in flagrante* and had him buried alive.' His smile faded. He leaned forward, planting his elbows on the map-table, his big face solemn.

'Where *you* can help, my dear fellow, is by reading Holkar's mind. No one knows him as you do. What is his strength? Where will he strike next? If we knew that, we would be ready and waiting.'

Quinn shook his head. Who could read a madman's mind? Like a cannon loose on a gun-deck, Holkar charged here and there without reason. His strength lay in his very unpredictability.

'Well, Colonel?'

'I cannot guess where he will strike, sir, but I may be able to find out. If I may recruit *hircarrahs* to gather intelligence – '

'Recruit whom you please, my boy. I give you *carte blanche*. Pick and choose among my officers as you like.'

'Thank you, sir.'

'I need hardly stress that the matter is of the first urgency. *I* cannot gallop here and there with my country on my saddle-bow, as Holkar claims to! Nor can I besiege twenty fortresses in the hope of finding him there. I need information, Colonel, and look to you to provide it.'

'I will do what I can, sir.'

As they discussed ways and means, Quinn was favourably impressed by Lake's direct manner and quick grasp of essentials. Here was a man he could work with, who understood *sepoys*. It was a pity he was ill-served by his subordinates.

When Quinn rose to leave, the Commander-in-Chief put out a hand to detain him and said in his bluff cordial way,

'I was told of your own sad loss. Your wife, I understand? Permit me to offer my condolences.'

Quinn bowed. 'I should have sent her away to safety. There were signs, God knows. I must have been blind.'

'No use blaming yourself, my boy,' said Lake consolingly. 'We all make mistakes. Who can tell when a dog will run mad? You have my sympathy, believe me.'

Quinn murmured an acknowledgement and took his leave. Poor pretty foolish Lakshmi! He had not been the husband she wanted. Perhaps if she had had children to occupy her, she would not have fallen for Sirji Rao's blandishments. He had squeezed all the information he could from her, and tossed her aside; she had died along with Dodd, Vickers, Ryan, and all his brother officers who refused to fight their fellow countrymen. His own life he owed to Ned, who had ridden by night to meet him and warn him of the massacre. Together they had fled north, with Holkar's men hot on their heels. It had been at the swollen Chumbalee river that Ned and his horse were swept away in the raging water. Of all Holkar's mercenaries, Quinn alone had survived.

When he begged help from Samuel Barnes, he thought the missionary less than pleased to see him; he had been firm in refusing Quinn's suggestion that Kate would be safer at General Lake's headquarters. It was plain he was in love with her, and anxious to see the back of any possible rival.

'She is safe enough here. The Marathas have never troubled us before – why should they do so now? I must tell you, Quinn, Mrs Gisborne and I have an . . . an understanding. There are difficulties, but in time, with God's help, we shall overcome them.' For a moment his voice had faltered, then he said very firmly, 'I know I can make her happy.'

His candid blue eyes met Quinn's, and in them blazed a message quite at variance with his words: Hands off. She is mine. Take your troubles elsewhere and leave us alone.

'I wish you both most happy,' Quinn had murmured, since there was nothing else to say. 'Certainly you deserve it. Now, about that horse? I fear my poor beast can go no farther.'

The relief on Samuel Barnes' face had been unmistakable. He led away the lathered bay and saddled his own countrybred, eager to do anything that would speed the departure of this unlooked-for, unwelcome visitor.

In the evening sun the mission looked sturdy and secure, its wide wings welcoming. Kate would be safe here, thought Quinn. Samuel Barnes would look after her. He wondered why the reflection gave him so little pleasure.

A month passed, during which Quinn worked hard to establish his network of intelligence on the fringes of Holkar's territory, which expanded almost daily as more small chiefs flocked to join his army and avail themselves of the rich opportunities it afforded for looting the property of any landowner foolish enough to remain loyal to his treaty with the British.

Like a bull tormented by gadflies, General Lake's army – complete with ordnance and baggage train – lumbered here and there, attempting to pin down the quicksilver Maratha cavalry, but the task was hopeless. British prestige was at its nadir; Wellesley's victories in the Deccan and Lake's own in Hindustan were now no more than memories, fast fading as Holkar's star rose. Even reports of his increasingly frail grasp of reality did nothing to diminish the awe in which he was held. Sanity was no prerequisite for a warleader: rather the reverse. How many of history's greatest conquerors had been touched by God?

In such a climate of opinion, it was taxing work to squeeze information from headmen and harlots, *banyas* and *ghari*-drivers, naked fakirs, sepoys, peddlers, peasants and all the flotsam of India's multi-racial society, whose fragments of knowledge pieced together might yield the secret of how Holkar might be destroyed.

'We are poor men. Our families cry for food. Why should we bring the wrath of the Marathas upon our village?' was a common response to Quinn's enquiries. 'Ask your questions elsewhere, brother. We can tell you nothing.'

Nevertheless, he persevered, picking up a word here, a message there; gleaning and weaving these fragments into a detailed report to lay before the British Commander-in-Chief.

It was when he returned from patrol one October evening with the whirr of ducks' wings and haunting bassoon concerto of frogs rising from a nearby *jheel* bringing to mind pleasant thoughts of the approaching hunting season, that he ducked under the entrance of his tent and found his *charpai* already occupied.

The sight of the gangling length of Captain Sweeney stretched out on the string cot, dead to the world, sent Quinn's spirits soaring.

'Ned! By all that's wonderful!'

Yawning and rubbing his eyes, Ned sat up, grinning sleepily at his astonishment. 'Beg pardon for commandeering your bed, sir! Must have dropped off waiting for you.'

'Where the deuce have you been? I thought you must have perished.'

'Ah, you don't get rid of me so easily! Truth is, my horse got tangled in a net. The poor beast drowned, but I scrambled ashore . . . and here I am.'

'That won't answer, you wretch! Give me the full story,' commanded Quinn, and Ned's grin faded.

'It does not make pretty hearing. I followed the line of Monson's retreat – such carnage as I have never seen. You remember the mission near Chandargarh, on the bend of the Chambal?'

'What of it?' Quinn demanded, his voice sharp with anxiety.

'It took me five days to get there, and when I reached it I found nothing left but a blackened shell. Holkar's work. They said at the village that he had come without warning, dragged the patients from their beds and fired the thatch.'

'The missionaries?'

Ned shook his head. 'Barnes escaped across the river – only to fall victim to *Bhils* in the hills. The villagers found his body. More than that I could not discover. The *patel*

262

begged me to leave since my presence put his village at risk if Holkar returned. As soon as I could, I made my way here.'

What it had cost him to struggle fifty miles through hostile country Ned did not say, but it was easy enough to guess. His tall frame was painfully thin, with shadowed eyes and grooves around that normally insouciant mouth. Quinn decided against burdening him with his own fears for Kate.

'What you need is a square meal and a bed of your own,' he said, clapping Ned on the shoulder. 'After that we'll see what employment General Lake can find for you.'

Ned slept off and on for three days, and in his waking intervals provided Quinn with a good deal of information. In particular, he was able to tell him that Holkar's treasure chests had been removed from Indore and taken to the fortress of Dig only a few days before the execution of his British officers. Ned himself had commanded the escort for the laden bullock-carts that effected the transfer; no doubt Holkar had felt confident that young Captain Sweeney would not live to tell the tale. This was excellent news.

'Sooner or later Jaswant Rao must return to Dig for funds,' Quinn told the Commander-in-Chief. 'That will be our best chance of catching him. Without his treasure, Holkar will find himself less welcome among his allies.'

General Lake listened carefully and rumbled agreement. Ten days later General Frazer, together with Monson, thirsting to recover his lost reputation, was despatched with a strong force of infantry and two regiments of cavalry, with orders to capture the fortress of Dig.

The Jat Raja of Bharatpur, to whom Holkar had entrusted his hostage, was a handsome courtly old man of ample figure and easygoing nature, much addicted to opium and Persian poetry. In every way he was the antithesis of his turbulent Maratha neighbours. He did what he could to alleviate the misery of captivity for Kate, allowing her to associate freely with his wives and their children.

'There is no quarrel between us personally,' he was fond of saying, 'so why should I treat you as an enemy?'

She was grateful for his generosity of spirit; grateful, too, for the time he spared to play chess with her. Chance remarks dropped during these games told her far more of events in the world outside than she could glean from the ladies, for all their chatter. Such fragments of news brought little comfort. Holkar's triumphal progress continued unchecked. He seemed to have a charmed life. His cavalry flitted here and there, burning and pillaging, evading General Lake's attempts to catch them as easily as a gazelle outruns an ox. His threat to lay waste the British possessions between the Jumna and the Ganges now seemed a real danger. But cocooned in the thick-walled fortress, attended by servants and treated with every consideration, Kate knew the kind of luxurious captivity enjoyed by royal hostages in medieval England.

It was with considerable dismay that she learned in late November that she must change her quarters.

'I shall be most sorry to lose your agreeable company,' said her courteous gaoler. 'But Jaswant Rao demands it and I must comply.'

'Why must you?' Agitation sharpened Kate's voice. 'He is an upstart – a robber chief. You are the Jat Raja!'

He spread pudgy hands in a gentle deprecating gesture. 'In the days of Ahalya Bhai my father made an alliance with the house of Holkar. Now Jaswant Rao calls in the debt I cannot refuse him.'

'Where are you sending me?' she asked fearfully.

'Forgive me, that I cannot reveal.'

'When?'

'Tonight, I fear . . .'

'What if I should escape?' she said, testing him, hoping he would agree to turn a blind eye; but he answered with such seriousness that she knew the hope was vain.

'I earnestly beseech you to put such thoughts from your mind. No, no! Do not try Holkar's patience. He is a most violent fellow and when you leave Bharatpur I cannot help you.'

The look that accompanied his words, at once grave and pitying, sent a chill up her spine.

'A glass of wine?' he asked, seeing her shiver.

She forced a smile: a taste for expensive claret was one of the Raja's agreeable weaknesses.

'Thank you, Your Highness.'

The wine, when it came, proved a disappointment. Her first sip raised the suspicion that it was corked, or had otherwise suffered in India's unforgiving climate. Nevertheless for fear of wounding her kind host's feelings, she swallowed it bravely. Only when the furniture began to rock dizzily did it strike her that the wine was doctored, and by then it was too late.

'Sleep soundly, memsahib,' said the Raja with gentle regret as Kate's knees buckled and she slumped into a servant's waiting arms. With finicky care he adjusted the fringed shawl about his shoulders and making a half-ironical *namaste* towards the recumbent form of his guest, waddled majestically from the *zenana*.

Waterfowl rose in a scolding cloud from the tufted surface of the marsh that extended in a wide half-moon before the fortress of Dig. Whistling and quacking, they flew above the heads of Captain Sweeney and his detachment of Irregular Cavalry, before returning to settle on the water which glowed pink in the setting sun.

Ned cast them a longing glance. There was sport to be had here in plenty, but first men and beasts must be quartered and he must make his report to General Frazer.

Four days had passed since the gallant *sepoys* of the seventy-sixth had snatched victory from defeat by capturing the fortified village outside the walls of Dig. Under a punishing hail of round, chain and grapeshot, they had charged Holkar's batteries and chased his infantry inside the fortress. It had been a rough, tough, bloody affair. Twenty-two European officers together with over six hundred *sepoys* had been killed or wounded, while enemy losses were reckoned around two thousand.

Only an optimist would consider this a satisfactory state of affairs. What remained of Holkar's infantry was now firmly entrenched in a fortress whose eighteen-foot thick walls were impervious to cannon, while the flooded ditch that surrounded the stronghold made the use of scaling-ladders impracticable.

Holkar and his cavalry, meanwhile, remained free to ravage the countryside, defying all General Lake's attempts to catch them. Day after scorching day the Company cavalry rode in pursuit of their elusive foe, only to have him slip through their fingers. Once it was the clattering of steel scabbards that alerted the Marathas in the nick of time; once a stallion neighed to a lovelorn Maratha mare and aroused the camp. Nevertheless –

'Tonight we'll nab 'em,' muttered Ned, standing up in his stirrups to ease his aching back after thirty miles in the saddle. 'This time they won't get away.'

A week of careful reconnaissance had brought Colonel Quinn's mounted force within striking distance of Holkar's latest camp, and so far the Marathas seemed oblivious of their enemy's presence.

'If they run, it will be for Dig,' Quinn had decided, tapping the position of the fortress on the map. 'Farrukhbad has fallen to us, Nina and Shahganj are in our hands. It must be Dig this time.'

Whereupon he had despatched Ned with twenty *sowars* and a message warning General Frazer of his intentions. 'We shall fall on them in the dark. If Frazer will turn out his cavalry in support, we should bag the lot.'

Ned rode hard, knowing the success of the manoeuvre depended on closing the jaws of the pincer simultaneously. He reached the British camp outside Dig before nightfall, but there a double disappointment awaited him. Not only had General Frazer been killed in action while leading the charge on the second range of Maratha guns, but command had devolved upon the newly-promoted Brigadier-General Monson, Quinn's most vociferous adversary, and ten minutes in this choleric officer's company was enough to damp Ned's hopes of his cooperation.

Brave, opinionated, and stubborn as the most refractory mule, Monson held the whole breed of military adventurers in deep contempt. He had watched with angry jealousy

Quinn's rise in favour with General Lake, and now saw an opportunity to discredit him.

'You ask me to turn out my cavalry at night on the orders of Colonel Quinn?' he said testily, throwing down the despatch and fixing hot brown eyes on Ned. 'Indeed, I will do no such thing! He should know better than to make such a request.'

'But, sir, you must!' cried Ned, too tired and disappointed by this refusal to guard his tongue. 'We may never again get so good a chance to lay Holkar by the heels.'

'*Must*, Captain Sweeney? *Must*? Is this the mode of speech you are accustomed to use to your superiors?'

'I beg you, sir, to reconsider.'

The damage was done. A vein rose vertically in Monson's forehead: his face darkened to a dull puce.

'And I tell you plainly, Captain Sweeney, you would do well to remember where you are. These insolent manners may be permitted in a decadent oriental court – I cannot speak for that – but you are making a great mistake if you think they will answer here. In *my* camp you will accept *my* decisions – is that clear? I do not intend to turn out my cavalry on a wild goose chase at your request or Colonel Quinn's.'

Too angry to trust his voice, Ned saluted and stamped out. The fool! The damned fool! he raged, and cursed himself for his want of diplomacy. This decision had spiked Quinn's guns with a vengeance: there was no time to warn him that Monson had refused his support. The pincers would not close; he must return at once and tell Quinn just how his civil request had been received.

Despite the protests of his *daffadar*, Ned ordered his men to remount their weary horses. An hour after arriving there, he rode away from Monson's camp.

The humped forms of the sleeping Marathas stirred from time to time and grumbled in their dreams under the diamond-studded sky, but Holkar could not rest. His head ached fiercely, throbbing as much with half-formed schemes and thoughts of revenge as with the cherry brandy he had swallowed recklessly, striving to drown the bitter taste of defeat.

Bad news had been brought by a trembling *hircarrah* just as darkness fell. His infantry had been defeated and thirty pieces of ordnance lost. The great fortress of Dig was besieged – and by whom? Not Wellesley, or Lake, or any great British general with whom it would be an honour to do battle, but by that blundering red-faced ox Monson, whom he had chased from the Mokundara Pass to Agra.

How had it happened? Who was to blame?

Treachery! he thought, and the red tide beat at his temples, making his cheek jump and twitch. Wherever I go, wherever I turn, I am betrayed.

Like vultures gathering above a kill, the ghosts of all who had betrayed him circled round his head, wings flapping, naked necks obscenely stretched. The Frenchman Dudrenec . . . Vickers and Dodd . . . Quinn, Quinn who had sworn to be his brother . . . Foam flecked his lips as he beat off the winged scavengers, smothered by their feathers, suffocating in the rotten stench of their breath.

'Treachery!' he shouted, struggling unsteadily to his feet. 'Awake, brothers! To arms! We are betrayed!'

Colonel Quinn heard the hoarse shout as he sat tense in the darkness a hundred yards beyond the dying campfires, his pistol cocked ready to give the signal as soon as he knew his men were in position.

'*Mount, brothers! To arms!*'

Quinn could not believe it. They had made their approach with silent stealth, bits muffled, hoofs soundless on the sandy soil. Not a horse had snorted or a man hawked and spat; his own ears had detected no smallest variation in the bullfrogs' lovesong, no tiny disturbance that might put Maratha pickets on the alert.

Yet here was Holkar's husky unmistakable voice, roaring to rouse his men. Was he an animal, able to smell danger in the air?

'*To arms! We are betrayed!*'

There was no help for it: though his men could not yet be in position, Quinn raised his pistol and fired. Before the echoes died, his cavalry swept forward and pandemonium broke out among the sleeping Marathas. Shrill screams split the air as they struggled to unroll from their cloaks and snatch up weapons. The clash of steel and clang of over-turned cooking-pots mingled with the terrified neighs of horses entangled in their picket lines.

Where was Holkar?

Skirting the mêlée, Quinn spurred towards a small knoll crowned by trees outlined against the starry sky. As he reached it he saw his instinct had not failed him. A knot of men, already mounted, milled about the knoll; in the dark it was impossible to distinguish faces but Holkar's stallion was easy to identify, an ivory ghost among black shadows. Without hesitation Quinn pushed into the press and seized his reins close to the bit. The blacker shadows shoved and grunted, wheeled and reformed, melting away with the fluidity of *ghee* as they merged with the surrounding dark-ness leaving Quinn alone with his captive.

'Surrender, Maharaja!' he commanded.

A muffled laugh answered him. Striking a match, Quinn leaned forward to peer into his prisoner's face. An unknown boy's face, beardless and smooth, the eyes alight with mockery.

'Foxed, by God!'

Quinn dropped the boy's rein and set off in pursuit of the fleeing horsemen, cursing himself for falling for so hoary a ruse. The diversion had spoiled his chances. Angry and disappointed, he abandoned the chase and rode back to the ruin of Holkar's camp.

A number of Marathas had taken refuge in a grove of trees by the stream, and his victorious *sowars* were amusing themselves by shooting these outsize birds from the roost, cheering whenever one tumbled off his perch.

Curtly Quinn bade them desist, and gave orders for pris-oners to be marched to General Lake's headquarters. It was hard to admit, even to himself, that he had failed again. But there was still a good chance that Holkar would ride straight into the arms of Frazer's cavalry, assuming that Ned had accomplished his mission. In no very good temper, Quinn turned his own horse's head in the direction of Dig.

The days of luxurious captivity were over. Penned in a narrow stone cell below the level of the moat, where only a dim greenish light filtered through the barred window, Kate spent a week in discomfort and fear such as she had never known.

The dank walls oozed moisture. Her pallet of dirty straw was alive with bugs, and iron rings set into the floor hinted at more sinister practices than mere incarceration. She tried not to think how many poor captives must have suffered and died in this subterranean gloom, chained to the rings, unheard except by their uncaring guards. At least they had left her free to pace the length of the cell, six steps back and forth until she feared the repetition would drive her mad.

By the third day she was shivering with ague, determined to risk anything to escape, even if it meant facing Holkar himself.

'Take me to your master,' she ordered the surly guards who threw food into the cell at intervals. 'I have important information for him.'

'The Maharaja will send for you when he desires,' one told her curtly, and she thought they took pleasure in her misery. With insolent looks they withdrew, and she lay down on the mouldy straw, fighting panic. No one would know if she died here. She must keep calm, keep her wits about her. Somehow she must escape.

On the seventh day the guns began. At first a distant rumbling that could have been thunder, then muffled crashes that shook the walls and brought clouds of red dust drifting through the barred window. It settled in a fine film, rendering the air so thick she feared she might suffocate. Worse, it floated into the brass pot containing her ration of drinking water. Though she hastened to cover it, the damage was done. She shouted for more, but no one answered.

All day the bombardment continued and no one came

270

near her. Kate crouched in the corner farthest from the window, muffling her face in the folds of her sari. When at last the guns fell silent, an eerie stillness settled over the fortress. She fought down the fear that she was alone and forgotten, left to rot in this castle of the dead.

At last she heard the tramp of boots, quite different from the soft shuffle of native guards, and her spirits soared, believing the British must have triumphed and would set her free.

'Help, Help! Let me out! For the love of God, let me out!' she called, her tongue thick and furred with dust, her voice a husky croak.

Lamplight streamed into the cell as the door swung open. With it came an avalanche of uniformed men, bumping and shoving and ducking their heads to avoid cudgel blows as they were herded into the confined space.

The words died on Kate's lips as she stared in speechless horror. Five – six – seven men; blood-stained, smoke-grimed, manacled, beaten. Not rescuers, but captives like herself.

'Water!' groaned a young ensign. The bone of his shattered arm showed white through the smoke-darkened skin.

A guard aimed a blow at his head and he sank to the floor. Clouds of disturbed dust swirled in the lamplight, mingling with the bloodstains. With grunts and imprecations the guards lined their prisoners against the wall and set to work to shackle them in pairs. Each captive had one hand free, the other was manacled to a short chain by which he was attached to his neighbour. This chain ran free through the iron ring in the floor, so that while one man's hand was close against the floor, his partner enjoyed a yard of freedom and vice versa.

Kate huddled in her corner, greatly fearing the guards might take it into their heads to shackle her to the seventh man; but they ignored her. Their task completed, they left the cell, leaving the prisoners in darkness.

As their footsteps died away there was silence; then a clipped authoritative voice demanded: 'Who's here? Speak

271

up and identify yourselves. Name and regiment. I am Captain Parker of the Seventy-Sixth.'

A confused babble of voices responded, made unintelligible by the groans of the injured men.

'One at a time. From the right.'

'Corporal Bennett, zur,' came a slow Devonian drawl. 'Sixth battalion, Queen's Own.'

'Private Evans. Twenty-Fifth.'

'Captain Boniface, farrier-surgeon to the Highland Regiment.'

'Sergeant Pearce. Eighty-Eighth.' After a pause the last speaker added, 'This 'ere's young Mr Wilson of my regiment, sir. We was standing together when the shell 'it us. Reckon 'e's 'urt bad. An' the horficer in the corner is poor Major Sanderson.'

'Thank you, sergeant.' Kate heard Parker mutter in a lower tone, 'Jaw shot clean away, poor devil. Doubt if he'll last the night.' Aloud he said, 'Well, as senior officer present – acting, that is – I take command. The first thing to decide is how to get out of this hellhole.'

'Not so loud, sir – beggin' yer parding, sir,' hissed Pearce. 'What abaht that black bint a-settin' there listening?'

'*Black bint?*'

'Over there, sir. By the door. I see'd 'er the minute I come in, for all she set so still. They've left 'er there to spy on us, you mark my words.'

Strangely, now the time had come to identify herself, Kate found it difficult to speak.

'I am English,' she said at last. 'My name is Katherine Gisborne.'

There was a moment's astonished silence, then Captain Parker cleared his throat. 'Forgive me, ma'am. We did not know – had no idea – *what* did you say your name was?'

'Gisborne. Katherine Gisborne.'

'Wife to the former Resident in Attaganj?'

'Yes.'

When Captain Parker next spoke his tone had changed subtly, the surprise replaced by a disapproving, inquisitorial

272

edge. 'Perhaps, ma'am, you will be good enough to explain to us how *you* come to be here?'

As briefly and simply as she could, she told her story, feeling their disbelief growing, knowing with a sinking heart that George's treachery must be execrated throughout the Company service. It would take a good deal to convince his former comrades-in-arms she was not tarred with the same brush.

'A strange tale, indeed,' said Captain Parker coolly when she finished. 'Mrs Gisborne, I congratulate you.'

'Why should you congratulate me?' She did not like his tone.

'I am lost in admiration of your power of invention. A *tour de force*, ma'am. A real *tour de force*. 'Pon my word, you should go on the boards. You would make your fortune there.'

With difficulty she restrained her temper. 'What can you mean?'

'Why, simply that you might have had difficulty in explaining how you survived your husband without concocting some such cock-and-bull tale!'

'Survived my husband?' Shock robbed her of breath like a blow in the midriff.

Parker went on in the same sarcastic tone, 'So the Begum pensioned you off, did she? Provided for you as she did for poor George Thomas' brood? She has a reputation for charity to the relicts of her mercenaries.'

'Are you telling me my husband is dead?'

'My dear ma'am, do not take me for a fool! Do you seriously expect me to believe you are unaware of it?'

'I had no idea,' said Kate quietly. 'Whether you believe me or not, that is the truth.'

She pressed her hands to her face. Her cheeks were burning, partly from emotion, partly because the temperature in the cell was undoubtedly rising. Too many bodies packed into the confined space had made the air foul, and it was rapidly getting more so. She tried to say a prayer for George, but all she could think was that if the guards did not soon open the door they would all be dead by morning.

273

The farrier-surgeon shared her anxiety. He said roughly to Parker, 'Leave the lady be. Gisborne's sins are the least of our worries just now. This place is like an oven. Mrs Gisborne, if you have any influence with these devils, get them to open this door.'

'But I have no influence. I am a prisoner like yourself!'

'You're the only one among us with the freedom to move. Shout, ma'am! Pound on the door. Tell them they'll have no hostages to bargain with if we die of heat in here.'

She did as he asked, little dreaming it would have any result, but the door opened soon after she began to beat at it. The guard listened with his usual air of surly impassivity to her complaint, and went away. When he returned he was accompanied by a smiling Sirji Rao Ghatke.

'You wish to ask me something, memsahib?' he said in his soft, insinuating way, stooping to bring his narrow rat's face close to Kate in the light of the lamp held high by a guard. The stink of garlic on his breath repelled her. She would sooner face Holkar himself than this soft-voiced monster of depravity. Sirji Rao it was who had inspired all Scindia's most notorious acts of cruelty and was commonly regarded as his evil genius; but having once summoned him she was bound to voice her complaint.

'Of your favour, my lord, give orders that these men may be untied so I may dress their wounds. We are too many here; we cannot breathe. Truly, if your prisoners die you will make no profit from them.'

She spoke in the Maratha language and he answered in the same tongue. 'The memsahib is wise. There are too many prisoners here.'

Fastidiously he picked his way through the tangle of legs and bodies until he reached Captain Parker. He stared down at him with a speculative smile.

'Well, Englishman? Will you dance for me tonight?'

Parker did not understand and made no reply. Flying into a sudden fury, Sirji Rao kicked him viciously in the stomach, shouting, 'Dog! Do you defy me? Answer when I speak.'

Parker roared with pain and doubled up, writhing against his chain. 'What's the matter? What does he want?'

274

'He asks if you will dance for him,' said Kate tremulously. The blessed relief of air entering the cell made her head swim.

'Dance? Damn fool question! How can I – ? Ow! Stop him! Call him off. Damn you, this is your doing,' he snarled at Kate as he was unchained and dragged bodily past her. 'May you rot in hell along with the rest of them!'

The door swung shut, cutting off his shouts.

Kate said in a shaking voice, 'I said nothing, I swear. I tried not to anger him. They are mad – all mad!'

'I believe you, ma'am,' said the farrier-surgeon sombrely, 'but the fact is, you're the only one of us who can talk to them. Isn't that right, lads? Like it or not, our lives are in your hands.'

Three days passed – three hot interminable days with little to drink and less to stay their gnawing hunger. During the first night Major Sanderson died, and the next day the wounded ensign fell into a delirium, sobbing and calling for his mother so heartrendingly that it was almost a relief when he too gave up the ghost.

Though Kate pleaded with the guards to take away the dead bodies they refused absolutely to touch them, and with Captain Parker's disappearance fresh in mind, she was afraid to press them too far. Fat bluebottles hummed through the bars to cover the faces of the corpses with an iridescent moving blanket. Corporal Bennett and Private Evans, each still linked to a dead man, bore the horror stoically, rarely speaking except to ask Kate if she would moisten the strips of cloth torn from her sari which they all laid across their mouths in an attempt to filter the stench. A vain attempt. The foul miasma of corruption filled their lungs and permeated their whole bodies.

Tough, sun-hardened survivors of a dozen tight corners, Bennett and Evans cursed quietly from time to time, nursing their reserves of strength, determined to stick it out until their comrades stormed the fortress.

'Can't be long now,' muttered Sergeant Pearce as the guns began their daily bombardment. 'Once ole Lake brings up 'is siege train, 'e'll knock 'ell out o' the black bastards, see if 'e don't. All we got to do is 'ang on.'

The farrier-surgeon grunted. It was too much effort to speak. Between the remaining prisoners all barriers of rank and sex had vanished. Male and female, officer and enlisted men, they existed rather than lived in a limbo punctuated only by the alteration of light and darkness, noise and silence.

When the dish of scraps and single brass *lotah* with their day's ration of water were thrust through the door, Kate divided the food into five equal parts and crawled from man to man, distributing the miserable rations. In helping them eat and drink, she tried to avoid touching the putrefying corpses, but moving about the cell disturbed clouds of bloated flies, which buzzed sickeningly about her face and hands.

The task completed, she would fall ravenously upon her own share, trying to eke it out and at the same time fend off voracious insects. Too soon it was finished, though her stomach still growled with hunger, and she felt her strength ebb daily.

Hang on, she thought. He is right. We must all hang on. The sun moved across the cell and the temperature rose. The long hours stretched emptily ahead with nothing to do but doze and scratch, dream and pray, endure and wait . . .

18

'To our esteemed and beloved Brother – Greetings!

Too long have dark clouds of misunderstanding hidden from us the radiance of your Presence, while serpents' tongues poison our ears and defile the clear waters of friendship . . .'

Quinn grinned sardonically as his eye ran over the flowing Persian script. Old Munshi Babu's hand, if he was not mistaken, writing at Holkar's dictation.

'Esteemed and Beloved . . .' I *have* gone up in the world, he thought. So Jaswant Rao is ready for some horse-trading and needs my help. Well, I've done stranger things. Let's see . . .

As he read on, his smile faded. By the time he laid down the letter his expression was grim. The devil! he thought, and his hands slowly clenched. I am caught between two fires. What am I to do?

Stripped of its flowery prose, Holkar's letter was a simple plea. Quinn was his brother who had sworn loyalty to his house and been well rewarded. Had he forgotten their shared youth? Their triumphs? The charges knee-to-knee and the victory feasts? Had he forgotten his pledge to Ahalya Bhai? Would his brother see him die penned between walls like a sheep in a slaughterhouse?

Then to the plea he added a bribe . . . and a threat. He was prepared, he wrote, to free the British prisoners chained in the dungeons of Dig, if he was permitted to depart from the fortress unmolested. But if this offer was rejected, he would have no choice but to execute his prisoners on the battlements, within sight of their comrades-in-arms. This he would do not from malice, but because his brother had forgotten him, and on his brother's soul their deaths would lie.

Monson would never agree to such a deal. Quinn knew that without asking. Obstinate, strait-laced, self-righteous, he would reject any hint of favours granted for favours received. Quinn himself placed no reliance of Holkar's good faith; but there was one factor he could not ignore. Holkar claimed that among his prisoners was a white memsahib. The devil of it was that the claim might be true – and it might be Kate Gisborne. The villagers of Chandargarh affirmed that she had been taken away alive, and a Maratha liked to keep an ace up his sleeve. It was entirely possible that Holkar had kept her all this time for use as a bargaining counter.

Quinn knew the terrible dungeons of Dig. The thought of Kate chained there for months on end turned his stomach. A woman who survived such incarceration would be lucky to retain her sanity.

Or was the story of the memsahib just a bluff – a desperate gambler's last throw? The siege train was on its way from Agra. When it arrived, Lake would pound Dig's walls to powder, and there would be no room for argument. Without Holkar the Maratha menace would crumble. How could he, Quinn, even contemplate setting the mad dog free?

But how could he let Kate Gisborne die?

In the corner of the tent the messenger squatted, patient and alert as a hunting cat. One of Sirji Rao Ghatke's catamites, thought Quinn, eyeing with disfavour the youth's pouting lips and soft bulging thighs. The old guard who had been his friends were mostly dead or disgraced, replaced by sycophants of Sirji Rao's choosing.

'What proof have you that there is a memsahib among the prisoners?' he demanded.

Silently the *vakil* rose. From the breast of his tunic he drew a small silk-wrapped parcel and handed it to Quinn with an obeisance at once servile and mocking.

Quinn snapped the threads and shook open the scrap of silk: a hard round object dropped out and rolled across the table. He picked it up. A ring: plain dull gold; narrow, undistinguished. . . . He held it close to the lamp, his eyes blurring as they strove to decipher the tiny letters.

G.L.G. – K.M.C. 1.II.1800

George Lovelace Gisborne to Katherine . . . Irrelevantly he wondered what the M stood for. The *vakil*'s sly eyes met his glancingly before resuming their study of the carpet.

'I must consider,' said Quinn, subduing his desire to catch the fat throat and shake the truth out of it. That would not help. Guile must be met with guile, treachery with treachery. 'Leave me,' he ordered.

'My master bade me – '

'Go!'

Quinn half rose and the *vakil* fled. He sank back on the camp-stool, staring unseeing at the letter, while his thoughts raced like demented squirrels.

The ring proved nothing. To Marathas, lying and cheating were natural weapons. Winning by treachery was a matter for pride, not shame. Holkar's warped sense of humour would delight in pretending Kate was alive long after she was dead. How he would gloat if he could trick Quinn into conniving at his escape by making promises he had no intention of keeping. And yet . . . And yet . . .

General Lake had given him a chance. There would not be a second. If he betrayed his trust now, his career in Company service would be finished for good. Could he throw it away on the chance – the slender chance – of saving Kate?

Lake was a wise man. He knew how divided loyalty could tear a man apart. Quinn's head knew Holkar was a menace, a cruel treacherous brigand, a mad dog; yet how could his heart break those bonds of shared comradeship? Wild and free they had roamed the Deccan. Must Holkar die trapped like a caged wolf, with never a chance to outrun his foes?

Clenched in his hand, the ring had grown warm, as it must have been while she wore it. No woman parts willingly with her wedding ring. How long since it had been wrenched warm from her finger? He remembered the sly mockery of the young *vakil*'s smile and the conviction grew on him that Kate was dead.

Very well, he thought. Two can play that game. I shall return the ring and call Holkar's bluff. Only a thrice-damned fool makes bargains with Marathas.

He rose and went to the tent's opening. In the bright moonlight the walls of Dig rose black and forbidding, domes, towers and turrets starkly outlined against the paler sky. Around the base a chain of glowing campfires marked where pickets were posted, while armed patrols ranged ceaselessly, checking posterns and bridges. Monson was taking no chances. The net was drawn close round Dig, but even a net had holes in it . . .

'Colonel Sahib?'

The *vakil* had been crouched in the shadows, watching the tent's opening. Now he glided to stand at Quinn's elbow.

Return the ring to your master. Tell him I do not bargain with mad dogs. That was what he meant to say, but his voice would not utter the words. Nor would his fingers unclench to release the ring round which they had locked as securely as a bulldog's jaws. He heard himself say, 'Tell Jaswant Rao to bring the prisoners to the Eastern Gate at dawn. If they are released unharmed, I will leave the gate unguarded one hour. No more. That is my final word.'

'It is understood, Colonel Sahib.' Ghostlike, the *vakil* melted away.

For a moment longer Quinn stood staring at the fortress' dark forbidding bulk, wondering at his own folly. Then he turned and strode down the line of tents. Only one person would understand his madness. There was much to do before dawn.

The brilliant flash of orange that lit the paling sky a mile to the east of Dig was followed by the dull thump of an explosion. Faintly in the distance the bloodcurdling Maratha war-cry drifted to the ears of the bored and restive Captain Hawkes whose men had been posted at the Eastern Gate.

'What's that? What's happening?'

Hawkes trained his glass on the spot from which the explosion had come. Thick black smoke rose in a column above the blurred mass of treetops.

He turned at the sound of approaching hoofs and saw a slim figure in a staff officer's cocked hat approaching at full gallop. Hawkes peered at him in the half-light.

'What the devil's up?' he demanded.

The young officer saluted smartly. 'The Marathas have attacked the baggage train. You are ordered to support Captain Napier in immediate pursuit.'

Hawke's narrow face lit up. He was a bruising rider; nothing could be more to his taste than a chase. He shouted to his *daffadar* and hastily mounted his own leggy bay. 'What about this damned gate?' he called over his shoulder.

'That's all right, sir. Captain Goodison is sending a troop to relieve you. They'll be here directly. I passed them on my way up.' As Hawkes hesitated, he added, 'You need not delay, sir. I will remain here until they come.'

'Much obliged to you, Captain – Captain – ?'

'Brown, sir. Thomas Brown of the Bombay Europeans,' said Ned glibly, knowing of five Tom Browns at least in that regiment. As Hawkes and his troop streamed away whooping in the direction of the smoke, he permitted himself a grin. Now for it! Quinn's *hircarrah* ruffians would lead Hawkes a merry dance chasing shadows in the jungle before he found out the attack was a sham; by the time he rounded up his men and returned the business should be safely done.

'Good work, Ned.' A shadow cantered out of the trees. It was Quinn, dark-cloaked, his horse lathered on neck and flank. No one who had seen Quinn sinking bumper after bumper last night in the mess-tent would dream he had spent the hours since laying a gunpowder train to an ammunition tumbril and positioning his ragged crew of *hircarrahs* where they would best cause a diversion.

Together they approached the Eastern Gate.

'Send out the prisoners,' called Quinn in the Maratha tongue. 'It is I, Sikander sahib, who speaks.'

The great walls loomed over them, impenetrably secret, but behind that massive façade Ned had an impression of intense activity. Unseen eyes were watching every move they made.

For a moment nothing happened; then slowly the great studded door swung open. A party of horsemen dashed through, bunched close as if running a race, wild hoofs striking sparks from the stones. Behind them rumbled a bullock-*ghari* packed with uniformed men – uniformed scarecrows, thought Ned, as the strengthening light revealed the ravages of their imprisonment. Some were sitting, some lying. Pale skin stretched like parchment over their bones, their eyes were dark hollows like the sockets of skulls. At first he feared they were all dead and this was one of Holkar's grim jests; then they moved, and waved, and called out feebly, and he knew with a surge of thankfulness that for once the Maratha had kept his word.

'You've done it, sir!' he cried, turning to Quinn with hand outstretched in congratulation. 'You've saved them.'

But Quinn sat silent and unmoving, his face set in an expression of bitter disappointment. Ned looked more carefully at the ragged crew in the bullock-cart and understood.

'He has tricked me,' said Quinn, as his eyes still searched for the one face that mattered. 'By God, he shall pay for this in blood.'

He turned away. Ned rode towards the cart which was pitching over the rough ground like a ship in heavy seas with the prisoners clinging to the sides. The reason for its erratic progress was plain. The rope passed through the yoked bullocks' nostrils that served to guide them had fallen from Sergeant Pearce's skeletal fingers and the animals, undirected, were lumbering towards the nearest trees. Ned leaned from the saddle and caught the trailing rope.

'Whoa there!' He hauled the vehicle to a halt, and addressed himself to the ragged figure in a sergeant's stripes perched on the driving seat. 'Where is Mrs Gisborne?' he demanded. 'Was she not among the prisoners?'

'Poor lady!' Pearce spoke in a faraway voice, but he alone among the ragged crew seemed to have retained the power of speech. His companions stared vacantly before them like living dead, apparently oblivious of their surroundings. Ned shrank from meeting those dull horror-shocked eyes.

'Where is she? Why haven't they sent her with you?'

'Poor lady!' Pearce repeated. 'A real lady, she was, whatever Cap'n Parker said about 'er. Without 'er, we'd all be dead, and that's a fact.'

'*Where is she?*'

'Dunno, sir. Took 'er away, didn't they? Tore the ring off 'er 'and an' took 'er away.'

'*Alive?*'

Ned turned to find Quinn beside him, his tired face vulnerable with hope. The Sergeant stared at him numbly.

'Answer me, man!'

Pearce blinked and made an effort to collect his wits. 'Give me a message, 'e did. Message for Sikander Bahadur. What was it now? Danged if I remember.'

He swayed on his perch. Dismounting hastily, Ned scrambled into the *ghari* and put an arm round Pearce's shoulders.

'Here. Give him this.' Quinn passed across his flask. The liquor made Pearce cough, but after swallowing a mouthful his eyes focused more clearly and he said almost briskly, 'Sikander Bahadur. That's what they calls Colonel Quinn, ain't it? I wasn't to tell nobody, only 'im.'

'I am Colonel Quinn. Give me the message.'

In the cart, the living dead stirred and mumbled.

Pearce said slowly, 'That one-eyed devil 'Olkar said as 'ow 'e'd set 'er free at Lallakotah. Said 'e'd leave 'er with the Brahmins and you'd find 'er there.' He passed a hand across his eyes. 'Not that she was in any state to ride, poor lady. Weak as a kitten, like the rest of us. Begged 'im to let 'er go, I did. Begged 'im to take me instead. 'E wouldn't listen. Said Sikander Bahadur 'ad broken 'is pledge and must remember the tears of Ahalya Bhai. Those were 'is words. "Remember the tears of Ahalya Bhai." '

Quinn's face drained of blood. Ned thought he looked suddenly old. 'I must go after them,' he said and wheeled the black horse. 'Holkar has some devilry planned . . . Fool that I was to have trusted him. Raise the alarm, Ned, and cover for me here, there's a good fellow.'

'What will you do? Let me come with you!'

Ned spoke to empty air. Quinn had already set his spurs to the black horse's flanks and with a wild drumming of hoofs they were gone. Following the path the Marathas had taken, horse and rider vanished into the trees.

*

The small village of Lallakotah, whose steeply stacked houses line the north bank of the Kuwari river five miles below the Goolla Falls, owes its relative prosperity to the ferry that plies across the broad placid stream and carries the greater part of the traffic between Dig and Bharatpur.

A curtain of mist hung low over the valley that December morning as Quinn rode wearily on a borrowed Deccani countrybred down the winding track that led to the ferry. It had taken him a day and a night to cover the fifty miles from Dig, owing to a series of mishaps; all hope of catching up with Holkar had vanished when, cantering too fast in uncertain light, the black horse had stumbled on loose stones and risen from the fall with both knees streaming blood. There could be no question of riding him farther, and Quinn was obliged to leave him in the care of the local *zamindar* and accept whatever his host could offer in the way of a replacement. This proved to be a raw-boned bay mare as deficient in mouth as she was in manners, but as soon as she and Quinn reached an understanding her battered legs devoured the miles, and when dawn broke the following day a thin sour thread of woodsmoke drifting to his nostrils told him he was nearing his destination.

Reining the mare to a walk, he approached the ferry. Early as it was, there were travellers astir; he counted more than fifty men and brightly clad women standing in knots upon the southern bank, chattering and laughing, waiting to cross. Their clothes and convivial manner indicated some festivity afoot – a wedding, perhaps. The big festivals of Dasehra and Dewali were past, but now was the season of marriages, and certainly this crowd had an air of pleasurable anticipation. As he approached, however, they fell silent, covertly glancing at his horse and uniform and muttering sullenly in response to his greeting. Country people whose land had been despoiled by marauding bands of armed men throughout the past decade had no reason to admire the military.

They think I have come to put an end to their fun, he thought without surprise, seeing the women adjust their saris to conceal their ornaments, and the men tighten their grip on their wretched bundles. Well, one cannot blame them.

All the same, he regretted the effect of his uniform upon their spirits, and when they stood back to allow him to board the ferry first, he accepted the courtesy with rather more elaborate thanks than the gesture merited, and led his mare forward to stand alone in the bows.

The rest crowded in the stern; the brawny ferrymen cast off their flat-bottomed vessel and began to traverse the stream at an angle to the current.

Behind him the hum of talk continued, voices pitched low. Too late he wished he had not revealed his knowledge of the Maratha tongue but stamped aboard like a *sahib*, elbowing the peasants aside. Then they would have spoken freely and he might have learned something regarding Holkar. Now they were on their guard, leaving him isolated in the bows even though it meant an uncomfortable crush in the stern.

Pulling a pencil and notebook from his pocket he began to write columns of quite meaningless figures and study them with close attention. In the polished brass dish propped against the rail, the reflections of the people behind him swam dizzily. No one can mumble like a Malwari peasant fearful of eavesdroppers, but seeing him absorbed in his book, gradually their voices rose.

'Are we in time, brother?' a withered grey-beard in a long shirt of Mhowa green with the crossed belts of a *shikari* demanded tetchily of the fat *babu* beside him. 'Curse these laggardly boatmen!'

A handsome broad-shouldered young Sikh standing near them chuckled. 'What's your hurry, grandfather? Why don't you lend them a hand on the oar? With your strength we should fly across like eagles!'

'He is an old fool.' The *shikari*'s stout wife twitched the fold of her gold-bordered sari closer about her mouth. 'All he cares about is ogling girls, and ogling's all he's capable of these days.'

A sharp scolding voice to Quinn's right began a diatribe against the greed of priests. 'Those Brahmins think only of what they can squeeze from us. What good were their prayers when my boy fell ill, though we paid in gold?'

'The boy was sickly, marked to die,' her husband grunted. 'You could have saved the gold.'

'My only son!'

'Hold your tongue, woman! Would you have all the world know our affairs?' When she was silent he went on in an eager gossiping tone, 'They say the priests demanded half a *crore* from Holkar, in case of trouble with the – '

'Hush!'

Quinn imagined the nudge, the pointing finger. 'Why has *he* come? Can we do nothing without the eye of the Sircar falling on us?'

'Hush!'

By now he had a fair idea of where they were bound and for what purpose. His anger rose but he was careful to let nothing show on his face. The smallest display of interest would sent them scuttling into the narrow alleys like startled rabbits: peasants had their own ways of thwarting official interference.

Closing his notebook with a snap, he thrust it in his pocket and addressed himself to the brawny ferryman as he began to swing the craft's blunt bows into the landing stage.

'Tell me, brother, which way lies the road to Ranjghur?'

Behind him there was a sudden hush; then the whispers broke out in a low babble. He heard 'Ranjghur' repeated several times. The sahib was riding south, away from Lallak-otah; they need fear no unwelcome interest in their activities.

'Follow the road to the fork and take the right-hand branch,' grunted the boatman, his shoulders shining with sweat as he hauled on his rope.

'I am going that way. I will guide you as far as the fork,' said the young Sikh, twirling his moustache, and Quinn knew that he, at least, was not involved.

Glancing once more in the polished dish, he saw the others exchange covert smiles. As soon as the bows were secured, they hurried ashore, clutching their bundles, and disappeared along the narrow path beside the river.

Quinn allowed the Sikh to guide him as far as the fork in the road, but as soon as the burly figure was hidden by a bend, he doubled back towards Lallakotah again, striking through the maze of streets at an angle he judged would bring him to the river-bank a mile or so downstream of the houses. If he then rode back towards the ferry, he was bound to encounter the old *shikari*'s party. With luck he would catch them before they began their grim work. Though he was alone, the threat of reporting the priests to the military post at Manpuri should be enough to deter them. Brahmins liked to keep on the right side of the British authorities; they had too much to lose by risking General Lake's wrath, and his attitude to their darker religious practices was unequivocal. Anything offending Christian principles must be stamped out.

Faintly in the distance he heard the long-drawn sonorous hoot of a conch, and the hairs rose on his neck. The procession was on its way. He had no time to spare. Urging the tired mare to a shambling trot, he hurried in the direction of the sound.

As he neared the river, the trees thinned. He heard shouting and the cries of women, wailing horns and the whine of viols mingled with the blood-stirring thump of the drum. Rounding a corner he came to the river. The mare stopped short, and Quinn swore softly.

He was standing on a rocky shelf some twenty feet above the river. Before and below him was the scene he had anticipated: a noisy excited throng of Hindus gathered about a square-built pyre of logs, neatly ranged tier upon tier to a height of five feet or more. Tall jars stood near the pyre and a garlanded priest was pouring oil from one of these over the logs. Though he could see no corpse on the pyre, amid the massed flowers it was possible to distinguish the outline of a heavy cartwheel.

Approaching from the direction of the village came a straggling procession led by conch blowers and musicians, in the midst of which a chair borne shoulder-high by four stalwart men showed plainly above the jostling throng. The ritual burning of a widow – just as he expected. But what

287

he had not expected was that an arm of the river – a full-grown tributary – separated him from them, and there was no bridge.

How far upstream would he have to ride to find one? Even if the mare had been fresh he could hardly have forced her into so rocky and turbulent a stream. Jaded as she was, any attempt to swim her across would drown them both.

Baffled, he let the reins drop on her neck. The woman would burn, and he could not prevent it.

Why should he worry? This was Hindu tradition. He was no proselytizing missionary bent on thrusting Christianity down heathen throats. He had no right to interfere. A woman conditioned from girlhood to regard self-immolation as the supreme example of wifely love would not thank a passing stranger for robbing her of her moment of glory, and in so doing condemn her to live out her days in wretchedness. Once the reddened palm-prints of a *sati* had been impressed on the lintel of her earthly home, she had no place there. If this widow survived, it would be as a disgraced and casteless drudge, a slave in her son's house.

Forget her, his reason urged. Ride on in pursuit of Holkar. You can do nothing here.

But his eyes were riveted to that sinister cartwheel. A widow who went willingly to meet death should not have to be tied to a cartwheel's spokes. When he had watched Muchta Bhai, only daughter of the great Ahalya Bhai, climb her dead husband's pyre, she had gone smiling and garlanded like a bride, a lemon in her right hand and a mirror in her left. Though her mother wailed and gnawed the hands of the Brahmins who restrained her, Muchta Bhai had crooned a lullaby as she set a burning brand to the logs and mounted the ladder to sit with her husband's head in her lap as the flames roared up with a scorching wind.

It was a crime to force an unwilling widow into the fire . . . yet how often did it happen? Family honour demanded the sacrifice. He thought of Serinda, who had rebelled and escaped, and then of Muchta Bhai, who had

288

preferred death to widowhood. The choice was the woman's. How could he guess this one's state of mind?

The chair-bearers circled the pyre, while the crowd cheered and threw flowers in their path.

'*Ram, ram, sati!* Hail to the virtuous wife! Victory to Ranchor! Victory to Umba.'

Quinn watched with narrowed eyes. The woman might be too old and infirm to walk round the pyre in the traditional way; or she might be gagged and stupefied inside the litter, listening in uncomprehending fear to the shouts and music.

His eyes measured distances. No horse could cross that boulder-strewn torrent. An active man might, he thought, with a fair pinch of luck, jump and scramble from rock to sloping rock above the waterfall at least as far as midstream. Beyond that he would have to swim and would very likely be drowned for his pains. He would be mad to risk it, and yet . . .

Almost without meaning to, he found he had dismounted. Old wounds nagged, his bones ached from the long ride. Never had he felt nearer his half-century. On the opposite bank the widow was being helped from the chair; helped – or dragged? His suspicions sharpened. This was no willing sacrifice.

He bent to unbuckle his spurs, then ran forward without giving himself time to reflect on the folly of what he was doing and sprang down to the nearest slab of rock jutting out of the water. He was committed now, he thought, landing safely and glancing back at the rocky shelf from which he had launched himself. There could be no going back.

The Deccani mare lowered her head and snorted in mild surprise at this unexpected behaviour, but already Quinn was gathering his strength for the next leap. One – two – three jumps brought him in a zigzag manner almost to the midway point where the chain of rocks ended. Now he must lower himself to a slanted slab, treacherously green, just below the surface before attempting to reach the centre island. As he put his second foot on the slab, the first slipped; the next instant he lost his balance and fell sideways into the churning water.

Struggling and kicking, he clutched at one rocky projection after another as the current sucked him away, but his fingers scrabbled in vain without finding a hold. Tufts of reed broke away as he grasped them; within seconds he was whirled into a deep narrow gorge a hundred yards downstream of his entry point and he knew with grim certainty that if he was swept over the waterfall he would surely drown.

Then his feet caught in a tangle of branches below the surface – the remains of a tree stranded upon rocks as the monsoon floods receded. It was water-logged now, the wood pulpy and rotten. One branch gave way as he grabbed it, but the rest held. Inch by cautious inch he hauled himself out of the main current into the backwater formed by the tree, and suddenly his feet struck bottom. Floundering forward chin-deep, arms outstretched before him, he reached the opposite bank and collapsed, panting and spluttering as he coughed water from his lungs.

The bank was below the level of the pyre. Absorbed in their gruesome ritual, no one in the crowd had seen him cross.

'Halt, in the name of the Sircar!' shouted Quinn, bursting among them, dripping and dishevelled, and those on the outskirts of the crowd gave him one horrified glance then turned and ran.

'Forward, men!' He waved on non-existent followers. Unable to believe a sahib would come on such a mission alone, the crowd swayed and jostled in blind panic, their ranks thinning magically as he pushed his way into their midst.

'Seize them! Arrest the priests! Arrest them all!'

Arriving at the very foot of the pyre, Quinn saw one of the priests bend swiftly and touch a lighted brand to the oil-soaked logs, but as the flames took hold with a crackling roar he was already climbing the ladder to the top of the pyre where a white blur half-hidden under drifts of marigolds showed where the widow awaited her fate. His knife was in his hand, his sodden clothes smoking as he hacked with desperate speed at the bonds tying her to the heavy wheel. She did not move; only the wide terrified eyes under the bridal veil showed she was conscious.

Smoke billowed up in a strong thick column from the centre of the pyre, and flames ringed them. They were alone in the heart of the fire, untouched, a pair of phoenixes unconsumed by the raging inferno around them.

'Come!'

He severed the last bond and swung the limp body across his shoulder. Holding a fold of her muslin robes gripped in his teeth to filter the choking clouds of smoke, he looked round for some break in the wall of flame, but there was none. The ladder by which he had ascended was well ablaze, half its rungs already consumed, and the ring of fire was advancing swiftly inward. Any second it would engulf them.

Pain seared his hands. He felt a tongue of flame run rapidly over his head, taking hair and eyebrows and whiskers in a single lick. The logs were shifting, tilting under his feet. If he delayed they would crumble into the red heart of the blaze. There was nothing for it but to jump, clutching his awkward burden and praying they would land clear of the fire.

Locked together they fell, hair blazing, clothes sprouting flames. Quinn rolled and stamped and beat at the woman's voluminous draperies, then seized her shoulders and dragged her down the bank into the water. As her body submerged in a hiss of vapour, her charred robes disintegrated. He stood waist-deep in the stream, staring blankly at white shoulders, long white legs trailing in the current.

Other people were running along the bank, reaching out to take the limp form from him.

'Here, sir. Give her here,' said an English voice, and thankfully he surrendered his burden.

Cursing himself for a mad fool, he plunged his head under water, conscious now of the stinging, blistered skin and inescapable pain in his hands. The thick wet uniform had saved his body, but his face, neck and hands were badly burned and the touch of water was a torment.

291

By degrees the pain eased. He rose charred and dripping, and waded to the bank where the watchers cried out in horror at his appearance. He saw a troop of sturdy Moslem *sowars* in the red turbans and sky-blue sashes of Mackenzie's Horse holding their mounts at the water's edge. With gentle hands they helped him up the bank.

'Does the woman live?' he croaked. Drawing air into his lungs was agony.

'She lives, Allah be praised!'

They had covered her with a horse-blanket; Quinn stared down at the face he thought he would never see again, and his heart seemed to fill his chest.

'Kate!'

The bull-necked, brick-faced Sergeant rose from his knees beside her, brushing dust from his breeches. 'You know her, sir?'

'I know her. I am grateful – most grateful – for your opportune arrival, Sergeant – '

'Wilkes, sir. Sergeant Wilkes, Mackenzie's Horse.' He stared with a mixture of fascination and revulsion at Quinn's raw face, and said hoarsely, 'Do you mean to say you're alone, sir? You tackled those devils on your own?'

'When I saw what they were about, I had no alternative.'

'Don't try to talk, sir,' said the Sergeant kindly. 'Your hands are burned something cruel.'

'I must know how you came to be here.'

'You can thank the Bishop's lady for that, sir. She got wind of mischief afoot, don't ask me how, one of her rice-converts blew the gaff, I'd guess. A holy terror is the Bishop's *mem*, and dead set against *sati*.' He permitted himself a conspiratorial smile. 'She made Colonel Howe's life a burden until he ordered us out on patrol . . . just on the offchance, as you might say. Well, she was right this time, and no mistake! A white woman, too. This will be a nine-day wonder. Are you sure you're all right, sir? Those hands – '

Quinn was not listening. Kate had begun to stir, her eyes flickered and then opened, startling sapphire against her

292

blackened skin. They rested on his face in silence, then her cracked lips parted. He bent low to catch her whisper.

'They said I was going to find my love,' she said, her voice a mere thread of sound. 'I never guessed they meant you.'

19

'Gentlee-man to see memsahib,' announced old Mustafa, or Bootlair Sahib, as he preferred to be called, though Eugenia declared his airs were insufferable and refused to pander to his vanity.

'Mrs Stacey is out, Bootlair Sahib. You know that.'

'Not wanting Memsahib Stacey. Seeing Mem Kate.'

'Oh . . .' Another sensation-seeker, no doubt. Kate sighed and pushed nervously at the lock of hair her *ayah* had trained to wave low over her brow, concealing the shiny red patch from which even the best bred visitors seemed unable to avert their eyes.

There had been a great many visitors since it became known that the 'white *sati*' was convalescing at the Bishop's Palace. Eugenia frankly enjoyed the attention and the chance it gave her to air her views on the evils of Hinduism; but Kate was tired of being exhibited as living proof of the mysterious ways of the Almighty and Eugenia's miraculous intuition. The tale of her rescue from the burning pyre had been told and retold until she was sick to death of it.

To be fair, Eugenia gave due credit to Sita Ram, the tale-bearing young Christian convert on whom she relied for information and who had warned her about the rumoured *sati*.

'The difficulty I had to persuade Colonel Howe to take the matter seriously!' she would say. 'Live and let live is his philosophy but I told him it was more likely to be die and let die! Men! They won't look at what's under their noses! He said it was very likely a hum, and he didn't believe in interfering with the natives.'

She would pause while her pale eyes travelled around the audience like a juggler's monkey, collecting admiration rather than coins. When she considered herself sufficiently recompensed, away she would go again, telling how Colonel

Howe had sent out patrols and how, after riding all night, Sergeant Wilkes and his troop had come on the dreadful scene. And how they had brought Kate to the infirmary, wrapped in a horse-blanket since the clothes had been burned off her . . .

Kate would smile and try to answer civilly when the ladies begged her breathlessly to tell them *exactly* what she had felt and thought, while the gentlemen tugged at their collars, imagining how she must have looked, naked on the river-bank.

She could not give them much satisfaction. The last thing she remembered was the sweet smile of the old woman who had bathed her at the end of that long terrible ride from Dig, massaging the stiffness from her muscles with scented oils. She had given Kate milk to drink, warm rank-tasting buffalo milk, saying she must keep up her strength. The journey was long, but at the end of it she would find her love.

At this point her memory blurred into a disconnected sequence of dreams. Suffocating darkness, fear and pain; then light, noise, and intolerable heat. The nightmare of trying to move leaden limbs, followed by the strange conviction that comes at the end of a nightmare, that when she woke she would find it was only a dream. She wished she could have talked to Sergeant Wilkes. It might have dispelled her sense of unreality and put paid to the nagging suspicion that Eugenia had not told her the whole truth. But Wilkes and Mackenzie's Horse were far away by now, pursuing Holkar to the gates of Bharatpur whence he had escaped through the perfidy of Colonel Quinn.

'Once a traitor, always a traitor,' Eugenia would declare, pursing her thin lips. 'To think this war might be over and Holkar in chains if General Lake had not trusted that scoundrel! He and his ragged ruffians of *hircarrahs* enticed Captain Hawke from his post outside Dig's east gate. When he returned the gate was still closed, but the bird had flown! Poor Captain Hawke! When the story got out, he was lucky to escape court martial.'

'At least he saved the prisoners,' said Kate.

The gooseberry eyes rested on her a moment. 'I warned you against Colonel Quinn, do you recall? Never trust a *mustee*.'

'I'd like to meet that fellow and give him a piece of my mind!' declared the Bishop vigorously. A large silver-haired man of imposing presence with a full, melodious voice, he was putty in Eugenia's hands and faithfully echoed her views. Kate had soon learned his bark was worse than his bite.

'Took it upon himself to let Holkar go free. Not a word to his superiors. If anyone faces a court martial it should be Quinn. They say Monson's out for his blood.'

Kate did not admit to Eugenia or anyone else that the face of Colonel Quinn loomed large in her nightmares of the pyre. Had he been there? Had mere longing conjured up an image of that scarred face wreathed in smoke?

Such talk made her scars itch. Pushing aside the concealing hair, she would pick gently at the scabs, but nothing escaped Eugenia's eye. 'Katherine! Remember what Doctor Brown said. If you can't stop touching those burns, we must bandage your hands. It's for your own good.'

'Memsahib?' Mustafa coughed gently to recall her attention. He hovered in the doorway, clutching a salver though she could see no card upon it.

'Tell the gentleman I am Not At Home,' she said wearily, and picked up her book to show the matter was closed.

Not at home . . . but before many months she would be. Eugenia had made all the arrangements. Gazing out of the window at the heavy-headed roses drooping in the noon heat, she felt an almost physical longing for the damp russet woods of Overton, the misty drizzle of an English December day.

Mustafa still hovered. 'Sahib say most urgent matter,' he wheedled, and she guessed the sahib in question had offered a handsome bribe.

Am I such a freak that people will pay to see me, she wondered. The notion tickled her fancy and Mustafa, encouraged by her smile, edged further into the room.

'Show sahib up?' he suggested.

'Wait! Who is he? Did you ask his name?'

'Sahib not giving name. Returning memsahib's per-opertee!'

Mustafa sidled closer and offered the salver with a flourish.

'My property?' Mystified, she stared at the small gold ring; then picked it up and read the inscription. She caught her breath and leaned back on the cushions, deathly pale.

'Memsahib!' exclaimed Mustafa in alarm.

'I – I am all right.' She breathed slowly, trying to steady her racing heart. 'You had better show the visitor in.'

As he padded from the room she leaned against the cushions, heart thudding, the gold circle clutched so tight that it impressed itself on her palm. The ring that had sealed her ill-starred bargain with George. The tangible symbol of his betrayal. Where had it been since the Maratha guards wrenched it from her fingers? Who had brought it back?

Hardly had she framed the question before the answer was with her, handsomely dressed in a cutaway coat of fine blue cloth with gold – surely gold? – buttons set with brilliants, a cravat of foaming lace, impeccable breeches, buckled shoes. His close-cropped head gleamed blue-black as he bowed over her hand.

'Dear Kate! How glad I am – how very glad – to see you recovered!'

'Colonel Quinn!' She started up, snatching away her hand, manners and composure flown out of the window. 'What are you doing here? How dare you creep in unannounced? If Eugenia knew – '

'She would have me thrown down the stairs,' he agreed with his twisted smile, placing his hat on a table and seating himself beside her. 'With your permission? However, as she is not here I propose to make the most of her absence. She has already kept me away as long as she could, and poisoned your ears against me, I have no doubt.'

His confidence unsettled her. She said less certainly, 'How did my ring fall into your hands?'

He smiled. 'A low trick,' he acknowledged, 'and one for

297

which I beg forgiveness. The truth is, I feared if I sent up my name you would refuse to see me.'

'Small wonder, after what I have heard of your exploits.'

'Tell me what you have heard.'

'Why, that you lured the guard from the gate and let Holkar escape from Dig! Eugenia thinks you should face a court martial. And to show he still had teeth and would carry out his threat to lay waste British property, Holkar ordered me burned alive!'

'Is that all they told you?'

'Isn't it enough?' She stared at him. She was back in the smoke-filled nightmare, but it was changing, assuming new clarity, and the scarred face was looming nearer . . .

'Tell me the truth,' she begged. 'I don't remember. I don't know what is real. You were there, in the smoke . . . ?'

'I pulled you from the flames.'

'You!' The shifting pictures locked into place. Her gaze fell on the gloves he had not removed, the strangely lashless eyes, and she sighed deeply. 'I knew . . . but I could not believe . . . Were you badly hurt?'

He flexed the gloved hands. 'They will mend, given time. My fighting days are over – for the moment, at least.'

'You saved my life.' Her voice shook as memories of the horror came flooding back. 'How did you find me? How can I ever thank you?'

He took her hands, gazing at her so intently that she caught her breath. 'Don't speak of it, my love. You owe me no thanks – on the contrary, I am to blame for your suffering. It was to punish me that Jaswant Rao placed you on that pyre.'

'Why should he do that?'

'Can't you guess?' Abruptly he released her hands and rose to pace the room. Returning, he said more calmly, 'He blamed you for my defection.'

'Blamed *me*?'

'Yes – and the devil of it was, he was right. His instincts are keener than those of any animal. He can smell treachery in the wind. It is how he has survived so long.'

'But that is absurd!' she protested, as the blood rose in her cheeks. 'I did nothing – said nothing – '

Quinn shook his head. 'No, he was right. Before I met you and saw our life through your eyes, it seemed all glory and adventure. After I recognized the futility . . . the suffering . . . the wanton destruction, I could not serve Jaswant Rao as I used to. That was when my influence with him waned and he turned instead to Sirji Rao Ghatke.'

'I am sorry to have been the cause of your fall from grace.'

'I tried to stay away from you, but you were never out of my thoughts.'

Kate drew a deep breath and faced him squarely. 'Did Lakshmi know?'

'She guessed.'

There was a silence. At last Kate asked, 'What will you do now?'

'Oh, there is more to life than fighting! General Lake has accepted my resignation – '

'Your *resignation?*'

His smile was mischievous. 'He could hardly condone so flagrant a breach of discipline! However, he has agreed to overlook Ned's part in it, and says he has the makings of a general. He is young. He will adapt to Company ways. I learned my soldiering in a different school. General Lake even offered to secure me a pension, provided I swore I would never take service with another native prince. I refused; but it was kindly meant and we parted friends.'

'Why did you refuse?' she asked, and he laughed openly.

'Dearest Kate, I am a military adventurer! I have not fought for nothing all these years. My conscience is robust; but even I could not accept alms from Lord Wellesley after giving him so much trouble. As old De Boigne said to me many years ago, "What is the good of earning money if you don't live long enough to spend it?" '

'So now you will play the nabob and squander all you have earned? I wish you joy!' said Kate, laughing in her turn.

He made mournful eyes. 'Impossible, without your help.'

299

Kate took herself in hand. This would never do. She said decidedly, 'Colonel Quinn, my passage is booked.'

'So I heard. It is why I have come hotfoot –'

'Within a month, God willing, I shall be on the high seas,' she continued as if he had not spoken. 'If you need someone to help you squander your ill-gotten gains, I can think of a dozen ladies who would be happy to oblige you.'

'There is only one I want, and I have wanted her a long time.'

As his gaze travelled over her, blood mounted in her cheeks. 'Why, Colonel Quinn, what are you saying?'

'I am asking you to be my wife.'

The air hung still and heavy. It seemed to Kate that time had stopped between one heartbeat and the next, as a spell might fall on an enchanted castle, freezing life where it stood. Whirring insects, chattering servants, the caw of crows and creak of the waterwheel were hushed. She gazed at the face she had once thought hideous, and knew she wanted him more than anything in the world.

She stretched out a hand, and the next moment was in his arms, his lips against hers, urgent with desire which woke a long-buried response.

The servants, she thought, and then: what do I care for the servants?

'Will you marry me, Kate?'

'I am going to England . . .'

Even as she spoke, the vision of the green smiling land that she had cherished over the past months faded as if a veil of mist had swirled across it. Grey fields sodden under weeping skies; smoking fires that never warmed the chill in the bones. There was no comfort there. India was in her blood now. She would not find happiness in England.

'Come with me, Kate,' he murmured. 'I will show you a world no memsahib ever sees; a paradise for our children to inherit. Come with me . . .'

Carriage-wheels rumbled across the paved courtyard and drew up with a clatter of hoofs and chinking of harness. A moment later Eugenia's clear penetrating voice floated up to them.

'A visitor? How charming! I will go up at once.'

Quinn cursed under his breath and released Kate. He looked round but there was no escape. 'Mustafa swore they would not be back for an hour!'

'Leave this to me,' said Kate, laughing at his confusion. He gave her a darkling look. 'I would sooner face a charging leopard.'

'For shame, Colonel!'

She moved a little apart as Eugenia, smiling and majestic, sailed into the room. The Bishop followed at a measured pace, hands clasped behind his back.

' "Put not your trust in horses!" A wheeler went lame not a mile from home . . .' Eugenia darted a questioning glance at Quinn, whose back was towards the light so she did not immediately recognize him.

'Your servant, ma'am. Your Grace!' He bowed, and at the sound of his voice her arched brows lifted a fraction.

'I believe you are acquainted with Colonel Quinn, Eugenia,' said Kate, suppressing an unseemly desire to laugh.

Eugenia's bosom swelled. She snapped shut her fan and shot a look of pure venom at Quinn. 'Who let you in?' she demanded. 'I gave orders you were not to be admitted. Katherine, if this is your doing, I warn you – '

'One moment, Eugenia.'

Kate turned to the Bishop, whose face had turned the red of a turkey-cock's wattles, and who was making much the same gobbling sound.

'I have often heard you express the desire to meet Colonel Quinn,' she said, smiling. 'I know you have certain views to express to him. But first, there is something you should know.'

She took Quinn's gloved hand and drew him forward, feeling in that strong clasp both comfort for the present and a pledge for the future.

'Colonel Quinn has asked me to be his wife. Will you give your blessing to our marriage?'

The Bishop's chiselled nostrils flared delicately, scenting money. No man climbs the slippery ladder of ecclesiastical

301

preferment without learning which side his bread is buttered, and the Church in Lallakotah was in financial straits. His large spiritual eyes surveyed Kate's suitor, seeing things his wife did not. Two of those diamond buttons would pay for a *pukka* roof to replace the disgraceful tin structure that barely kept the monsoon rains off the altar. The buckles on Quinn's shoes must have come from a raja's treasure-house. Clearly rumours of his large fortune had not been exaggerated.

The Bishop ruminated, weighing the probable benefits of such a nabob's goodwill against the certainty of Eugenia's wrath. The balance hovered, but he had a soft spot for Kate.

'Bless your marriage, my dear?' he said, smiling benignly. 'I will do better than that!' Ignoring his wife's gasp of outrage, he offered two fingers to Quinn, saying, 'Well, Colonel, I have heard a great deal about you and am glad to make your acquaintance at last. So you are to marry Kate? I wish you both most happy. I will conduct the wedding ceremony myself. Nothing would give me greater pleasure.'